THE TAJ
CONSPIRACY

Dear Anushka &
Manav,

happy reading!

Manreet

13 Jun '12.

THE TAJ
CONSPIRACY

Manreet Sodhi Someshwar

westland

westland ltd

Venkat Towers, 165, P.H. Road, Maduravoyal, Chennai 600 095
No. 38/10 (New No.5), Raghava Nagar, New Timber Yard Layout, Bangalore 560 026
Survey No. A - 9, II Floor, Moula Ali Industrial Area, Moula Ali, Hyderabad 500 040
23/181, Anand Nagar, Nehru Road, Santacruz East, Mumbai 400 055
4322/3, Ansari Road, Daryaganj, New Delhi 110 002

First published in India by westland ltd 2012

Copyright © Manreet Sodhi Someshwar 2012

All rights reserved

10 9 8 7 6 5 4 3 2 1

ISBN: 978-93-81626-13-9

Typeset by Arun Bisht

Printed at Manipal Technologies Ltd., Manipal

For my brother and sisters,
and the conspiracies of childhood.

And as always, Malvika and Prasanna,
the loves of my life.

Schematic representation of the Taj Mahal complex

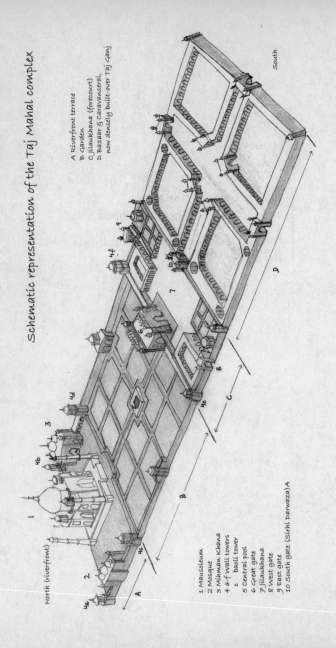

North (riverfront)

South

A Riverfront terrace
B Garden
C jilaukhana (forecourt)
D Bazaar & caravanserai,
   now densely built-over Taj Ganj

1 Mausoleum
2 Mosque
3 Mihman khana
4 a–f Wall towers
   c baoli tower
5 Central pool
6 Great gate
7 jilaukhana
8 West gate
9 East gate
10 South gate (Sirhi Darwaza) A

Schematic section of the mosque with side wing & flanking towers

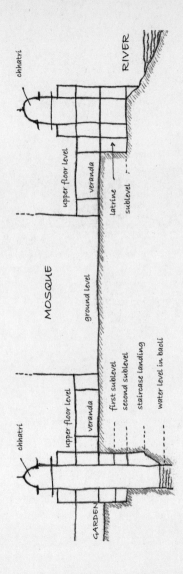

chhatri

upper floor level

veranda

MOSQUE

ground level

RIVER

latrine

sublevel

NW CORNER

GARDEN

chhatri

upper floor level

veranda

first sublevel

second sublevel

staircase landing

water level in baoli

SW CORNER - BAOLI

Agra

It was the new moon's thirteenth night in the month of Magha. In the moonless dark, a fine January mist hovered over the Taj Mahal like a veil. A man walked down the pathway to the monument, his jacket collar upturned as he cut his way through the mist that parted—seemingly in deference, or fear. Ahead, the marble edifice loomed in all its splendour, immune to the diaphanous vapours shrouding it, to the cold wind that rose from the river, tearing at it with ghoulish howls, immune as well to the man striding towards it, quicksilver coursing through his body.

Much like that common metal—the only one that is liquid at room temperature—this man was singular, elusive. Now as he watched the dome, its marble eerily aglow in the moist haze, he reflected on its grandiose beauty. Taj Mahal: a monument to love built by an emperor griefstricken at the loss of his wife. And yet, an emperor with an entire harem for his personal pleasure, inconsolable over the loss of *one* wife? An edifice of glittering marble inlaid with a filigree of precious stones whose sole use was to house a gloomy mausoleum? The man squared his shoulders and breathed in deeply. How much history lay obscured and sealed under that marmoreal gloss in a centuries-old cover-up?

History, after all, was written by victors—a rewrite was long overdue. What he knew about the Taj Mahal would divide the nation in two—again.

❋ ❋ ❋

Two men sat in the sparse room, in the triangle of warmth provided by a radiation heater glowing red in one corner. They had known each other for some time; there was an easy familiarity in their manner. One of them had brought along biryani for dinner, in two pre-packed Styrofoam containers, having consumed which they sat across from each other, their sated appetites contributing to the genial atmosphere. A little saffron-coloured rice remained in one Styrofoam container, where it now sat congealing, the ghee glazing individual rice grains.

On the wooden table between them was a celadon plate, blue-grey, a fading floral motif testimony to its age. Outside, the mist hung close to the glass windows, eavesdropping in the colonnaded corridor, spying on the unfolding scene.

'I thought you'd appreciate it. The gardener brought it in. A bored bull dug it up with his hoof!' He gestured towards the foliage that extended beyond the corridor to a corner where a bullock cart used for lugging material was standing. 'Can you believe it,' he laughed, 'even the bulls of India are archaeologists by nature!'

'Well,' the man opposite responded, 'what would you expect, in a land littered with history and artefacts?'

The first speaker nodded. 'Much of it, unfortunately, buried over time.' A curious look passed through his eyes—which the other man noticed—before his customary sanguine expression returned. 'Here,' he slid the artefact across the table, 'take a closer look. Perhaps you want to hazard a guess as to its age?'

The other man leaned forward, squinting in concentration as he observed the even glaze, the minor chips, the gloss that would shine through after a thorough cleaning. His left hand tugged at his collar as he proceeded with his examination. He licked his lips, jerked backward and started to inhale open-mouthed. His breathing turned rapid, his face reddening as both hands struggled to unbutton his shirt. His eyes became glassy. He stuttered faintly, 'W-w-what ... help ... d-d-doctor ...'

The first speaker observed the frantic gesticulations as the man writhed and gasped. With a deliberate slowness, he leaned forward and took the celadon plate. He flipped open the Styrofoam container's lid, took a pinch of the leftover saffron rice, held it up to the gasping man and then deposited it on the plate. The blue-grey colour bleached into an opaque greyness. A sharp intake of breath punctured the laboured breathing of the other man.

'Honestly,' the first speaker trilled, 'for someone with your knowledge, you can be awfully dense at times...'

Understanding dawned on the writhing man, his hands now attempting to tear at his chest even as he doubled over with the effort to get air into his lungs. In a desperate attempt to stand, he grasped at a wooden chair, the veins in his hands bulging blue.

'A celadon plate,' the first speaker instructed, his voice carrying censure for an ignorant pupil, 'also called a poison plate. A handy tool used by the Mughal emperors: prior to each meal, a sample was sprinkled on the plate— even a trace of poison and the plate would change colour. Or—'

A loud pop sounded as the celadon plate cracked into two jagged halves.

'—break,' the first speaker completed, pleased with the demonstration. The next instant, the writing man convulsed, before his head hit the wooden table and his body slumped.

Pakistan-occupied Kashmir

Inside, Jalaluddin, leader of the militant Kashmiri organisation called Islamic Jihad, was in his rock bunker. He squatted on a wool rug, a map spread out in front of him. The large map, almost a square metre in size, showed a meticulously detailed plan of the Taj Mahal, the mausoleum, the twin buildings flanking it, its Charbagh gardens, the riverfront scheme, the four entrance gates. Inserted into the architectural details was precise information about security at the monument, with numbers: metal detectors, barbed-wire barricades, police personnel and vehicles.

Jalaluddin had been in Pakistan's Inter-Services Intelligence until, one day, they were ordered to sideline the Kashmir cause to ferret out the Saudi sheikh Osama bin Laden. He quit and rallied a force of Islamic Jihadis—

IJ as they came to be known. The agenda he set was simple and straightforward, without the bureaucratic baggage of the ISI: liberate Kashmir from Hindu India.

And in the decade since, Kashmiris had learnt that when all else failed, the person to turn to was the man who had first stood up to the Indian security forces. Two young women who had left home to tend to their family's apple orchard had gone missing; their battered bodies were found in a stream the next day. The police refused to register a case and fired on the protesting family instead. When news reached Jalaluddin, he left his snowy hideout at night and sought out the girls' father, from whom he learnt that a shopkeeper with a store near the stream had seen a police truck parked on the bridge and heard women crying for help. Within the following week, five more bodies were found in the stream—all of men in uniform, all decapitated. Soon it was public knowledge that the police camps lined along the stream, shielded by razor wire and sandbags, had lost five personnel. And the legend of Jalaluddin was born, a saviour living up to his name by upholding the glory of his faith.

Now his ex-general, a dreaded ISI man who planned simultaneous peace overtures and terror attacks, had embarked on an outrageous mission and sought his help. As he pictured the marble monument in his mind, Jalaluddin saw rivulets of blood streaking it crimson. He watched the flurry outside with satisfaction: snow had begun early, which was a good omen. It heralded a severe winter, one that would freeze the mountains and kill the kafir soldiers on Kashmir's slopes.

Agra

Mehrunisa Khosa parked her car at the designated spot for motor vehicles and decided to walk the one kilometre to the Taj Mahal. In any case, at that hour, pre-dawn, there was no horse carriage or government-operated electric bus to transport her to the monument. Arun Toor, the supervisor, had suggested the time—this way they would get an hour or so before the monument opened to the general public at sunrise. She had left Delhi at two in the morning, and the drive, free of traffic, had taken less than two hours.

Mehrunisa looped a turquoise Pashmina shawl around her neck, dug her hands into the pockets of her tan leather jacket, and looked around. She had walked this route frequently in the last six months—the Taj was integral to her research, and Arun had proved helpful. And yet she had a feeling of disquiet. The early hour, and the dense fog which swallowed an outstretched arm, had rendered everything unfamiliar.

She clutched the shawl for reassurance—it had been her mother's—and it came to her that 'pashmina', the

Indian word for cashmere, was derived from the Persian 'pashm'. Mehrunisa's research on the Persian influences manifest in contemporary India's architecture, food, language, and culture was ostensibly an attempt to connect with her Persian mother who had succumbed to cancer a year back, but as a child who had grown up between cultures, it was also a search for her identity. Squaring her shoulders, she jutted her chin, holding it at that angle which her father would tease befitted a Persian princess, and started walking.

At the entrance to the Taj Mahal, a police patrol was dozing. When Mehrunisa had succeeded in waking a policeman and shown him the special pass provided by Arun, he stared at the lone woman, the mist swirling around her, and leered, 'You want entry?'

That would have bemused Mehrunisa a year back when the thirty-year-old had moved to Delhi from Florence to live with her godfather, the famed historian Vishwanath Kaul. Professor Kaul was the only scholar the Government of India had permitted to measure the Taj Mahal, a monument he had worked on for most of his fifty-odd years as an art and architectural historian. His book, *The Taj*, was regarded as a definitive work on the monument.

Though Indian by nationality, courtesy her Punjabi Sikh father, Mehrunisa had always lived overseas. After her mother's death, she had decided to live in India for a while, to get to know the country that was supposedly home. The intervening months in Mother India's lap had recalibrated her bullshit detector, especially with regard to the Indian male. One way to subvert a patriarchal society that had rendered the average man a chauvinist, was to foist class on him—in the hierarchy of Indian prejudices, class and caste were still supreme. The typical male in authority—policeman, government officer, bureaucrat—suffered a feudal mindset, and Mehrunisa, equipped with a fair complexion, hauteur on-demand, and an exotic accent, could project upper caste-class with élan. Holding her five-foot-nine frame erect, with a toss of her black hair and a flash of her grey-green eyes, she punched her mobile phone, feigned a call to the Taj supervisor, and angled the handset towards the policeman, 'Your boss.'

The constable recoiled, working the saliva in his mouth; meanwhile, his drowsy companion sat upright. Seeming to recognise her, he straightened his shirtfront and said to his colleague, 'Why waste time—don't you recognise Madam? Only yesterday the supervisor mentioned that she'd arrive early.'

Mehrunisa rewarded him with a smile.

'Inspector Javed, of CISF,' he said, referring to the Central Industrial Security Force that had been guarding the Taj Mahal since 2002. He got out of the van and motioned her towards the side entrance. With quick steps he marched her to a grille-iron door, where, after a routine security check, he stretched his arm in the direction of the Taj Mahal. A powdery mist mingled with the central canal and shrouded the tree-lined walkway, at the end of which the marble monument, framed by four slender minarets, seemed suspended in ether.

'I've seen it daily for five hundred days now—you'd think the effect of its beauty would decrease,' Inspector Javed said. 'Forgive my colleague's behaviour,' he continued, gesturing in the direction of his vehicle. 'The Taj is a national treasure. We have to guard it,' his eyes darkened, 'from fanatics.'

Mehrunisa walked down the central walkway towards the mausoleum, the mist ponderous over the gardens, and shivered involuntarily. As a child she had accompanied her godfather to the monument frequently. One summer, however, while exploring the complex, she had stumbled upon a basement room. As she probed the dank interiors, the door clanged shut and no amount of shouting fetched help. Ultimately, she was located at dusk, by which time she had petrified. Thereafter, Mehrunisa had developed a fear of basements, refusing to ever enter one. In an attempt at perspective she acknowledged that fear with a moniker: 'basement issues'. She cast a glance around: most visitors fixated on the marble monument didn't realise that a vast labyrinth of rooms, corridors and basement stairways ran beneath their feet. In the Mughal era, the subterranean levels had a functional inner life. Now, they were closed to visitors.

Inside the mausoleum, at the door that led to the tomb chamber, Mehrunisa paused. It was ajar; Arun had told her he would leave it open before he retired for the night. Beyond lay the paradisiacal house of Mumtaz Mahal, the beloved wife for whom Emperor Shah Jahan had put all elements to work—even sound. The large domed chamber with its perfect acoustics was renowned for one of the longest echoes of any building in the world. She had seen visitors test it with their screams during the day, ignoring the need for repose amidst the tombs. Until now Mehrunisa had only heard about the 'sound of infinity'—now she waited to experience it. It was an unusual privilege accorded to the first visitor: as soon as the person walked in, vibration caused by air moving through the huge ventilated dome reverberated through the room. Now, with eager anticipation, Mehrunisa stepped inside and shut her eyes. A faint whoosh filled the air. Mehrunisa glided across the room, the sound trailing her every movement. It transported her to the snow-clad Zagros mountains, standing atop a summit, one hand clasped in each of her parents', as in the quiet they heard the mountain breathe. A smile lit her lips—it was magical! She stood still, the sound getting fainter with each ripple, until the sacred moment was over and she opened her eyes.

The large hall, together with the tomb chamber over the actual burials below and the outer dome above, was the Taj Mahal's core. A bronze lamp hanging above the cenotaphs cast a golden glow. During the day nobody noticed the lamp, even fewer were aware of its romantic history. A gift from Lord Curzon, a viceroy of British India, it was inlaid with silver and gold, and modelled on the design of a lamp that hung in the mosque of Sultan Beybars II of Cairo. The story went that on a visit to the Taj, Lord Curzon was so dismayed by the smoky country lanterns used by his guides to show him around, that he resolved to present the Taj with worthy lighting. For a century now, Mehrunisa reflected, an Englishman's love had illuminated the imperial Mughal tomb.

The faint light filtered into the main chamber through the marble filigree screens that formed an octagonal periphery around the two cenotaphs. The marble was cold beneath her woollen socks and Mehrunisa curled her toes. A quick glance at her wristwatch showed 4.30 a.m.—at best, she had an hour-and-a-half or two before she had company. She intended to spend the time studying the exquisite pietra dura on the cenotaphs in the tomb chamber, an impossible task during regular hours. Access to the tombs through the marble screens was through a low gate. It was closed to the public, but Arun had promised to open it for her.

Where *was* he? She scanned the entrance doorway—Arun should be joining her any time. Perhaps he was preparing tea in his office near the great gate, inside the Darwaza-i-Rauza? Tea would be good in this chill, Mehrunisa acknowledged as she dug into her voluminous Birkin bag for a torch. Depositing her bag in a corner, she switched the torch on.

Its powerful beam cut a yellow swathe through the chamber as Mehrunisa approached the gate in the marble screen. Mumtaz Mahal's cenotaph was in the middle, as per the original plan. However, on his death, Shah Jahan was buried alongside his wife and his cenotaph rested next to her, disrupting the famed perfect symmetry of the Taj. The original tombs were in a basement chamber below, a common practice in mausoleums of the period. Mehrunisa shone her torchlight on the cenotaphs, eager to get into the hallowed space—and her heart contracted. She sucked in her breath.

How had she failed to see it?

A body lay on the marble floor beside Mumtaz's tomb. Motionless. Mehrunisa moved her torch in a shaky arc, trying to focus the light on the supine body. As it revealed the face, a scream tore from her throat. The cry sailed up the soaring marble dome, rebounding in a powerful echo. Arun had first demonstrated to her the high-domed chamber's remarkable acoustics, saying her name loudly, so all around her had cascaded, like droplets, *nisa-isa-sa-sa*. Now her scream fell on her like shards as, six feet away, she saw Arun Toor, dead, his blood streaking the marble floor crimson.

Agra

The echo faded away, no feet hurried to the mausoleum, the Taj returned to silence. Mehrunisa stood there, her heart hammering inside her. Was the murderer still around? She took a breath and tried to calm herself. The blood on the floor had congealed, which meant that the murder had probably been committed several hours back. It was unlikely that the murderer would still be lurking around. She should summon security, but she owed it to Arun to get closer, to see if there was any sign of life.... Even as she thought that, she knew it was futile. A deep breath and Mehrunisa opened the latch to the low gate. Gingerly, she stepped inside, the torchlight guiding her.

She shone it on his face and immediately turned away, feeling nauseous. Whoever had done this to him had been violent. The entire left side of his face, beneath his beard, was bruised and swollen. She forced herself to look again, and noticed, this time, that there appeared to be something on his forehead. What she saw her mind registered at once but refused to comprehend. Shaking her head as if to clear it, she studied the drawing in red—blood?—on the lined skin above Arun's brows. A vertical eye had been traced in the middle of Arun's forehead: an oval with a central circle, the blood encrusted unevenly.

A *third* eye?

Mehrunisa, half-Persian, brought up in the Middle East and Europe, schooled in Renaissance art, was nevertheless familiar with her paternal heritage, thanks to her father's insistence that young Mehr holiday in India every year. Mehrunisa's favourite time was with her godfather, where an average day could include an exploration of a world wonder, a camel ride through a desert hamlet, or a shadow puppet performance of stories from the *Mahabharata*.

Mehrunisa pondered the third eye, the mind's eye, the inner eye.... A sign of enlightenment, it adorned the foreheads of Hindu sages as vermilion or sandal paste marks. But this drawing was more specific, the circle in the centre indicating an open eye. Shiva was usually depicted with his third eye closed, the opening of which was regarded as calamitous. Why had Arun drawn the eye on his forehead? Had *he* drawn it?

Mehrunisa's gaze fell on Arun's left hand that lay on his chest, index finger crusted with blood. Had Arun used it to draw on his own forehead? But Arun was right-handed.... Her eyes trailed to the right arm prone beside the body. The white bandage that bound his right hand—he had accidentally cut his palm the previous week—was bloodied. A gash on the wrist from where blood had seeped was still open. His wrist slashed and left to die? Did people die from a slashed wrist?

She bent down and peered. A thin trail of blood led to his right thigh where a penknife lay. Mehrunisa recognised the little folding knife Arun carried in his pocket; the perfect utility tool, he called it, as he used it to open letters, cut cardboard boxes, trim fingernails. Had Arun cut his right wrist to draw blood to write with his left hand because his right hand was bound? But why not draw blood from another part of the body that would be less painful?

Mehrunisa bit her lip and moved the torch in a circular sweep around the body. The left pant leg had ridden up, revealing a swollen ankle and purplish flesh—Arun had taken a severe beating. She came to a pause near his feet, encased in white Nike sneakers, where she could see some writing on the marble floor. It was of uneven thickness, a scrawl, but legible. Three words in Hindi and the ink—blood—had exhausted twice, once after the first word and again at the third, for the last letter in each was faint.

Chirag tale andhera.

The dark beneath the lamp. Mehrunisa was a linguist, fluent in six languages—still, it was baffling. Which lamp? She glanced above at Lord Curzon's bronze lamp beneath which were the two cenotaphs—the 'dark' being referred to?

It was all so bizarre. A dying man sketching, using his blood as ink, his index finger as implement, trying to convey something. And convey what?

As the riddle zapped through her mind, a putrid smell assailed her and the realisation that Arun Toor, her friend and the Taj's caretaker, was dead hit her. She recoiled in horror, staggering.

The next instant the entrance door was flung aside as a man darted in. In the shaky beam of her torch, Mehrunisa saw a luxuriant moustache unfurling outwards from under a slim nose, in stark contrast to the clean-shaven chin. The compact body was dressed in a policeman's khaki uniform. The outstretched arm held a pistol levelled at her.

Agra

Mehrunisa was in custody in a police station. She had been there for a couple of hours. Her back ached from sitting upright in a wooden chair and her backside was sore. Her stomach was queasy from lack of food and the worry gnawing her insides. In the eyes of SSP Raghav, the man who had barged into the mausoleum and brought her in for questioning, she was a suspect.

He'd woken early that morning, he told her, and as he drove by the Taj Mahal, he'd seen a lone car parked in the complex. Suspicious, he'd headed inside when a scream shattered the air and he raced in to discover a bleeding corpse. And Mehrunisa standing over it.

It took a lot of will for Mehrunisa to project calm, regurgitate the same answers to questions that had been repeated in one form or another since dawn. She licked her lips and reminded herself to breathe deeply even as she pretended not to notice the curious glances directed at her from the policemen lounging about. SSP Raghav headed an Anti-Terror Squad—the nameplate on his table said so—and he had hinted darkly about increasing terror attacks, and the Taj Mahal being a prime target.

Leading her out of the mausoleum, he had shouted rapid-fire instructions to Inspector Javed who was watching the action from the door. 'Call your constables and order them to guard the place. Also, delay the entry time to the Taj Mahal until noon—provide some official-sounding excuse. That will give us enough time to secure the crime site and gather evidence.'

Deep breathing did not seem to be helping, for her senses were assailed by the stench of sweat and piss that permeated the police station. She was swivelling her neck slowly to relax the muscles when a voice behind made her head snap up.

'I walk in and see you crouching over a dead body, blood spilled on the floor. It appears to be a crime scene.' SSP Raghav rounded the table and stood in front of her, one thumb hooked in his belt loop. 'If the body on the floor is the victim's, who is this other person? Did the murderer disappear, or was she caught in the act?'

Mehrunisa found herself shaking. Stay calm, she counselled herself, you have done nothing wrong. It was typical police behaviour—overbearing, dismissive, brutish. She couldn't seriously be considered a suspect. Inspector Javed must have confirmed the time she'd arrived at the Taj, and the coagulated blood was clear indication that the murder had occurred some hours back. Reassured by her reasoning, she looked up, angled her chin, and regurgitated once more that she had arrived early to study the cenotaphs before the public was allowed in. Arun Toor was to meet her at the mausoleum. Instead she had found his corpse.

'When was the meeting fixed?'

'Two days back. I called yesterday—'

'What time?'

'Eight p.m. I reconfirmed the appointment, we chatted briefly and then he excused himself. He said he was expecting a visitor and had to prepare for the meeting.'

'A visitor? That late? Who was the supervisor expecting?' The SSP furrowed his brow as if he had not heard the information previously from her.

'Someone called Aurangzeb.'

'Hmm. Aurangzeb. Are you sure you heard correctly?'

'I think so.'

SSP Raghav leaned over the table and spun a glass paperweight with trapped air bubbles inside. As it rattled on the table he peered at her closely. 'I know one Aurangzeb related to the Taj Mahal. But he died three hundred years back. You know any modern one?'

Mehrunisa gulped and shook her head.

'Ever heard his name from the supervisor before? From anyone else at the Taj?'

Mehrunisa shook her head again.

SSP Raghav lifted his brows and blew air out of his mouth, making his moustache quiver. 'Terrorist, possible? One of the jihadis our neighbour exports routinely?' With that he proceeded to pace the room, hands interlocked behind his back.

A slap of slippers sounded as a peon came up to Mehrunisa, plucked a glass of tea from a wire rack and deposited it in front of her. A plate with a greasy omelette and toast appeared beside it.

'Eat,' the SSP barked. 'I don't want you fainting. I have more questions to ask.'

To humour the SSP, Mehrunisa took a few sips and nibbled at the toast. The waft of fried egg mingled with the police station's distinct vapours left her feeling like she had bitten into bread extracted from under an armpit. As she quelled nausea, a loud wail rent the air followed by thrashing sounds. Turning in her chair she saw a policeman walk in dragging a young man by his hair, his sweater ripped and blood trickling from his head. Mehrunisa felt her stomach heave. Clutching it, she doubled over a potted palm in one corner of the room and vomited.

SSP Raghav let her use the bathroom. It was passably un-dirty. She quickly rinsed her mouth, splashed water on her face and darted out.

'Tell me again about what you saw.' SSP Raghav was waiting outside the door and walked her back to his desk. A policeman watched her, his lips twisted in a smirk.

Once again Mehrunisa recounted the three things she had noticed: the eye sketched on the forehead, the slashed wrist, the bloody scrawl.

'What do you think they mean? The eye and the writing?' The SSP probed his bushy moustache as he pinned her with his dark eyes.

Mehrunisa shrugged. 'If he was the one who was responsible for the writing—it could have been the murderer.'

'Let's assume it was the supervisor. Atleast we have some insight into what his motivations might have been. You knew him—what do you think he was trying to say?'

'He was a Shiv bhakt—which is why the sketch on the forehead made me think of Shiva's third eye. Otherwise ...' she trailed off.

'Hmm ...' He joggled his brows at her. 'And the slashed wrist?'

Mehrunisa shrugged. 'If we assume he slashed his wrist, then why? For blood to sketch and scrawl? Arun was a right-hander, why would he slash his *right* wrist and write with his left? Yes, his right hand was bandaged, so that might have forced him to use the left to write, but if his intention was to draw blood, why cut the right hand that was already injured, why not another part of the body that would be less painful.... No,' Mehrunisa shook her head slowly, 'the slash on the right wrist was meant as a clue as well.'

Mehrunisa straightened as she continued, 'And Arun did lay a lot of store by the number three. According to him it was an auspicious number: symbolic of the Hindu trinity, a symbol of Lord Shiva who is three-eyed—trinetra, with three braids of hair—trijata, carries a trishul ... In fact,' she nodded at the recollection, 'he was so caught up with the number that when he ordered tea for two people, there was always an extra cup.'

'He was paranoid?'

Mehrunisa shrugged. 'Superstitious.'

The SSP spun the paperweight again, a scowl on his face. 'Well, anyway, the important thing is to find out how Toor was killed. A post-mortem will tell us that.'

He nodded at the token woman cop who had been hanging around desultorily; she led Mehrunisa away to be fingerprinted. Finally Mehrunisa was permitted to make a phone call. An agitated Professor Kaul promised to contact the ASI director-general right away, after which he would proceed to Agra.

It had been several hours of interrogation and Mehrunisa was so overcome with fatigue that her senses were numb. The SSP, trailed by the woman cop, led her to an adjacent room where two other women were being held. One was a complainant of dowry harassment, the other had beaten her drunk husband and fractured his ribs, she was informed. 'Wait here until your uncle arrives. I have to return to the Taj Mahal. But remember, until we find the murderer, you're on call,' he added darkly.

Agra

Hundreds of young men in khaki shorts and crisp white shirts stood to attention in the sprawling Sadar Bazaar stadium, their bamboo sticks at their sides. It was the final day at the training camp.

The speaker was dressed in a muslin kurta and dhoti, despite the severe winter. 'In the last twenty days you have learned to be Real Men. Real Men, proficient in the art of self-defence. And none too late. Anti-Hindu forces—national and international—are determined to finish off the Hindus ... and everything we can be proud of.'

Shri Kriplani surveyed the audience, his toothbrush moustache quivering. A senior leader of the Bharatiya Hindu Party, the BHP, he was the popular face of resurgent Hinduism. He was also the chairman of BHP shakhas, the community camps for training Hindu youth. Its ostensible agenda was to sensitise the young people of India to its cultural heritage, which, they said, was endangered by the twin onslaughts of fundamentalist Islam and American hegemony.

'The greatness of our motherland has never been in doubt. However, over the years, we, her weak-willed sons, have allowed her to be tainted and defiled. But,' Shri Kriplani's head arched over his audience, 'better late than never. The time has come to re-establish Ram Rajya, the rule of Lord Rama, the golden age of India! You want to know why? Thousands of years ago, Ram Rajya was more advanced than today's world. Listen.

'Operation Desert Storm? Where Saddam Hussein and America went to war the first time. Saddam thought he would win the war with his Scud missiles. But the Americans with their Patriot missiles tracked the Scud's trajectory and destroyed it in mid-air. Impressed? But haven't we all seen this before in our historic land?' His outstretched arm invited them to answer him.

Not getting a reply, he shook his head dolefully. 'You know, *each* one of you knows. The problem is—you have chosen to forget. Had not Lord Ram's arrows similarly destroyed those fired by the evil demon Ravan?'

Vigorous nodding and whispers disrupted the order.

'Satellite pictures have shown that between Rameswaram in southern India and northern Sri Lanka exists a bridge. It is presently beneath sea level. People talk of London Bridge, Golden Gate, so on. Yet, we constructed an engineering marvel across the sea two millennia ago!'

Noticing the impact on his audience, Shri Kriplani puffed his chest, his neck stretching thin like a turkey. He surveyed the gathering.

'Want to know more? Shivling! The mark of Lord Shiva! Do you know that the Shivling is shaped like the dome of a nuclear reactor?'

A collective gasp emanated from the stunned trainees.

'That's why I say: don't forget the Vedas of our ancestors. They contain all the information you and I and the world will ever need. Ram Rajya! Vedic Shastra! These will take us forward. Always remember. I congratulate you on your graduation. Go forward, spread the light. And never forget: the defence of Mother India rests with her original inhabitants, her real children. The foreigners in our midst are sons of Babur. *They* are not *us*.'

Deep inside Chhattisgarh forest

The cop reclined against his jeep as he smoked and studied the clearing in front of him. Tall sal trees towered over him. Enmeshed with lush bamboo, they choked daylight and at dusk it was pitch dark. The only light was from the vehicle's headlights and the glowing cigarette end.

The man listened, his ears attuned to the various sounds filtering through the forest. Venturing into the dense jungle at night was fraught with danger—even the roads were reclaimed as panthers prowled, reptiles crawled, sloth bears hunted and the deep cawing of the jungle crow signalled a tiger kill. However, predators in the forest came from more than just wildlife—and this other sort liked to hunt policemen for their heads.

Nothing in the man's seemingly relaxed bearing revealed his coiled readiness. Tense as a cat, his ears picked up a rustle of bamboo apart from the sporadic bird twitter and flapping of wings.

A shadow peeled itself from a tree across and noiselessly approached the clearing. The man was dressed in fatigues, a gun slung on one shoulder and his eyes, visible through a black shroud, were fixed on the cop who blew smoke into the night air. He had the stealth of a wild animal as he loped forward, one hand holding the gun in place, the other visible across his abdomen.

Something about the angle of the visible hand was not right—the cop had only seconds to register that thought.

The man was five metres away; the cop whipped out his pistol and shot him point-blank. The shot rang out in the forest. Vigorous flapping sounded as birds took flight amidst alarmed trilling. The man slumped to the ground.

A frantic head bobbed out of the jeep on a wail. 'But our instructions were to take him alive!'

The cop, R.P. Singh, approached the fallen man, his pistol ready. Satisfied, he bent down and searched the man's shirt pockets. The wailing man now stood behind him, flailing his arms in protest about government talks planned with the Naxal leader, craning his neck as he furtively eyed the dead body.

Straightening up, Singh grabbed the aggrieved man's palm and deposited something on it. 'Gift for the party from your Maoist friend!'

The man scrutinised the oblong greenish metallic object in his palm, his eyes widening in panic. 'G-g-grenade,' he sputtered, gulped and rapidly emptied his hand.

R.P. Singh snorted, grabbed the grenade and, turning to the shocked man, patted his shirtfront before depositing it in his upper pocket. 'It's not live,' he said with a brief smile. 'But your Naxal friend meant to roast us alive with it even as he pretended to surrender.' He motioned for the man to collect the body.

'Rule number one: never negotiate with terrorists.'

Delhi

Mehrunisa curled her feet beneath her as she sat cross-legged in a leather armchair, dug her hands under her armpits and wondered when she would stop shivering. It was not *that* cold. Besides, a heater—albeit inefficient—was glowing red in one corner of the room. It reminded her in some ways of her Florence apartment, a frigid en suite she rented in an old stone house on the banks of the Arno.

The city was situated in a draughty valley but in the winter months the cold rolled across in tidal waves. Her job as a tourist guide, which she'd taken up after majoring in Renaissance studies, necessitated a place in central Florence. The short walk to work and the charming views from her room window offset the steep rental she dished out every month. Traversing the cobblestones of Florence, soaking in the giddy-coloured Duomo, feasting on Michelangelo's David five days a week, Mehrunisa had been happy. It didn't last long. An urgent summons arrived from Rome: Maadar was dying.

An inoperable brain tumour had left her mother with a three-month lifeline. And Maadar was insistent that she would not submit to any radiation nonsense. 'I love my hair too much,' she grinned, her voice faintly brittle. Continuing with the adamancy, she announced that she wanted to spend her remaining days in the town she still called home: Isfahan, Nesf-e-Jahan. At that point in time, Isfahan was not just one half of the world, as the Persian proverb went, it *was* the world.

Mehrunisa sighed and shifted in the chair. Maadar's sudden desire to visit Isfahan had been difficult to fulfil. In the thirty-odd years since she had left Iran, Maadar had returned only for an occasional visit. In any case, all that was left in Isfahan was Uncle Massoud, cantankerous with age and infirmity that impeded his painting, and the rambling house. But impending death had made Maadar stubborn. An old family friend visiting them from Tehran had agreed to become the official sponsor for the visit. Mehrunisa had accompanied her mother on the trip, her life in limbo: she was journeying to a past that had been lost, with a mother who, in the near future, would also be lost. However, at Immigration, the authorities had refused them entry. Thus had ended Maadar's last flight to Isfahan, and with it, her life....

It was during that trip that her mother had divulged that Mehrunisa's father, the suave ex-diplomat businessman, had in fact been an undercover agent. A career spy, he had been captured by the Pakistanis once and tortured—the threat was to behead him and display his head on the Line of Control for the Indian Army to see. But he had managed to escape. How, he had never revealed—the fewer details his family knew, the better. And the scar was thereafter masked by the designer stubble.

The disclosure was prompted by Maadar's desire to see Mehrunisa shake off the past and find closure. If her little girl who had doted on her father never put his sudden disappearance behind her, how would she get on with her life, find a man, marry and settle down.

Enough! She shook her head and reached for the lip balm in her bag. Except her hand found her wallet. Withdrawing it, she caressed the picture encased within a plastic sheaf: a couple on a marble bench with the Taj Mahal as the backdrop. Papa had brought Maadar to Agra for their honeymoon, the land of the grandest gesture of love in the world. They were madly in love; enamoured with each other, with life, with art. In fact, art was what brought the two together and was to be an abiding passion thereafter.

Papa had been in Tehran on work and, during a lunch break, had wandered into an art gallery off Laleh Park. The featured artist for the exhibit was painter, sculptor and muralist, Massoud Abgashi, the flyer informed him as he began a tour. He found the paintings intriguing, he always maintained, the abstract work incorporating traditional elements. However, what entranced him was the elegant gallery owner, who approached him as he gazed at a three-dimensional collage of inks, watercolour and porcelain. 'What do you think?' she'd asked.

He turned to see a woman dressed in an emerald silk shirt and black pants, her green eyes sparkling with some internal mischief even as she smiled at him politely.

'It's mystifying,' he managed to reply, mystified that he had managed to speak despite feeling tongue-tied.

'What is?' Noticing his incomprehension, she elaborated, 'What is mystifying?'

'Oh! The porcelain,' he shrugged.

She burst into laughter before regaining her composure, and responding, 'Yeah?' Only her teeth biting her lower lip showed that she was laughing at something.

It was then that Papa decided to brazen it out. 'Look, why don't you spill the secret so I can join in the laughter, and then I would like to ask you out for lunch.'

Maadar swore that line had come out at jet speed, though Papa always maintained that, while internally quavering, he had affected calm. Nevertheless, the result of it was a long lunch, a brief courtship and a quick marriage—the prospect of a Sikh-Muslim wedding equally unappetising to both sets of parents. Massoud Abgashi was Maadar's cousin, an eccentric genius who, when unhappy with his work, hurled pots of paint at it. These canvases Maadar rescued and displayed in her gallery. They amplified the artist's 'abstract' compositions, thereby enhancing his prestige. Uncle Massoud, whom Mehrunisa had not met for several years, was now in retirement while the value of his work continued to skyrocket.

Mehrunisa felt like sobbing, as she often did on such reminiscences; told herself *No!*, and proceeded to shut her eyes tight. With Maadar's passing, she had decided to come to India to her godfather Professor Kaul, in whose Delhi home she had spent many summer vacations as a child.

It was Maadar who had divulged how the professor, who was neither family nor colleague, had become a close friend of Papa's. When Harinder Singh Khosa joined Intelligence, he was sent to Professor Kaul for lessons in Persian culture and language. Later, when he became romantically entangled with Maadar, he sought out Kaul to learn the nuances of Persian culture, and a friendship had developed between the two men. When they married,

Kaul was the person Maadar conversed with in Farsi, and when Mehrunisa was born, with both their families still sulking at the undesirable marriage, it was inevitable that he'd be their daughter's godfather. As Papa became increasingly involved in his work, which kept him away from home for extended periods, Mehrunisa started to spend summers with Professor Kaul where her father could zip in and meet her—it was also where her father knew she could get exposure to Indian culture.

Since she'd moved to Delhi, Professor Kaul had taken her under his tutelage, and she'd begun work on her project researching Indo-Persian linkages. It was a conscious effort to connect with her roots, the legacy of a Persian mother and a Punjabi father. Of course, she was still figuring her way in the antipodal environment she had moved to. She bemused her countrymen: half Muslim-half Sikh, decidedly Non-Resident-Indian in her bearing. To Mehrunisa, however, these were all irrefutable parts of her self, a self she was attempting to comprehend. Nevertheless, the answers she was looking for continued to be elusive. She was aware of a persistent sense of disquiet and loss.

Still, her project gave her comfort, as did assisting Kaul uncle with his ongoing work on the Taj Mahal. It hadn't taken her long to feel at home working on the world-famous monument. The Taj was like her: of mixed parentage—built on Indian soil by a Mughal emperor, its architecture and design reflected its hybrid heritage—Persian, Islamic and Indian; and a monument to loss—built by an emperor in memory of his lost love.

Yes, the Taj Mahal and she were rather congruent.

On that comforting thought, she noticed the grey dawn light of winter outside the window. An hour back, she had woken up from some dreadful rehash of the day's ordeal and sought the reassurance of her godfather's presence.

Now she looked in the direction of her saviour, her godfather Professor Kaul, who was snuggled in his thermal blanket. He had insisted he was not sleepy, but a day on the road had taken its toll on him. She was glad to be ensconced in her godfather's warm house after those hours of interrogation.

It had helped that the professor was one of India's foremost historians. Upon her call he had contacted his friend, Raj Bhushan, the director-general of ASI, who had personally vouched for Mehrunisa over the phone to the SSP. Professor Kaul had driven down, and upon assurances to SSP Raghav that she would be available for further questioning if the need arose, she was released.

She shuddered at the memory, in need of some sleep herself but preoccupied with the state of her godfather. To all apparent purposes he was healthy and alert but Mehrunisa, who had been living in his home, had witnessed some startling changes in him. He seemed to forget mid-sentence what he was saying; at times, he would fail to recognise the neighbours. Just a fortnight ago, when Mehrunisa had been rifling through his well-stocked study, he had walked in on her and, noticing the book in her hand, had queried, 'Who is Sharmila?' Mehrunisa had thought he was joking: Kaul's harmless rivalry with India's other eminent historian, Sharmila Thapar, was well documented. She had been about to laugh when she realised he was serious.

An abrupt movement from the bed drew Mehrunisa's glance. The professor had bolted upright. Eyes alert, he looked around abruptly, seeking something. Sighting Mehrunisa in a corner, he summoned her with an abrupt flick of his right hand. Mehrunisa walked over and sat on the bed's edge.

In a clear, quiet voice the professor said, 'I need to tell you something while I am still lucid. Don't interrupt me—it might break the thread of my thought. In which case, I might descend into the abyss again. First,' he paused, as if summoning all his strength for what he was about to disclose, 'I think I am losing my mind...'

With a sinking heart Mehrunisa watched the man who reminded her most of her father. Losing both parents was clearly no insurance against more loss.

Professor Kaul's hands twitched where they rested atop the wool blanket. He was looking straight ahead. Mehrunisa followed his gaze. On the wall opposite the bed was a triptych frame with three mesmerising pictures of the Taj Mahal. Shot by the famed photographer Raghu Roy, it showed the Taj in various moods: pre-dawn, in the bright sun, on a full-moon night.

'Tell me again about Toor's body and all that you discovered with it,' Kaul urged now, looking Mehrunisa in the eye.

Earlier, on the drive back from Agra, Mehrunisa had disclosed to her godfather what she had seen at the mausoleum that morning. Kaul had met Arun Toor, though he could not claim to have known him well. He travelled to Agra infrequently, and it had been the ASI director-general who assigned the Taj supervisor as the point person for Mehrunisa's project as a favour to Kaul. The professor was a long-term consultant to the ASI on Mughal-era monuments, and with Raj Bhushan, the acquaintance had developed into friendship. The fact that they were both bachelors in the same city helped; aided, no doubt, by their deep love of Indian history. That they were a quarter-century apart in age did not seem to have come in the way.

Mehrunisa had the precision of a tour guide and the trained ability to summarise pertinent facts. Once again she recalled for Professor Kaul her discovery of Arun's body and what she had seen: the third eye drawn on his forehead, the slashed right wrist, the bloody scrawl by his foot that said, 'Chirag tale andhera'.

When she finished, Kaul's face was impassive, his jaw slack—a sign he was churning something in his mind. Mehrunisa, who knew better than to interrupt, waited. As she studied her godfather, she thought what an impressive figure he cut despite his seventy years. His steel-grey hair was swept back from a side parting revealing a high, wide forehead, his brows arched upwards from eyes that could be regarded as too big were they not balanced by the rest of the face. The nose, prominent, angular, was what could be called typically Kashmiri—the kind deployed by cartoonists to caricature Indira Gandhi. The mouth, medium-sized and bow-shaped, rested atop a surprisingly firm chin. His skin was unwrinkled, except for the forehead and the laughter lines around the eyes. What a splendidly handsome man, Mehrunisa thought, and wondered why he had never married.

'Don't eye me like that—someone might mistake it for love.'

As Professor Kaul's eyes crinkled, Mehrunisa started to giggle. This was the man she had always known, not the confused person she had witnessed earlier. Relieved, she clasped him in a hug.

'Chirag tale andhera,' Professor Kaul said after Mehrunisa had pulled a chair close to the bed. 'What does it mean to you?'

'Literally,' Mehrunisa began, 'the darkness underneath the lamp. The proverb is used to convey that something is amiss where it should not be.' She paused and looked at her godfather, who urged her on.

'So, why would it be scrawled near Arun's body? What was he trying to say?'

'Either of two people could have written it: Arun or the murderer,' she replied. 'The motive for each would be different, and we can't determine who wrote it until the forensic report comes in.

'So let's focus on the text for now. What is it telling us? There is one chirag, lamp, right where the body was found,' Kaul said, referring to the British viceroy's gift.

'Lord Curzon's lamp,' Mehrunisa nodded.

'And what is literally beneath Curzon's lamp? The two cenotaphs, which we know are false graves. The actual bodies were buried in a chamber underneath. Are the words referring to that chamber? What are we expected to find there?'

Kaul ruminated for a while before turning to Mehrunisa. 'How do you think Toor died?'

'I don't know,' she shook her head, 'but he was badly beaten. The wrist was the only open wound I saw.'

'Yes, the wrist.... Wouldn't a man who has the strength and alertness to cut himself and then write with his blood, attempt to walk out and seek help? Toor knew the night guards were not too far off—why not try and reach them, instead of expending energy on some writing? And wouldn't the murderer want to make sure Toor was dead before he left? If he had even some familiarity with the Taj, he would know that the supervisor could alert the night security.'

'Well, perhaps the murderer thought Arun would be too weak to call anyone considering how much he was beaten. And perhaps he was; maybe he only had the strength to leave these clues.'

Kaul shook his head and said, 'Then why not just write the murderer's name?'

'Because he was a stranger? He was wearing a mask that hid his face? He was ambushed and didn't get to see his killer...'

There was a note of desperation in her voice that the professor didn't miss. The strain of the past twenty-four hours and the lack of sleep were showing. Quietly, he suggested they wait for forensics to reveal the cause of death. 'That should clarify a few things,' he said.

After a few moments of silence, he continued, 'You should go meet Raj Bhushan, thank him for the phone call to the Agra police and discuss what you saw with him. But wait for him to get better, though.'

'Get better?'

'He wasn't in office yesterday when I called, and he wasn't answering his cell phone, so I went over to his house and found him in bed, all covered up, hoarse voice.... A bad case of flu—all that travel, I think.'

Mehrunisa knew he was alluding to Raj Bhushan's work on a UNESCO project on World Heritage Management, wherein contemporary Delhi, with its rich heritage and rapid urban growth, was a case study for conservation. That, coupled with his programme to upgrade the ASI, kept him travelling across the country and overseas—so much so that Mehrunisa had never met him.

'I don't think I've seen him like that before,' said Professor Kaul, his face clouded with uncertainty, 'he looked ... unusually unwell. Perhaps the news of the supervisor's murder—'

Just then, the housekeeper, Mangat Ram, walked in and handed the telephone handset to Kaul. 'Call from Agra, Sahib.'

Professor Kaul, his face registering mild anxiety, spoke into the phone. Mehrunisa could catch some indistinct voice, punctuated by static. As Kaul listened, the colour vanished from his face. He hung up and and cradled the handset in his lap, deep in thought.

'Uncle. Kaul uncle,' Mehrunisa urged softly, 'who was that on the phone?'

Eventually he looked up, his eyes vacant until they fell on Mehrunisa. 'You must be careful, my child.'

Mehrunisa watched, unsure. She slid her hands forward and found them now in her uncle's firm grasp. The professor seemed to recover from his abulia. 'It was SSP Raghav. The forensic tests cannot be performed. He wants to question you again.'

'Why can't the tests be done?' Mehrunisa asked in a shrill voice.

'Because they no longer have a body on which to conduct the tests. Arun Toor has disappeared from the hospital morgue.'

Agra

Jara stood in the undergrowth bordering the Yamuna's bank, opposite the Taj Mahal. Nothing much ever happened in these abandoned fields. The spot came to life occasionally as a vantage viewing point for visitors to the famous monument who did not want to pay for the entry ticket but were keen on photographs to flaunt back home. However, they never ventured too far into the thick undergrowth, which was just as well. Jara's mind went over the events of the last several hours...

Through the day, mist had hung over the river, circling the Taj and winging its way over the gardens. Midday, the chill had driven people indoors for the warmth of a quilt, and late at night he did not expect to bump into anyone. At the morgue the lone guard, too cold to sit in watch over his dead charges, had deserted his metal chair, probably for the comfort of his little shed at the entrance gate.

Jara, a brown monkey cap shrouding his face, had slipped inside. Locating the corpse was no problem; he had specific directions, and the corpse was still in its distinctive pink kurta. The city of Agra was not exactly teeming with forensic experts, he was told, and a doctor was scheduled to examine the body only the next morning.

Jara hated the smell of formaldehyde and the cold, slippery feel of the dead, but an order was an order, and he had never disobeyed one. A stiff, long, male human body was not the easiest thing to transport so he had brought his tools along. These were rather basic: a hammer and a saw, the teeth of which he had sharpened that morning.

A couple of determined blows to the knees saw the kneecaps break. That would enable him to fold the legs the way he wanted. Next, he struck at the shoulder blades, which proved tougher, taking several hard knocks before splintering. With pressure, he managed to fold the chest. The trickiest bit followed—sawing the body in two. Lifting the kurta, he chose the spot at the waist, keeping the navel as a benchmark. First, he tied down the corpse's head and thighs with separate leather belts, fastening the straps under the narrow steel bed. The body was frozen—rigor mortis had set in—and he knew no blood would gush out. Yet he looked away as he took the saw to the waist.

The body was rock-hard and he realised with a jolt that it would require more strength and time than he had foreseen. He glanced at the clock in the morgue, its loud ticking the only sound to be heard above his breathing. Steadying himself, he resumed hacking, holding the blade at a forty-five degree angle to the taut flesh covering the bones. Since he was aiming for the spot between the rib cage and the pelvis, the one bone he had to cut through was the spine—his boss had illustrated it on a skeletal chart of the human anatomy. The one thing he was unprepared for was the vile odour. As he focused on the task, trying to keep the smell out of his mind if not nostrils, bile rose in him. The next instant a shower of vomit shot out of him, spraying the corpse, the floor, his shoes. When he was done, he looked around. In the room's far corner was a sink. He removed his sweater and wiped the vomit from his shoes and the floor with it. The corpse, he let be. The smell would prove a useful bait. Next, he stuffed the sweater into the large black plastic bag he had carried with him.

The water at the sink was a trickle. He rinsed his mouth clean and washed his face. His hands shook, but the sight of the mauli, the spiritual Hindu thread in red and yellow, on his right wrist steadied him. Wasn't that the instruction? Whenever he felt weak, he was to touch it—strength would surge within him.

Back at the corpse, he resumed sawing with manic energy. The human body is a precise piece, and just as he had been instructed, the body came apart at the navel, falling into two clean, saw-tooth-edged halves. He folded the two halves and shoved them into the capacious black bag.

Now, taking a quick look around and seeing no one, Jara dragged the black bag deeper into the mist-wrapped green cover until he reached a spot where the grass grew as tall as him. He shone a torch around, scrutinising the ground below. Yes, the grass at the peepul tree's massive base lay flattened. Jara flung the bag towards it. Falling in a soft thud, the thin plastic rent to reveal the chopped body. The crisp winter air amplified the foul vapours of drying vomit and decaying flesh. He whistled, a low, long whistle that permeated the mist, and waited.

A couple of minutes later a faint rustling sounded. A brownish-green reticulated python came into view, its body writhing behind. It had grown to fifteen feet in the ten years that he had been raising it on a diet of dead meat. The python smelled the body. It was hungry, he knew. He had not fed it in weeks. And the python liked regular meals, he was used to it. He should know—he had trained it since it was a baby. He also knew the python would appreciate the gift that was ten times the size of his regular meal, a rabbit. It slid around the corpse now, opening its mouth wide until the upper and lower jaws were almost vertical, and made to swallow the meal in front of him.

The python would do a clean job, Jara knew. He had seen to the one thing that could have made it problematic for the snake: human shoulders can be too big for a python to swallow whole. Once he had seen a python that had attempted to swallow a young man. The pressure of the shoulders had ripped its stomach open.

In this instance the python would finish the job, the smashed shoulder blades ensuring a smooth passage into the snake's belly. Thereafter it would disappear from view, satiated, and hide in the bush for weeks as it digested the cadaver.

Agra

SSP Raghav was irate. The head of the Anti-Terror Squad had spent the past couple of hours questioning Mehrunisa Khosa once again in the murder of the supervisor of the Taj Mahal. Could the woman be a suspect? An accomplice? Or had she just been at the wrong place at the wrong time?

In any case, he had learnt nothing new. In the process, though, he had exhausted fifteen cups of unsweetened masala chai, half his daily quota of thirty, well before noon. That irked him. Raghav was a tea addict and the only way he had figured he could control his addiction was to ration it himself and eliminate the sugar—before a doctor mandated it.

Earlier, the crime scene examination had not revealed her fingerprints on anything incriminatory, no weapon had been discovered except for the pen knife; in fact, the corpse itself had disappeared! And the woman appeared as perplexed by the entire sequence of events as he. He had shown her the broken celadon plate that had been discovered in a dustbin in the supervisor's room—she could shed no light on that either. In any case, one of the attendants at the monument had earlier shrugged and said, the discovery of such bric-a-brac was not unusual in the complex's extensive gardens. To add to Raghav's woes, Mehrunisa's credentials were impeccable: both the ASI director-general and that eminent historian Kaul had vouched for her. Except for the fact that she had been found at the crime scene, there was nothing really to tie her to the crime.

In which case, the focus shifted to the mysterious Aurangzeb who had visited the supervisor. Was he another terror export from the Western neighbour?

SSP Raghav had been given charge of ATS only recently. This new outfit was to be modelled on the ATS Mumbai—the first to be formed in the country in 2003 in response to the increasing incidents of terror. SSP Raghav's initial area was what the ASI called 'Agra Circle'. The objective was to monitor the safety of an area dotted with three World Heritage Sites.

His first case, he rued, and he had been unlucky enough for it to involve a murder, that too in the Taj! If there was one monument that could define India—like the Eiffel Tower did Paris and the Statue of Liberty did the US —it was the Taj Mahal.

It was rather inconvenient that the supervisor had popped it right inside the mausoleum. The Taj had had to be closed to visitors for a full day. The abrupt closure had caused such a furore amongst tourists who had arrived— many foreigners having booked in advance, for winter was peak season—that he had been summoned by his boss, the deputy inspector general, to offer an explanation! And then to top it all, the dead supervisor had managed to vanish from the morgue. The guard on duty swore he had seen no one arrive in the night. Having been in the police department for two decades now, Raghav deduced that was entirely feasible, the guard likely sleeping on duty. That knowledge, though, didn't help him, for the body had vanished leaving no trace behind. Except, yes, some dried vomit on the concrete floor close to the raised steel bed on which the body had lain. So now there were further additions to his existing list of questions regarding the murder.

Who had murdered Arun Toor?

How?

Why?

Was it personal enmity? or

Was it linked to his role as the Taj supervisor?

Who had taken the body of Arun Toor?

Why was the body taken?

Where was it taken?

SSP Raghav had a hunch as to why the body had been taken. It was due for a post-mortem. The forensic examination would have revealed the cause of death. Since the body had disappeared, perhaps the murderer did not want the real cause of death to be identified.

Again he returned to the mysterious Aurangzeb who might have been the last person to see Arun Toor alive. And the one to have murdered him. Yet, no one at the monument had heard his name with regard to anything, nor could the security confirm that such a man had visited the supervisor that evening.

How exactly, Raghav scratched his luxuriant moustache, had this Aurangzeb entered the office unnoticed, and where had he vamoosed?

SSP Raghav acknowledged to himself his casual use of that word: vamoose. In his job of chasing criminals and interacting with low-lifes, he liked to be reminded of his English (Honours) graduate degree. It recalled gentler times and distinguished him from his peers who could not construct one sentence in English that was not mangled. His command of the language had impressed the DIG who often roped him in to prepare presentations. As head of ATS, Raghav's career trajectory had only one way to go—up. With fundamentalist Muslims and rabid Western superpowers, terror was a growth industry. He wished he had a larger force to command though; with two constables reporting to him, how much terror could they handle?

The clearing of a throat brought SSP Raghav back to the present. Mehrunisa was sitting upright, her hands clasped together, her brow puckered.

SSP Raghav bristled at the quietly confident demeanour—the woman was involved in a murder case, yet he could not help feeling that she was reproaching him for keeping her waiting. He bolted upright and briskly gathered his police cap.

'We shall visit the crime scene,' he cocked a brow at Mehrunisa, 'to reawaken any dead memories.'

Agra

'What do you make of the clues your *friend* left behind?' SSP Raghav asked Mehrunisa as they walked the concrete pathway to the mausoleum. Being a Friday, the monument was still closed to general visitors, entry permitted to Muslim worshippers alone. But it was past the time for prayers at the mosque and the monument stood silent.

Mehrunisa disliked the policeman's tone that pitched her simultaneously as Arun's accomplice and adversary. She shrugged, her mouth a straight line. 'Does that mean you've ruled out the possibility that it could be the murderer's doing?'

'The murderer was a violent man who beat the supervisor black and blue. He doesn't strike me as the type who'd hang around sketching clues for us.'

'But why wouldn't Arun write the murderer's name, if he had a chance?'

'Maybe he didn't know his real name. How many people do you know who are called Aurangzeb? Maybe a terrorist was on a recce of the monument, maybe the recce went wrong...' he muttered. 'So, what do the clues mean?'

'They mean as much to me as they do to you.'

'The eye on the forehead implies a calamity, because—?' Raghav paused with a questioning look at Mehrunisa.

'Because the eye sketched on the forehead was open. Shiva's third eye is usually closed; its opening means destruction, a calamity.'

'Okay,' Raghav said. 'The slashed wrist?'

'I keep returning to it,' Mehrunisa said thoughtfully, 'and what is significant is that Arun chose the *right* hand. Why? The right hand is regarded as the pure hand, the hand used to eat, to make a religious offerings, etcetera. Maybe, then, cutting off the right hand, notionally, would be a desecration? A desecration of something considered pure?'

The SSP had been listening with narrowed eyes. 'So the clue is implying that something will desecrate the Taj Mahal?'

As they entered the mausoleum, the two constables took guard outside. Lord Curzon's lamp cast its yellow light over the cenotaphs. SSP Raghav flashed his torch at the lamp and said, 'That, I guess, is the chirag.' His loud voice echoed in the vaulted dome, compounded by the still air that had lain undisturbed overnight. He was referring to the proverb Arun, presumably, had scrawled on the floor: Chirag tale andhera.

Now the SSP swivelled the torchlight towards the cenotaphs: '*That*, we can assume, is the darkness beneath the lamp.'

'If you take it literally,' Mehrunisa said.

SSP Raghav narrowed his eyes. 'Meaning?'

'Well, the proverb is generally understood to mean that something is awry where it should not be.'

Abruptly, the SSP barked, 'How much Indian blood is in you?'

'Half,' Mehrunisa said. 'My father is Indian.'

'Mother?'

'Persian.'

The SSP regarded her darkly as he pondered this revelation.

'What do you think is awry with the Taj Mahal?' He pointed his torch at the cenotaphs. When Mehrunisa looked puzzled, he added, 'If the supervisor hinted something was wrong, he was obviously alluding to this place, right? So, what is out of place here?'

'How would I know?' Mehrunisa shrugged her shoulders in helplessness. Yet, even as she said that something struck her: the SSP's usage of 'out of place here'. The one thing that was out of place was the second cenotaph, Shah Jahan's. At the end of his reign, the emperor was imprisoned by his son Aurangzeb and placed under house arrest in Agra Fort where he spent the rest of his life contemplating the Taj Mahal from a window. On his death, Aurangzeb—out of pity, remorse, or piety— ultimately united Shah Jahan with his beloved Mumtaz by placing his tomb adjacent to his wife's. However, that charitable act forever spoiled the mausoleum's famed symmetry.

Mehrunisa opened the low gate and let herself into the octagonal chamber. The SSP followed, handing her his torch, the weak light of a winter day proving insufficient.

Mehrunisa first shone the torch on Shah Jahan's cenotaph, to the west of Mumtaz's. Bigger than his wife's, it reflected the same elements: a larger casket on an elevated base decorated with splendid lapidary and handsome calligraphy. Her eyes skimmed over the cenotaph, the sheer beauty of it once again entrancing her. On the casket's lid was a sculpture of a small pen box, a traditional Mughal funerary icon for a man's casket. On Mumtaz's cenotaph a writing tablet was similarly sculpted, the traditional icon for a woman.

As a teenager, in the summer months of tutorship under Professor Kaul, Mehrunisa had burnished her knowledge of the Taj Mahal. It had started off as plain curiosity. However, her evident enthusiasm for the task and organised approach had prompted Kaul to take her on as an assistant as he had embarked on an ambitious project: the first full documentation of the Taj Mahal. The result was his authoritative work titled, *The Taj.*

'Well?' the SSP prodded.

'Nothing here.'

'Perhaps the other one?' SSP Raghav indicated Mumtaz's cenotaph.

'The one out of symmetry is Shah Jahan's.'

'So you say,' he acknowledged, 'but in popular wisdom, it is the *man* who gets the central place. Here, rather unconventionally, it is the woman. Since we are examining the asymmetry of things, we should look at the other one too.'

Mehrunisa shrugged—the SSP was spouting folk wisdom, so it was no use pointing out to him that the tomb owed its existence to the memory of a *woman*—and turned her attention to Mumtaz's cenotaph, placed at the chamber's centre.

On a rectangular marble base, about 1.5 metres by 2.5 metres, was the oblong marble casket. Once again, the base and casket were inlaid as though embroidered with golden, silver and multicoloured metal threads of zardosi, an ancient Persian art form successfully transplanted to India. With a sigh Mehrunisa thought of her current project on Indo-Persian linkages. Her godfather was hopeful she would be able to create a book out of it; Mehrunisa's goal though was more personal. Arun had been so helpful with the project—now, he was dead and she was embroiled in the investigation of his murder....

She returned to her examination. The base was decorated with registers of interlacing hanging flowers, the top and sides inscribed with Quranic verses. The common theme of the verses, Mehrunisa knew from her earlier study, was to comfort the soul of Mumtaz with the prospect of paradise. The programme began at the north (head) end. At the south (foot) end, in the lowest element of the plinth was the epitaph: *The illumined grave of Arjumand Banu Begum, entitled Mumtaz Mahal, who died in the year 1040 (AD 1631).* Satisfied, Mehrunisa returned the torch to the SSP when something niggled at her. Surely not! She grabbed the torch back.

The geometric floor patterns and the floral screen motifs threw shadows on the cenotaphs. Mehrunisa's gaze cut through those as she scrutinised the lettering in the epitaph. She was fluent in both the languages used: the Quranic verses in Arabic and the epitaph in Persian, the official language of the Mughal Empire. Besides, the flowing lines of the calligraphy had become all too familiar to her over past visits.

Something was horribly wrong...

SSP Raghav heard Mehrunisa's slight gasp. 'What is it?' he asked urgently. 'What do you see?'

Mehrunisa raised her left hand, a request for silence, and continued to peer at the marble. A minute back when she had read the inscription on the south side she had failed to notice the change. She shut her eyes, blinked several times, then focused on the inscription, even as memory raced ahead: The illumined grave of Arjumand Banu Begum, entitled Mumtaz Mahal, who died in the year 1040.

Except, that was what it *should* say...

She knew the script by heart. Mumtaz's epitaph was styled in naskh—as opposed to the sulus script used for Shah Jahan's epitaph. Naskh was a simpler script than sulus, which was regarded as the mother of the cursive styles of writing. It was the predominant calligraphic style for epigraphs in the seventeenth century. The Quranic verses, however, on the top and sides of the cenotaph were written in sulus.

She bent closer, willing the discrepancy to vanish. No. Crouching a half-foot from the cenotaph she fingered the calligraphy, something she strictly abstained from usually, and shone the torch on her finger. It was white dust.

'What!' the SSP growled. 'What is so fascinating?'

Mehrunisa heard the curt rebuke but her mind was in turbulence. There *was* no mistake. Glancing at him she said slowly. 'The epitaph, it has been ... altered.'

'Altered? You mean tampered with? In what way?'

Mehrunisa's tongue peeped out to touch her upper lip as she collected her thoughts. 'The inscription here,' she pointed at the area of scrutiny, 'says, *Marqad Masnooee Arjumand Banu Begum Mukhatib bah Mumtaz Mahal Tanifiyat ferr sanh 1040 Hijri.*'

'Wait a minute,' said the SSP thrusting his right hand forward. 'You mean to say you can read all this?' His hand swivelled in circles over the cenotaphs. 'I have been told there are parts in Arabic and parts in Farsi, Persian that is.' He scrutinised her, his left eyebrow quizzically aloft.

It was a question she was used to; people were surprised that she could speak Arabic and Persian. To their minds, the two were probably as different as Swahili and French—the answer, therefore, confounded them further. 'I do—read and speak both languages,' she said in a firm-gentle voice. 'Anyway, the Persian script uses all the letters of the Arabic script, plus four.'

The SSP looked stunned. 'You mean, mostly, the scripts are the same?'

Mehrunisa nodded.

He shook his head in wonder. 'Okay. So, you said, something-something Banu Begum ... so what about it?'

Mehrunisa took a deep breath. This would take some explaining. 'It should say *Marqad Munavvar Arjumand Banu Begum Mukhatib bah Mumtaz Mahal Tanifiyat ferr sanh 1040 Hijri.*'

'*Should* say?' SSP Raghav blinked hard. 'Didn't you say the same thing both times?'

Mehrunisa shook her head and motioned him to examine the south-end epitaph on Mumtaz's cenotaph. Pointing to a particular word she said, '*Masnooee.* Persian for counterfeit. Fabricated. False.'

'What is counterfeit?'

'The epitaph should read, "The illumined grave of Arjumand Banu Begum, entitled Mumtaz Mahal, who died in the year 1040". Except now it reads, "The counterfeit grave of Arjumand Banu Begum, entitled Mumtaz Mahal, who died in the year 1040". In Persian, "marqad munavvar" is the illumined grave—that has been switched to "marqad masnooee", the counterfeit grave. Now you see?'

SSP Raghav clucked in exasperation. 'But this *is* a false grave. The actual one, for both Mumtaz and Shah Jahan, is in the lower tomb chamber. That is a well-known fact. And until some years back, tourists could descend and view it for themselves.' He regarded her now. 'So what's the big deal?'

Mehrunisa tried to stay calm. Perhaps she was mistaken. Perhaps it was all a figment of her imagination. She cast a downward glance at the epitaph. In the aureole of the torchlight, the alteration seemed to glare at her.

'Sure, the upper cenotaphs are false graves, as widely known. But the epitaph has never stated that it is a *counterfeit* grave. It calls it the *illumined* grave. This entire mausoleum,' Mehrunisa's gesture took in its sweep the cenotaphs, the screen, the vaulted dome, 'is built to commemorate the death of Mumtaz Mahal. Calling it "masnooee" is akin to blasphemy.'

'But this ... this ...' the SSP pointed to the epitaph, 'was written three hundred and fifty years back. How can it be different now? Surely, you are mistaken!'

'No. The word "munavvar" has been switched to "masnooee". It is minute—it takes little to change it from one word to the other. But ...'

The SSP looked unimpressed. 'Look, perhaps we should call in a Taj attendant and enquire discreetly. There has to be an error—'

'No,' Mehrunisa held up her hands, 'please, listen. This could be sensitive. Let me examine the rest of the cenotaph.' Loath to connect the two, yet desperate to underline the criticality of the situation, she said, 'Just four days back, the supervisor was found murdered here, right at this spot.'

SSP Raghav gave her a long, hard look. 'Chirag tale andhera.'

Mehrunisa bit her lip. 'I don't know. But what I have stumbled upon needs closer examination.'

The SSP exhaled his fury. Clearly this thing, whatever it was, was not going away. 'Go on,' he said, rolling back his shoulders. 'Read ahead.'

Mehrunisa returned to scrutinising the calligraphy on the tomb as SSP Raghav watched. She had circled around the tomb and was now at the head, the north end. Hunched over, she read the invocation: *He is the everlasting. He is sufficient.* Following that was a line from the Quran—*God is He, besides whom there is no God. He knoweth **what is concealed and what is manifest**. He is merciful and compassionate.*

At the same moment her heart snowballed into her chest. She stared at it, for there, in front of her eyes, unmistakably, specific words in the passage had been made bold.

'What do you see now?' SSP Raghav asked anxiously.

Mehrunisa pointed to the part of the Quranic verse that had been highlighted, and stood in bold relief from the rest. She rubbed a finger against it and examined the blackish hue on her skin. 'Several coats of black paint over the original calligraphy, which is done with jasper.'

SSP Raghav's brows took flight above bulging eyes. 'Nonsense! An entire mausoleum built in memory of Mumtaz Mahal, and now her own tomb questions where she lies buried!'

On Mehrunisa's urging he peered hard at the calligraphy. He had to admit: it was beautiful, but incomprehensible. He shrugged, uncomfortable with looking ignorant and out of control. 'So, this tampering—you are *absolutely* certain?'

Mehrunisa nodded as she dug out a digital camera from her bag. 'There is one man whose judgement I trust more than mine. I'll take some photographs to share with him.'

'Your uncle, the historian?'

Mehrunisa nodded and as she began clicking pictures, the SSP contemplated aloud, 'Why would someone do this? What was the motive behind these changes? Was it mischief? Blasphemous as it is to us, perhaps it is somebody's idea of a joke. A stupid one, yes, but a joke.' He looked at her for assent.

Mehrunisa pursed her lips. 'First a murder and now these changes to three-hundred-year-old calligraphy ... no,' she shook her head, 'I think it's more than that.'

Pakistan-occupied Kashmir

'All this newfound brotherhood and camaraderie— where is it going to take us?'

The young mujahid knew better than to answer. In the first place, it was not a question: the Commander liked to air his views aloud. In the second, Jameel Jalaluddin was not a man to be interrupted.

His remarkable eyebrows were a thick curve that dipped over the bridge of his high nose but rose to continue unbroken over the other eye. It gave the impression of two scythes sitting next to each other, their curving blades scrutinising everything in view. His eyes were small and round like prayer beads. The upper lip shaven, his chin was shrouded in a rough beard.

'Are we going to forget our Kashmiri brothers? Turn our back on a struggle of five decades because the president of Pakistan wants to warm his chair till he dies? What about the new initiatives?'

He glanced at the sheet of paper in his hands and read aloud. 'An agreement has been reached by India and

Pakistan to start a bus service across the ceasefire line in Kashmir. To put life back into a flagging peace process and give Kashmiris a chance to have a say in their future.' The nostrils of his distinctly Pashtun nose flared to impressive size until his firm mouth opened to spit, 'Betraying the blood of the Kashmiri mujahideen!'

The link between jihadi ideology and the Pakistan army was old. In 1948, Pakistan was stinging from India's refusal to hand over Kashmir, and people were angry. But the angriest were the conservative Pashtun tribesmen in Pakistan's Northwest Frontier Province, hundreds of kilometres away. They held tribal jirgas and for hours the elders sat, sipped tea, and debated. They waited for the Kashmiris to revolt, and when that didn't happen, they scrambled together a volunteer army in the pioneering use of mujahideen to liberate Kashmir.

Jalaluddin strode down the narrow room, hands clasped behind. To calm his mind he focused on the mission that his ex-general in the ISI had assigned him. He smirked as he pictured a marble monument in his mind, bustling with kafirs, and then exploding the next instant, showering dust, skin and bloodied limbs. He turned to the young mujahid and spat out, 'First the Hindus demolish Babri Masjid. Then they give us the carnage of Godhra. Now a "bus of peace". In turn we'll present these Hindus with something *they* will never forget. Something so huge it will shake their complacent dal-eating selves! And ridicule them in the eyes of the entire world.'

Diary

I *killed my father the day I turned six.*
It was after he had gifted me my brand-new Hero bicycle, its shiny red colour heralding what was to unfold. He was unaware, of course, and had chosen the particular colour after consulting me. 'Apple-red,' he had smilingly endorsed, 'for the apple of my eye.' But apples have worms in them, sometimes. An apple is also a dangerous fruit: don't Christians and Jews believe that one bite condemned mankind to death? Anyway, apple-red it was and I picked the colour because it is the colour of blood—though, I have to admit, the varied symbolism of 'apple' that I learnt as I grew struck me as particularly appropriate.

The bicycle was brought home and I rode it in the veranda, then the lawn, to the proud applause of my parents, and the guarded enthusiasm of the gardener, the cook, and my ayah—frequent victims of my childish pranks. Ayah, though, was privy to some of my 'oddities'—a term my father used to describe some of my behaviour.

Like the fact that I still suckled at my mother's breast, despite father's explicit command to discontinue the practice.

But I liked to nestle against my mother's softness, her long black hair veiling my face, the red bindi aglow on her smooth, fair forehead. She liked it too, the times when I nibbled a nipple and she winced, making as if to smack me, instead arching her back as I strengthened my suckling. It was what I had seen father do to her. On hot, sultry afternoons, when father returned for his siesta and my mother and he retired to their cool bedroom, I pretended to sleep in my room. After Ayah left, I would sneak into the rambling garden outside the windows of my parents' room. The windows would be shuttered but one slat was broken—enough for a peephole. I did not like what my father did to my mother, but my mother seemed to enjoy it. I studied that look on her face and strove for it when I suckled at her breast.

But returning to the birthday present.

After I had ridden my bicycle and eaten the celebratory dish of halwa-poori, my father retired for his customary evening bath. It was the middle of February, a wintry dusk had brought darkness and cold in its wake. My father liked his bath water steaming hot—tepid was for the weaklings, he scoffed—and would always check the water by dipping a hand into the bucket. To heat the water we relied on electrical heating rods, a bathroom geyser being a rarity in those days. The rod was immersed in a bucket of water, and guaranteed to have water boiling within a half hour.

So my father went inside for his bath, trailed by the cook. In a standard ritual, my father bunched up his pyjamas, took off his slippers and stepped into the bathroom where the large bucket sat spewing vapour into the air. Cook unplugged the cord from the bedroom wall outlet and waited for father to dip his hand in the bucket. Post which, satisfied with the water's temperature, he would flick his fingers in dismissal.

That day, however, he grunted in disapproval; the cook trembled his way to the bucket, checked for himself and re-plugged the immersion rod. Despite the steam, the water was not at the required temperature because a jug of cold water had been added surreptitiously.

My father changed out of his clothes, sat bare-chested on the bed, his temperature rising as he waited for the water to boil. Cook stood in forlorn guard at the doorway, willing the water to heat up quickly. When my mother summoned him from the kitchen—the curry paste was burning, how had he forgotten to add water?—my father harrumphed, sent the cook on his way and marched to the bathroom, unplugging the rod on his way in. As he shut the door behind him, he failed to notice his son, who had been watching from the veranda, sneaking in on his rubber-soled Bata slippers. My father's hand was in the bucket when current leapt at his fingertips from the water, then went rocketing through his body.

A horrible scream summoned everyone to the bathroom. The wooden door, secured from inside, took a while to be forced open. When it was, inside lay father, stone-cold, a trickle of red oozing out of one nostril.

Hands were raised in puzzled query—the immersion rod lay limp in the bucket, its cord safely unplugged from the bedroom outlet.

Delhi

Mehrunisa sighted Professor Kaul in his favourite winter spot beneath the mango tree in the manicured garden. But it was nearly dusk and chilly and the professor should be indoors. As she crossed the lawn, a troubled Mangat Ram hurried towards her from the patio. 'Sahib is unwell,' he said nodding toward Professor Kaul. 'He's been sitting there since lunch. Not lifted a finger to drink or eat. I served him his lunch at one, then four o'clock tea—all untouched. When I asked, Sahib, is something wrong, he gawked at me, then, then ...' Mangat Ram's voice went tremulous, 'he said to me, *who are you?*' The housekeeper clasped his mouth with his right hand.

Mehrunisa did not know what to make of this revelation. Perhaps Professor Kaul was just pulling his leg? He was known to occasionally joke with the housekeeper: if I needed a wife, I would have married, right? But Mangat Ram took it in his stride. In the years he had been in Kaul's service, he had developed the temperament of a phlegmatic spouse, ignoring Kaul when needed, otherwise steadfastly delivering good food and keeping house. But then she saw the professor hunched in his chair, the darkness creeping around him, and his words floated into her head: *I think I am losing my mind.*

Now, as the housekeeper watched her, Mehrunisa grimaced, and said, 'Let's take a look.'

Kaul did not react to her approach. He sat like a Buddha, but with his legs extended, pondering space.

'Uncle,' she murmured, 'Kaul uncle.' Mangat Ram, his hands clutching the edges of his sleeveless brown wool jacket, stood behind her. When the professor stayed impassive, Mehrunisa delved into her bag and pulled out her digital camera. She was scrolling through the images when Mangat Ram leaned forward. Looking at the photographs, he asked glumly, faint remonstration in his voice, 'You visited the Taj Mahal, bitiya?'

Mehrunisa knew what he was implying: hadn't last time been trouble enough? She did not grudge him that, having known him as long as the professor. Besides, it was Mangat Ram who had initiated her into flying kites and playing marbles during the long days of summer. She flashed a reassuring smile.

Meanwhile, Professor Kaul's head had jerked in their direction. His eyes were fixed on them in a blank stare. Then he cried out in agony and reached for his legs resting atop a jute stool. Mangat Ram rushed forward, clucking. 'Sitting in meditation like some sage atop a mountain—haven't moved your legs for hours now. No wonder they have gone stiff.' With a brisk movement of his palms, he set about bringing the circulation back into the professor's limbs.

The professor's eyes had yielded their former glaze to a frantic ferret as they spun about. 'Kaul uncle?' Mehrunisa queried again.

'Mehr?' he said, and looked about him as if searching for the source of the voice.

Mehr: it was his term of endearment for her, one he used to calm her when she was upset as a child. One he still used, but infrequently. Right now, it was he who sounded distressed, child-like. She lowered herself to the ground, placed a hand on his shoulder and said softly, 'I am here, Uncle.'

Professor Kaul looked down; when his gaze fell on Mehrunisa, his eyes lit up. He pulled himself upright and promptly withdrew his legs from Mangat Ram's ministrations, remonstrating, 'Stop fussing over me like an old hen!'

A perplexed Mangat Ram backed off, questioning the air with his hands. 'My stomach feels like a cave, get me some food!' the professor said, then turning to Mehrunisa, he lowered his voice and quizzed, 'Did that policeman call you for questioning again?'

Over tea, Mehrunisa recounted the events of her trip to Agra: the police station, followed by the Taj Mahal, and the perplexing discovery she had made there. An attentive Professor Kaul was all ears. It seemed improbable that just a while ago he had misplaced his mind.

'So, what do *you* think?' she asked apprehensively. 'Mischief or malice?'

Professor Kaul shook his head. 'The difference in the script of the two words is marginal, except to a trained eye. Yours is, but most would miss it. Why would an attention-seeking prankster or a deviant artisan go to such lengths for so little? For something a casual observer would never grasp even if he stared at it for eternity...'

Professor Kaul interlaced his fingers and continued, 'From what you have narrated, and from your photographs, the alteration appears to be artfully executed. In fact, only a master craftsman, an expert karigar, would be able to accomplish those changes with such finesse. But who is this artisan? And why did he do it?'

'You think his identity is critical?'

Professor Kaul's thumbs circled each other as he thought. 'Yes. You see, most karigars are Muslim—it is a family art that has been handed down through generations. There are some families in Agra who claim descent from the original craftsmen who worked on the Taj. So, why would a Muslim agree to tamper with a verse from the Quran?'

'Well, strictly speaking, he has not *tampered* with a Quranic verse, only the epitaph.'

'Sure,' Kaul nodded. 'Except, remember that the Taj Mahal is esteemed as the foremost symbol of Islamic art, and is particularly renowned for its paradisiacal vision of heaven on earth. The fact that the monument is decorated with Quranic verses adds to the monument's piety. The artisan therefore knew what he was doing, unless he couldn't read the script.'

'Unlikely—if he could change "munavvar" to "masnooee", he could read the verse.'

Above them, birds were hastening homewards in a darkening sky. A bus horn sounded through the dusk.

'When could he have got access to the tomb chamber?' Mehrunisa wondered aloud. 'And how much time would it take to make those changes?'

'A couple of hours.'

'That's a narrow window. Late night, when the Taj is closed—somebody who could access—'

'The artisan was not alone.'

'Why do you say that?'

'The average artisan is schooled in what is a family tradition and isn't well-educated. The import of the changes, however, suggests an erudite mind. The change is minor, but the *significance* of the change is immense. Masnooee is an intriguing choice of word. It conveys a lot. Forged. Made in imitation of something else with intent to deceive.... *Deceive*. Therefore the questions arise: deceive whom, and why?'

With an index finger he tapped the Persian text. 'The original epitaph conveys: Here lies Arjumand Banu in her illumined grave. The changed calligraphy says: This is a counterfeit grave. The import? You, the visitor, have been deceived. So, the question arises: if not Arjumand Banu, then who is lying here? And if she does not lie in this grave, then this mausoleum was not built for her. If it was not built for her, then the story behind the Taj Mahal is false.'

Mehrunisa wagged her head. 'The tampering turns the story on its head.'

'Exactly. Striking at the very foundation of the Taj Mahal. The person behind the change wants the public to question whether Arjumand Banu, the heroine of the Taj Mahal, ever did lie in the tomb chamber. And if she did not, how accurate is the claim that the Taj Mahal was built by Shah Jahan in memory of his beloved Mumtaz?

'The second change, in fact, adds weight to the question that has been raised by the first change. Listen: *what is concealed and what is manifest*. The person is stating now that things are not as they seem—something has been hidden while another has been revealed ... If that weren't bad enough, it's an inscription from the Holy Quran...'

'If word got out that it had been tampered with, it would create serious trouble.'

He nodded.

'Chirag tale andhera.' Mehrunisa whispered. 'If this is what Arun Toor was referring to, we already have a murder linked to the tampering.'

'A bloody potboiler. Only this one's too close to home.' Professor Kaul snorted.

Around them, night had fallen. Bats had emerged and flew about, some frighteningly low, Mehrunisa observed. Their thin cries sounded in the air. Mangat Ram, who had come to gather the tea things, clucked his exasperation, muttering about shrieking bats and bad omens.

Unknown to him, both members of his audience were already aware they had encountered something ominous. They sat in silent contemplation until Mehrunisa spoke. 'That someone is trying to discredit the Taj seems obvious. The questions then are: who, and why?'

'Lord Bentinck?'

She frowned. The name sounded familiar, yet not quite. Professor Kaul allowed himself a half-grin. 'Lord William Bentinck, governor-general of British India, from 1827 to 1835. You see,' he leaned towards Mehrunisa, 'through its three hundred and fifty years of history, the Taj has had its detractors. Hatred against the Mughals, who were seen as invaders destroying Hind's heritage, spurred them. In the early eighteenth century, the Jats from nearby Bharatpur ransacked the monument, taking away two chandeliers that hung over the cenotaphs, the silver entrance doors and lavish carpets that adorned the mausoleum floor. Later the gold shield over the fifteen-foot high finial at the top of the main dome was removed. But the British proved to be the most dangerous. Lord Bentinck, ostensibly in India as a British administrator, was to find his calling as a scrap-dealer when he planned the demolition of Taj Mahal for its marble.'

'Demolition?'

'In 1831, *John Bull*, a Calcutta newspaper, reported that the governor-general wanted to demolish the Taj and auction its marble,' the professor nodded. 'But the highest bid was only 150,000 rupees and the Taj was saved. By the 1850s the monument had become a "pleasure resort" for the British. The mosque and assembly hall were rented to English honeymooners! And daily picnickers came armed with chisels and hammers to extract fragments of agate and carnelian from the flower-inlays.'

Mehrunisa listened, rapt. With her godfather, history was a series of nested narratives like the *Arabian Nights*.

'However, another Englishman, Lord Curzon, came to India as the viceroy in 1899. The English have a way of redeeming themselves,' he laughed. 'Curzon oversaw a massive restoration—'

'And gifted the bronze lamp, which illuminates the tombs to this day,' Mehrunisa finished with a smile.

Kaul nodded. 'In the history of the Taj's detractors, you'll agree, Bentinck was the worst. So far.'

'Meaning?'

'Bentinck's folly was ignorance and greed. Both made him blind to the monument's beauty. However, the Taj's current enemy is driven by a more deadly sin. He is knowledgeable, subversive and cunning. And how do we conclude that? Conversant with Persian and Arabic, therefore knowledgeable. Striking at the Taj Mahal's very foundation, therefore subversive. A minor change that carries a huge import, therefore cunning.'

Professor Kaul settled back in his armchair. 'I don't know why, but it seems like you've discovered the tip of an iceberg, Mehr.'

He paused and Mehrunisa saw that he looked drained, as if the last hour of analysis had leached everything out of him. He spoke slowly, his voice faint, as if he was summoning remaining reserves of energy to complete his thought. 'During the Second World War, they had to cover the Taj's dome with scaffolding to protect it from German Luftwaffe, and later the Japanese air force. Similarly, during the Indo-Pak wars of 1965 and 1971. Looks like the Taj is in trouble once again, Mehrunisa.'

He contemplated the lint on his cardigan.

'I'll be there with you, always—but I can sense my mind is beginning to dodder. There are times when the mist settles so dense that I do not see ... it will be your challenge, Mehr.' He looked at her. In his eyes Mehrunisa saw grief. If Shah Jahan had loved Mumtaz enough to build the Taj, Professor Kaul had loved the Taj enough to devote a life to it.

Mehrunisa tussled with the enormity of what she was hearing: her godfather's reiteration of his illness and the grave danger to the Taj. The professor sat up and clasped her hands.

'Until you unmask him, think of our mystery man as Bentinck. It'll help you remember the fate that could have been, and might still be, the Taj Mahal's.'

Mehrunisa felt her stomach cave in. The Taj Mahal was emblematic of her mixed heritage, a stolidly reassuring presence as she navigated life in a country that was home, and yet, not quite. Working there had given her direction, a sense of purpose. And the monument was precious to the man who was the only family she had left.... Now it looked like she could lose them both.

The thought filled her with panic. She wanted to howl and wake up from the nightmare to be comforted by Maadar and Papa.

But she had lost them too.

Delhi

The ASI director-general had a slim frame that made him appear taller than he was. When he smiled, his mouth curved upwards like a monkey's, his lips disappearing into a faintly comical semicircle. At that point, it was difficult to fathom whether he was smiling or grimacing, Mehrunisa thought as he greeted her, indicated a sofa and requested she wait while he dispensed with some urgent paperwork. Professor Kaul would have accompanied her, but that morning, finding him restless, she had summoned the doctor who had administered a Calmpose shot and put the professor under watch.

Mehrunisa had never met Raj Bhushan before, yet he looked vaguely familiar, perhaps from the group photograph in her uncle's room. In the two years since Raj Bhushan had headed ASI, he had sought out the eminent historian as he attempted to invigorate India's architectural heritage. Raj Bhushan had a reputation as a counterfactual historian—his version of British rule in India as an era of social progress and modernisation of infrastructure was a subject of some controversy amongst historical commentators.

Seated in the carved wooden armchair in the large room, Mehrunisa studied the milky tea in front of her, brown from over-brewing, and decided to leave it halfway. She liked tea the Persian way, with a hint of sugar and a slice of peach or a segment of orange. It was a family tradition, the memory of which racked her. In the evenings, after Papa returned from the Consulate, Maadar would prepare what he called an aperi-tea-f for him: a tall glass with peach slices, a splash of rum, ice cubes, and tea. In that sense her father was old-fashioned: he mourned the pace of modern life, the cost of which was the gradual disappearance of customs like the aperitif. His own disappearance, though, had been abrupt. Mehrunisa was fourteen at that time, and while her friends hung out at al fresco cafés, her shrine of choice became the Trevi. The Baroque fountain, where tourists gathered for the time-honoured custom of throwing a coin into its water and thus guaranteeing a return to Rome, became her talisman. Varying her routine daily— eyes closed, prayer on lips, back to the fountain, toss with the left hand over the right shoulder—she willed her Papa's return. A year passed in which the coin collection at Trevi swelled and hope seeped out of her.... *No!* Mehrunisa shook her head. *No!* She would not think of Papa—going down that road constricted her chest and filled her eyes until she choked. *No!*

She forced herself to concentrate on the artefacts in the elegant room, the majority of which—whether paintings, brass statues or wood carvings—were representations of Shiva. One particular bronze sculpture caught her eye: Shiva, in a circle of flames, his left leg raised, the right balanced on a demon, as he performed his divine dance of creation and destruction.

'You fancy the Nataraja?' Raj Bhushan remarked as he walked towards her over the coir carpet. Dressed in a tweed jacket, a muffler thrown around his neck, gray flannel trousers and stylish leather oxfords, he cut a very dapper figure. His spectacles were thick-rimmed black, which would have been nerdy once but now were decidedly geeky-chic. 'My favourite though is the Ardhanarishwar. Are you familiar with it?'

'Sure.'

'The lord who is half-woman. It is the synthesis of Shiva and Parvati into one: the left side is female, the right male. One entity with its male and female elements in harmony—a powerful, postmodernist concept, wouldn't you say?' He laughed, a high-pitched, boyish laugh that ended as a gurgle as if it had been hurriedly snuffed out. Returning to his table he summoned Mehrunisa. 'Take a look at this,' he said as he moved some papers out of the way, aligned them neatly, stacked them in one corner of the table, plucked a case of fresh mints aside and arranged it atop the papers.

Below the table's glass-top was a painting in which, framed against a black backdrop, was a figure split vertically down its middle into two separate yet conjoined halves. The left, draped in red, was a female form; the right, a tiger skin wrapped around his waist, was a male form with a blue body. The colours were striking in their contrast and the two separate figures, despite their disparate forms, looked in complete harmony.

'It is beautiful,' Mehrunisa assented.

'You know,' Raj Bhushan said as he walked towards the corner sofa, 'in Hindu mythology we have over three hundred million gods and goddesses. Rather superfluous when you realise that just one would suffice. Shiva. He is the complete God.'

Mehrunisa tipped her head.

'I trust you are better now?' Taking the chair opposite her, he smiled. 'It was unfortunate, you getting embroiled in the business of murder. I guess you are here with regard to your project work—anything I can help with? You may need to lay off the Taj for some time, but in a week or so it'll return to normal.'

'I doubt that,' Mehrunisa said.

Raj Bhushan raised his brows. 'Really? Could you elaborate?' He popped a fresh mint in his mouth and slid the case towards Mehrunisa.

Declining, she proceeded to explain her recent trip to the Taj Mahal and the changes she'd seen in the calligraphy.

Raj Bhushan's face was impassive as he listened. When she finished there was a long silence before he spoke. He adjusted his spectacles and studied the floor. 'This ... change,' he said, his right hand quizzing the air, 'how certain can you be? I know you are literate in Persian and Arabic, but the contemporary Perso-Arabic script—the one you would be familiar with—is nastaliq. And the script used in the calligraphy of the Taj is not nastaliq.' He crossed his leg, his mouth arching upwards in some semblance of a smile. Momentarily, Mehrunisa was distracted by that smile.

'Hmm?' Raj Bhushan queried, as he stroked his boxed beard.

'Mumtaz's epitaph is written in Persian, the court language of the Mughals, and styled in naskh. The Quranic verses on the top and sides of the cenotaph are in Arabic, the language of the Holy Book, and written in sulus.' Mehrunisa paused, trying to assess the director-general's response. If there was one thing that irritated her, it was a patronising tone. Now, she drove her point home. 'Contemporary Persian texts, ninety-nine per cent, are published in a typography that is based on the naskh style. Nastaliq has become popular with its recent computer implementations. But it has readability issues, so its usage has been limited to school books on Persian literature.'

Raj Bhushan sat still, his index finger resting vertically across his lips. To Mehrunisa, it appeared as if he was trying, albeit unconsciously, to shush her. Now, he tapped that finger against his mouth a few times before clearing his throat and speaking. 'Kaul has trained you well.'

For the briefest instance Mehrunisa thought she saw something like concern in his eyes. But he was shrugging as he said, 'You will have to forgive my ignorance—I am not a scholar of either language, Persian or Arabic.'

'But you have a basic understanding?'

'Very elementary.' Again that smile. 'Nothing to rival yours. However, learned as you are, my dear, I still have my doubts as to the alteration. It seems like too much effort, and for what? Nobody who visits the Taj gets close enough to the tombs to read the calligraphy. That is, *if* they could read it in the first place. Then why bother with such a change?'

Quietly, Mehrunisa said, 'Because of its implication. The *illumined* tomb versus the *counterfeit* tomb.'

Raj Bhushan's neck recoiled in incredulity. 'Forgive me, dear, but this sounds like a conspiracy theory. The alteration in the calligraphy, if indeed there is one, will be investigated right away. I have in my department a bright young fellow who would be up to the job. In the meantime, I'll request that you treat it as a curious occurrence—harmless, really.' With an elegant shrug he held out his palms.

Mehrunisa shook her head. 'I think it's more than that, especially when you consider that it's one of a series of incidents: the supervisor's murder, his body vanishing from the morgue, and now someone has changed the epitaph...'

The director had a solicitous expression on his face. 'You seem rather distraught over the murder of Toor?' His eyes studied her.

Once again, Mehrunisa felt something—something she could not put a finger on. It was almost as if the director were *watching* her.

'He was a friend.'

'But of course. Listen, I personally do not see a link between the murder of Toor and the,' his fingers wiggled the symbol of inverted commas in the air, '*altered* calligraphy, but rest assured, it'll be examined. Now,' he said, rising, 'if you'll excuse me...'

Mehrunisa slung her bag over her shoulder, thanked him and walked out. As she reached the door, Raj Bhushan called out, 'Convey my regards to Professor Kaul. And wish him a speedy recovery.' He stood there, hands tucked in his pockets, wearing that peculiar smile.

Outside, Mehrunisa rubbed the back of her neck. Neither the SSP nor the director-general seemed to believe that the calligraphic changes were important. *Was* she overreacting?

Delhi

When Mehrunisa returned from meeting the director-general, Mangat Ram informed her that Pamposh, Professor Kaul's niece, was waiting inside. They had spoken over the phone frequently since Mehrunisa's return to India, but had not seen each other for five years.

Now, standing in the patio, Mehrunisa wondered how much Pamposh must have changed. They were twelve when they were first thrown together in the professor's rambling house. She remembered how, one day, Mangat Ram had returned from the market carrying a pup with the groceries. He had found it mewling outside a neighbour's gate, he'd said, abandoned.

'Why?' the girls quizzed in unison.

The housekeeper examined the scrawny mutt and said, 'Probably because he's a mongrel.' When asked to clarify, he explained that a mongrel was a mixed breed.

Pamposh had nodded and said, 'Like Mehroo.'

The next instant the door opened.

In that flash it takes us to size up people we have known well, Mehrunisa realised that Pamposh was much the same. Dressed in an elegant ivory-coloured Kashmiri knee-length phiran, her riotously curly hair cut short, Pamposh greeted her with a smile bookended by deep dimples.

'Mehroo!' she cried, using the name that harked back to their childhood. A quick hug later, her eyes did a swift appraisal, she gave a naughty wink and said, 'You look as fetching as ever.'

'And you,' Mehrunisa smiled as she draped an arm around Pamposh and led her inside. When they were seated on the living room sofa, Pamposh, with worry in her eyes said softly, 'What's up with Kaul mama?'

Mehrunisa apprised her of the professor's deteriorating health, which was increasingly marked by periods of forgetfulness.

Pamposh's eyes widened. 'You mean to say he forgets who *he* is?'

Mehrunisa paused as she attempted to describe the situation accurately. 'It's as if he enters a vacuum,' she shrugged, 'where he is aware of nothing.'

'You mean,' Pamposh said, 'he doesn't recognise people around him? Even people he knows well—like you, and Mangat Ram?'

Mehrunisa nodded, her lips pursed.

'Oh dear!' Pamposh said in that strangely excitable voice. Mehrunisa was accustomed to it—in childhood she would teasingly call her Drama Queen. Not surprisingly, Pamposh had leveraged that trait into a vocation. She was a trained actor; not the sort, however, who perform for affluent audiences in air-conditioned halls. A theatre activist, she staged feminist street plays at various corners and squares of Jaipur with her troupe of actors drawn from secondary schools and her own school. A play centred on the issue of female foeticide became so wildly popular that it started to register on the itineraries of foreign tourists. Traffic in front of Jaipur's Hawa Mahal stalled whenever her troupe performed, leading the municipal authorities to order her to take her play elsewhere, preferably within the four walls of a theatre. But Pamposh refused. The suppression of the play led to protests from parents, concerned citizens, tour guides and travel agents. By popular demand, Pamposh's troupe was back.

Pamposh tugged at her chin thoughtfully. 'Perhaps I should move in for some time. I could keep an eye on Kaul mama and we could be together, eh?' Before Mehrunisa could answer, she continued, 'But what would happen to my children?'

Pamposh also ran an orphanage for children who had been the victims of riots. Expectedly, most children were from minority Muslim families. To help calm the mind and develop mental toughness, the children were taught yoga. In meditation class, which Pamposh often conducted, the children were taught to recite Om, and various Sanskrit shlokas, as an aid. When the unsuitability of teaching Hindu hymns to Muslim children was broached, Pamposh's answer was typically pragmatic: what better way to redress the sectarian violence they have witnessed than by emphasising that God is one, no matter in what form?

'I'm here,' Mehrunisa said simply. 'Come when you can, like today.'

'Today, right!' Pamposh clapped her hands and hopped off the sofa toward the table where her bag sat. She rummaged through it, extracted a paper and handed it to Mehrunisa. 'Read it, while I ask Mangat Ram to get tea.' She spun on her high heels in the direction of the kitchen.

Mehrunisa scanned the flyer for a 'Delhi Kashmir Sammelan', which listed Pamposh Pandit as a keynote speaker and carried her profile. After she had finished reading it, Mehrunisa reflected how the little girl who had been her summer companion had matured.

At any given time, Pamposh was a living contradiction. A coin-sized red bindi contrasted sharply with the peaches and cream complexion of her Kashmiri skin. The forehead decoration was a trademark and always worn, whether Pamposh was in a starched cotton sari, jeans, flowing skirt or salwar kameez. Another characteristic feature was the dejihors she sported: a rather distinctive ear ornament, it hung from the helix and was traditionally worn by married Kashmiri Pandit women. Pamposh was not married and the reason she gave for wearing it was, 'So I never forget where I come from.' An aureole of black curls framed her heart-shaped face and her triangular chin jutted out in some signal of defiance. Pamposh, whose name meant lotus flower, had no truck with lotus-eaters, nor could the adjective 'lily' apply to her. In her diminutive frame—she was five feet-two inches—she packed the energy of a dynamo.

Pamposh also ran a website called Kashmiri Pandits for Peace in Kashmir, a repository of information on culture, language, religion, and matrimonial services. 'Displaced Kashmiris' was a popular section which provided a network for Kashmiris who had fled their homeland in the wake of the Pakistan-backed Muslim insurgency to re-establish connections with people they had known or left behind.

There were those in the Kashmiri community in Jaipur who regarded Pamposh as emblematic of all that was good and beautiful about Kashmir. A typical Kashmiri beauty—some called her Kashmir ki kali, in a nod to the popular '60s Hindi film that showcased the beauty of Kashmir to the rest of India—she had the fire of a blazing chinar in her and a deep-seated love for her homeland. Her website was lauded for its attempt to highlight the plight of Kashmiri refugees to a disinterested India.

Pamposh's heels clacked down the hall before she appeared with a tray laden with tea.

'Ta-daa! Look what I got you Mehroo, your favourite!'

Soon they were digging into the pyaz ki kachoris, sipping ginger tea and chatting as of old. As Pamposh was updating Mehrunisa on the Kashmir Sammelan, she licked some tamarind chutney off a finger and shook her head exasperatedly. 'But there is this one guy in the organising committee who hates me. Last year he raised such a ruckus, and for no fault of mine.'

Mehrunisa lifted her brow in question as she savoured the caramelised onion filling.

'Because,' Pamposh wagged her fingers in the air to indicate quote marks as she switched to speaking in a wheezy voice, '"Ms. Pandit is the niece of the famed Kashmiri lover of Muslims, the historian Vishwanath Kaul. In fact, so besotted is that Kashmiri Pandit with the sons of Babur that he has spent a lifetime researching and writing about the very barbarians who have made the Kashmiri Pandits homeless. Oh, what shame!"'

Pamposh clutched her stomach and began to shake with merriment as Mehrunisa guffawed.

Holding up an index finger, Pamposh sputtered, 'And that's not all.' In a whispery voice she mimicked, '"And why is Ms Pandit, at thirty, still single? Because the households with eligible Kashmiri boys privately wonder what they would do with a daughter-in-law like her?!'"

Pamposh burst into another fit of laughter.

Mehrunisa returned her teacup to the tray and said, 'Sounds like the convention gets some wolves. Why would you want to be there?'

Suddenly Pamposh sat up, back upright, looking rather serious. 'Because Mehrunisa, Pamposh Pandit is a brilliant representative of Kashmiriyat, the ethos of social and religious harmony which is the true spirit of Kashmir. Why, Mehroo, I love you even, and you are half-Persian!'

Agra

'You do understand the import of what I am saying, Kriplaniji,' Professor R.N. Dixit said, gazing eagerly at the man seated opposite him. A folder was open on the table and papers containing diagrams and text in Hindi and English were strewn about.

Kriplani did not reply. He studied the man in front of him dressed in a worn blue blazer, an improperly buttoned shirt, grey pants that could do with ironing and greasy silver locks that fell to his shoulder. All the trademark signs of a mad scientist. To that extent, he reflected, Dixit had not changed much since the days when they both taught at Benares Hindu University. Professor R.N. Dixit was acknowledged as a brilliant chemist who, lost in his laboratory, had to be reminded of each class he tutored. At home, he forgot to eat his meals and his wife, sick of the reheating, wondered if he'd know the difference if she served him sawdust. However, to Dixit's credit, the flipside of his forgetfulness was his laser focus on each project that caught his fancy. He had several patents to his name and retirement had brought him a sought-after consulting practice.

Kriplani massaged his clean-shaven chin and pondered. The obvious gleam in Dixit's eyes was due to the project he had just outlined—like him, it was mad, outrageous and yet, if it succeeded.... His toothbrush moustache quivered, vibrating sympathetically to his machinations. At last he spoke.

'You realise what you are asking me to do? At stake is a historical Indian monument. Not any monument, but the most famous one. Any wrongdoing will bring infamy to the person involved. Me.'

Dixit watched the ex-minister with manic eyes. 'When it succeeds, imagine what it'll do for the great glory of Hindutva.'

And for the glory of himself and his party, Kriplani thought, remembering the dismal result of the general elections six months ago. Perhaps it could provide them with a pivot around which to rally the Hindu vote bank.

'How can you assure me of your absolute secrecy in this matter?'

Professor Dixit wagged his head knowingly, his silvery locks astir. 'You're right to be concerned—you head the largest opposition party in the country. But friend,' he leaned forward and twitched his bulbous nose, 'this is me, the same Dixit you've known for most of your life. In these troubled times of terror and human bombs, I've decided to put my genius to better use. My concern is shining light upon the great and glorious religion of this land. Our home-grown Hindu faith. Taj Mahal—'

Kriplani held up a hand. 'Have your tea, Dixitji. I do not doubt you. Still, I would be risking a great deal by agreeing to your plan.'

The proposition tantalised Kriplani, though. He was an Agra boy, having grown up—like any Agra resident—in the perennial shadow of the Taj Mahal: a weekly family outing meant a visit to the marble mausoleum; eager outstation relatives were duly chaperoned to the world-famous monument; and all school picnics were conveniently held in its sprawling Mughal gardens. Perhaps it was the excessive viewing, or a case of familiarity-breeds-contempt, but even as a child he had found the monument squat and ungainly and the colour of spoilt milk. As an adult he had found it compared poorly in aesthetics with the grandeur of a Meenakshi temple or the Kandariya Mahadeva temple at Khajuraho—both predating the Taj by centuries. It was the Western historians, drunk on Mughal grandeur, who opined ceaselessly on the Taj Mahal's beauty. To any discerning Indian there were more worthy monuments in the nation. The only thing about the Taj Mahal that Kriplani had enjoyed as a child was the game of hide-and-seek in the monument's bowels—the belly was at that time still open to visitors. Now it was locked and barricaded, but Kriplani knew it well. The immense potential of it now started to swim up to his consciousness.

Dixit slurped his tea as he looked around the room. A framed portrait of Krishna on one wall caught his eye. He replaced the saucer with a clatter on the table and pointed his chin in its direction. 'Do your duty, Kriplaniji, and leave the rest to him.'

Kriplani smiled. The mad scientist was oblivious to the hive of possibilities his initial idea had germinated in Kriplani's mind. The government of India did not sanction the procedure, so God had sent a transgressor his way. Leaning forward, he asked, 'Carbon dating the monument, you said? How will it work?'

Raipur, Chhattisgarh

The commissioner of police Arvind Pradhan had the good looks of servicemen who made it to the position of ADC to the state governor. R.P. Singh could easily picture Pradhan standing stiffly behind the governor, gazing straight ahead, oblivious to cameras. Besides looks, Pradhan had the smarts to make it to that coveted position. It was not luck that had led to his appointment as commissioner of police in a state locked in a battle with its own people, the embattled Maoists. Pradhan knew how to pick resourceful subordinates, was unsparing in the demands he placed on them, but protected them fiercely. In that cabal, R.P. Singh was a favoured lieutenant. But this time around, Pradhan's handsome brow was knitted.

He clucked his tongue before glaring at R.P. Singh. 'You've gone too far this time. The instructions were clear—bring the goddamned man in. The CM wants to hold talks with the Maoists, simple. Media was agog, there was advance talk of a breakthrough, we had everybody taped up—human rights people, journalists, activists—and then you go and screw things up!'

He shook his head. 'Bad! Things are looking very bad for you.' His eyes goggled at Singh for his apparent passivity as he sat across from his superior, hands resting on his lap, a picture of serenity.

It was not the first time R.P. Singh was taking the rap and there was nothing new he could add in his defence. The commissioner had been briefed and he was aware that if the Maoist leader had not been killed, he would have killed Singh—either way, there would have been no Maoist leader engaging in talks to parade before the world. Only, Pradhan's best resource—who had delivered several of the 'hits' that had zoomed him up the career ladder—would have been felled.

However, walls have ears and Pradhan was ensuring that the CM's umbrage was conveyed in no uncertain terms to his errant subordinate. It had become difficult to open a daily and not find a photograph of the slain man or read a headline about the government's atrocities.

'I have gone through the report you submitted,' Pradhan glanced at the computer on his desk, paused as he settled back into his red chair, 'and have forwarded it to the CM's office. They want to order a probe to investigate whether you acted rashly.'

R.P. Singh listened intently as he sat relaxed, one leg resting atop a knee.

'Meanwhile, they want you sent on leave.' The commissioner moved his tongue against one cheek. 'However, that would be a waste of time, right?'

'Sir,' R.P. Singh responded with respect.

'Instead you'll spend the next six months with the CBI in Delhi, Special Branch.' Pradhan watched him with reproach before lowering his voice. 'I am parking you there Singh, keep your head below the radar for once,' he hissed.

'Sir,' R.P. Singh said.

One of the three phones on the desk rang. The commissioner eyed it briefly before picking it up. The tone of his voice informed Singh that he was speaking to a senior journalist. Singh groaned inwardly—only a political scandal or a battle between the Bollywood Khans would energise the media away from this Maoist death. Perhaps it wouldn't be so bad to get away from it all for some time. Delhi would be a pleasant diversion. The metro was buzzing with fresh drinking holes, the alcohol available was world-class, and women were no problem.... That facet of his life was entirely lost to him since he had been posted to the badlands of Bastar. A day lounging in the air-conditioned hum of a high-end bar was the polar opposite of lurking in dense vegetation on the trail of a Maoist with reptiles and bison for company.

He was seeing happy visions of Delhi when the commissioner replaced the phone, swore and looked up. He mimicked a high-pitched voice as he said, 'Naxal movement is growing because it is people's struggle transformed into a power struggle—would you agree, Sir?'

R.P. Singh pursed his mouth to prevent the laughter from bubbling out.

Pradhan blew air and shook his head vigorously. Turning his attention to Singh he continued sotto voce, 'Six months of paid holiday, Singh. Relax in Delhi and cool that head of yours before you are back.' Raising his voice, he said, 'You'll pick up some strategic skills with the CBI which will come handy when you return. Remember the battle with the Maoists will not be won overnight.'

R.P. Singh nodded quietly. A break from gaandu Maoists wouldn't be bad. Besides, he had a license to chill!

Agra

Mehrunisa drove to Agra from Delhi in pursuit of the only lead she had. Despite the misgivings of the SSP and the ASI director-general, she was intent on identifying the artisan who had altered the calligraphy on Mumtaz's tomb. She would start by meeting the two families in Agra claiming direct descent from the artists who had worked on the mausoleum in the seventeenth century. The finesse of the alteration suggested someone hailing from either clan, and Professor Kaul had supplied the names of the two patriarchs: Hafeez Gul and Hajji Nizam Naqshbandi.

At the entrance to the narrow lane in which was located one address, she parked her car. Marble stores and craft shops, many of which had adjacent open courtyards that served as workshops, flanked the alley. Mehrunisa could see inlay-workers squatting on low wooden slats, barefoot, their heads bent in concentration, cutting hardstones with bow saws, the technique unchanged since Mughal times. Extreme skill was needed to saw stones such as agate, jasper and heliotrope into tiny crescents, circles, ovals and other delicate shapes. A lapidary sat fitting the minute pieces into a tabletop, arranging them in place before fixing them with glue, to create the desired pattern. The work took its toll on the eyes of craftsmen, who usually quit after twenty-odd years to avoid going blind.

She came to a halt outside a nondescript house whose nameplate said Hajji Nizam Naqshbandi. The door was open. Stepping over the threshold she saw a woman hanging clothes on a line. 'Salaam-e-lekum,' Mehrunisa called out.

'Walekum as salaam,' said the woman as she dried her hands on her cotton dupatta and came forward, her face questioning.

Mehrunisa recollected the information Professor Kaul had provided on this artist. Apparently Hajji had overseen the replacement of damaged or deteriorating pieces in the Taj all his life, supervising the men who worked under his keen eyes. A follower of the Naqshbandi Sufis, an ancient order of Islam, he had kept up the traditional involvement of the mystic Sufi brotherhoods in his art.

Mehrunisa introduced herself to the woman and explained that she wished to meet Hajji Nizam Naqshbandi. She was doing a project, she added, on the Taj Mahal, and needed to speak with the man who had worked on the monument for forty years.

The woman scrutinised Mehrunisa, taking in the straight black hair, the grey-green eyes, the fair complexion. 'You are Persian,' she said.

'Yes,' Mehrunisa said, taken aback at the certainty in the woman's voice. 'I'm half-Persian—my mother's side. How did you know?'

The woman snorted. 'My husband has spent a lifetime carving Persian beauties. High forehead, large eyes, sharp nose, prominent chin. You have a strong face. Your parents couldn't have named you anything else.' She pointed to a chair opposite a string bed. 'Sit down. I'll make some tea.'

'There's no need,' Mehrunisa protested.

'Then how will we talk? Hajji saab has gone to see the doctor—he'll be a while.'

'Oh! Is he unwell?'

The woman walked to a room located in a corner of the central courtyard. It had a chimney and a narrow window through which a steel object glinted. Probably the kitchen, Mehrunisa thought.

'He's as unwell,' the woman's voice floated out, 'as any man who has lost a son.'

The family was bereaved and she was intruding on them! What should she do? She looked around, noticing the stone-paved patio, tufts of grass springing through the crevices, paint peeling from the walls, the clean but sparse quarters—Mehrunisa could see that the chief artisan of the Taj Mahal was a poor man indeed. The woman reappeared with two cups of tea and a plate of spicy potato puffs on a tray. She deposited it on a wooden table beside the bed, handed Mehrunisa her cup and lowered herself slowly on the bed. Poor knees, she indicated with a wry smile.

'I am so sorry,' Mehrunisa murmured. 'I had no idea, otherwise I would not have intruded.'

The woman waved her apologies away. 'No, no. Not the way you think,' she sighed, 'thanks to Allah! Only, our son seems to have lost his mind.' She mopped her brow with one end of her dupatta. 'So many times I told my husband, don't train him to be a karigar, don't. Hajji saab has devoted his entire life to the monument's upkeep, and what does he get in return? After forty years of service, he is still employed on daily wages by the Indian government! A skilled artisan treated like a common labourer. But Hajji saab loves his work.' Her eyes filled with pain, her mouth crushed with sadness as she sat, hands folded in her lap.

The shrill horn of a vehicle sounded in the distance, piercing the stillness. Mehrunisa noticed the woman's well-worn clothes, the dupatta that had thinned from many washes, the sagging bed on which she sat. It was not a house that had ever seen prosperity.

'My boy,' the woman sniffled, 'Nisar, he has a lovely voice. He sings often with a local qawwali troupe, Khusro's songs especially...' As her voice trailed off, her eyes returned to the table. Urging Mehrunisa to drink her tea she offered her the puffs, adding 'home-made' to reassure her. She sipped her tea and over the teacup enquired, 'You are familiar with Khusro?'

Mehrunisa nodded. It was impossible to live in India and be untouched by the legendary poet. His compositions—in Hindi, Persian, a mix of Persian and Hindi—continued to be equally popular with folk singers, pop stars and Bollywood. Credited as the founder of Hindustani classical music and qawwali, he was born of a Turkish father and an Indian mother.

The woman shook her head. 'You should hear my Nisar sing to understand why I was keen for him to develop that into a profession. But no, he had grown up watching his father chisel and sand and coax stone to beauty. So he followed in his steps. And there too, he showed his skill. What a fine craftsman he was turning out to be! The Taj supervisor himself complimented his work.'

At the mention of Arun Toor, Mehrunisa felt a stab of pain. 'So, did he get to do any special work at the Taj?'

'He would go daily with his father. Then Hajji saab fell ill and had to be hospitalised for two weeks. We are poor people—how could we afford the cost? Fortunately Nisar landed a prestigious project at the Taj. The next day he returned with one thousand rupees that he had made on the special commission.' The woman flicked her palms open in bewilderment. 'But within days of that he became morose, stopped working, started muttering under his breath ... Hajji saab recovered and returned home, but my boy, he took to his bed.'

Mehrunisa's pulse was racing but she attempted to speak normally. 'How long ago was this?'

The woman grimaced. 'Less than a month ago.'

'And now—where is he?'

'Hajji saab left him with relatives in Nizamuddin in Delhi. They live close to the dargah. He thought a chance to spend time in the saint's calming shade might work. Daily the mausoleum resounds to Sufi hymns—surely the saint's blessings will come upon my son and distract him from this wretched work of an artisan! Even in his delirium,' she bunched her dupatta in one fist and buried her mouth in it, 'he muttered *rauza-i-munauwara, rauza-i-munauwara*, over and over.'

Mehrunisa placed a hand on the woman's shoulder to comfort her. The mother's agony was written all over her face. Though her voice had been muffled through the thin cotton of her dupatta, Mehrunisa had heard correctly. She was onto something now, she knew. She had to find the son in Nizamuddin and talk to him. The woman may not have understood, but Mehrunisa had got the import of her son's feverish muttering.

Rauza-i-munauwara.

The illumined tomb.

Agra

SSP Raghav was in his office when his mobile rang. Mehrunisa Khosa, the screen flashed.

'SSP Raghav,' he said in his arrogant voice.

The woman sounded excited as she informed him that she might have tracked down the artist who had altered the calligraphy.

'You are in Agra!' Raghav could not hide his surprise. He had given the woman a hard time and here she was in the city, calling him of her own volition when any other person in such a situation would give him a wide berth.

'Where else would I meet the artisan?' she said gaily as she detailed her encounter.

Raghav listened even as his mind rejected the theory that Mehrunisa was trying to prove. The woman believed it sufficiently to have come traipsing down, but he was convinced that the tampering—if indeed there was any; after all, the woman could be mistaken—was a harmless prank. Who would make a change that in the first place none would notice and in the second, upon noticing, would fail to comprehend? Agra, indeed the entire country, was not exactly brimming with people literate in Arabic or Persian—nor were these first languages for the thousands of visitors to the Taj.

Instead, he had been focusing on the mysterious Aurangzeb. Was he an Islamic jihadi? But no one had taken credit for the murder, something a terrorist group would have done. Or was it premature—perhaps there was more to come? Did the calligraphy tampering link up with some bigger plan, as Mehrunisa alleged?

He had assigned a constable to go through the files and books in the supervisor's office for any mention of an Aurangzeb, the person Toor was supposed to have met the evening he died. But the constable had not come up with anything.

Arun Toor—or the murderer—had scribbled 'chirag tale andhera' before dying as a warning, or as a clue. Raghav believed he had meant the basement rooms and had those searched for explosive devices but found nothing thus far. The rooms continued to be under surveillance. On his advice, his boss had stepped up security at the Taj Mahal: there was an additional team in the Yellow/outer zone, tourists were being frisked more thoroughly, and the Red/inner zone protected by the CISF was put on high alert.

A constable walked in with the latest cup in his daily tea-a-thon. Raghav questioned him with raised brows as he rotated his index finger atop the teacup in a stirring motion. The constable waved both palms in panic as he mouthed 'no sugar'. Satisfied, Raghav nodded him away.

Meanwhile, Mehrunisa was going on about the chief artisan's son; she would try and locate him in Delhi, she told the SSP. And then there was a long pause.

The inviting aroma of tea wafted up. SSP Raghav grunted as he collected his thoughts. Privately he thought it was a dud, but it would be good to keep the woman within reach—after all, he didn't have any concrete leads on which to proceed.

'Sure, do that,' he humoured her. 'When you do track this Nisar down, keep me posted.' On that he switched the phone off and sipped his tea.

These artists, he smirked, so woolly-headed. In their world, terrorists wielded chisels and not guns!

Agra

The Taj Mahal stands on a white marble platform atop a red sandstone terrace, surrounded by four octagonal minarets, flanked on the left by a mosque, and on the right by an identical assembly hall. Behind it flows the Yamuna, and in front stretch the Mughal gardens. Since the land slopes down towards the river, the sandstone base rises four feet above the garden on the riverside; a fact indiscernible when the monument is approached from the gardens. The two minarets to the north have stairs that lead down to exits at the riverside. Since the towers are no longer open, visitors are unaware of the two doors that can be used from the riverside to enter the Taj. These lead to stairs and rooms inside the towers, and from there to the upper level, granting access to the mausoleum.

Tonight, moonlight glistened off the rippling Yamuna and shone on bare muscled arms that cut through it with noiseless strokes. All around lay quiet. Jara emerged from the water like a sea creature: thin loincloth plastered to his posterior, droplets cascading down his bare skin, muscles flashing with every tread forward. Hunched over, he ascended the slope towards the monument's rear and made for the door to the right, which would lead him into the northwest tower. From the folds of his loincloth, he extricated a heavy iron key.

He had his orders: there was work to be done inside the hidden rooms of the Taj Mahal.

❋ ❋ ❋

The next morning the idle gossip of tourists floated down below. On the paved sandstone terrace above him, near the base of the two northern riverfront minarets, steps descended to the rooms where Jara was. However, the stairways were closed off with iron railings. It was not unusual to find tourists gawking at the railing, speculating on what lay beneath.

Precisely what a group of tourists was doing at that very moment.

A woman had put her face to the grille covering the blocked staircase as she attempted to peer into the dark. Unable to sleep, Jara had idly wandered beneath the railing. Now he could hear the woman's laboured breath as she squirmed to see what was below. Above her, others urged her to move on and give them a turn. Initially, Jara had chuckled when he heard their wild speculation on how far the underground tunnel went: to the Agra fort! No no, all the way to Delhi! Guides spiked the debate by adding that the staircase was the means by which Shah Jahan had the architect and workers of the Taj Mahal transferred to dungeons, thus preventing a replication of his magnificent monument.

The truth, though, was more prosaic: the stairway gave access to seven rooms arrayed along the Yamuna. Jara had been told that, at one time, the river could be viewed through the rooms' generous arches. But now the once airy space was walled up, offering no natural light. That suited him just fine: a creature of the dark, he didn't care much for the beauty that the visitors gawked at. No. He knew the Taj from inside out, and its bowels, dungeons, and terrace rooms, which were closed to others, were of late his quarters. In the shadows Jara knew he was safe, but he did indulge an errant thought sporadically: what if he were to quietly ascend the steps, and near the railing reveal his face? Would fuel be added to the legend of the Taj's resident ghost?

Ten years ago, Jara had been driving his boss' police jeep through the streets of Srinagar when a suicide bomber had rammed his explosives-laden car into the vehicle believing that the director-general of police was the man sitting beside the driver. In fact, the DGP was delayed at home but had sent his jeep ahead with an inspector carrying the files needed for the noon meeting with the chief minister.

Jara remembered a thundering jolt that threw him against the steering wheel, a deafening blast and an instant inferno that engulfed him. By the time he was rescued, flesh from his face had melted. He spent the next year in the Military Hospital. After five rounds of surgeries, his face was reconstructed, in a manner. From salvaged tissue, the surgeons had given him a mouth. He had cavities which functioned for eyes and ears, and twin vents for a nose. His shattered skull was replaced by a plastic dome and his brain had suffered such that parts of it were irreparably damaged. His complexion was limestone-white, rather ghost-white.

That was what children called him, ghost, and ran screaming *bhoot, bhoot*—when they didn't start shrieking at the sight of him. He so unnerved the people around him that he decided to become less human in his habits. As he shunned daylight, night became his friend. When others slept, Jara was free to walk the roads. However, even the roads at night-time were not free of living creatures: the omnipresent soldiers guarding the nooks and crannies of Srinagar gawked at him or slapped him around, attempting bravado; the dogs yelped when they saw him; the homeless began to mewl. Lonely, frustrated, his brain fighting through fog for days on end, he had been losing himself when someone took him under his wing. With time, Jara learnt how to live in the world with his new face and found a new mission.

He retreated into the dark rooms now; the resident ghost of the Taj Mahal had certain housekeeping chores to do.

Jaipur

Pamposh Pandit was busy with her weekly ritual: cleaning the mahogany model temple in her prayer-cum-study room. A miniature of a north Indian temple, it was built on a square base with a high wooden ceiling atop which arose a tapering spire. The wood had a smoothness that comes from being tended over the years.

It belonged to Pamposh's mother—she had brought it with her as part of a young bride's dowry when she married Omkar Pandit. It had formed an integral part of her mother's morning ritual as she bathed, draped a fresh sari, gathered flowers from the garden—tucking one behind an ear—and offered them to her God. As she lit the two silver lamps and burnt incense, she would summon her husband and young Pamposh. Omkar Pandit did not much care for invocations to God; his belief was karma, the doing of one's duty, and everything else would get taken care of. But he also believed in indulging his spouse and good-humouredly ribbed her about her one-on-ones with God as he accepted the prasad and vermilion. For young Pamposh, it was a time to ask God for anything and also to ring the tiny silver bell before she could decamp with a sweet.

Now, once a week, Pamposh cleaned out the temple and the idols it housed: pot-bellied Ganesha, lotus-seated Saraswati, and a framed picture of matted-haired Shiva, a serpent coiled around his neck. It was her way of connecting with something that was lost to her forever. Unlike her mother, Pamposh lit the lamps and the incense stick only once a week; a daily ritual would evoke too many memories.

The temple's base housed a narrow drawer that her mother had used for storing cotton wicks, a box of matchsticks, aromatic incense. Pamposh only kept an oak ring box in the drawer. Now she took it out with care. Nestled on a red satiny cloth was a single tooth, an adult molar. Her gaze lingered on it before she returned it to the drawer and stepped back to scrutinise the temple. The lamps were aglow, the smell of sandalwood wafted from the incense stick, the gods looked radiant: Yes, her mother would be happy.

Fighting the lump that rose in her on every such occasion, Pamposh settled on the day bed with her favourite book. Every Sunday the tooth took her to the scene of carnage: a concrete road strewn with metal pieces, glass shards, petrol streaks, bloody blotches where a car bomb had vaporised director-general of police Omkar Pandit. He had hunted terrorists in the strife-torn state of Kashmir with mounting success that had resulted in several attempts on his life. Finally, they had succeeded. The only part of himself that Omkar Pandit left behind on that day was a tooth, a single molar. A forensic team recovered it from the site and confirmed it belonged to the DGP. The news so devastated her mother she had to be admitted to the long-term care of specialists of trauma victims.

Pamposh tried not to think of her parents through the week as she attempted a semblance of a normal life. Only on Sundays did she allow the bitterness, which sloshed within her like vitriol, to spill over. Her parents had been good people. And yet, Pamposh thought, their gods had let them down—assorted Hindu deities, her mother, and karma, her father. No wonder then that Pamposh's favourite book was the world's oldest written treatise on military strategy: *The Art of War*, written by Sun Tzu in the sixth century BC.

Pamposh clamped her eyes shut, breathed deeply and banished everything from her mind. Opening the volume at the bookmarked page she began her reading as customary with the last verse of the third chapter.

So it is said that if you know your enemies and know yourself, you will win a hundred times in a hundred battles. If you only know yourself, but not your opponent, you win one and lose the next. If you do not know yourself or your enemy, you will always lose.

Pamposh had many demons to conquer.

Agra

In front of the Taj Mahal is a large courtyard called the Jilaukhana. In the olden times, visitors to the tomb would dismount from their elephants and horses and assemble here before entering through the great gate. Today tourists to the Taj queue up here, their eyes scouting northwards for a glimpse of the famed wonder, as they wait to be frisked by security men.

Seldom, if ever, does a visitor investigate the area south of Jilaukhana called Taj Ganj, originally an integral part of the Taj Mahal. Once a bazaar teeming with stalls selling precious stones, silks and perfumes, today it is crammed with shops hawking Taj trinkets, cheap reproductions of marble inlay work, ubiquitous Agra sweets, drugs. The formal architecture and grandeur of the Taj Mahal stands in bold relief against the utilitarian squalor of Taj Ganj.

It was in this quarter that Jara, the emissary, had gone forth seeking suitable candidates for his mission. The qualifications were simple: they had to be devout Hindus, male, young, illiterate, in menial jobs, if not jobless. The critical criterion, however, was that they had to have suffered in the recent Hindu-Muslim riots. Taj Ganj was inhabited by both Hindus and Muslims, and six months ago, a Muslim celebration had turned funereal when a truck had rammed into the procession, killing several Muslim men and children. The rumour went that the Hindu police had deliberately permitted the truck to proceed through the narrow alley, already congested by the procession. Riots had ensued. Policemen and Hindu shops were targeted. A curfew was declared and the Taj Mahal remained closed for a week. Hindu-Muslim tensions, however, continued to simmer.

All that the emissary had to do was look for glowing embers. He had located ten eligible candidates for the first session. Each qualified with his own gruesome story. One came from a buffalo stable that had been ravaged—the inferno had consumed the boy's water buffalos as well as his parents. Another had a brother whose brains were pulped by a hurled brick. Yet another was an aspiring arsonist who had initiated target practice on street strays. He had witnessed his constable father being set ablaze by a mob, the charred carcass later strung from a lamppost.

Taj Ganj was restive. All it needed was a prod.

Delhi

A flower-seller thrust marigolds in Mehrunisa's face. She averted her head and saw a hawker beckoning her to his wares—rosaries and embroidered caps—laid out on a green sheet. She pretended not to notice, retreating into the bubble she had learnt to create during her time spent in India. From within it she could observe everything even as, to a casual observer, she appeared remote, glacial. It worked, granting her the space she needed to function in the teeming milieu of her adopted home.

Mehrunisa crossed her arms as she waited for the boy who had escorted her to emerge. He was carrying the note of introduction that Hajji Nizam Naqshbandi had kindly consented to write. Mehrunisa had found the old artisan's company delightful. In his quiet dignified manner he had recounted his association with the Taj Mahal over forty years, not once betraying any bitterness despite the obviously shabby manner in which he had been treated by its custodians. She had requested he mention in the letter to his son that she was fluent in both languages used in the script of the Taj Mahal: Arabic and Persian.

Now Mehrunisa glanced in the direction her young guide had disappeared. A medieval-looking archway led to a veranda that fronted the tomb of Amir Khusro. Tucked away in the shade of a five-star hotel, residential bungalows and a looming flyover, Nizamuddin was one of Delhi's oldest, continuously inhabited areas. It housed the tombs of Nizamuddin Auliya, a Sufi saint, and Amir Khusro, his disciple and one of India's greatest poets.

The next instant she felt a tug at her elbow. Her escort had surfaced and was pointing a short distance away to where a young man slouched, a faint beard covering his face. 'Nisar,' the boy nodded and stuck out his palm. Mehrunisa planted a ten-rupee note in the outstretched hand, steadied her bag and walked forward. She raised her right hand in the traditional Muslim greeting, aadab. Nisar did not respond nor did he make a move to depart. He just stood there, regarding her blankly.

Mehrunisa decided to join him at the mausoleum entrance. She removed her shoes and tied a patterned silk scarf over her head before entering the dargah. Approaching Nisar, she spoke in Urdu, informing him of her meeting with his parents and conveying their blessings. When she mentioned the Taj, Nisar turned and walked away.

Mehrunisa followed as he headed for the filigreed screen surrounding the tomb. Around them milled barefoot men and women, heads bowed, lips moving in silent invocation. A throng of devotees was tying colourful threads to the screen and young children wove through, their high-pitched voices floating above a distant recitation. When she caught up with Nisar, she reeled off her introduction as a student of Mughal art, the time she had spent studying the Taj Mahal, and her particular interest in the tomb itself, taking care to refer to it as *rauza-i-muqqadas*. At the mention of the 'holy tomb' Nisar's eyes flickered nervously.

Mehrunisa decided to take a chance. Who had instructed him to change the calligraphy on the rauza, she asked.

Nisar trembled visibly, but remained quiet. Wheeling around, he hurried into the courtyard where a waterseller, leather bag slung on one shoulder, roamed with drinking water. Rushing up to him, Nisar cupped his shaky hands to drink. Mehrunisa caught up with him and said sotto voce, 'Speak to me, Nisar. I know about the changes. Between "munauwar" and "masnooee" is a world of difference, and you know that, right? No one has noticed it so far, no one except me.'

Nisar's eyes were focused on her.

'But I don't blame you Nisar. I know you are a *mureed*.'

Mehrunisa paused to gauge Nisar's reaction. Since he appeared to be a devotee of Nizamuddin and Khusro, she had used the Sufi term for one who was committed to a spiritual teacher. Had she had any effect on him? Two children scampered between them, chasing each other in the courtyard. Mehrunisa noticed that a troupe of qawwali singers had gathered and were readying their musical instruments in the courtyard. A crowd had started to gather around them. Nisar went to join them. Mehrunisa followed and sat beside him.

The next instant, to her great surprise, Nisar started humming a tune. As she looked on, he began chanting and the clarity of his voice impressed her. He was singing one of Amir Khusro's compositions that had become a rage when a Bollywood lyricist had adapted it for a Hindi film song. Listening to it, she realised something curious: Nisar was singing the even lines from the song, leaving the odd ones out.

duraye naina banaye batiya...
... na leho kaahe lagaye chhatiyan
by blandishing your eyes and weaving tales...
... why do you not take me to your bosom

As Mehrunisa watched him, he stole an occasional glance in her direction. Was Nisar hinting at something? Of course, *of course*!

Nisar had chosen to sing a peculiar number, one that the erudite Amir Khusro had composed simultaneously in two languages: Hindvi, a version of Hindi, and Persian. The first line was in Persian, the second in Hindi and thus it continued, the two languages alternating through the song.

Nisar was testing her! Not taking his father's word for it, or hers, he was gauging for himself whether he could trust her. And what better way to do it than by checking the veracity of her claims? Through this one verse Nisar could determine how conversant Mehrunisa was with Persian, with the Sufi tradition, with Amir Khusro. She smiled: despite his perplexing behaviour, he was fine.

Mehrunisa was no singer—but what the heck! She recited the Persian lines:

Zehal-e miskin makun taghaful...
... ki taab-e hijran nadaram ay jaan
Do not overlook my misery...
... My patience flows over the brim

Nisar showed no sign that he understood what Mehrunisa was doing. A brief pause, and he resumed his singing.

In the background, the qawwal was singing tirana now: tananana, tananana he sang, lyrically rendering another innovation of Amir Khusro which had become a tradition in Indian classical singing. It was an indication to people that the singing would commence soon. The faithful were now streaming around them, making their way to the qawwal.

Careful not to draw the attention of the people around, she whispered, 'Nisar, you have to tell me who it was. Who instructed you to change the epitaph and verse? Surely somebody supervised you as you worked.'

Nisar's face remained impassive

'Tell me,' she pleaded. 'For the sake of the rauza to which your father has committed his entire life.'

Nisar's mouth quivered as his eyes moistened.

Had the mention of his father hit home?

Meanwhile, the qawwal was addressing his audience, asking for any special song with which to commence his performance. Abruptly, Nisar responded with a request.

The singer acknowledged him. Someone said, *Wah! Wah!* in appreciation. Mehrunisa sat, her hands in her lap, biting her lip as she wondered how to get Nisar to divulge his secret. Her eyes skimmed the sea of Van Gogh colours that encompassed her: white marble pillars topped with gold work, an ochre wall of sandstone, red rose petals on the tomb's emerald green cover glimpsed through the white filigree.

In the meantime, the singer was midway through his recital, and the crowd was responding with fervent rhythmic clapping. On the periphery of the gathering an old man had risen and was beginning to sway like a dervish. He was experiencing the trance that is often brought about by qawwali—people under its influence said later that it was akin to flying. The singer started to build the song to a crescendo, the applause got more vigorous as torsos began to sway to the forceful beat. As the singer dwelt on a phrase that seemed to have struck a resonant chord, chiming it, Mehrunisa glanced at Nisar. He was immersed in the music, eyes closed. The persistent chime drew her to the lyrics that in her distraction she had ignored thus far. The singer was alluding to the one who had hidden beneath a veil, who had drawn a covering over his face...

Uska mukh ek jot hai, ghunghat hai sansar, ghunghat mein woh chhup gaya, mukh par aanchal dar.

The words made Mehrunisa scrutinise her companion. Nisar moved his left palm in front of his face in a deliberate motion. To an onlooker it would signify nothing but to Mehrunisa, it suddenly dawned why Nisar had requested that specific song! The lyrics, in conjunction with Nisar's particular gesture, meant something. For an instant Nisar looked straight into her eyes before shifting his gaze. He understood that she had understood. And he would reveal no more, for he bowed his head and was lost in the music.

Mehrunisa's heart pounded in rhythm with the surrounding frenzy. Nisar's choice of song coupled with his palm gesture meant one thing: mask. The man Mehrunisa was seeking wore a mask, a mask he had removed for Nisar, and what had been divulged had so spooked him that he had almost lost his mind.

Agra

The youth were lured to the one-room tenement in Katra Omar Khan in Taj Ganj with the promise of a sign-on bonus of one thousand rupees for a prospective job. In return, all they had to do was to watch a film.

The man on the screen wore orange robes. From beneath the V-neck of his cotton kurta, curly black chest hair crept out. His face was austere and handsome with a flowing black beard, like a meditating sage from the TV serial *Mahabharat*. Despite the plainness of his garb and the looseness of his robe, the man's muscular frame was virile, and his eyes seemed to study the seated men in front with a piercing intensity. He folded his hands in an elaborate namaskar, elbows jutting out, forearms parallel to his chest. When he spoke, his deep voice resonated throughout the room.

'You are gathered here today to learn of the biggest hoax that has been perpetrated on you. The hoax that you, in particular, have grown up with. The hoax that is the shame of our great nation, Bharat. The hoax that is the collective tragedy of all Hindus.'

The voice paused, the eyes gored the audience. Then in the manner of those fearless saints who dictated to kings and courtiers, the sage continued to thunder. 'The time has come to strip off the curtain of falsity that shrouds your eyes. So that you, brave sons of a holy mother, will know how your mother has been defiled by the *grrr-eat* Mughals. The terrible tyranny of the invaders shall be revealed to you. Once you have learnt the truth, you will be free to choose your path. You can choose to avenge your honour, and thereby, the honour of Mother India. Or—' another long pause, '—you can continue to suffer the tyranny of the Mughals. The sons of Babur live in your neighbourhood and they burn you, they loot you and they kill you—at their will.'

The audience watched in silence. The words had found their mark, embedding like shrapnel in the young men's raw riot-ravaged selves.

The orange-robed sage lifted his right palm in benediction. 'It is time to begin your education.'

Delhi

Mehrunisa shivered as she stepped inside the twelve-pillared marble hall. Pulling up the collar of her jacket, she peered around. The hall would close in fifteen minutes—Nisar had chosen this particular time for their meeting. Clearly he was not one for small talk. She glanced at the scalloped arches—in the fading light of dusk they seemed to hover like the mammoth wings of a bird.

After her first meeting with Nisar in the shrine of Nizamuddin, Mehrunisa had twice attempted to ferret out information on the man in the mask. Thus far, though, she had not been successful. Nisar appeared unmoved by her repeated pleas. Except, as Mehrunisa had made to leave the shrine during her last meeting, he had shoved a scrap of paper in her hand.

Diwan-i-Khas, Monday, 5 p.m.

Diwan-i-Khas, the Hall of Private Audience, was located within the Red Fort. It was the chamber within which emperor Shah Jahan would hold private audiences with selected courtiers to discuss important affairs. Over the corner arches was inscribed the famous verse of Amir Khusro: 'If there be a paradise on earth, it is this, it is this, it is this'. Nisar, qawwali-singer, Sufi-poetry-lover, was a tad dramatic, Mehrunisa had concluded as she speculated on his choice of venue.

Standing now in the barren hall she realised the location was appropriate: on a cold winter day near closing time, the Hall was devoid of people and secluded. In their interactions, Nisar had appeared petrified, refusing even to open his mouth in acknowledgement, as if he was being marked. But where *was* Nisar?

The sunless day was briskly morphing to night and she thought to retrieve the torch from her bag as she surveyed the cavernous shadowy hall. Situated in the rectangular chamber's centre was a marble platform on which her eyes squinted in concentration. At one time, atop the platform had stood the hall's centrepiece, the fabled Peacock Throne, Takht-e-Taus, of solid gold adorned with peacock figures, their iridescence resulting from countless inlaid precious stones. Mehrunisa was aware, ruefully, of another Indo-Persian linkage in this story: the Shah of Iran, Nadir Shah, had carried off the throne in 1739 during an invasion! The pedestal was barren as a result, but a bundle of some sort appeared to be lying there.

Mist floated in from the arched, open doorways into the chamber. As she approached the pedestal, she realised that the bundle was a huddled human; some homeless vagrant who had sought shelter in the hall? Her feet echoed and Mehrunisa felt a chill that was not due to the weather. The figure, perhaps Nisar, was crouching, head resting on his knees. She called out to him, her voice sounding tinny to her ears. What nonsense! Mehrunisa reprimanded herself for being dramatic. She touched her kara, the steel bangle that was a gift from her father as a symbol of his Sikh faith, which she wore on her right wrist. She swallowed, hoisted her shoulder bag, and walked to the figure.

'Nisar?'

He did not move.

Bending down, Mehrunisa shook his shoulder. The body in repose slumped forward. On a gasp Mehrunisa recoiled. Blood pounded in her ears as she grabbed the man's shoulders and turned him over. Her shriek curdled in her throat. The front of Nisar's blue sweater was blotched red. His body was cold and slack. Horrified, she registered the expression on the boy's face—it was one of frozen terror.

Out of the corner of her eye, Mehrunisa sensed movement. She looked around quickly. From a marble column to the pavilion's right, a shadow unglued and stepped into view. It was a man, dressed in a thick brown overcoat; a brown monkey cap covered his face and head.

There's no reason to panic, Mehrunisa told herself. He could be a tourist, or perhaps a guard, wearing a knit balaclava to protect his head from the evening chill. Even as she bolstered her confidence, her feet urged her to flee. Meanwhile, the man walked with mincing steps towards her. The thick monkey cap—a purple pom pom perched incongruously on top—obscured his face, covering not just the jaw but the mouth as well.

As Mehrunisa wondered what to do next, the man's right hand went below his jaw and tugged at the brown cap. In one swift motion it was off and the face was covered no more. It was all the impetus Mehrunisa needed. On a shrill scream, she turned and sped from the marble chamber, aiming for the nearest archway. A leap from the plinth landed her on the green grass. Not a soul was in sight in the garden or the misty courtyard beyond. As she steadied herself, Mehrunisa glanced back. The man was re-masked and marching towards her.

Momentarily rooted, Mehrunisa watched him. For the first time in her life she had seen a human face with no human features! A blotchy blank frontispiece with two holes for eyes and a slit for a mouth. The man was now less than five meters away and in his right hand he held a knife tipped red.

Delhi

Mehrunisa ran. Naturally lithe, she had never faced weight issues, but at that instant her body seemed curiously ponderous as she thundered down the length of the Red Fort. The building was rectangular and Mehrunisa would have to traverse one full length of two kilometres before reaching Lahore Gate, which would lead her out into the teeming Chandni Chowk market. On any other day, she could have counted on the presence of eager spectators queuing to watch the evening son-et-lumière. But it was a Monday, the one day of the week when there was no sound and light show.

A backward glance showed that her pursuer was still in chase, though her sprint had lengthened the distance between them. Now Mehrunisa was passing the Diwan-i-Aam, the Hall of Public Audience, another rectangular structure on a raised plinth. She swung around a corner and, shielded by the plinth, did a quick reconnaissance. To her right, in the distance, was a vaulted arcade, the walls of which were lined with souvenir shops. Mehrunisa could count on human company once she reached there. To her left was the approaching masked man—there was no let-up in his powerful strides.

She had two options: she could strike out for the large open space that led straight to the vaulted shopping arcade on the west. Or, she could cut across the courtyard of Diwan-i-Aam and make for the Drum House on the eastern side directly across from Lahore Gate. The first would expose her to her pursuer; the second would keep her in the shadow of buildings but take longer. Mehrunisa decided time was of essence.

Besides, what could the man do except break into a sprint?. He seemed to have avoided it thus far, perhaps because of his bulky woollens. She would just have to outrun him. Taking a deep breath, clamping her bag under her arm, she plunged into the open.

Mehrunisa ran diagonally across, making for the large north-south street that bisected the open space. Once she reached the intersection she would swing right to the shops. She glanced behind to gauge her pursuer's response. He seemed to have come to a standstill. Surprised, she continued to look back even as she ran forward. The awkward angle caused her to lose her footing and fall to her knees. The next instant something whizzed through the air, straight overhead. Instinctively, she ducked, clutching her head in her hands. The missile made a soft landing in the gravel. It was a knife. Had she not taken the tumble, it would have found her back!

She leapt up, screaming, 'Help me! Help me!' Her cries rang out in the open space as she raced along, tears streaking her cheeks.

Her shrieks brought an old man to the vault's mouth where bright bulbs were diffused by the darkness and mist. As Mehrunisa plunged towards the arched entrance, he held out his arm to steady her. He regarded the flustered woman who was casting uncertain glances behind her as she panted to a halt. Whatever was in the rear seemed to have been swallowed by the mist.

Mehrunisa doubled over, clutching her abdomen and drawing lungfuls of air. Ahead, some stalls were still open, the wooden jewellery boxes and ivory-inlaid artefacts glowing in the amber light. A few curious faces were turned towards her. She straightened, whispered her thanks to the man who had steadied her, and stumbled out into the melee of Chandni Chowk.

The honking traffic, the clatter of mule-drawn carts, the bustling pedestrians, the clamour of street vendors— for once it was comforting. Mehrunisa stood there panting, perspiring, shivering. She felt her stomach heave. As she bent, a liquidised version of her lunch flew out and spattered the soil and her moccasins.

Agra

SSP Raghav had just finished updating his boss on the Taj supervisor's murder case. Since there was no breakthrough to report, he spent time emphasising the leads they were pursuing. That did not cut ice with the DIG who was curt in his rebuke: next time I call, I want results not lecture-baazi!

Stung, SSP Raghav attempted to drown his anger in three cups of specially-ordered 'sugared' tea. While most men treated stress with cigarettes, Raghav's substitute was tea. Now he drank the sweet tea with relish and nursed his chagrin when the phone rang: Mehrunisa. He glared at the glowing green screen—the gall of that woman!

'What?' he barked.

In a subdued voice the woman informed him that the artist Nisar was dead.

'What! Nisar who?'

She explained that Nisar was the young son of the chief artisan of the Taj Mahal, the one who had been assigned to make the changes to Mumtaz's tomb. She had sought him out in Delhi, as she had promised. They had set up a meeting but someone had murdered him before she reached the venue.

'Murder?' Raghav blinked hard. A second murder...

Yes, the woman replied, and started to explain how she had found Nisar with blood on his sweater when Raghav interrupted her.

'Slow down, okay. Tell me everything from the beginning. Start with how you established contact with this Nisar,' Raghav prompted as he thought how the woman seemed to be making a habit of finding corpses. This was the second corpse she had found in ten days. And in both cases she had fixed a meeting with the deceased. Something was fishy here....

Having heard her out, he asked if she had informed the police.

Well, that's why I am calling, she said, taken aback.

He had meant the Delhi police but he didn't say anything. The woman did sound shaken.

'I want you to stay put,' he said in a severe tone. 'First the supervisor, now this artisan. Meeting you is proving dangerous for people.'

As he hung up, he thought furiously through what she'd told him. Were the two cases related, in which case there was credence to Mehrunisa's view about the changes in the tomb's calligraphy. Was the woman intrinsic to the two deaths? And who was this 'masked' man who had terrified Nisar and pursued Mehrunisa with a knife? The man was either fearless or a lunatic. While he had planned the attack around closing time, it was still a gamble that there would be no people around. The city of Delhi heaved with humanity round the clock.

By now—he glanced at his wristwatch, it had been a couple of hours since the murder—the Delhi police would've been alerted. He would call an old friend in the department and see what leads he could get.

Delhi

That night, Mehrunisa slept fitfully. The full moon placed a spotlight on every object, making it glint in the dark of her bedroom. Soft edges acquired sharpness, amorphous shapes became shadowy forms, and red splotches seemed to erupt out of everything, even her white duvet. Nisar's slack, cold body swam in front of her eyes before it was replaced by the memory of his mother as she offered Mehrunisa puffs and tea and spoke lovingly of her son's gift for singing. An anguished Mehrunisa sat up in bed sobbing. How would Nisar's parents cope with the murder of their young son?

Finally, she vacated the bed for the armchair where she huddled, arms wrapped around her legs, chin atop her knees. Mehrunisa knew loss and guilt but, for the first time in her life, she had known terror. The knowledge that she had been a second away from being impaled made her shudder again.

She had returned home, managing to maintain a façade of normalcy even as her heart was in a cold clutch.

Mangat Ram, distracted by Professor Kaul's condition, had refrained from conversation as Mehrunisa headed straight for the bathroom. It took a few brushings and gargles to expunge the bitter aftertaste of vomit. Assuring the housekeeper she had eaten outside, she checked on her uncle who was asleep in bed, his face wan. His situation was steadily deteriorating; the lucid periods were fewer.

Now, pre-dawn, bereft of sleep, Mehrunisa took stock of her situation.

Just a few days ago she had been leisurely researching an architectural masterpiece, assisting a renowned historian, recuperating in the comfort of a loving household, and suddenly, it had all unravelled.... Her godfather was seriously ill; she was attempting to solve a mystery for which she was ill-equipped; two men she knew had been murdered, and in her pursuit for answers, she had almost gotten killed. She was out of her depth here, and the enemy—Bentinck, as her uncle had called him—knew that. A woman trained in Renaissance art, with two elderly men for family, and few friends—how would she fathom the Taj conspiracy? After all, she had no training to solve mysteries, no skills of detection or surveillance or self-defence.

All she had was a knowledge of languages and a love of art—twin legacies of her upbringing. Maadar spoke to her in Farsi, Papa in Punjabi, teachers and friends in Arabic, Italian, English and Hindi. The different faiths of both parents, neither of them didactic, had osmosed into her, yet, Mehrunisa had her first spiritual experience in a museum. The genius of great art was that it influenced one involuntarily. Mehrunisa's first sighting of *The Pieta* by Michelangelo was a moment that seized her. That man could conceive and sculpt an image of such beauty, tenderness and power, which she, hundreds of years later, could witness, was in itself transcendental. That feeling of simultaneous humbling and upliftment was to recur as she encountered more masterpieces. Having lived between worlds, art was her anchor; it grounded her, whether she was in Italy or India. Which was why it hurt, this attempt to discredit the Taj. As she ruminated, a thought struck Mehrunisa. She sat upright.

The situation was decidedly grim, but even in that darkness there was a glimmer....

Bentinck had tried to kill her. That could only mean one thing: she was on the right track. As the memory of her flight through Red Fort surfaced, Mehrunisa shuddered but stayed focused. Bentinck had demonstrated cunning, stealth, and ruthlessness. He was no ordinary adversary. Yet, he was feeling threatened by her....

How does a major in Renaissance studies, a linguist, a student of Indo-Persian linkages manage to scare an opponent like Bentinck? As she mused, Mehrunisa rolled her kara back and forth on her right wrist.

Chaturanga. The word popped in her mind. Chaturanga. Shatranj. And a section from her Indo-Persian project floated into her mind.

The game the world knew as chess had originated in India as chaturanga. In the sixth century, the Persians learnt the game, and when Persia was conquered by the Arabs, it dispersed through the Middle East under the name shatranj, the Persian corruption of chaturanga. Chaturanga, meaning an army of four divisions, was first mentioned as a battle formation in the Indian epic *Mahabharata*. Arguably the world's most intellectual game, chess was at heart a battle simulation. Therein lay her answer.

In the battle with Bentinck, the battlefield was the mind.

And there was one way to defeat him: mentally.

❋ ❋ ❋

In the morning, Mehrunisa decided to go for a walk in the gardens of Humayun's Tomb. Recently renovated and declared a World Heritage Site by UNESCO, it was an oasis in the bustling metropolis. Savouring the sun of a winter's day, the breeze whispering in the palm fronds, the soothing hum of distant traffic, she willed herself to believe she could restore things in her world.

When she returned home, she went to see how her godfather was doing. Professor Kaul was sitting up in bed, propped against two pillows, his arms prone by his side, head upturned.

'Kaul uncle,' Mehrunisa said.

He continued with his scrutiny of the ceiling.

She bit her lip. 'When did this happen?'

'He was fine when he woke up,' Mangat Ram said. 'His friend Raj Bhushan came over. He said he would have come earlier but he had a relapse and was laid up with flu again—he had a thick muffler wrapped around his face. I served them tea. They were together for an hour or so. After Bhushan sahib left, I came to collect the tea things and found him like this.'

Mehrunisa sighed. Time to summon the doctor again. She looked in the bedside drawer for the diary that held Professor Kaul's important phone numbers.

Mangat Ram stood murmuring to himself. 'It is a day for strange things. First, the milk split. Then the neighbour's boy broke the living room glass pane. Next,

Raj Bhushan asks for more walnuts. And now, sahib taking to bed like this...'

Mehrunisa was flipping through the diary, not paying particular attention to the housekeeper's babble. However, the thing about walnuts stuck in her mind—Professor Kaul was partial to them. It helped him think, he said, the process of selecting a walnut, examining where to apply pressure, cracking the shell into two neat halves, retrieving the intact nut, scraping off the skin, and munching on the chewy kernel. Mehrunisa did not share his passion but her godfather had been merrily feeding her the 'king of nuts' since childhood.

She turned to ask the housekeeper, 'What was it about the walnuts?'

Tch! Mangat Ram clucked his tongue. 'Bhushan sahib never eats walnuts. In fact, the two of them,' he pointed with his chin at Professor Kaul, 'would argue over the dry fruit. He never liked it and Sahib would always urge him to eat some. But today,' Mangat Ram looked mystified, 'Raj Bhushan ate a bowl of walnuts!'

'How do you know? Perhaps it was Kaul uncle.'

'No. Raj Bhushan came to the kitchen looking for me. He handed me the empty bowl, said he loved them and could he have some more. I told you—a day for strange things!'

Delhi

'Look here, read this news,' Shri Kriplani waved the newspaper at his assistant. 'Why do we always need the West to endorse us, to remind us of our greatness!'

Prodding his spectacles up his nose until his lashes flicked the lenses, he held the paper up and read aloud, in the manner of a professor lecturing his students. Old habits die hard, and Shri Kriplani had been a professor at Benaras Hindu University for years until, with increasing middle-class affluence and aspirations, a fundamentalist Hindu party that had hitherto been at the political fringe was catapulted onto centrestage. Realising his oratory skills and degree in Sanskrit could be leveraged for greater glory in such a political party, he had switched careers.

'The hottest chilli in the world is Indian,' he now intoned. 'The Chili Pepper Institute in New Mexico has confirmed that the bhut jolokia, or "ghost chilli" measuring at one million SHU—a measure for chili heat—beats the hottest chilli measured so far.'

Shri Kriplani glowered. 'When in doubt, consult history. Do you know why the Mughals could never conquer the Deccan? They were used to a diet of pulao, almond sweetmeats, and rich fruit, so they had become soft and ineffectual. That is why they proved to be no match for the Marathas, whose bellies were on fire with chilli juice.'

Leaning forward he opened a round steel container. Within it glistened thumb-sized, bright-red chillies. A warm, smoky aroma arose. 'Bhut jholakiya,' Shri Kriplani displayed it with a flourish. 'Here, taste it for yourself.'

The assistant eyed the chilli, his throat constricting in anticipation.

'Just place it on your tongue, don't swallow,' urged his boss. 'Do you know,' his voice dropping a few decibels, 'the army is thinking of using it in weapons?'

The assistant took a chilli, bit a tiny shard and placed it on his tongue. Heat started to singe his gums and tongue and flared down his throat.

Shri Kriplani studied him. 'It will do the boys good. Inform the shakha supervisor—the boys must chew a chilli before each meal. For a warlike and determined character.' He dismissed the assistant who, once he was out of view, sprinted to the washroom.

Meanwhile, Shri Kriplani rose from his chair and made for the sideboard. Atop it rested his daily tonic, a glass of pale yellow liquid. He reached for it and, in a single movement, downed the entire glass. Once, he had found it distasteful, but the health benefits had convinced him otherwise. Urine therapy. After all, hadn't his mentor lived to the ripe age of ninety-nine? He eyed himself in the mirror: the spare, slender frame was packed with the vitality of youth, his eyes were clear and his mind was sharp. In the days ahead he would need all the alertness and energy within him. He had found a way to bring the Hindutva agenda back on track. Pseudo-secularists had derailed it once....

In 1992, Hindu faithful had succeeded in destroying the Babri Masjid, which had been erected by the barbarian Mughal conqueror on the site of Lord Ram's birthplace. So consumed had the sainiks been in their passion for Lord Ram, that they had torn down the mosque with their bare hands!

Yet, the construction of a Ram temple had been stalemated by pseudo-secularists when they moved the Supreme Court. But now Kriplani had found another lever, one long enough to prod awake the apathetic masses throughout India. He replaced the glass on the table and licked his mouth. His mind went to the absentminded professor who had arrived unexpectedly offering his services—God fulfilled himself in many ways!

Thus far, all was going according to plan.

Agra

It was late night in Taj Ganj when a group of men filed into a nondescript room in the run-down market Katra Omar Khan. Inside the dimly-lit room, they took their position in front of the TV, cross-legged, attentive. Their hunger for education would be difficult to match even in the finest classrooms of India—privation and revenge were their spurs.

In his deep voice, the saffron-garbed guru on TV began. 'You have grown up in the shadow of the Taj Mahal. Living in your pitiful homes, you have been dwarfed by the grand monument. Its marble shimmers and changes colours with the changing light through the day, while your quarters look drab in any season. The Taj has acres of green gardens flowing with water. You have not a tree to shade you in the blistering summer and get rationed water, when lucky. The grand Taj is a mausoleum, the tomb of a dead queen built by an emperor. Your hovels are living quarters for you, the living dead.'

He paused, his eyes piercing them.

'For what else are you, but the living dead? Condemned in the twenty-first century to live like abject Hindu subjects of a seventeenth-century Mughal king! All your life you have looked at a lie, and understood nothing! Nothing. What if I told you the Taj is rightfully yours? It is yours for the taking!'

The men turned to exchange bewildered glances.

The guru had paused in anticipation. Realising the TV had gone silent, they turned to the screen again.

'Yes. The Taj is yours. It belongs to you. To me. To all our Hindu brothers and sisters … because like you and me, it is *Hindu*. Shah Jahan did not build the Taj Mahal. He converted Tejo Mahalya, a Shiva temple, and built his wife's tomb on it.' The guru's face was thunderous. 'The Mughals were invaders. Barbarians. They knew how to loot, not build. Wherever they went in India they destroyed our temples, beheaded our idols. Who can forget what Ghazni did in Somnath? He personally hammered the gilded lingam of Shiva, the temple deity of Somnath, to pieces, and carted the fragments to Ghazni where they were embedded in the new Jama Masjid's steps. *Our* lingam, powdered into *their* steps. What can be more heinous?'

The guru's eyes blazed at the gathering. Now he lowered his voice, sounding more ominous as he resumed. 'Where they did not destroy the temple, they converted it into a mosque. Such was their treachery. The Taj Mahal is one such example. It is a Muslim tomb built on a Shiva temple. A Shiva temple that is no ordinary temple. It is called Tejolinga. Do you know why? Because it is the missing thirteenth jyotirlinga! Jyotirlinga. A place where Shiva first manifested himself. The twelve shrines of Shiva are well known, so well known that the Muslim invaders destroyed them, again and again and again. Kashi Vishwanath, holiest of all pilgrimage sites in India, destroyed by Aurangzeb. This legendary temple of Shiva was ransacked several times! And we rebuilt it, again and again. But—what if there was one Shiva temple, one Jyotirlinga that was so completely transformed that people forgot it was ever a Shiva shrine? So complete was its conversion that people even forgot it was a temple once, and not a dead queen's tomb! So completely were the Hindu people brainwashed that they recalled only twelve jyotirlingas, and erased the rightful thirteenth!'

The cross-legged audience of spindly young men sat in stiff concentration as the message of their impotence and misery was hammered into their comprehension.

'Tejo Mahalya! Where *you* should be worshipping the great Lord Shiva. Instead you have got the Taj Mahal. Where you bow your head to a dead mortal, that too Muslim. Tch!' The guru spat in fury.

'And Shiva? His worship has been consigned to a hole in the wall of the Taj Mahal!'

Was he referring to Ghat Mandir? the audience wondered.

As if the guru could read their thoughts, he wagged a knowing head. 'Yes, that apology of a Shiva temple that now goes under the name of Ghat Mandir. A temple to Mahadeva, the great lord of the trinity, Lord Shiva—and where is it located? Atop the pipe that brings water from the Yamuna into the Taj! Shame! Shame! Such utter shame!'

Om Namah Shivaya. Om Namah Shivaya. Om Namah Shivaya.

I surrender to God.

The chants rumbled forth from the screen as an agitated guru attempted to calm himself.

The seated men fidgeted, unsure what was expected of them, and looked about. A whispering started. Was this true? What was the proof? Who would believe them?

The voice from the TV surged again. 'You will get answers to all your questions. Every single one. The myth of the Taj Mahal was not built in one day. The Mughals ruled over us for three centuries. Three hundred years in which they enslaved us, gagging and blindfolding us to our true heritage. But why continue to be slaves?

'The time has come to seek the truth. Because only the truth will set you free.'

Delhi

The neurosurgeon at the All India Institute of Medical Sciences delivered a diagnosis that devastated Mehrunisa: Professor Kaul was suffering from Korsakov's syndrome. It was a case of a deep and, perhaps, permanent devastation of memory.

The professor's history of severe migraines could have caused the impairment, the doctor said. Or, it could have resulted from the alcoholic destruction of mammillary bodies in the brain—the professor, though by no counts a heavy drinker, was fond of his daily Scotch. Whatever the cause, amnesia seemed to have overtaken him. The illness had advanced to the extent that the patient seemed to have forgotten a large chunk of his life. He recognised his book on the Taj Mahal, but for the most part everything else seemed to have been erased from memory, except, occasionally, when his mind surfaced from the fog.

He had exhibited a history of 'little strokes' in the lead-up to the final collapse. Mehrunisa had witnessed some of those, but perhaps he had experienced others while she had been away.

The notion that her uncle, the renowned scholar, the man who could tell such fascinating, layered tales, was lost to her was like a physical shock. That such a man could lose a chunk of his rich life was horrifying. For Mehrunisa, it was a double whammy. Kaul uncle, the genial, loving godfather was the last link in a chain that connected her to her lost father. And she had lost her only ally—Professor Kaul was her guide and confidant in the attempt to unravel the incidents at the Taj. Whom would she turn to now?

Agra

SSP Raghav was unhappy. The one-day match between India and Pakistan had gone in favour of Pakistan, the enemy having snatched victory on the last ball by hitting a giant six.

Saala! The match was rigged all right. All these cricketers making money on the side. Who could blame them for indulging in what was, after all, a national pastime: the quest for illicit income? But surely these men could rein in their greed at least when playing The Enemy? Was there no patriotism left nowadays?

Disgusted, he strode to the narrow portico that ran along the colonnaded front of the police station and spat. The station was quiet, with just two constables and him on duty. He didn't have a family to go home to—his wife and children were in Salem because the boys, in secondary, needed a stable school environment. Besides, he had followed the cricket match and he felt compelled to compensate for the lost hours of work. If only, he shook his head once again, if only Team India had won.

This wasn't helping. He marched to his room, grabbed his cap, felt for his motorcycle keys in his front right pocket and strode out.

At the gate he turned to the right and sped down the empty road to the Taj Ganj area with nothing specific in mind. The Taj issue had not stopped troubling him. There was more than one thread to the story, of that he was now convinced. The ASI director-general Raj Bhushan had supervised the examination of the change in the epitaph and Quran verse and proclaimed it 'minor vandalism'. Mehrunisa, though, had been unconvinced. To which the director had quipped, 'You believe there is a conspiracy afoot! The Taj Conspiracy, shall we label it?'

He had been a policeman too long to be a conspiracy theorist, but something was awry. Where did the second murder, of Nisar the artisan, fit into the equation? What linked Nisar to the supervisor was the Taj Mahal. Were the masked man and Aurangzeb two different men or one?

No wonder he needed the crisp night air to clear his head.

Raghav was cruising down the lane that led to Sirhi Darwaza, the south gate of the Taj complex. It was narrow and lined with shophouses on both sides, their façades painted red in harmony with the Taj forecourt's red sandstone. That was about all that was harmonious between the utilitarian bazaar and the elegant Taj Mahal. Beyond these lay a jumble of tenements that made up Taj Ganj. He cast a disdainful look at the shops he was passing: Gyan Bookbinders, Aditya Sweets, Arun & Bros. Chemists, A1 Guest House, Taj View Motel, Mumtaz Ladies Tailor, Rocky Music. Built by Shah Jahan as a bazaar where a variety of merchandise brought from all over the world could be sold, it was now a miserable market. As was characteristic of small-town India, where man and animal co-existed, there was a large buffalo stable in the lane and an abundant monkey population residing on rooftops. A smattering of cheap hotels and restaurants catered to backpacking tourists. The budget lodges showcased Indian ingenuity: multiple floors piggybacked on narrow plots of land until they could provide a view of the Taj Mahal! Raghav snorted as he veered his motorcycle around a series of festering cow dung cakes.

The Taj Ganj area, raucous with human and animal traffic through the day, sat quiet. Raghav passed a bonfire whose embers glowed dully. A stray dog raised his head to glance at him and a string of lights pulsed intermittently atop a signboard as people slept in the warmth of their homes. He was nearing the arched wooden gate at the lane's end when he spotted shadows crouching on the right. Their hesitant shuffling aroused his curiosity. Bringing his motorcycle to a stop, he pointed the vehicle's light in their direction.

'Who's there?' he called out.

A scramble ensued. A hushed, yet frantic, *Police!* sounded. The shadows were racing now, away from him, toward the crowded shophouses. He hastily put his motorcycle on its stand and gave them chase. His physical ability belied his forty years—it had been a factor in his selection for the ATS, aided by the patriotism he wore on his sleeve. At annual functions, when booze flowed and beer bellies jiggled in carnival bonhomie, it was common to toast, 'Fit as a fiddle, Raghav has no middle!' The 'middle' alluded to both his trim waist and the fact that in a culture of 'anything goes', he was a fastidious man.

Now Raghav drew closer. The lane was ill-lit but he could make out two men, probably youngsters, but their frantic dash was no match for the SSP's trained sprint. He was closing in when one of them cast a quick backward glance, yelped, dropped what he was carrying and doubled his speed. Raghav neared the bundle that had fallen to the ground with a dull thump, a stack of loose sheets. As he glanced up, he saw the boys were scaling a low wall. Beyond it would lie the narrow courtyard of a house. Doubtless the miscreants would scale more walls in their getaway—the area beyond was a maze of dwellings. He glanced in their direction—they must be local, the swift manner in which they had vaulted across and vanished. Raghav knew it would be futile looking for them in the dense labyrinth of houses. Besides, they had left their booty behind, which he now bent to retrieve.

A4 size paper, printed sheets—it was too dark to read. Screwing up his eyes, he walked to the nearest lamppost that was ten metres away. The light was dull, moths trapped within the glass case reducing the effectiveness. He stood beneath the flyblown lamp and strained his eyes to read what looked like a pamphlet: white background, bright orange lettering and a headline in bold.

As he read it, SSP Raghav knew his instinct had been right. The 'Taj conspiracy' was not a hypothesis—it was a work-in-progress! And, if the headline was to be taken at face value, the evil behind the conspiracy was Hindu, not Muslim. His eyes bulged with shock as they scoured the text again:

The Taj Mahal is a Hindu Temple
Brothers and sisters of Agra! You have been fooled for too long. The most famous monument of our city, the world-famous Taj Mahal, is

not a Muslim monument built by a Mughal emperor! No! Its actual name is Tejo Mahalya—a Hindu temple that, as per the tradition of conquerors, was converted into a Muslim monument.

Do not take our word for it, we beg you. Read the proof that follows and form your own opinion.

No. 1:

Point to Ponder: Who built the Taj Mahal?

Lie: Shah Jahan

Truth:

- **Shah Jahan had an affair with his daughter Jahanara after the death of Mumtaz!**
  Is this the state of a man pining for his wife and building a monument in her memory?

- **Shah Jahan bought a beautiful building from Jai Singh.**
  In his own court chronicle, Padshahnamah, Shah Jahan admits that an exceptionally beautiful building in Agra was taken from Jai Singh for Mumtaz's burial.

- **Using captured temples for burial was a common Mughal practice.**
  For example Jama Masjid, Delhi; Arhai-din-ka-jhonpra, Ajmer; Gyanvapi Mosque, Kashi … the list is endless!

No. 2:

Point to Ponder: The name: Taj Mahal

Lie: Named by Shah Jahan

Truth:

- **The Taj Mahal is a distortion of Tejo Mahalaya.**
  The term Taj Mahal does not occur in any court papers or chronicles during or after Shah Jahan's time. That is because the building is an ancient Shiva temple with the Sanskrit name Tej-o-Mahalaya.

- **How can a burial place be called a mahal?**
  A mahal is a mansion.

No. 3:

Point to Ponder: Sealed rooms in the Taj

Lie: Serve no contemporary purpose

Truth:

- **Shiva idols hidden within sealed rooms in the Taj.**
  Shiva lingams and sacred Shiva idols lie in the sealed rooms on the south side of the long corridor! Who filled in the doorway with masonry? Why are scholars not allowed to enter to examine?

No. 4:

Point to Ponder: Hindu design of Mughal monument

Lie: Trident pinnacle atop the mausoleum dome—unique to Indo-Muslim architecture

Truth:

- **A sacred Hindu motif atop a Muslim tomb?**
  The trident pinnacle atop the dome is also inlaid in the red sandstone courtyard to the east of the Taj. It shows a kalash holding two bent mango leaves and a coconut.

No. 5:

Point to Ponder: Correct age of the Taj Mahal

Lie: Repairs in the Taj in 1652, thirteen years after construction— normal wear-and-tear

Truth:

- **The Taj Mahal was built hundreds of years before 1652!**
  In a letter by Aurangzeb to his father dated 9 December 1652, he reports serious leaks in the Taj Mahal in rainy season. Why should the Taj, only thirteen years old, show symptoms of decay? Wouldn't it be more reasonable to believe that by 1652 it was already hundreds of years old and was showing normal wear-and-tear?

- **ASI does not permit carbon dating.**
  Why has the Archaeological Survey of India not allowed the verification of the exact date of the Taj Mahal through the widely-accepted scientific method of carbon dating?

Hindu Brothers and Sisters, the time has come to put an end to this gross injustice. Time to tear off the veil of lies and untruth. Read this proof, pass it on—as a Hindu, it is your sacred dharma! Let the ripples of truth spread through Agra city and to the whole of India!

Jai Shiv Shankar! Jai Ho!

Delhi

R.P. Singh was in the office of the CBI director special operations where he had been summoned urgently.

'JCP Rana Pratap Singh. Your middle name is trouble,' the director said sharply.

His middle name was 'Pratap', given by his parents in honour of their famous clansman, Maharana Pratap Sisodia. The Rajput warrior was a thorn in the side of Mughal emperor Akbar through his life, and as R.P. Singh studied the bearded man in front of him, he wondered what he had done to irk the CBI head.

Dressed nattily in a tweed jacket over a maroon pullover, a thick gold watch strapped to his wrist, the director gave the impression of having been interrupted at a party. The wall behind was decorated with framed photographs of the director with dignitaries.

'Three days into the job and the home minister has assigned a task for you. High priority...' He twisted his mouth into a sneer.

Then he proceeded to tell Singh that the Agra police had come across a pamphlet that alleged that the Taj Mahal was a Shiva temple. Ordinarily the police would have consigned it to the wastebasket, but the yet unsolved murder of the Taj supervisor had occurred within the mausoleum less than a fortnight back. The two might well be unconnected events, but the Agra police had panicked, pressed the alarm button and called the home minister. And now, the director snorted, the matter has been offloaded upon us.

R.P. Singh groaned inwardly: from the frying pan into fire. He hadn't even begun savouring Delhi—a relaxed head shave at a fancy barber's, one leisurely visit to Capitol bar, barely enough time to enjoy the women, who had surprised him with their daring new dress sense, and now he was being sent off to chase a crazed right-winger!

Nonchalantly, he patted his shiny pate and said with a half smile, 'When a bald guy shows up, something is bound to happen.'

The director special ops kept his mouth pursed in a grim line. His brow darkened as he wagged an index finger in R.R. Singh's direction. Finally, he said in a raspy voice, 'You report directly to me.'

That hoarseness indicated a weakness for alcohol. Hmmm ... supercilious *and* incompetent. R.P. Singh settled back into his chair, crossed his leg and returned an even gaze that did not reveal his thoughts. The force was filled with men like the director, chutiyas in police uniform, who needed men like him. He treated them with casual disdain and they suffered him because, when it came down to the wire, someone had to keep the streets clean. For his meritorious service they gave him medals, souvenirs that he stowed in a drawer in his wardrobe. R.P. Singh had made a habit of going down sewers and exterminating the rats. Precisely why he had been summoned for the task. It was pest control time again.

'I accept the assignment,' he said. 'Two conditions. I get the resources I ask for, no questions asked. And I report back when I have something concrete.'

Delhi

SP Raghav wrapped up work at 3 p.m. and set out for Delhi. It was a sunny, cloudless day, rare for winter, yet the policeman's face was a thundercloud.

As soon as he had seized the blasphemous pamphlets, he'd rung his boss to update him on the latest twist in the case. It rattled the DIG enough to inform the chief minister who had panicked and shifted the onus to the home ministry. The case was now out of his supervision: the CBI would be crawling all over it soon.

Raghav pursed his mouth bitterly. If only he had paid more attention to that woman Mehrunisa.... Bloody hell! What a bizarre case—the Taj a Shiva temple! But there were enough lunatics in the country and he had forgotten the basic principle of police work—you follow *every* lead. A donkey cart swerved into his way and he swore loudly at the driver. As he craned his neck to glare at him he saw a cowering boy, hands lifted abjectly.

He would be in that position when the CBI officers arrived to lord over him and rub his incompetence in his face. To say nothing of the implications of this failure for his career....

Raghav was still upset with himself when he reached the ASI director-general's office. He was assigned with updating him and discussing security arrangements in view of the new development.

Raj Bhushan, however, showed little enthusiasm at his presence. The SSP, in his crisp policeman fashion, slid the pamphlet across the director-general's table adding where he had found it.

Raj Bhushan's jaw muscles clenched—perhaps the reason why the remaining colour seemed to drain from his already wan face—as he studied the leaflet. After a period of contemplation in which the director's head was bent over the pamphlet, and SSP Raghav—not having been offered a chair—stood upright, Raj Bhushan deposited a paperweight on the leaflet and looked up. He interlocked his fingers, rested his arms on the table, and with a look of mild perturbation asked, 'So, what can I do for you, Inspector?'

Raghav was taken aback by the director's casual response. However, he offered politely, '*SSP* Raghav, Sir. And if I may, this pamphlet,' he pointed to the offending leaflet trapped under the director's elbow, 'seems to be another attempt to discredit the Taj.'

Raj Bhushan gave a thin smile. 'Thank you for your concern, *SSP*. I am happy to note the attention that you are devoting to Agra's foremost monument. But clearly, recent events seem to have unduly influenced you—after all, in your trade people get killed all the time. I see no reason to link this leaflet to the supervisor's murder.'

'And the changes in the calligraphy?'

Tch! the director clucked in exasperation. 'Those aren't *changes*. Just some tampering, probably by a local lout with time on hand. I suggest you dismiss any conspiracy theory you might have in mind.'

Raghav reined in his response. Perhaps, for a man responsible for hundreds of monuments in India, each in varying stages of decay, a threat to the Taj Mahal—arguably in robust health and perennially under the tourist scanner—was too fantastic. Quietly, he informed him that the case had been moved to the CBI.

'Oh!' Raj Bhushan said, a sudden look of concern on his face. He glanced down swiftly at the pamphlet, pushed up his spectacles, and after a few seconds he looked up. 'SSP,' the director shrugged, attempting amends, 'the Taj has always had its detractors. Just a year ago some Agra businessmen started this campaign "Taj Hatao, Agra Bachao"—remove the Taj and save Agra! Do you know why? Because they feel that business is being driven out of Agra since the courts have ordered the removal of polluting factories. Then there are those nutcases who are asking for a share of the annual revenues the government earns from the heavy tourist traffic to the Taj! A share of the profits.' He snorted his disgust. 'How ridiculous can people get! But what can we do? Increase security, add a few more guards.' He eyed the policeman. 'What would I advise, though?'

He crushed the leaflet into a ball before flinging it across the floor into a bin. 'Ignore them.'

Agra

'Myself, Govind guide.' The man grinned at the security-frisked couple at the entrance to the Taj Mahal. 'Ajucansi, Sir-Lady, one oph the wonders oph the world.'

The Emersons had by now experienced enough Indian-accented English to conclude that they would ask for clarification only in dire circumstances. So they nodded and studied the glowing white pearl that loomed before them. In any case, they had read about the Taj, and Mrs Emerson clutched a copy of *Lonely Planet India*.

Holding up his right palm, Govind guide continued, 'Now, Taj Mahal has phive main design elements: darwaja or main gate, bageecha or garden, masjid or mosque, mihman khana or rest house, and rauja or Taj Mahal mausoleum.'

Mrs Emerson, comprehension dawning with a phase lag, nodded.

The Taj stood in front of them on a raised square platform with its four corners truncated, forming an unequal octagon.

'186 × 186 pheet,' Govind rattled off helpfully, 'size of the platpharum.'

Mrs Emerson was the more enamoured party. 'We read that the unique Mughal style combines elements of Persian, Central Asian and Islamic architecture,' she enquired slowly, seeking elucidation.

Govind muttered, 'Un-huh,' unequivocally, and rattled off another series of numbers. '41.6 metres, or 162.5 pheet—height of the phour minarets, set, ajucansi, symmetrically about the tomb. Now, the structure, ajunansi, is octa-gonal. Meaning to say, eight sides. Add to that one pinnacle pointing to top, and one foundation. Total ijs therephore ten.' He held up both palms, the fingers outstretched. 'Right?'

When the Emersons again looked blank, he continued, 'Ten is a sacred Hindu number. You see, Hindus believe in ten directions. Any building to do with the royal or divine has this number.' He smiled smugly.

The Emersons exchanged curious glances but before they could confer, Govind launched a broadside. 'The central dome, like a bulb, is 58 pheet in diameter and rises to a height of 213 pheet. It is surrounded by phour chhatris, domed can-opies. Now this,' he leaned forward, 'is a pheature seen mainly in Hindu buildings.' Drawing back he glanced from Mr Emerson to Mrs to gauge their response. There was none, except irritation. Govind guide rolled his shoulders, gestured to the path ahead with his open palms, and walked in front. His job was to spread the message—the rest was up to people.

They walked down the path leading to the Taj, majestically reflected in the watercourse, when a howling erupted from the garden to the right. A man, his arms flailing, was emitting strange noises. At his feet was poised a rhesus monkey, his face cocked at the man. The next instant a pebble came flying though the air, landing on the monkey's hind. With a yelp, the monkey bounded off. As the Emersons watched, Govind guide shook an exasperated head. Tapping his forehead with his right hand, he added, 'These monkeys are a menace. At timej they run with tourist camera.' Pointing to the Canon slung around Mr Emerson's neck, he said, 'You take care,' and started to briskly lead the way again.

'But why doesn't the administration remove the monkeys?' a concerned Mrs Emerson asked.

'How many monkeys to remove? And put them where?' the guide smiled at her. 'Madam, in this country we worship monkey. For us it is the avatar of Hanumanji.'

When the Emersons looked bemused, he supplied helpfully, 'Monkey God, Hanuman, rescuer of Sita, wife of Lord Ram, hero of *Ramayan*,' and resumed walking.

As they approached the mausoleum, the guide resumed his tour-speak. 'Built in white marble, phull building. And notice the delicate pietra dura work—stone inlay. At one time, precious and semi-precious stones were embedded here. But then, the Birteesh held picnic parties here and for amusement scratched out the stones.

'Okay,' he rubbed his hands together, 'I have something to show you, something special. Not many people know it.' He led the way in a perambulation of the monument, stopped in front and pointed to the top. 'See the dome. Now look at the top. What do you see?'

The Emersons crinkled their eyes and peered. As Govind eyed them, they shrugged. 'A pinnacle, perhaps?' Mrs Emerson offered lamely.

'On top of the pinnacle—the design you see?'

Mrs Emerson shook her head.

'No prablum,' Govind assured them. 'An exact replica is available. I will show you. This way.' He walked towards the red sandstone building flanking the Taj to the right. In the red stone courtyard, he pointed to a sketch on the floor. 'Replica of the pinnacle on the dome. Look closely. A coconut resting on bent mango leaves placed on a kalash, a pot of water.' Govind straightened from examining the sketch and declared, 'A popular Hindu design.'

'Then *what* is it doing in the Taj Mahal?' Mr Emerson demanded in exasperation. He had come to see a famed Mughal monument; instead he was getting some religious spiel. 'Is the Taj not a Muslim monument, built by Mughal emperor Shah Jahan?'

'No.'

Mr Emerson looked incredulous. 'Did you say "No"?'

'Yes. No.'

'We are seeing the Taj, right?' Mrs Emerson's right index finger drew circles in the air. 'Yes?'

'Yes,' Govind nodded, lowered his head and spoke conspiratorially. 'But everything is not what it seem—'

'Speak up, man!' Mr Emerson commanded.

'The Taj Mahal is actually a Hindu temple.'

Mr Emerson's eyes narrowed as he sought to determine whether the guide was mentally all there.

'The truth, ajucansi,' he pointed to the sketch on the floor, 'has been hidden for long. You tell me, what Muslim building, mosque, will you see the design of kalash or mango leaf, which is Hindu by nature.' He leaned forward conspiratorially and said sotto voce, 'The writing on Mumtaz's tomb itself says it's fraud, fake!'

Mr Emerson caught his wife's forearm, took her aside and whispered urgently into her ear. Turning to Govind guide, he handed him his fees with a measly tip, and said,

'Thank you. My wife would like to rest. We don't know how long before we will resume our tour.'

'Sir change mind, okay.' Govind guide pocketed the cash, evidently happy, said, 'Salaam, Bye-bye,' and sauntered towards the entrance seeking the next set of visitors.

'A conspiracy theorist, likely. Forget it, darling!'

However, Mrs Emerson looked unconvinced. 'There is some monkey business going on. I have a good mind to report him—spreading such lies! As if,' her voice hushed, 'there isn't enough trouble in this country.'

✳ ✳ ✳

Night-time in the Taj complex saw increased security: both the CISF within and the police force outside had been strengthened. SSP Raghav was liaising with the police teams that secured the Taj Mahal on a regular basis even as a CBI team was expected to arrive any moment.

He had no jurisdiction over the CISF, which was responsible for the security of the monument within the complex, but Inspector Bharadwaj of that force was onboard and cooperating with him. The inspector had been informed that there was a fresh threat to the Taj Mahal and the complex therefore was put on high alert.

On the sandstone platform, a newly-posted CISF constable patrolled the north side watching the inky Yamuna as he walked. The area beyond was a black swathe and the thin mist did not help matters.

'Why're you wasting time here?' a harsh voice stopped him in his tracks.

The young constable recognised Inspector Bharadwaj of the CISF who was striding down towards him. He looked angry.

'Do you see anybody enter the Taj Mahal from the riverside?' he asked. 'Those were the days of the emperor when he floated up in his fancy boats. Where is the emperor now, hanh?' He let out a low, sneering laugh.

The constable, visibly nervous, wagged his head.

Bharadwaj patted the policeman on his back. 'Happens, you're new on the job. Go,' he nodded towards the gardens in front, 'patrol the east wall.'

Delhi

SSP Raghav was at the residence of Professor Kaul to discuss the pamphlet with Mehrunisa. The 'proof' offered that the Taj was a Shiva temple had confounded him—if it could fool him, what would happen if it fell into the hands of the public? He needed Mehrunisa to tell him truth from lies.

She, in turn, was surprised at his sudden appearance. His contrition seemed genuine however, and when he handed her the pamphlet it plain knocked her out. She led her unexpected guest to the living room where they sat now.

As she frowned at the leaflet, Mehrunisa nibbled at a cheese wedge. The low table to her right was aglow with a low-wattage bulb concealed beneath the inlaid marble top; lapis lazuli, agate, jasper, malachite shimmered in intricate arabesque on a marmoreal sea. *Vatican Masterpieces*, which Mehrunisa had been browsing when she was interrupted, rested atop it. Perusing the leaflet, she reached for the wine beside the book. SSP Raghav, sitting upright in an armchair, glowered at the bulbous wine glass.

She had graciously invited him in and offered—*wine*! Raghav was no prude, but the idea of a woman so boldly offering him a drink offended his sense of decorum. He had grown up in a culture where men drank—always to inebriated stupor—while women prepared the savoury accompaniments and afterwards assisted the tottering men to their beds. Anyway, wine was too new-fangled for him.

'It is rich and fruity,' Mehrunisa had recommended the Montepulciano red she was drinking with a smile. That was another strange thing—the alcohol he knew was bitter and brisk. So instead he had accepted the offer of tea, which Mangat Ram had appropriately infused with ginger.

Having finished consuming his cup of masala chai, SSP Raghav rose, hooked his thumbs in the loops of his belt, and enquired, 'Well, what do you make of it?'

'Clever,' Mehrunisa said, a note of pique in her voice.

'Yes, as a layman, I almost believed it.'

'It is the argument of a sophist: plausible but fallacious. *Aria fritta.*'

'What?'

'A lot of hot air, really.'

SSP Raghav started pacing the carpeted floor. His manner was of a medium-weight wrestler anticipating the arrival of his competitor, a heavyweight champion. 'Look!' he paused, his right hand cradling the holster on his hip. 'I don't think you understand. The people of Agra town, the daily wage-earner, the businessman, the grocery store owner, the housewife, they don't understand logic and sophisticated arguments in the manner of intellectuals! If we have to prove this pamphlet false, we need to provide concrete proof in layman's language. You understand?'

Mehrunisa regarded the policeman from her armchair. He was trying not to sound his usual overbearing self, and she detected a note of concern.

'SSP Raghav, have you heard the story of Michelangelo and a man called Biagio da Cesena?'

The policeman stared at Mehrunisa, his eyes goggling. His expression clearly indicated what he thought of stories, especially those with strange-sounding firangi names! With some effort he kept his composure. 'Stories are for children and, perhaps, scholars. For a policeman, there are cases to be solved. I came here thinking that you might be able to shed light on the unusual claim made by this leaflet. Perhaps I am wasting my time.'

With an extended arm, Mehrunisa indicated the chair. 'Please do sit, SSP Raghav and make time to hear a short story. Trust me,' she flashed a quick smile, 'you will find it enlightening.'

Raghav hesitated before sitting on the chair's edge.

Mehrunisa flipped the pages of *Vatican Masterpieces*, tabbed a page, and handed the book to the policeman.

He glanced at the picture. *The Last Judgement*, it said, by Michelangelo. A lot of nude men, and some barely-clothed women, hovering in a blue sky.

As if she was in the Vatican leading a tour group, Mehrunisa began. 'Biagio Martinelli da Cesena was the Pope's master of ceremonials. When Michelangelo was painting the Sistine Chapel wall, Biagio criticised the nudes as immoral. Michelangelo, however, was magnifying the Creator's work by illustrating his finest creation, Man, in his pristine form. Besides, the Last Judgement also means the Resurrection of the dead, and surely, they would not arise from their tombs in clothes! Biagio, however, persisted with his criticism. The fresco was nearing completion when Michelangelo was painting Minos, a mythical king, at the entrance to Hell. Tired of Biagio's carping, he gave his profile to Minos, adding two ass's ears!

'Now, this Minos had a serpent for a tail. If you examine the painting's bottom right-hand corner,' Mehrunisa urged the policeman, 'you'll see how Michelangelo got even!'

SSP Raghav peered at the picture and located a figure with a serpent twined around it. On further scrutiny, he inhaled sharply. The serpent's head was biting the poor man's private parts! He was taken aback. Obviously, this Mehrunisa was a rather forward woman, urging him to look at pictures such as this. Squaring his shoulder, he asked gruffly, 'The purpose of this story?'

'*The Last Judgement* was painted five hundred years ago. Each year, millions of Vatican visitors gaze at the Sistine Chapel. Both the painter and his critic are long dead, but Biagio da Cesena has remained forever the guardian of Hell, with ass's ears and a snake-bitten member. So, the moral of the story is?'

SSP Raghav continued to regard her mutinously.

'Don't mess with an artist!' Mehrunisa couldn't help laughing, despite the pompous miffed look on the policeman's face, or because of it.

'Biagio's criticism created problems for Michelangelo. So what did the painter do? He inverted his perspective, and created in turn, a problem for Biagio—one that not only made him a laughing stock of sixteenth-century Rome, but turned him into an enduring gag on the Vatican gig!'

With a straight face SSP Raghav enquired, 'And how does this help us?'

Mehrunisa uncrossed her legs and in one elegant move, stood up. In her long black cashmere sweater, black leggings—ringed at the bottom with multicoloured leg warmers, flowing black hair framing a marmoreal complexion, she looked as fetching as a sculpted Venus, and as resolute as stone. She rolled the pamphlet and tapped it against her open left palm. 'That the Taj Mahal is a Shiva temple is Bentinck's personal grievance. This pamphlet makes it public.'

Crossing her arms in front of her chest, she looked straight at the policeman. 'We need to make the problem *his* alone.'

'How?' SSP Raghav was leaning forward from the chair in which he sat grumpily. 'And who is this Bentinck?'

Mehrunisa narrated the story of Bentinck, the greedy governor-general of British India who had tried to sell the Taj Mahal for its marble, and how her godfather had suggested they call the person behind the conspiracy Bentinck.

'The Taj Mahal sure has its detractors,' SSP Raghav said and divulged the ASI director-general's response to the pamphlet.

Mehrunisa paced the carpeted room, the scroll in her hand. 'Bentinck is trying to shift the burden of responsibility. He believes, for some reason, that the Taj Mahal is a Shiva temple which has to be reclaimed. However, that problem is solely his since the public is unaware and unconcerned about the,' she wagged quotation marks in the air, '*Hindu* origin of the Taj Mahal.'

She reached the table, paused to sip wine before turning to her guest, the wine glass dangling from her hand.

'SSP Raghav, when you have a problem, a problem relevant only to you, what is the response of others around you?'

'They don't care.'

'Why?'

'It doesn't affect them.'

'Exactly! People are never interested in the problems of others. The only way to hook them is by demonstrating how the problem affects them—upon which it becomes theirs.'

SSP Raghav nodded. 'And by claiming that the Taj Mahal is actually a Shiva temple, this Bentinck fellow is trying to arouse the religious sentiment of the Hindus. In effect, making it a problem of the masses.'

He cracked his knuckles. 'So what is your plan to tackle him?'

'By using the same logic. Bentinck's appeal is to the *Hindu* in Agra residents. Perhaps, there are other elements in their nature that can be appealed to? What is Agra best known for? What puts Agra on the world map? What is the source of livelihood for a large number of Agra residents? One answer: the Taj Mahal.'

SSP Raghav cleared his throat before adding, 'And recently, it has been declared one of the seven wonders of the new world.'

'Why would Agra residents jeopardise their potential prosperity for a crazy right-wing allegation? Especially,' Mehrunisa chewed the last morsel of cheese, 'when it is brought to their notice that the builder of the Taj Mahal, the Mughal emperor Shah Jahan was three-quarter Hindu?'

'*What?*'

'He was born to the Rajput princess Jagat Gossain. His father, Jahangir, was himself born to a Rajput princess, Akbar's wife. And Akbar allowed his wife to remain a Hindu and to maintain a Hindu shrine in the royal palace. Occasionally, he participated in pujas she performed. So Jahangir's mother and Shah Jahan's grandmother was a practising Hindu. As was his wife: Jahangir persisted with Akbar's religious policy.'

SSP Raghav clucked his tongue. 'For a fact, it is well concealed.'

'I guess the Mughal-equals-Muslim tag works as an effective shroud. In fact, most historians agree—Professor Kaul definitely does—that the Mughal family tradition was one of cultural openness and religious cohesion. Babur, the founder of the Mughal Empire in India, was descended from Changez Khan on his mother's side. Changez Khan participated in Christian, Buddhist and Muslim observances. Timur, the paternal precursor—Babur was descended from him on his father's side—was inclined towards Sufism. And Sufism, as you know, is a mystical sect that derives from the sensibilities of other faiths. Babur and Humayun were both rather practical about the place of faith vis-à-vis power. Akbar was a syncretist who created a new religion, Din-i-Ilahi, a sort of melding of Muslim and Hindu sensibilities.

'Imagine if Shah Jahan had opted to follow that part of his heritage. After all, he was more of Rajput-Hindu extraction than Turko-Mongol,' Mehrunisa said. 'A tantalising thought. Or a case of counterfactual history.'

When the policeman gave her a puzzled look she explained, 'It is Raj Bhushan's favourite form of history. Quite a few historians believe in revisiting the past through reasonable speculation. The Harvard historian Niall Ferguson is a leading champion of counterfactual history, and Raj Bhushan has studied under him.'

SSP Raghav stroked his moustache. 'You mean to say that the ASI director-general might agree with this speculation that the Taj Mahal is a Hindu temple?'

'Not *agree* exactly. But he believes in a healthy spirit of enquiry. So he likes to speculate, "What if the Taj Mahal was a Hindu temple converted to a mausoleum?"'

The policeman shook his head. 'Tell me, what is the difference between the writer of this pamphlet and these counterfactual historians? Both are imagining alternative scenarios!'

Mehrunisa's response was a shrug. Raj Bhushan was consistent: he had dealt similarly with both the issues that attempted to invalidate the Taj Mahal—the calligraphic changes and the pamphlet. He either set great store by the general delinquency of idle Agra youth, or was the possessor of immense sangfroid.

SSP Raghav muttered darkly, 'Clearly the job of managing India's monuments does not consume him...'

Turning to Mehrunisa, he said, 'What would you suggest?'

'Design a pamphlet of my own. One that advertises the Taj Mahal as a Hindu by-product, almost. And a rich cash cow for milking. I can count on your support, right?'

'I'll check if the pamphlets have already been distributed or if I managed to catch them before the act was committed. I can ensure a quiet and effective distribution of your pamphlets. When do you begin?'

'Now.'

'Now?' A quick check of his wristwatch showed 8.30 p.m.

'What better time than now? Mangat Ram will rustle up a meal—you haven't eaten, right?—after which we'll begin. I'll prepare the pamphlet but it would have to be transcribed, as you mentioned, into layman's language.'

SSP Raghav sat there mulling over her suggestion. 'No point in us distributing a rebuttal if this original isn't around. In which case, we shall wait for him to play his next card and if it involves the leaflet, we have a counterattack ready."

'Also,' Mehrunisa continued, 'you must investigate the underground labyrinth of the Taj complex once again—'

'One minute,' Raghav interrupted her, an index finger aloft. 'What do you mean by "underground labyrinth"?'

It was Mehrunisa's turn to look surprised. 'Oh! I thought you had examined the basement area for a bomb...'

'Yes—the lower tomb chamber, beneath the ceremonial tombs, the cenotaphs. We checked those thoroughly. What else is there that constitutes a labyrinth?'

Mehrunisa went very still for a moment. The memory of a young girl huddling in the dark against a cold basement wall as hours crawled by chilled her. She shivered, then shook her head determinedly. 'SSP Raghav,' she said quietly, 'get ready for an all-nighter. You need a refresher on the Taj complex. In the case of the Taj Mahal, what you see is not what you get. And the conspirator is clearly someone who knows the Taj inside out.'

She walked out of the room and returned with a stack of thick hardbound books that she placed on the dining table. Briskly flicking through one, she beckoned the policeman.

'The Taj Mahal has several subterranean levels. In the Mughal era these had a functional inner life. Now, of course, they are closed to visitors...'

Agra

SSP Raghav stood in front of the Taj Mahal mausoleum, his eyes glued to the walkway. He had reached Agra late morning armed with a 'proof' pamphlet that listed incontrovertibly that the Taj Mahal was indeed a Mughal monument, and with a new appreciation of the underground layout of the Taj Mahal.

However, the DIG had busted him with a command to report to the CBI officer assigned to the case who would await him at the Taj. Raghav had hotfooted it here, but he had been waiting for an hour now and there was no sign of the CBI officer. Lack of sleep and the bright noon sun were making him grumpy as he glanced at his watch again.

The son-of-a-gun had instructed that they meet directly at the monument. Rana Pratap Singh, ex-JCP Chattisgarh, now with CBI, was two ranks senior to him, several ranks notorious, same age—forty—and his new boss on the Taj case. If the average Indian prayed not to get involved with the police at any point in their life, it was because of officers such as R.P. Singh. His mobile beeped.

'I don't see you SSP,' a voice drawled.

Raghav scoured the gardens, 'I am right here, Sir.' It being lunch hour, tourists were few.

'Where?'

'In front of the mausoleum.'

'The enemy I know sneaks up from behind.'

Raghav spun on his heels and dashed to the northeast side of the platform. A boat was drawing up, a tall man astride at the prow. The sun glinted off his bald pate and his aviators.

Talk about arriving in style, Raghav observed with disdain before he hurried to meet him. The riverine traffic in winter was usually low. However, that year the Yamuna's level was higher owing to heavy monsoon rains that had caused the river to flood several plains.

With a lithe jump the man landed at Dassehra Ghat, straightened and walked up to the waiting SSP. As they shook hands, Raghav registered a firm grasp. As he led the way up to the platform R.P. Singh resumed the conversation like they had never been interrupted. 'Shah Jahan, it is said, had a river patrol. Do *we* have one?'

'Sir?' Raghav was not sure he had heard correctly. It did not help that his new boss was six-foot plus, which forced him to tilt his head up as he spoke.

R.P. Singh came to a halt at the north side of the platform. He crossed his arms across his chest and surveyed the Yamuna. 'The water level is high enough for boats. Put a constant watch here; I don't want even a dog to swim up. Understood?'

Raghav looked at him, but could only see his reflection nodding its head rapidly in the CBI officer's dark glasses. 'Yes, Sir.'

Then R.P. Singh proceeded to walk around the complex as Raghav detailed the security arrangements that had been put in place. When they had finished a complete tour, R.P. Singh rattled off additional security he wanted: erection of watchtowers, a twenty-four-hour patrol of the riverside, dedicated monitoring of the CCTV cameras.

Finally, they halted in front of the Jilaukhana. Tourist traffic had begun to build up and a long queue snaked in front of the entrance. They walked to the east gate outside which R.P. Singh hailed a vendor and bought a paper cone of roasted chana. Raghav refused the offer of chickpeas as they stood watching the security guards frisk the visitors. His new boss had fantastic aim, Raghav grudgingly acknowledged as, from the corner of his eye, he saw him toss chana from waist-level to his mouth and never miss. What had he heard about Singh competing in the Asian Games shooting competition...?

'Who is Aurangzeb?'

The question came out of nowhere. Now, as Singh observed him, his face bland, a discomforted Raghav had to confess he had no idea.

'Hmmm. At least you'd know who *was* Aurangzeb?'

It was the oldest trick in the police manual. R.P. Singh had deliberately caught him off-guard and was now driving home who was boss.

In a tight voice Raghav said, 'Mughal emperor. Shah Jahan's son.'

'Traitorous chutiya,' R.P. Singh drawled. 'Did an inside job on his father. This Aurangzeb is a mole inside the Taj Mahal. Start looking for him, SSP. We find him, we'll solve the Taj conspiracy.'

Delhi

It was time to meet Mehrunisa, R.P. Singh decided, and wearing his best private-school demeanour he descended on the professor's house.

The CBI officer who likened his job to that of a jamadar—keeping the streets clean of terrorist-Naxalite-fundoo rubbish—and whose name figured on the hit lists of several militant organisations, had another side to him.

An alumnus of Mayo College, the private boarding school pitched as the Eton of India, Singh kept that facet in habitual abeyance. It served no purpose when chasing Maoists in mosquito-infected jungles or when interrogating low-lives. This particular feature was switched on when he was meeting genteel folks or superiors who could help his career trajectory.

Dressed in grey slacks, a black cable-knit wool sweater and black patent leather loafers, he stood at Professor Kaul's doorstep early morning. When the door opened he saw a statuesque woman who surveyed him with grey-green eyes. Surprised, he switched the skirt-chaser within him to sleep mode and brought to life the occasional gentleman. Showing his identity card to an unsure Mehrunisa, he informed her that the 'Taj conspiracy case' had been assigned to the CBI and that SSP Raghav was reporting to him.

Mehrunisa led him to the patio that looked onto the garden, motioned to a cushioned cane chair, and asked, 'How can I help you?'

R.P. Singh sat down, tipped his head in thanks and said, 'Let's start at the beginning. Perhaps you can take me through the calligraphy changes and their import.'

Mehrunisa recounted her discovery of Arun Toor's body at the mausoleum, the three things she had noticed with it, and the changes in the epitaph and Quran verse.

R.P. Singh heard her out without interruption, listening intently with his black eyes narrowed.

She had finished recounting how she had located the artisan Nisar, when Mangat Ram interrupted them. Mehrunisa excused herself to oversee Professor Kaul's breakfast in the dining room.

R.P. Singh observed the well-preserved lawn as he mulled over all that he had heard. The woman made sense. Why hadn't SSP Raghav seen it? Because he was convinced of an Islamist angle. That was what happened when you headed the Anti-Terror force, you saw everything through the filter of terror. Raghav had heard of 'Aurangzeb' and his mind—programmed to go on high alert at the mention of a jihadi—zoomed into a probable terror plot.

R.P. Singh did not blame him. If he was back in Chhattisgarh and heard of the incidents around the Taj, he'd have blamed the Naxals! The gaandu Maoists were all he ate and shat—they had totally engulfed his worldview....

Now, he had the benefit of an outsider's perspective. He would see things clearly for a week, after which he'd probably also be too deeply involved to pull back for a different perspective.

He was itching for a smoke. However, that would ruin the persona he was carefully presenting to Mehrunisa whom he could see from where he was sitting on the patio. He observed how the professor seemed to be performing his actions as if asleep. After she had fed the professor, Mehrunisa and Mangat Ram escorted him to a spot in the garden. A weak winter sun was trying to grin its way through a smattering of clouds. Mehrunisa placed a shawl on the professor's lap, tucking the folds on both sides. On re-joining him, she made sure to sit such that she could glance in her uncle's direction.

'Shall we?' R.P. Singh asked her and Mehrunisa nodded.

'This man who pursued you in the Red Fort—he would have caught up with you unless you are a trained athlete? I am not doubting your story, please understand. I am trying to get a picture of this alleged murderer.'

'He seemed to shuffle, as if the bulk of his clothing was hindering his movement.'

'Hunh. And did he say anything?'

'No. Nothing at all. In fact,' Mehrunisa paused as she remembered the man wrenching off his woollen cap, 'now that I recall, he appeared curiously soundless. No grunt, no exclamation...'

R.P. Singh pinched the bridge of his nose, his eyes closed. 'The face with no features is probably due to severe burns. The fact that he shuffled indicates a problem with walking. He might have some sort of brain injury...'

'How's that?'

'Severe charring that erased all facial features could have damaged the brain of this monkey-cap—'

'*Monkey-cap*!' Mehrunisa smiled. 'You make him sound comical.'

'Oh no,' Singh said hastily, 'it was just a descriptor. What would you call him?'

'Bentinck.'

'Bentinck? Why?'

Mehrunisa narrated, again, the story of the British governor-general.

'And you think he is Bentinck?' R.P. Singh asked.

Mehrunisa shook her head. 'No. Bentinck would not risk exposing himself. His strength is that he is hidden. An unseen enemy is more powerful, and he knows that. Monkey-cap is more likely Bentinck's henchman...'

Abruptly a drizzle started. Mehrunisa ran into the garden. As she attempted to lift Professor Kaul to his feet, R.P. Singh appeared at the other side, steadying him. As they shuffled to the house, Mangat Ram joined them with an unfurled umbrella. The winter monsoon, which had hovered reluctantly in the skies for the past few days, had finally opened up. The thin rain, so contrary to the deluge of summer, fell noiselessly over the garden.

In Agra it had rained through the night and the sky had still been overcast when R.P. Singh had departed for Delhi that morning. The showers brought to mind a surging Yamuna, a vision that bothered him for some reason.

Agra

SP Raghav checked out the security at the Taj Mahal again, to the visible consternation of Inspector Bharadwaj. Raghav put it down to territorial angst: Bharadwaj probably appreciated his intruding upon his territory as much as he did the CBI. He shrugged and walked on, leaving the CISF inspector in the gardens where he was checking the central walkway. It being a Friday, the monument was closed to visitors and Bharadwaj had taken the opportunity to run a thorough check of the premises.

Most people are unaware that inside the Taj Mahal complex is a functioning mosque that is open only to Muslim worshippers every Friday. Raghav himself had discovered this upon his posting to Agra. Shah Jahan had conceived the Taj Mahal as Mumtaz's home in paradise and the mausoleum set in a garden was ultimately a tomb chamber. How had the woman Mehrunisa described it— he scrunched his eyes in recollection—ah! 'the pinnacle of Mughal funerary architecture'.

Pleased with his memory, Raghav perambulated the mosque. It was shortly after noon. The worshippers, around a hundred men, had washed themselves at the ablution tank and were inside the red and white building.

Raghav, dressed deliberately in plainclothes, donned a skullcap that he had carried in a pocket and stepped inside the vaulted building. The worshippers stood facing one wall—Kaaba, he presumed. Those in front knelt, others stood behind them, all with their hands cupped, eyes shut.

Raghav scrutinised the men—all perfectly ordinary, lower-middle class, residents of Taj Ganj most likely.... Finding everything in order he crept out. It was then that he sighted a lone man skulking around the northwest tower behind the mosque. The towers were not open to visitors.

When Raghav crept up on him, he saw him clicking pictures, but his camera was focused on the riverside. Raghav clamped one hand on the man's shoulder and with the other snatched the camera.

'Hey!' The man rounded on him angrily and swore.

Raghav's hand shot out and caught the man by the scruff of his neck. 'What are you up to?'

'Let me go,' the man squirmed and pointed to his skullcap. 'I came for the prayers.'

'Is that so? Then why are you not in the mosque?'

'Neither are you!' The man pointed at Raghav's head and started to wriggle harder. But Raghav's hold was firm. The next instant he smashed his foot hard on Raghav's and twisted suddenly to free himself. Instead he found his wrists handcuffed behind him.

Raghav brought his face within inches of the man's and said darkly, 'Time to start praying!'

He hauled him to the police station for questioning. Several hours of interrogation, questions interspersed with blows, yielded nothing. The man, bruised and battered, insisted he was a worshipper, yet could provide no proof of residence. And the digital camera had revealed his peculiar photographic preoccupation—the photos were all of the north side of the monument capturing its rear, the terrace gallery and the views of the monument from across the Yamuna.

This unusual interest bothered Raghav and he wondered if he had missed this man's accomplices, one of whom might be Aurangzeb....

Delhi

Mehrunisa and R.P. Singh sat quietly under the patio awning, sipping tea as rain fell around them. At one point, Mehrunisa looked up and yelped in surprise. Professor Kaul's face was framed in the window of his bedroom, which looked out onto the patio. He was gazing in their direction, his eyes alert. She clasped her mouth in amazement—Professor Kaul had not got out of bed of his own volition for almost a week.

She hurried towards the main entrance. Striding down the hall in his dressing gown, hair awry, was Professor Kaul. Like a wild animal that had escaped its cage, he tossed his head around, without taking notice of Mehrunisa where she stood or Singh where he sat a few feet away on the patio.

'Kaul uncle?' Mehrunisa made to touch him.

Turning at the sound of her voice, he asked abruptly, 'Where is Mehrunisa?'

She was too stunned to speak.

He looked through her as he queried again, 'Has anyone seen her?'

'I am standing right in front of you, Uncle.'

'Rubbish!' Professor Kaul shook his head. 'What sort of joke is this? Mehrunisa is a girl, twelve-thirteen years old.' Once again he cast furtive glances around him. 'I was looking to tell her a story. A,' he lowered his voice and tipped his head conspiratorially, 'special one.' His voice rising, 'Find her, quickly. Before I forget the story.' Panic seized his face, contorting the handsome visage into one of terror.

Taking his arm gently, Mehrunisa guided him towards the seat she had just vacated. 'Why don't you tell me the story, before you forget. That way,' she continued in her calm voice, 'I will make sure the story reaches her.'

He eyed her doubtfully, but seemed to decide that she was trustworthy for he began to talk, words gushing forth as if from a burst dam, steamrolling any pause or punctuation.

The story was a familiar one—Mehrunisa had heard it many times in her childhood. A popular incident from the *Mahabharata*, the story was narrated with such rapidity that it probably made no sense to R.P. Singh who was observing the professor as if he were a laboratory specimen.

Yudhistra, the eldest Pandava, was made the crown prince of Hastinapur. This made his cousin Duryodhana jealous. With the help of his maternal uncle Shakuni, Duryodhana made a plan to kill the Pandavas. He persuaded the five Pandava brothers to attend a grand fair in the town of Varnavat where he had a lac palace built for them. Lac burns easily and he planned to kill the Pandavas in their sleep. However, their uncle Vidura learnt of this plot and warned them in time. He also had a secret tunnel dug, through which the Pandavas could escape. The five brothers, with their mother Kunti, stayed in the palace during their visit. Bhima, the second

*Pandava brother, himself set the palace on fire. Then they
escaped safely through the tunnel, leading Duryodhana
to believe they had perished in the fire.*

On finishing his rapid-fire narration, Professor Kaul
gulped lungfuls of air. After which he slumped in the
chair, and all Mehrunisa wanted to do was to hug him.
She made to lean forward, draping an arm around his
back when he bolted upright.

His eyes were round with fear as he clutched her wrist
and whispered hoarsely. 'Tell her, tell Mehrunisa when
you find her, to watch out. Watch out for Aurangzeb!'

❋ ❋ ❋

An enervated Professor Kaul, totally spent after his narration,
was back in his room. While Mangat Ram watched over
him, a pale Mehrunisa had returned to the patio.

R.P. Singh's eyes narrowed. 'Aurangzeb again. For a
historical figure to suddenly go contemporary would
require a reason.' He hunched forward and looked at her
meaningfully.

Mehrunisa nodded thoughtfully. 'Aurangzeb is clearly
not a militant—the urgency, the intimacy, with which
Kaul uncle mentioned his name makes me believe he
knows his true identity...'

'So why doesn't he disclose it?'

'Because he is unable to,' Mehrunisa suggested. She
disclosed that the professor was diagnosed with a syndrome
that had robbed him of a large chunk of his memory.

'But he is clearly afraid,' R.P. Singh patted his bald
pate, his mouth pursed in contemplation. 'The professor
is afraid for you.'

Mehrunisa lifted her shoulders in a helpless shrug.

Was he mistaken, or were her eyes green? Singh wondered. Mentally shaking himself, he said, 'This story that your uncle narrated—is there a relevance?'

'I don't know,' Mehrunisa said in a shaky voice. 'He has always been an ardent storyteller. All my knowledge of Indian mythology comes from the stories he has told me. My father had little interest in them. This particular one that he narrated, I've heard before.'

'Are patients with this syndrome known to recall their lost memory?'

'Yes, the doctor mentioned that Kaul uncle could recollect fragments of his past which he would vocalise without any apparent context.'

'See,' R.P. Singh sat up excitedly, jabbing the air in between them with an index finger. 'I'm wondering if some stimuli triggered the professor's recall of that story, and the warning about Aurangzeb.'

'You think the two are related?'

'Perhaps.'

Mehrunisa sat there trying to figure what the story of the lac palace had to do with Aurangzeb. When R.P. Singh requested her to recount it for him, she did so slowly, all the while looking for a link.

'A fascinating story,' Singh said. 'Old rivalry, a plan to kill, ingenious escape.... What do you think is the most critical element in the story?'

'The escape?'

R.P. Singh's right index finger probed the air as if attempting to locate something before it came to a halt. 'Masking the escape. That, to my mind, is the crux of this matter.'

Delhi

The man at the centre of the Taj conspiracy was the murdered and corpse-gone-missing Arun Toor. R.P. Singh had a sketchy idea of the man from the file SSP Raghav had developed on him. It contained some photographs, a record of his work experience, educational certificates, testimonials of people who worked with him and had known him. His house had been searched, twice; his colleagues and acquaintances questioned—a couple of constables had travelled to Benares and Etawah to interview Toor's relatives; another constable was working through the list of contractors who carried out regular repair and maintenance work at Taj Mahal, and yet—nothing. Nothing had turned up which shed light on why somebody would want to murder Arun Toor, bachelor, history major, and Taj supervisor. What he needed therefore, was a better sense of the man, his personality, his friends and enemies. Since Mehrunisa had spent time working with him, and they'd been friendly, he decided to talk to her about Toor. 'Why don't you tell me more about the Taj supervisor?' he asked. 'This all began with Arun Toor, and I know nothing about him.'

Mehrunisa nodded but suggested they continue the discussion over some food, and R.P. Singh, having left Agra before breakfast, readily accepted. He was enjoying the company of this woman—she struck him as vulnerable yet resolute, engaging and erudite. As Mehrunisa led the way and he followed, his eyes on her shapely rear, he reminded himself not to get carried away. The Bastar badlands was to be blamed for his sensory deficit—back in the civilised world, his male hormones were in overdrive, he thought, grinning to himself.

The housekeeper brought in a fresh pot of tea, scrambled eggs and a rack of toast. Mehrunisa indicated that he help himself.

As he buttered a toast thickly, Mehrunisa started talking.

When Mehrunisa first met Arun Toor they had got talking like old friends. That was surprising, considering how unlike they were, in both demeanour and upbringing: she was elegant and composed, he was unkempt and gregarious; she had a cosmopolitan upbringing in the Middle East and Europe, he had grown up in the ancient Indian city of Varanasi. What they had in common was a love of Michelangelo, though they were to discover that only later.

One evening, after Mehrunisa had been frequenting the Taj Mahal for over a month, Arun had suggested dinner. He knew a place that served authentic Unani, Persian, food. The legend went that the chef's ancestor had travelled with the Persian ambassador in the entourage sent by the Shah of Persia to Aurangzeb in honour of his accession to the Mughal throne. The chef's ancestors had served in the royal kitchens, and now that royalty was dead, the family survived on the patronage of Agra's citizenry. Only, Arun added, giving her a once-over, you may find the place short on ambience.

'If the food is good, I've been known to trade atmosphere for it,' Mehrunisa smiled.

The eatery was a tiny ill-lit place in Taj Ganj where they sat on creaking wooden benches opposite each other as steaming berry pulao and abgusht was deposited on the table. The food, Mehrunisa discovered, was surprisingly good and authentic—the specialty, pomegranate soup, superlative. They savoured lamb morsels against the background drone of evening traffic and swapped stories. When Mehrunisa finished recounting her student days in Florence and her pursuit of Renaissance art, Arun Toor surprised her by concluding, 'And your favourite artist, no doubt, is Michelangelo.'

'How did you guess?'

'You strike me as a person I like to call "classic"—the things that attract them are of enduring excellence. Look at you. Your clothes, your speech, the manner in which you conduct yourself,' he said, stretching an imaginary thread between his fingertips, 'elegant, authoritative, but also,' he winked, 'typical. Which means, your favourite artist has to be either of the three acknowledged Renaissance greats: Leonardo da Vinci, Michelangelo or Raphael.'

Arun Toor chewed noisily on a green chilli, as above them moths fluttered around a light bulb dangling from a nearby bamboo pole. 'You mentioned your love for Florence, so it would be logical to deduce the artist would be Florentine. That rules out Raphael. Of the two Florentines, I would bet on Michelangelo.'

Mehrunisa pulled out a wet wipe from her bag and wiped her hands. Arun raised his eyebrows in mock surprise and with his chin indicated the corner basin. Smiling, Mehrunisa shook her head and asked, 'Why Michelangelo? Leonardo is acknowledged as the complete Renaissance man, and if, as you claim, my taste tends to the classic, surely I'd veer to him?'

Arun nodded, 'Well said. I would say you had picked a hole in my deduction, except,' he held up his right index finger, stained yellow from the turmeric in the paste, 'Michelangelo was the one with a tortured soul.'

Mehrunisa sat still.

'And I would say,' Arun continued happily munching his food, 'that Mehrunisa Khosa shares an empathy with that tortured soul.'

'Why would you say that?'

'Your project, Mehrunisa—Indo-Persian linkages—it is a search, isn't it? A search for answers—to yourself, perhaps?'

'And you, my friend, have all the answers?'

'I have offended you. Well, if it helps, let me divulge that my favourite artist is also Michelangelo!'

Arun guffawed at her obvious astonishment. 'The *other* one. Michelangelo Merisi da Caravaggio. You are wondering where and how I got to study Caravaggio? A poor brown boy from the boondocks!' Arun's smile had gone static on his face.

Taken aback at the unexpected venom in his voice, Mehrunisa almost flinched.

The next instant Arun snorted, before pointing his index finger at her and grinning cheekily, 'Got you!'

Growing up in Varanasi, the cultural capital of India, Arun divulged, he had encountered many young backpackers who came to the holy city by the Ganga to discover Hindu spirituality. Somewhere their enthusiasm had infected him and he had resolved to one day travel to a place about which he had little knowledge and immense curiosity—Italy, the fount of Renaissance.

'Mark Twain said Varanasi was older than history, older than tradition, older even than legend, and looks twice as old as all of them put together! But a true appreciation of home comes when you have travelled far. I wanted to see if my wanderings in that *other* land of such immense culture would build my appreciation for the art of India. After all, I was infatuated enough to want to pursue a career in it. It seemed like a good test—this exploration of another world and its artistic palate.'

Arun described how he had spent a summer backpacking his way through Italy, studying the sculpture and art in its various museums, working in restaurants to earn money whenever he ran out of it, sleeping on benches in public parks. When he returned he considered himself an amateur on Western art and architecture—at least he could tell a Romanesque church from Gothic, he finished, grinning.

'So that's where you discovered Caravaggio?'

'Yes!' Arun said, his eyes bright. 'His paintings were so monstrously vivid. I would be standing in the Uffizi in Florence, in front of a Caravaggio, and there, on the wall, I could imagine a scene out of one of Varanasi's little lanes being played out on the canvas. In his paintings I saw people with grubby soles. I knew those feet—they were the feet of people who spend their days and nights barefoot. And those half-shadows in which he painted his characters, their faces simultaneously conveying one emotion and masking another. The brilliant interplay of bright with dark—chiaroscuro, as they call the technique—it mesmerised me. I, for one, had never seen anything like that before. That made him unique to me. On my return I scoured the Banaras Hindu University library for literature on Caravaggio, his paintings, his life, anything and everything.'

It was Mehrunisa's turn to smile. 'It fits. Your propensity for Caravaggio.'

'Why? Should I be peeved at your value judgement?'

Mehrunisa waved her hand in dismissal. 'You know what I mean.'

'Yes. A guy with a scruffy beard, grubby hands, and loud laughter would best appreciate the unpretentious, manic genius of Caravaggio. Not to mention the can-blow-smoke-through-the-nostrils bit...' Arun laughed, throwing his head back, snorting. It drew interested, amused glances from the other tables.

'Caravaggio lived a rough-tough life and his paintings are full of the grime, ordinariness and lust of life. Why,' Arun guffawed, 'even his Cupid had dirty toenails! The beggars, the prostitutes, the menacing shadows—what a relief from the piety and soft tones of Botticelli, or—pardon me—the musculature of Michelangelo who put muscles even on women! The Delphic sibyl—you recall? Face of an angel, and the biceps of a giant!'

It was a sticky night, the air ponderous with the impending monsoon. Mehrunisa and Arun remained quiet for some time, immersed in the quiet companionship that comes from sharing. A mosquito came droning in front of Arun's face. He clapped it between his palms; the spell was broken. With a snap of his fingers, Arun ordered paan.

Mehrunisa had seen its orange juice spat merrily in the streets and declined the offer. Grinning mischievously, she rested her chin on her palm. 'Some art historians say that Caravaggio's art is, ultimately, a murderer's confession. You must know he murdered a young man and spent his life thereafter running from the law.'

Arun smiled, a smile that got lost in his beard, but lit up his eyes and rounded his cheeks. 'He was a rough and ready guy—a street brawler, a gang member, a murderer.... You have studied his paintings so you would know what gave that luminosity to the brilliant white he used in his paintings.'

'White lead paint,' Mehrunisa replied quietly.

'And?'

'It is highly toxic.'

Arun's response was a shrug as he lit up a cigarette. 'When did genius ever play by the rules? His mantra: transgress.'

'It's interesting that you use the word transgress. I thought you'd say innovate.'

Arun Toor burst into one of his guffawing laughs, nodding his head in some secret merriment. 'That is the difference between you and me, Mehrunisa. The difference, let's say,' his voice went flat, 'between privilege and penury, between ideal and real. The genius in the underprivileged world does not innovate; he transgresses. Remember *that*!'

Mehrunisa acknowledged this with a lift of her brows. 'You do seem to have a strong empathy with Caravaggio. There are art historians who believe that it is his guilt, the burden of his oppressed soul, which lends his canvas such feverish intensity. Applying the deductive reasoning you demonstrated, what could be the cause for your empathy with Caravaggio the murderer?'

Arun went still. In a deadpan voice, he asked, 'Are you calling me a murderer, Mehrunisa?'

He leaned forward and whispered, 'Perhaps I do have murder on my mind.' Next he gave a slow, half wink, following it with a languid smirk as smoke curled out of his nostrils.

The paan juice that stained his lips a reddish-orange should have made him look ridiculous. Instead, with the deepening night sky in the distance, the iron rod used for plucking roti from the clay oven glinting against the brick wall behind, and the faint light casting Arun's face in shadow, his coloured mouth made him look faintly ghoulish. The scene, Mehrunisa realised, could be straight out of a Caravaggio painting!

When R.P. Singh left Professor Kaul's house after spending three hours being updated by Mehrunisa, his head was a little fuzzy. It had been an entirely pleasurable time—ambience, female company, food—yet what he had gleaned from the meeting had confounded him.

The Arun Toor that emerged from the anecdotes that she had recounted was a man of contradictions: a sloppy dresser yet fastidious arranger of files; a man who frequently changed the style of his beard but never of his clothes; a Benares boy who was in awe of an Italian painter; a history scholar who headed the drama club in college; a practical man who was nevertheless obsessed with the number three; devoted to the monument yet aware of his Jat heritage that had once ransacked the Taj.

He was not sure if he had heard about one man or two....

Delhi

Mehrunisa was studying an upside-down Ardhnarishwar as she sat opposite Raj Bhushan. The ASI director-general was on the phone. He had called her that morning to share some news. Since he was occupied, Mehrunisa studied the two-that-are-one-form of Shiva for which he had earlier exhibited great enthusiasm, and wondered if there was a woman in the director's life, a Shakti to complete his Shiva.

'Yes.' Raj Bhushan grinned as he rubbed his hands. 'It is good of you to come at such short notice, but I thought it might interest you.' He paused. 'Would you care for a trip to Jaipur?'

'Jaipur?' Mehrunisa asked. 'Why?'

'For the Jaipur map. In the Maharaja Sawai Man Singh II Museum in the Jaipur palace is a large cloth map. In 1722, the Mughal emperor Muhammad Shah appointed Maharaja Sawai Jai Singh as the governor of Agra. At that time, the Maharaja was planning a new city at Jaipur and, for comparative study, he instructed that a map be prepared of the Mughal empire's old capital and its prominent buildings. The result,' Raj Bhushan said as he rested his elbows on the armchair, 'is an image of Agra much as it had been under Shah Jahan.'

'Oh!' Mehrunisa leaned forward in excitement. 'You mean the map shows the Taj Mahal?'

The ASI director-general's face broke into its peculiar broad smile, his mouth forming a humungous 'U' even as the teeth stayed hidden from view. 'Not just the Taj Mahal, but the entire riverfront scheme planned by Shah Jahan—of which many gardens, buildings and tombs are lost or have fallen into ruin.'

He opened the right-side drawer of his desk and brought out a case of mints. Flipping the lid open, he tilted the case towards his guest—who declined with a shake of her head—and popped a fresh mint into his mouth.

Amazing! Mehrunisa thought. This map would be further proof that the Taj Mahal was integral to an elaborate plan by Shah Jahan and not an isolated structure that could have been usurped.

Raj Bhushan smiled as he arranged the papers on his table and stacked them neatly to one side. 'I was correct in my estimation! Finally, something that cheers you! As a matter of fact, I have been in talks with the Jaipur royals to buy the map for the ASI.'

A bearer walked in with tea, and the director-general instructed him to deposit the tray near the corner sofa. 'Shall we,' he said, indicating the sofa to Mehrunisa.

Once they were reseated, Raj Bhushan began serving tea as he talked. 'It was Akbar who started to develop Agra as a riverfront city. However, it was during Shah Jahan's reign that the garden with buildings on a riverfront terrace, like the Taj Mahal, became the norm. The Jaipur map shows the chahar baghs as a characteristic of Mughal Agra's urban landscape: a square garden divided into four quarters by paved walkways and canals can be seen in many buildings. One popular example, considered the design predecessor of the Taj Mahal, is Itmad-ud-Daula's tomb, constructed by Nur Jehan for her beloved father.'

Raj Bhushan handed her an elegant bone china teacup.

'It would be worth a look. Besides,' Mehrunisa paused, 'Kaul uncle's niece lives in Jaipur. Perhaps I can persuade her to visit uncle for a while—it may help jog his memory.'

'His niece, hmm?' He had finished pouring the tea and replaced the teapot in the carved walnut tray. He eyed the placement, shifted the kettle marginally so the spout and handle were aligned in a straight line and sat back satisfied.

'Have you met Pamposh?' Mehrunisa asked. 'We spent several vacations together as children.'

'Briefly. Let's hope she can be of assistance to your uncle.'

Pakistan-occupied Kashmir

In his bunker, Jalaluddin scrutinised the folder that had arrived that day. From within it he retrieved several thick stacks of surveillance photographs. A kettle, glass and a bowl of candy stood to his right, so the carpet in front of him lay free of any items.

Tearing the rubber band off the first bunch, he laid out the pictures in a row on the carpet. The Taj Mahal lay spread out before him, the monument captured from several different angles: the façade and interior of the mausoleum; the two flanking buildings; the gardens and walkways.

Jalaluddin poured himself a glass of green tea. Over small sips he peered intently at each photograph, as if committing it to memory. Another set of pictures showed the security detail around the monument: sandbags, police in khaki uniforms with metal detectors, the barbed wire barricades, the CCTV cameras, the policeman inside his cell manning the cameras.

The photos were not the work of an ordinary tourist. What was captured was not the aesthetics of a monument renowned the world over for its beauty, but the security, or lack of it, around it.

Additionally, the photographs had been clicked at different times—the garments of the visitors and policemen switched from summer wear to sweaters and shawls.

His man had sent word that police had apprehended him while he was photographing at the monument—the last batch of photographs consequently were in their possession. Let off after a couple of days of questioning, he was lying low.

Jalaluddin harrumphed quietly as he finished studying the photographs. His jihadis were single-minded in their pursuit. He grabbed some candy and padded to the mouth of the cave where icicles had formed. Sucking on the sweet, he watched the falling snow with approval.

Agra

SSP Raghav looked around the cramped study where he awaited Professor R.N. Dixit. The constable given charge of going through Arun Toor's files had compiled a list of contractors and consultants who had worked on the Taj Mahal during Toor's tenure as supervisor. The name of the retired chemistry teacher had come up—apparently he had been consulted for the recent chemical cleaning of the Taj Mahal. It didn't seem like much of a lead, but the duty constable was unwell and Raghav had a couple of spare hours, so he decided to pay Dixit a visit.

The walls of the small room were lined with shelves bursting with books, files, folders, ring binders. Open volumes were splayed atop the shelves, the professor's desk, even his worn chair. The mess seemed to indicate a man preoccupied with something.... Raghav blinked hard; the musty air was suffocating him. Scraping his chair back, he stood up abruptly.

A framed photo on the wall above a bookshelf showed the professor with the famous BHP leader Kriplani.

Raghav squinted at another picture to its right—an old black and white college picture with names listed below. He walked up to it. Scanning the names, he did a double take: both Kriplani and Arun Toor were listed there. Hmm... so Arun Toor had been a student of Dixit's at Benares Hindu University; Kriplani, it was well known, was a BHU professor before he turned to politics.

As Raghav prowled the room his ears pricked up. Amidst the utilitarian household sounds—rhythmic swish of a broom, the wet slap of slippers, the pressure cooker's whistle—he caught a faint bubbling sound. He went still. It seemed to come from a tall almirah, the upper half of which had glass doors, the bottom half wooden ones. He put his ear to the wooden almirah—the noise was coming from within.

The wooden doors were bolted at the bottom. Curious, Raghav pulled the bolts and opened the doors, which yielded to reveal a largish storage area, completely barren, at the end of which he could see a wooden panel. Raghav's unease was growing by the minute. Crouching, he probed the panel. Applying pressure with both hands, he worked the edges. Suddenly, the panel flipped backwards. Raghav coughed. A chemical smell filled his nostrils even as the bubbling sound grew louder. He was staring into pitch dark.

Squinting into the darkness, he crawled forward. In the blackness, a blue triangle hovered, above which floated a spectral white. It was so eerie it filled Raghav with trepidation. He glanced back at the study. The almirah was a passage to a room that Dixit frequented. In which case, a light switch had to be close by.

Raghav breathed his relief and stretched his hand out of the almirah to probe the wall outside. Nothing on the right. On the left wall he found a switch, flicked it on and light washed over a white-painted room. Raghav blinked as shiny glass apparatus, orderly jars and beakers, tidy shelves and clean tables came into view. A beaker bubbled atop a Bunsen burner—the blue flame—that was reflecting off the surrounding glass.

The laboratory was immaculately clean, a sharp contrast to the mess in the study. From the almirah to the room was a two-foot drop and Raghav jumped onto the floor of the lab.

He approached the table where a yellowish liquid was bubbling, pinching his nose at the corrosive smell. The beaker was connected to a row of stainless steel cylinders, in turn rigged to pipes, rubber tubing and gauges. Stapled sheets lay beside the equipment. Raghav flicked through them. Some text on radiocarbon dating with accompanying diagrams. With a shrug he tossed it back and looked up.

Why did Dixit need a secret lab? Was his wife privy to it?

As he chewed on this thought his eyes skimmed over the room before returning to the table. He turned to leave when a smaller sheet below the stapled document caught his eye. Picking it up, he scanned a couple of hand-drawn sketches and a spidery scrawl that—he screwed his eyes to decipher the writing—said 'carbon dating the Taj Mahal using a piece of wood from a basement room doorway'.

Carbon dating the Taj Mahal!
Raghav recoiled in horror.

❊ ❊ ❊

At the police station, Professor Dixit insisted on his right to legal counsel. His mouth set in a mutinous line, he shook his head and refused to answer any questions. Raghav looked at the man with silvery locks, his fly open, his shirt buttoned up wrong and doubted his sanity. He let the professor rant and called R.P. Singh.

When Singh arrived he hollered at Raghav, even as he eyed Dixit, 'Have you shoved a bamboo up his backside yet?' Then, he grabbed Dixit by his collar and dragged him into an empty cell where he accused him of murdering Arun Toor. Patting his bald head, he clucked his tongue and drawled, 'Get ready for the gallows, Dik-shit—that's where you're headed!' He unclasped his leather belt, slid it out, and with manic eyes, cracked the leather on the brick floor. A stinging whiplash rang through the cell.

R.P. Singh's act was a throwback to the archetypal Bollywood villain—the kind even mouldy professors were acquainted with—and Raghav saw the effect as Dixit blanched visibly.

'I-I-I b-barely knew the Taj supervisor.'

With the next crack of the leather belt, R.P. Singh singed the hair on Dixit's ankles, striking it within a millimetre of his wrinkled skin.

Dixit sprang up screaming. Hands folded he sputtered rapidly, 'I was o-only l-looking to carbon d-d-date the Taj Mahal.'

R.P. Singh lunged at his throat. 'Gaandu! In order to prove it was a Hindu temple?'

Dixit bobbed his head as if his neck had grown a spring. 'P-p-professional curiosity,' he quivered.

Singh shook him like a chicken and cracked the whip again.

Dixit screamed. 'Ask Shri Kriplani, the BHP party leader, ask him.' Tears streamed down his eyes as he wobbled in Singh's clutches. 'He'll v-vouch for m-me.'

At that extraordinary admission, R.P. Singh and Raghav exchanged glances. The same thought had seized them both.

Was Kriplani the man behind the Taj conspiracy?

Delhi

Shri Kriplani's face was set as he went over his options. He had been at it for three hours now. That was when his PA informed him about a CBI officer who wanted to speak with him. Kriplani had taken the phone call and heard a confident drawl; the officer wanted to meet him urgently, he said, to discuss the Taj Mahal.

It was 9 p.m. and R.P. Singh would be in his office soon. Shri Kriplani had bathed and worn a fresh dhoti-kurta and a crisp khadi jacket. The cold never bothered him: not for him the sweaters and shawls that Delhites swathed themselves in during the short winter. Also, he liked to convey a spartan appearance—in a newly-consumerist nation, it evoked Gandhi's aura. He looked at himself in the mirror, the trademark red tilak on his forehead, and pleased with the result, he ambled to the sitting room.

His first sight of the CBI officer did not reassure him. The tall bald man was lounging in the sofa and, on his approach, stood up in a leisurely manner. The man extended his hand, Shri Kriplani folded his and indicated he sit down.

'How can I assist you?'

R.P. Singh leaned forward. 'What is the nature of your friendship with R.N. Dixit?'

In his smooth statesman voice Shri Kriplani said, 'Dixit is a colleague from BHU, from the days when I was a professor.'

'What can you tell me about him?'

'Many things,' Kriplani smiled blandly. 'Question is what interests you, Officer?'

R.P. Singh chuckled. 'At this time of the day, what interests me is a warm bed ... but work has to be finished, so here I am, doing my job. So, Dixit—are you two close?'

Kriplani did not rise to the bait. 'I've known Dixit on and off for several decades. He is a brilliant professor, but very absent-minded. In BHU, a clerk was assigned to remind him of every lecture he was scheduled to take. Absorbed in his lab, Dixit wouldn't remember to eat, forget lecturing the students.' Kriplani gave an indulgent smile. 'Archetypal mad scientist.'

'And a brilliant chemist, right?'

Kriplani stiffened slightly. 'Yes. I believe he has a healthy consulting practice. He told me so when we met last, after a long gap.'

'But you are in Agra frequently.'

'It is an important constituency.'

R.P. Singh acknowledged this with a slow swing of his head, his mouth a straight line.

'Do you know where Dixit is at present?'

Kriplani shrugged.

'In prison. For attempting to carbon date the Taj Mahal.' R.P. Singh leaned in, eyes fixed on the politician. 'It is an offence, you know, Kriplaniji.'

Shri Kriplani smoothed his kurta, which was as yet creaseless. Safety lay in absolute denial. Nobody was aware of his meeting with Professor Dixit. Besides, it was the chemist who had come up with the suggestion of carbon dating—he had just humoured him.

R.P. Singh's gaze did not waver. 'And when someone is conducting such experiments with the goal of inciting communal violence, you know how seriously the law looks at it...' Eyes intent on Kriplani, he slid a folded sheet out of his front pocket and passed it to him.

Ordinarily, Kriplani would be affronted at a paper being given to him thus. But this CBI officer was making him wary. Calmly, he proceeded to unfold the paper. It was blank. Anger rose within him and reddened his neck. Refusing to take the bait, however, he held up the sheet for R.P. Singh with a look of mild consternation.

'Oh! My mistake, Kriplaniji, apologies. Here.' Singh slid over another sheet, smoothed it out himself and spread it on the table between them.

The Taj Mahal is a Shiva temple!

Shri Kriplani's jaw tightened at the sight of the pamphlet. He adjusted his reading glasses, picked up the sheet and proceeded to read the text intently. A man walked in softly carrying a tray which he deposited on the table. On it was a plate of crisp samosas and a hot cup of masala chai.

The aroma of crushed clove and fried samosas dispersed between them. Shri Kriplani saw Singh's nostrils twitch even as he pretended not to have noticed the items clearly brought to soften him up.

As he pretended to read the pamphlet, Kriplani realised the problem was bigger than he'd thought.

'Oh! Look, I am forgetting to serve my guest.' He glanced at the wall-mounted clock which showed 9.30 p.m. and said in a paternal voice, 'Long day on the road for a police officer. You must be tired and hungry. Some food will do you good.'

R.P. Singh lifted an eyebrow in mock surprise, 'Thank you for the concern. But first, let's deal with this pamphlet, shall we?'

'Look, Officer,' Kriplani acted flustered as he thrust out his palms, 'I don't know why you're showing me this.'

R.P. Singh lifted one shoulder. 'That's simple. Dixit has given a statement that he was carbon dating the Taj Mahal on your orders.'

Kriplani flushed. 'That's a lie!' he said, sitting upright. 'You can examine my track record, Officer. I am a true patriot,' he ticked the finger of one hand, 'I have no truck with anti-national elements,' he ticked a second finger, 'and, surely, Dixit is making unjustified allegations,' he finished by ticking a third finger. He glowered at Singh, angry furrows in the red tilak.

'Whom will you believe? A lunatic chemistry professor or a respectable people's leader like me?'

'There is the recorded statement.'

'So, if tomorrow anybody makes an allegation against me, you'll record his statement?'

'Not just anybody. Ex-colleague, old friend, BHP member...'

'Nonsense!'

'Besides, nowadays these things are never hidden from the media. The police may close this case but what if media get wind of the allegation?'

Kriplani glared at Singh. 'I've always emphasised on national integration—Hindustan is the land of Hindus *and* several minorities who, however, need to accept that relationship in view of religious harmony.'

Silence hung between the men. R.P. Singh eyed the samosas, settled back into the sofa, patted his pate and regarded the BHP leader. A deeply rattled Dixit had been let off with a warning—he'd need time to recover from the police treatment. Playing this politician, though, was an altogether different ballgame.

Kriplani returned the gaze with a benign smile. In a voice smooth as white butter he said, 'Casting unjustified aspersions on the leader of the largest opposition party in the country is not a sensible course of action for a bright young officer's career. You know what they say: why pick a fight with the crocodile when you are destined for the pond?'

R.P. Singh nodded sagely. 'That is true,' he said with seriousness. 'Except, Kriplaniji,' he paused, 'I thought you'd give me Lord Krishna's advice.'

Kriplani's brow puckered.

R.P. Singh leaned forward to gather his aviator sunglasses from the table, and as he did so, said, 'Karmanya vadhikaraste...' Do one's duty, regardless of the fruits of the action—a shloka from the *Gita*.

The next instant he was striding out without any farewell.

Kriplani watched him go: for a big man he was very light on his foot. As his gaze returned to the table, Kriplani pursed his mouth. The food was left untouched. A brown film had developed on the milky tea as the fried samosas sat congealing on the ceramic plate.

Agra

On the outskirts of Mathura on NH2, the national highway between Delhi and Agra, was a dhaba that stayed open through the night catering to truckers and night travellers who needed to refuel their stomachs. As R.P. Singh left Kriplani's office he called SSP Raghav and summoned him there.

Two hours later the two men were sitting on a manji, the jute cot sagging beneath their weight as Singh had his dinner. Raghav, who had eaten earlier, sipped a cup of tea appreciatively from a kulhar. After a daily routine of sugarless tea in chipped glasses, the gingery, sweet, milk tea infused with the earthy texture of clay was heavenly.

R.P. Singh had finished updating Raghav on the meeting with the BHP leader. He bit into a green chilli, tore a bite of tandoor roti to scoop up a portion of chana masala and scarfed it down. Through the mouthful he asked, 'Is Kriplani telling the truth? What do you say?'

Raghav took a last sip and hurled the clay glass into a nearby bush. 'Does it matter?'

R.P. Singh's eyebrows rose. 'Explain,' he said.

Raghav tugged at his lush moustache as he collected his thoughts. 'Let's assume that Kriplani is the instigator of the Taj conspiracy. In which case, with your visit, you have called him out. Therefore, he won't risk continuing with the operation—in which case, the case is closed.'

A horn blared on the highway, its screech cutting through the cold night air.

'If, however,' Raghav resumed, 'Kriplani was trying some foolish carbon dating trip *but* is innocent of the conspiracy, then the question we still have to answer is: who is the conspirator?'

'Right,' R.P. Singh wagged his head. Satiated, he pulled back and eyed the steel utensils that had been wiped clean. 'I was hungry,' he smiled and burped. He motioned for a boy to remove the plates. Swiftly the cot was cleared and the boy brought a jug of water and a towel. 'Now this is real service,' R.P. Singh said happily. Having washed and wiped his hands, he settled back, resting his elbows on the jute cot. The boy reappeared with a bottle of Old Monk and two clay glasses. Raghav's eyes widened in surprise.

'What!' Singh laughed. 'A late night chat with no drink! Who died?'

He poured a tall peg in each clay glass, handed one to Raghav, clinked his kulhar and said, 'Cheers to chana masala!'

SSP Raghav grinned. 'Looks like somebody enjoyed his meal.'

R.P. Singh nodded. 'Last meal I had was breakfast. Crafty Kriplani! No sooner did my stomach rumble than samosas started to float in front of me.' He took a long swig which emptied the glass and refilled it. 'Now, the question for us: who is the conspirator? Let's see. What do we know about the conspirator? That he killed Arun Toor. Why?'

'Because the Taj supervisor had got wind of the conspiracy,' Raghav said as he sipped his rum. 'But the supervisor left clues to alert us to the conspiracy.'

'Yes,' Singh nodded. 'Bloody dramatic ones too! Using blood from his slit wrist. And the clues were clearly referring to a Taj Mahal equals Shiva temple equation: Shiva's third eye drawn on Toor's forehead as a sign of impending calamity. Chirag tale andhera—'

'But,' Raghav interrupted, 'that seemed to indicate the basement rooms, which, after Mehrunisa instructed me on the Taj labyrinth, we checked thoroughly and found nothing!'

Singh shook his head, took another long swig and drained his glass. 'You got that wrong. The "andhera" was pointing at the changes in the calligraphy.'

'Perhaps,' Raghav nodded thoughtfully and took another sip of his drink.

'Oye!' Singh hollered and stretched a hand in his direction. 'Why are you sipping rum like a lady at high tea? Bottoms up, man!' With that he drained his glass again. Raghav followed dutifully.

As Singh wiped his mouth with the back of his hand Raghav refilled their glasses. It was past midnight and the dhaba was still buzzing. On several cots men were stretched out under blankets. In the distance fields stretched out, mist skimming the crop. R.P. Singh liked the open; it reminded him of his father. A decorated war hero, he had been an army officer whose non-family postings kept him away for long periods, but when he returned, he'd take his son trekking and hiking and Singh

recalled many nights when they had slept in the open....
He shook his head and returned to the present.

'But then why did Toor's corpse vanish?'

'To avoid a post-mortem,' Raghav said, clearly
enjoying his drink. He had removed his shoes and was
sitting cross-legged on the cot now.

'Who would take the corpse?' Singh squinted in
concentration. The rum was affecting him. 'The murderer?'

'Aurangzeb?'

'I think this Aurangzeb is someone Mehrunisa knows
as well,' Singh said, and told Raghav about his visit to
Professor Kaul's house where he had witnessed the
professor warn Mehrunisa about Aurangzeb.

Raghav whistled. 'This gets interesting!'

'Listen,' R.P. Singh sat up. 'Do you know why they
assigned the case to me?

Despite several drinks, Raghav was sober enough to be
unsure how to answer.

'Go on,' Singh urged, 'speak your mind. Anything you
say this evening will be forgiven.'

That was all the encouragement an inebriated Raghav
needed. 'Because, JCP Rana Pratap Singh, you are a son-of-
a-gun, with a reputation for weeding out troublemakers.'

'I am the official chutiya, you mean? Ha!' R.P. Singh
gave a loud snigger. 'No. I am the jamadar, the cleaning
man. I have gone down so many sewers I can think like
the rats who live in those gutters!'

'So what do you think of Aurangzeb?'

The two men were sitting on either ends of the narrow
jute cot, their chests inclined towards each other, the
depleted Old Monk bottle sitting between them. To a
casual onlooker they would appear a pair of good-for-
nothing drunks.

R.P. Singh spoke softly. 'This Aurangzeb has two faces, one he shows the world—Mehrunisa, for instance—and the other is hidden. So, he is a composite of his known face and his hidden face. What is hidden, is in the dark. Therefore, we need to search the dark....'

He tipped his glass, finished his drink and tossed the kulhar on the ground. It slammed into the clay ground with a pop.

'What was designed as the complement of the Taj Mahal?' R.P. Singh looked up at Raghav and watched the light slowly dawn in his eyes.

Raghav's eyes widened as he recalled Mehrunisa's tutorial. A bazaar and caravanserai originally formed an integral part of the Taj Mahal complex—it was now obliterated by the city quarter known as—'Taj Ganj,' he said.

Agra

The next morning SSP Raghav was up at the crack of dawn. His head was fuzzy from the previous night's binge and lack of sleep, but it was nothing that a round of sit-ups and a cold shower would not fix. Two cups of tea and a breakfast of omelette-toast later, he was strolling in Taj Ganj as its residents awakened from sleep. Raghav had deliberately chosen the early hour for, as the day progressed, Taj Ganj became increasingly congested. He reached the streetlight under which he had seen the boys that night and looked around. A row of shuttered shops, a three-storey budget hotel—precariously perched on its narrow base, some cycle rickshaws parked for the night, the ubiquitous strays. Overhead electric cables crisscrossed the narrow street. He walked down, his keen eyes observing the pedestrian area for anything out of the ordinary.

Earlier, discreet enquiries regarding the incendiary pamphlet had revealed that he had pre-empted the boys. At the police station they had rounded up the usual suspects, hooligans and petty thiefs, but the two boys he had sighted were not amongst them. Thereafter, Raghav, in plainclothes, had done a round of Taj Ganj but the punks remained elusive.

Taj Mahal-Taj Ganj, he thought, mulling over R.P. Singh's hypothesis. He had to agree though: in this world, in the part of it that was India, beauty and beast co-existed, one never far from the other. The beautiful Taj Mahal, and attached to its side like a sore, the ugly Taj Ganj; the 5-star hotels and the budget hovels; the expensive marble souvenirs and their lowly craftsmen who went blind crafting them....

A buffalo grunted as he passed its stable and Raghav realised he had reached Sirhi Darwaza, the entrance gate to the Taj Mahal. Located close by was the wall the boys had clambered to get away. He walked up to it.

The street was now filling up with people engaging in their daily chores. However, his police uniform would ensure that they kept their distance. He glanced at his watch. He had a window of a half hour before patrons, animals, vehicles dispersed through Taj Ganj, rendering any further examination difficult.

The imposing carved wooden gate, decorated with iron knockers, stood under an arch beyond which lay the Taj Mahal's Jilaukhana. The main bazaar street terminated at this point. It was some days since the incident and he was unlikely to find anything, but Raghav examined the ground as he traced his steps from the gate towards the low wall the boys had scaled.

A dog was idling by the wall and he shooed it away. The ground beside the wall was dusty, unlike the concrete of the bazaar street, and Raghav sifted through the soil with his shoe. The cap of a Pepsi bottle, scraps of paper, a twisted plastic rag, a—locket?

He bent down, retrieved the locket and wiped it on his trouser leg. It was two-sided, one face showing Shiva, the other a series of temples on a riverbank below which was written Bateshwar 101.

Raghav was vaguely aware of the town located around seventy kilometres from Agra—a Shiva pilgrimage centre, wasn't it? The locket wasn't much to go by, but the presence of Shiva on it had him hooked. He decided to drive down to Bateshwar for a recce.

Meanwhile, he would instruct a plainclothes policeman to scour Taj Ganj, then check the weedy Yamuna bank opposite the monument. Nothing would come of examining that undergrowth probably, but he didn't want to come up short next time he faced CBI's Singh.

Inside Brijwasi Sweet House & Restaurant in Sadar Bazaar, Inspector Bharadwaj sat in a private booth awaiting the arrival of steaming mutton handi and fresh naan. He was hoping to impress his guest, a man of considerable girth—the sort that came from wrestling in an akhara from an early age—and bulging biceps, all of which he put to good use as an Agra strongman. Which, in turn, had brought him several encounters with the law but no jail time. For a policeman to engage openly in public with a known goon was one way to ratchet up his own public standing—this, after all, was Uttar Pradesh, where a thug as the right-hand man of a politician was the norm. And this particular strongman had links that went all the way from the local BHP unit up to the top.

The next instant mutton handi was placed on the table and Inspector Bharadwaj was pleased to notice the strongman's nostrils twitch. With upturned palms and an ingratiating smile he urged his guest to begin.

'And you?' the strongman grunted.

The inspector explained he was fasting, calling upon some obscure deity from the vast Hindu pantheon that desired Bharadwaj's specific abstinence.

The strongman grunted again and started to tuck in— in his presence, folks usually fasted.

Inspector Bharadwaj was a newish recruit who had proved his credentials six months back when the strongman, who ran a successful rent-a-riot outfit, had orchestrated a spectacular rampage at the Taj Mahal on the occasion of the Urs celebration at the monument. Bharadwaj with his posse of CISF men had flailed helplessly while the vandals did their job. The CISF had the mandate of securing Taj Mahal, yet, as the proverb went, *ghar ka bhedi lanka dhaye*. With a mole within, even Ravan couldn't keep his legendary Lanka safe.

That performance earned the inspector an entry onto the strongman's list, and hard cash. However, the job Bharadwaj was entrusted with now was vastly bigger; executed correctly, it would catapult him up the state police hierarchy.

Inspector Bharadwaj watched the strongman gorge, swallowed the saliva in his mouth, patted his shiny forehead that was enlarged because of frontal baldness, and waited for his guest to divulge the next step in the plot.

Delhi-Jaipur highway

'Are you keen on an intellectual exercise? Some mental aerobics?' Raj Bhushan popped a fresh mint into his mouth as he glanced at her.

'Why not?' Mehrunisa said, her eyes scanning the barren tract that bordered NH8, the national highway connecting Delhi to Jaipur. They were being driven in Raj Bhushan's official car, having left at dawn for the five-hour trip. 'It'll help pass the time.'

Raj Bhushan cocked his head. 'You remember the pamphlet that SSP Raghav found? I'd like to debate some controversial points it raised, especially with regard to the design elements of the Taj Mahal.'

'Why would you want to do that?'

'A healthy spirit of enquiry?' Raj Bhushan chuckled. 'Why does Shiva's trident rest atop the central dome of the Taj Mahal?'

Mehrunisa's eyes widened in disbelief as she examined her interrogator with frank curiosity. He was, as the cricketing term went, batting on the front foot.

'You know it's nothing of the sort! The pinnacle consists of a crowning element formed of lotus leaves—'

'Another standard Hindu symbol: the lotus! Vishnu is always depicted standing on a lotus. Goddess Saraswati sits on a lotus.'

Aria fritta! Mehrunisa said to herself silently. Clearly, although the ASI director-general was friendly with Professor Kaul, the two men had decidedly different approaches to their work. While Raj Bhushan believed in questioning history which sometimes necessitated being equivocal on historical matters, Professor Kaul was rigorous with the truth. *Rubbish*, he would have exclaimed on hearing the counter-argument just made by Raj Bhushan. His life's work had been built around the Taj Mahal; a small fraction of it dealt with speculation concerning the Hindu origin of the mausoleum, which in his mind, was the preserve of idle gossipers and greedy guides.

At its heart, the Taj Mahal was a syncretic creation. That the product of a mating between two vastly different beliefs and cultures had wrought a thing of such luminosity rankled the fundamentalists who'd rather see it as a mongrel. A mongrel was a stain on the purebred—it had to be stripped of its individual features until each element could be assigned its proper ancestry. The lotus flower was Hindu: how dare a Mughal emperor use it in his monument? The pot with overflowing flowers was definitely a Hindu kalasha, and damn the Mughals with their vision of paradise as a place filled with flowers! An old anger stirred within Mehrunisa and flashed briefly in her grey-green eyes before years of self-discipline asserted itself. She angled her chin at Raj Bhushan: if the Taj Mahal required an advocate, this Indo-Persian mongrel would fit the bill just fine.

'So, you're unaware,' she said in a mocking tone, 'that the lotus flower had become a standard motif of Islamic Indian architecture by the time of Shah Jahan? The Qutab Minar in Delhi, begun in 1193, is an excellent example of early Indo-Islamic style.'

Raj Bhushan smirked. 'Because twenty-seven temples were destroyed to construct the Qutab complex!'

'Shifting from architecture to political history, are we?'

'The two are linked, my dear.'

'Sure, but that isn't the point of this discussion. The point is that the Qutab Minar evolved out of an Islamic conception and a Hindu execution. Qutab-Din-Aibak built the first mosque in India, the Quwwat-ul-Islam within the Qutab complex. Because he was in a hurry, he did not wish to send for engineers to Iran—where arches and domes were well developed. Instead, he ordered the local Hindu architects to follow their trabeate system of horizontal beams. Partly due to the use of material from Hindu temples, and partly due to the work of Hindu craftsmen, the Qutab Minar is what it is.'

'Well said. But returning to the Taj, what about the shape of the finial atop the main dome? Which is a pot with overflowing plants, an ancient Hindu symbol of prosperity and wellbeing? What the Hindus call a kalasha?'

'Who's sounding like a conspiracy theorist now!'

Mehrunisa had propped her sunglasses atop her head since the sun was still not strong. Now she wished she was wearing them—she could do with a rose-tinted view of both the landscape and the ASI director-general. She forced herself to speak evenly, but her grey-green eyes registered scorn at the foolish query.

'Vases filled with flowers have a long tradition in Muslim culture, and in the Indian context they are also

214

related to the concept of prosperity. The Muslims were, after all, rulers to their large Hindu majority. Shah Jahan's vases had a further symbolism. Paradise in the Quran is imagined as gardens—jannat, rauza—full of trees, flowers, plants and flowing waters. Surely, you recall, the Taj Mahal was conceived and constructed as Mumtaz's house in Paradise?'

Raj Bhushan shrugged.

'Sometimes,' Mehrunisa said coldly, 'I wonder which side you are on.'

'No wonder in that, my dear,' Raj Bhushan said as he uncrossed his leg and straightened the crease of his wool pants. 'I am on the side of enquiry. You could call me a rigorous sceptic.'

'So you accept nothing with certainty?'

'Nothing,' he nodded. 'What we can do is to make a set of conclusions, and to each conclusion attach various degrees of probability. Now, it is most *probable* that Shah Jahan built the Taj Mahal from scratch. However, there also exist other conclusions which are less probable but nevertheless, have some degree of probability.'

'Such as the one you just espoused: the Taj Mahal as a Hindu temple?'

'Truth is elastic-plastic, Mehrunisa. Can you be sure of its coordinates? Between the Hindu kalash and the Islamic crescent, where does the finial of the Taj Mahal lie?'

Raj Bhushan picked at some lint from his sleeve and balled it, rolling it between his right thumb and index finger. Mehrunisa noticed his fingertips were curiously yellowish. Also, his breath had acquired a heavy odour—amidst the debate he had forgotten his mouth freshener, the mint pellets that he popped at regular intervals.

'The Mughals had a history of razing Hindu temples to the ground and building their mosques, tombs and palaces on them. It started, as you mentioned, with the construction of the first mosque in India within the Qutab complex. Aibak went on to demolish the gigantic Vaishnava temple at Ajmer and build a mosque that is known as Arhai-din-ka-jhunpra. Aurangzeb razed Kashi Vishwanath temple at Varanasi, a Jyotirlinga for the Hindus, and erected a mosque in its place.' Raj Bhushan's voice was hoarse. 'History books are littered with examples—' He choked on his words, his eyes watering. Clearing his throat, he reached for a bottle of water. 'Excuse me.'

Outside the air-conditioned car, traffic engorged the highway. Besides the trucks, tourist buses and cars, Mehrunisa spotted a camel-pulled cart, the animal majestically lumbering on the roadside, seemingly impervious to smoke or snarl.

'The Taj Mahal was a Rajput palace purchased by Shah Jahan!' Raj Bhushan capped the water bottle and turned towards Mehrunisa, his eyes alight with mischief. For just a brief moment she was reminded of her dead friend, Arun Toor, and his sparring, sportive style of debate. 'In his own court chronicle, *Padshahnama*, Shah Jahan admits it,' Raj Bhushan continued, holding his hand out, as if urging her to believe. 'He mentions that a beautiful grand mansion in Agra was taken from Jai Singh for Mumtaz's burial.'

Mehrunisa gasped. 'You know that is false!' she said.

Raj Bhushan smiled his monkey smile before settling back into his seat. 'Prove it.'

'The *Padshahnama* was written by Abdul Hamid Lahauri, Shah Jahan's historian. One statement by

Lahauri—"Va pesh az-in, manzil Rajah Mansingh bud"—has been misinterpreted by some to claim that there originally was a palace of Raja Man Singh of Amber which was taken over from his grandson Mirza Raja Jai Singh and converted. Lahauri never mentioned a palace. He recorded over and over again that it was a piece of land that was selected for the burial and it was acquired in exchange of properties from the emperor's Khalsah-lands, and that the work began from the very foundations.'

Raj Bhushan remained silent, meditative, his eyes pinning her from behind those fashionable spectacles. For a moment Mehrunisa was distracted by that penetrating gaze.

'Further, there is no record to show that Raja Man Singh ever built a magnificent palace such as the Taj Mahal at Agra. He did commission the temple of Govinda Devaji at Vrindaban in Uttar Pradesh, and a complete record exists of the construction, including the builders' names. Surely, if he had built something on the grand scale of the Taj Mahal, there should have been something on record in the family archives of the Jaipur royals?'

Raj Bhushan studied Mehrunisa. After what seemed like a long while, he tipped his head in an elaborate bow. 'Professor Kaul would be pleased with your scholarship, Mehrunisa. I myself am quite impressed. I must admit I had underestimated the depth of your research.'

At any given moment, Raj Bhushan was the epitome of suaveness, yet Mehrunisa could not shake off the feeling that although he had complimented her, he was somehow angry with her.

Bateshwar

Riding his motorcycle, Raghav was in Bateshwar within an hour. At the railway crossing he showed the signalman the locket and enquired about the temples. The portly railway employee said that locating the temples would be no problem once he passed the crossing—what else was there in the village? However, he was mystified by the locket and speculated that one of the newly-sprung tourist agencies might be behind it. Apparently, the riverside temples had only been getting attention of late.

The road into the village zig-zagged through the Chambal valley, once notorious for its dacoits. When he reached there he found himself, unsurprisingly, in a sleepy hamlet where everyone knew at once that he was a stranger. His policeman's uniform drew apprehensive glances. Good, Raghav thought as he parked in front of a temple and walked inside. The priest within gaped at him and enquired timidly if he was there for prayers. Deciding it would be one way to get the priest talking, he nodded. The next instant a plate with offerings was placed in his hand and the priest initiated the prayers, pausing to instruct Raghav in rituals, as a couple of temple assistants joined in the chorus. It was over quickly, after which Raghav was invited for a closer look at the presiding temple deity. Interestingly, he sported a moustache and turban, and was dressed like a rich merchant. What is the deity called, he enquired of the priest. Bateshwar Mahadev, a form of Lord Shiva, the priest said. Very different from the Shiva on the locket, Raghav observed, who was a standard blue, clad in tiger skin, Ganga springing from his topknot.

Raghav should visit at the time of the cattle fair, the priest advised, which was when the village came to life. And at the time of Maha Shivratri, of course. Further queries yielded some inanities on the abundant livestock at the time of the fair. He was looking to exit when there was a rustle as another worshipper walked in, and the priest hurried to him.

Outside the temple, Raghav descended the steps to the riverbank. A Naga sadhu sat meditating, his ash-smeared torso naked in the cold except for a shawl draped over his shoulders. A trident was planted in the ground, its three prongs decked with marigold. A shout sounded and Raghav turned to see a boatman waving to him from the ghat.

The boatman had few teeth but was very chatty. He wore a threadbare sweater, scrunched-up dhoti and a thin muffler tied turban-like around his head. Raghav could not turn down his offer of a ride up the Yamuna—a paltry twenty-five rupees.

As they glided past the whitewashed temples, Raghav learnt that there were 101 temples originally, of which less than half remained. He spotted several ash-smeared ascetics on the bank as well.

'Many Naga sadhus here?' he asked the boatman.

'Bateshwar is the home of Shiva, and they are his bhakts.'

The lack of teeth made the boatman's voice sound like a whistle. Raghav had to strain his ears to catch the words sprinkled in that breathy passage of air.

The boatman waved a scrawny arm at the cliffs rising around them. 'They live in caves in the mud walls of the ravine. You should see them at Maha Shivratri when they descend upon the ghats.' He gave a sly toothless grin. 'Then the cameramen from Delhi come to click more than just the temples!'

Raghav recalled a stint he had done at a Kumbh mela once. Ash-smeared, dreadlocked Naga sadhus were fiercely clannish and a fight had broken out between two groups. It didn't help that they were high on bhang, which they consumed religiously as Shiva's favoured drink.

'You get good business at that time?' Raghav asked the man.

'Na,' he shook his head. 'Those days when kings and royalty and noblemen used boats are no more. Who has the time? Where do you come from, Inspector?'

'Agra,' Raghav replied.

'And did you come down by boat? No, see! I could take you up to Agra, and drop you right beside the Taj Mahal. But would you be interested? No. No one has the time.' He clucked his dismay.

'Really?' Raghav said surprised. It was entirely logical, but he had always seen the Yamuna beside the Taj clogged with plastic and garbage. Here, of course, the water was bountiful. This year though, even the Yamuna behind the Taj was at its high mark. Something about that vision made him pause. He was trying to figure out why when his mobile beeped.

Constable Dayal. Whom he had instructed to examine the undergrowth on the riverbank opposite the Taj Mahal.

'Yes,' Raghav barked.

What he heard next made him forget all about Bateshwar, its temples and a leisurely boat ride back to Agra. Clamping a hundred rupee note in the perplexed boatman's hand, he was off like the proverbial Chambal valley dacoit. Weaving his motorcycle between grain trucks and laden trolleys, he was on site within an hour.

A shaken Dayal met him at the periphery and wordlessly started to lead him. Tall grass engulfed them as they crunched their way inwards where the growth was thickest. What Raghav saw next loosened his bowels—he had to either shit or vomit urgently. He believed he had seen a lot in his two-decade career—rape, murder, bestiality—yet, this plumbed the depths of human depravity.

Sprawled in the crushed grass were two large portions of a serpent, probably a python, ruptured in half. From within the split belly of the beast a partial human body was visible. All manner of bugs were crawling over the raw flesh. Raghav had to look away to keep the rising bile in check. He took several deep breaths and steadied his nerves.

'Sir,' the constable whispered, 'the corpse still has clothes on. See.'

Raghav forced himself to look. Bizarre as it sounded, the ruptured python had indeed thrown up a hacked, but clothed, human cadaver from its belly. The kurta was congealed in gunge, but the colour stood out: vibrant pink.

A frisson of electricity sped up Raghav's spine. The scene was ghastly, yet it had offered a glimmer of hope—

the Taj conspiracy case could be solved ... there was no mistaking that bright pink kurta. He had last seen it on the corpse of Supervisor Toor before it vanished from the morgue.

Diary

My mother has always been the centre of my life, and—despite her death ten years back—she still is. When she passed away, at the young age of forty-five, she had the well-preserved look of beautiful women who age so gracefully that their beauty grows, instead of diminishing.

I could not bear to be parted from her. However, death is a given for all mortals. It is also the case that the old die before the young and I knew my mother would exit this world before I did. Two incontrovertible facts that I had to fight. So I trained myself for the eventuality. And if you prepare well, it is amazing how much you can actually accomplish that would normally be deemed impossible.

Now, ten years later, my mother's presence in my life continues to be strong and I can see her as and when I like. Though, I must hasten to mention, I have to be discreet—I have lost my mother once, I cannot afford to lose her yet again.

She is central to my life and yet, even when scouting my home, none would be able to tell. It is our secret, my mother's and mine. The pride of my living room is in its centre. During a visit to the interiors of Rajasthan, I came across an old decaying haveli, its habitable areas apportioned into a teashop, a tyre-repair shop and digs where barefoot children ran about playing hide- and-seek. Amidst the general squalor, a remarkable wooden door still hung from an interior room. The panel was partitioned into sixteen squares, and within each square a different animal was carved in relief—a peacock, a pair of monkeys, a tiger, an elephant. It was rather unique and I had the panel pulled from the loose hinges. No one raised a brow; I was a government officer, and I handed out some dole in parting. Back in Delhi, I consulted another expert who confirmed my estimate: it was a rare piece dating from the early nineteenth century.

I crafted a centre table using my discovery. My large iron trunk, painted black, topped by the carved teak panel mounted with a thick glass panel. The complete piece looks rather attractive, modern yet traditional, and serves my purpose. Nothing less would do for my mummy. I am sure she is pleased.

Jaipur

Pamposh's residence—a sprawling haveli—never failed to amaze Mehrunisa. The Pandits had been residents of the city for generations since the head of the family had entered the service of the Jaipur royals. Pamposh had moved to Jaipur to live with her paternal grandfather after her father was killed in a terrorist attack in 1991. Since her father was an only child, there was no other claimant to the sandstone mansion except a reluctant Pamposh.

She did not like the undue attention and the concomitant assumption of wealth the haveli drew to her. She would sell it off, she complained, except where would she find her roots—that subterranean thing that secures us in this world? Srinagar, she would sigh, had been taken away from her, and Jaipur, she could not afford to lose. Officious relatives suggested she convert the haveli into a heritage hotel and live off tourist earnings. But Pamposh was a woman with a mind of her own. The reports of rising incidents of female foeticide in the state of Rajasthan caught her attention. While the underlying factor was a feudal mindset, it was compounded by the lack of orphanages. The nineteenth-century haveli was built around a central courtyard: Pamposh converted the east L-wing into an orphanage and children's school; the west served as her residence.

Mehrunisa had called from Delhi to inform Pamposh of her visit and had been invited, along with Raj Bhushan, to come over after their work was done and spend the night at the haveli. Now, standing at the nail-studded haveli door, Mehrunisa reflected how much had transpired since their last meeting: both the professor and his beloved monument were facing an insidious adversary.

Pamposh, dressed in an orange phiran, greeted her with a hug before turning to Raj Bhushan who stood behind Mehrunisa. Shaking hands with him, she acknowledged with a nod, 'We've met.'

Pamposh led them down a cold corridor to a large room that was fashioned like a study-cum-bar. In one corner, a fireplace was spitting softly, its amber glow gilding the frescoed walls. Mehrunisa had been in the room once before, when she had visited with Professor Kaul to pay their respects to the patriarch, Pamposh's grandfather. All Mehrunisa recalled from that visit was the old man's flowing whiskers and beard.

Now she stood entranced by the vibrant honey-coloured frescoes on the walls depicting women in swirling ghagras, bells on their ankles, their slim arms lifted in intricate dance poses. Another wall depicted three men ready to hunt, the central figure an archer taking aim.

'Beautiful, isn't it?' Pamposh interrupted her reverie.

'Wonder how I never noticed it before...'

Pamposh smiled and indicated an armchair with intricately-carved wooden legs. 'You were a child—there were other things to hold your attention.' Pinching the thumb and index fingers together, she tugged at the ends of her mouth.

Mehrunisa smiled at Pamposh's illustration of her grandfather's walrus moustache. 'You remember,' she said.

'Of course I remember,' Pamposh shrugged. 'I remember everything.' Looking straight into Mehrunisa's eyes, she said, '*Khosh amadid.*' It was Persian for welcome.

Mehrunisa acknowledged it with a tilt of her head, recalling the many days they had spent together as children under the roof of her godfather, Professor Kaul. They were sufficiently alike yet exotic enough to each other to enjoy their time together as they exchanged Persian and Kashmiri phrases, customs, stories. The only similar feature they shared was a fair complexion. Pamposh was a fiery electric beauty with sparkling dark eyes, dimples, curly hair and a saucy tongue. Mehrunisa, with her grey-green eyes, straight black hair and a quiet demeanour, could slip in the background as Pamposh held court. Pamposh's vivacity made others in the room fade.

They had shared a closeness that comes from being put in each other's company at an early age. In the last decade, however, the two had gone their separate ways, seldom meeting, and Mehrunisa wondered how much they had grown apart.

Meanwhile, Raj Bhushan had been studying the mural of the hunters and he now commented, 'It would date to the late nineteenth century—it has a mix of European and Rajput art. It is probably quite precious, considering the state in which it has been preserved.'

'My grandfather was fussy about maintaining his heritage,' Pamposh acknowledged. In the distance a bell rang. Indicating the bar, she excused herself.

Raj Bhushan proceeded to the side table on which a decanter, some glasses and glass bottles were ranged. He studied the offerings and said, 'There's cognac, whiskey, gin—what can I get you?'

'Ideal weather for a cognac, thank you,' Mehrunisa said, rubbing her palms together. Outside the window, the glass was foggy from a swirling noon mist. She had started on her cognac when Pamposh strode into the room and stopped, resting her right hand in an angle on her waist, her eyes wide with some hidden merriment as she looked at Mehrunisa.

'There is a man at my door enquiring after you. Claims he is a CBI officer.' She had a dancer's trained ability to widen her eyes without lifting her brows. On a whisper, she added, 'Why is the police after you, Mehroo?'

Mehrunisa shrugged and smiled, 'Not to worry,' and deposited her glass on a side table. How had R.P. Singh traced her to the haveli, and *why*, she wondered.

Meanwhile, Pamposh, apparently relieved by Mehrunisa's response, continued, 'He'd be quite handsome, except he's bald. I like a man with a full head and a beard, if possible—the fun is in figuring what all the fuzz conceals.' With that she gave a slow, naughty wink in the direction of Mehrunisa and Raj Bhushan.

Mehrunisa thought Pamposh's gaze lingered on Raj Bhushan's bearded face far longer than would be considered decent. In that sense Pamposh had not changed, she was still a flirt.

'So,' Pamposh asked perkily, her dejihor glinting as she angled her face, 'does Mehrunisa allow him entry?'

Glaring at her for the double entendre, Mehrunisa walked past saying, 'I'll have a word with the officer.'

❋ ❋ ❋

Mehrunisa could not believe her eyes, yet there could be no doubt. The photograph showed a giant python, some four metres long, ruptured in the middle. From the exploded belly stuck out the remains of a man's torso and head. Bile rose in her and she lunged for the main door. Throwing it open she rounded the threshold and heaved. As she straightened, R.P. Singh handed her a kerchief.

Mehrunisa wiped her mouth feeling sick and foolish: sick at the gory picture the officer had thrust under her nose, and foolish for having demonstrated weakness.

R.P. Singh studied her with concern. Mehrunisa was still shaking from the exertion. His right hand hovered as if to steady her, but changed course and started to scratch his chin. 'I'm sorry. I wouldn't have shown it to you if I could help it.'

Mehrunisa's mouth was sticky with acid and she wanted to rinse it out. Irritated, she asked, 'How did you know where to find me?'

Singh shrugged, 'I called your home.'

R.P. Singh would not have rushed to Jaipur to show her the picture of a ruptured python without reason, she thought, and asked, 'What's special about the picture?'

Singh produced a folded sheet from inside his jacket and handed it to Mehrunisa. 'Copy of the report filed by the investigating constable,' he said.

Python and dead body found on Yamuna bank opposite Taj Mahal

On Thursday, 20 January, I, Constable Bhole Prasad Dayal stumbled on the remains of a python, and the man it had tried to eat, in the grass on the banks of Yamuna opposite the Taj Mahal. The python was probably unable to digest the body, which caused its stomach to burst, killing it, and discharging the remains of the man.

Further, the body of the man appears to have been sliced in two, which would have had to be done before the snake tried to eat it. I alerted my superior, SSP Raghav of Anti-Terror Squad, who ordered the area to be cordoned off and the body was sent for DNA testing to help identify the person.

The area where the python was found floods easily in the monsoon, and locals have reported sighting a large snake in the undergrowth on occasion.

'Opposite the Taj Mahal...' Singh said softly.

Mehrunisa could not get the significance of either report or picture. Was her mind fuzzy from throwing up? She examined R.P. Singh's face.

'You don't see it, do you?'

'See what?'

'Here,' he pulled a cushioned stool from a corner and attempted to get Mehrunisa to sit.

Mehrunisa shrugged his hand away. 'Don't patronise me. What is it that I'm not seeing?'

Singh tapped his index finger at the gruesome picture at the spot where the man's torso emerged from the python's slit belly. It was a large colour picture and as his finger tapped it repeatedly, Mehrunisa noticed that the man's torso was clad in a pinkish shirt. As she peered closer at the grainy image, she noticed the man's face was bearded...

Mehrunisa's eyes opened wide. Her head jerked up and she looked into R.P. Singh's eyes. What she saw there confirmed the hypothesis forming in her mind. 'But ... but ... how could this be?' Mehrunisa murmured. 'Who, how-how did this happen?'

'SSP Raghav is on the case. A DNA test will identify the victim. But it'll take time. However, if we're all thinking the same thing, then perhaps we have an ID on the corpse already.'

'What would Arun be doing in this place?'

'You mean his corpse. Remember it vanished from the morgue.'

The next instant Mehrunisa's eyes filled with tears. Her last memory of Arun was the two of them walking back from the tomb towards the Jilaukhana as the supervisor escorted her to the exit. He was smoking, as was his habit. Dressed in one of his trademark colourful kurtas, his beard shaggy, his hair unkempt, he looked like an obsessive lover of the Taj Mahal.

That vibrant, energetic, messy man, full of life and passionate about history, was dead. Had been murdered. What was more gruesome was that his body was found in the belly of a hungry python. What trajectory of fate had taken the Taj supervisor from the splendour of the monument to the innards of a reptile?

A cold dread clutched Mehrunisa's heart as she eyed the picture again. Before she could escape to the door, she gagged again.

However, this time, the evidence of her dismay and weak stomach was splayed on the shirtfront of R.P. Singh.

Pakistan-occupied Kashmir

Jalaluddin curled his toes under a blanket as he studied the sheets in front of him. Outside, a howling wind hurled the falling rain with fury, routinely pelting some icy showers into the hideout. Stormy weather had cut him off from his courier for two days now. It made things difficult, but the inclement weather hampered the kafir army too....

The flashlight cut a bluish-white swathe through the dark and Jalaluddin peered closer to read. His brow line dipped over his hooked nose as he crouched closer. On the rough wall his shadow looked like a giant raptor swooping to seize its prey.

There were several options of attack. A sutli bomb was the noisiest—its explosion could be heard within a one-kilometre radius. It was easy to source, being a popular firecracker at the Hindu festival of Diwali. He gave a twisted smile. A sutli set off close to the entry gate would divert and distract police for enough time to allow a suicide bomber to smuggle himself in from the main gate.

Another would come in from the riverside. They would quietly bide their time until police reassured visitors that all was fine.

Jalaluddin's eyes moved to the rear of the cave. Nothing was visible in the pitch black but he feasted his eyes nonetheless on what lay covered beneath a tarpaulin. It had arrived two days back before the weather turned hostile. AK rounds, Pika rounds, some RPG rounds, two-and-a-half kilograms of RDX, twelve bundles of IED wire ... his chest swelled with the count. The ISI sure knew how to arm an operation.

A gust of wind made the flashlight wobble. Jalaluddin adjusted the beam and returned to the plan.

When the monument was throbbing with people again, two suicide bombers would simultaneously pull the plug. As the two men ascended heavenwards, the kafirs would be blown apart, their limbs scattered around their wrecked world wonder.

Jalaluddin stroked his beard, liking what he read. The scene of devastation made him puff up in satisfaction before he proceeded to study the next plan.

Jaipur

R.P. Singh cleaned his shirt as best he could and then joined the others in Pamposh's living room, warm from the crackling fireplace. He showed the photograph to the curious gathering, and as it was passed around, he watched their reactions closely: Pamposh, about to vomit, trotted on high heels to a washroom; Raj Bhushan tensed up visibly; Mehrunisa looked morose.

Pouring himself a large peg of Johnnie Walker—Gold Label, he noted appreciatively—Singh settled in a high-backed chair. Raj Bhushan's head was bent over as he read the police report intently. Singh sipped the whiskey, felt the warm silky texture down his throat, his eyes never leaving the director-general. The man intrigued him.

SSP Raghav had narrated how casually the ASI director-general had dismissed the pamphlet. If the police thought the threat was serious, then why was the man unconcerned?

Pamposh returned then, and standing in the centre of the carpeted room, raised a hand. 'No more gruesome chatter!' She gave a shaky smile, 'Unless you want me to puke and ruin the party.'

Turning to R.P. Singh, she asked formally, 'I realise you are here on work, and I don't want to come in the way of police business. So, how can I help?'

R.P. Singh stood up gallantly and shrugged. 'My work here is done. However,' he held up his whiskey glass, 'considering I've joined the party, may I stay?'

'Of course,' Pamposh smiled broadly before she walked over to a high bar stool and perched on it.

Meanwhile, Raj Bhushan had finished his perusal of the report and kept it aside stiffly. He joined the hostess at the bar, consulted her softly and when she pointed to the drinks cabinet, said 'Ah!', and proceeded towards it.

R.P. Singh decided to steer the conversation to the pamphlet alleging the Taj Mahal was a Shiva temple. Contrary to what he had declared to Pamposh, his work wasn't done until he had witnessed Raj Bhushan tackling the controversial subject.

'I heard you were shown the pamphlet confiscated in Agra—the one that claims the Taj Mahal is a temple. What do you think of it, Mr Bhushan?'

At his name, Raj Bhushan looked up from opening a bottle of Benedictine. He pursed his mouth before answering, 'As I mentioned to your colleague, the Taj has always had detractors. This is nothing new.'

Pamposh swivelled on her stool and excitedly asked R.P. Singh to divulge the new controversy.

When he had finished telling her about the pamphlet, she chuckled delightedly. 'I have always found Taj Mahal tittle-tattle rather fascinating. A story with all the right ingredients: sex, religion, royalty, greed and gossip!'

'Tittle-tattle?' R.P. Singh considered the phrase before lifting his shoulders, 'I'll have to confess my ignorance.'

'Enlightenment time,' Pamposh beamed. 'If you are the CBI officer in charge of the Taj investigation, you have to be aware of all the stories attached to the monument.'

She glanced at Raj Bhushan and Mehrunisa and started before either could consent. 'I don't think Shah Jahan built the Taj Mahal in memory of Mumtaz. How could he when on the death of Mumtaz he began an affair with his seventeen-year-old daughter.'

She turned to look at Mehrunisa. 'What you say doesn't need my endorsement,' Mehrunisa said.

'Oh come, Mehroo! For the sake of fun?' Pamposh pleaded merrily, before swivelling her bar stool in the direction of Singh again. 'Francois Bernier, a French physician and chronicler in mid-seventeenth century India, was a discerning reporter. Not only does he mention incest, but goes on to claim that some courtiers justified it saying that "it would have been unjust to deny the king the privilege of gathering fruit from the tree he had himself planted".'

'Which daughter of his was this?' R.P. Singh asked.

'Jahanara,' Pamposh supplied. 'Apparently, she was as beautiful as her mother Mumtaz, and,' she winked, 'younger. On the death of her mother, she took the responsibility of caring for her father. Shah Jahan, in turn, bestowed on her half of Mumtaz's property, and only the remainder on his six other children. Even the royal seal, which was in the custody of Mumtaz, was entrusted to her.'

'Wow!' Singh said. 'Some affection. I'm familiar with another story. That after Mumtaz's death Shah Jahan did not appear in public for one full week. When he did eventually emerge, his beard and moustache had turned completely white and his eyes were weakened from constant weeping.'

'Yes,' Raj Bhushan nodded, 'it is another in a legion of stories that surround the Taj Mahal.'

'Like the story that he chopped off the hands of all the artisans who worked on the Taj Mahal so it could never be replicated,' Pamposh laughed.

'B&B, anyone?' Raj Bhushan held up a snifter in which brandy was afloat amber Benedictine. Finding no takers, he walked to the fireplace. 'If I may add, the stories of Shah Jahan's dalliances come from Manucci and Bernier. These cannot entirely be taken at face value. They both arrived at the Mughal court towards the end of Shah Jahan's reign, and had no direct access to information about what went on in the palace.'

'No smoke without fire,' Pamposh shrugged again. 'At the very least they establish that there was gossip in court circles on these matters.'

'Aria fritta!' Mehrunisa said dismissively. 'The court chroniclers do not mention any such thing.'

Pamposh laughed. 'Come, come Mehroo, don't scold us in Italian! The silence of the chroniclers, all loyal officers, proves nothing. In any case, they were too busy singing hymns praising the great Mughal! And on that note,' Pamposh said, extending her left arm as if to emphasise her point, 'if Shah Jahan built the Taj Mahal, how come no records exist that give details of its construction? No direct information about its architects? And really, if the Mughals were the grand builders of their age, why is there no written proof of their architectural theory?'

Pamposh's speech was slurred. R.P. Singh wondered if she'd had too much to drink—after all, she was guzzling whiskey straight.

'Go on,' Pamposh urged Mehrunisa, 'tell me. Indians are excellent record-keepers. Ancient Sanskrit texts such as the shilpa shastras and vastu shastras still exist and provide to this day the Hindu canon of art and architectural theory.' Pamposh drew her hand in a wide arc, the whiskey sloshing in the glass held in that hand. 'Hmm? Director ASI, Mr Raj Bhushan—perhaps you would care to enlighten us?'

Raj Bhushan took a sip of his B&B, rested the glass on the side table, crossed his leg and looked directly at Pamposh. 'You are espousing a form of history which is gaining currency among a new breed of historians. Founded on the premise *what if*, it is counterfactual history. *What if* we were to believe the Taj Mahal was not actually built by Shah Jahan? *What if* the Mughals were not the great builders they are made out to be? Mind you, they claim they are doing this out of scholarly interest. History, after all, is written by the victors. Counterfactual history can, for instance, examine it from the vanquished man's perspective.'

Raising one palm in the direction of his hostess, he courteously enquired, 'Are you of the counterfactual history school, Ms Pandit?'

'Pshaw!' With a wave of her hand, Pamposh trashed the idea. 'I have no truck with history or historians. But I grew up in the overwhelming shadow of one,' she rolled her eyes, 'Professor Vishwanath Kaul, and he is such an obsessive Mughal lover that I think it is my rebellious right to refuse to be co-opted into his fan club.

'Besides,' Pamposh shrugged, her face taking on a melancholy look, 'as an Indian, you are never allowed to forget your history. It is not an option.' She cast her eyes around the room, resting them on Mehrunisa, Raj Bhushan and R.P. Singh in turn.

'Are you Hindu? Are you Muslim? Are you the descendant of Babur who took our land from us and made us slaves in our own country? Or are you a Hindu raja who presides over a Muslim people? Or sore with India, sore with Pakistan, you cannot decide which way to swing your Himalayan kingdom?'

Although Pamposh's last question referred to the king of Kashmir's vacillation during the partition of India, what showed on her face and her tremulous lips was the concomitant loss of home, parents and homeland she had suffered at a young age.

She tossed the remaining whiskey down and clucked loudly, 'Nope! Forgetting is not an option. We carry our histories in our blood and are ever willing to spill it.'

She rose and lurched. 'Refills, anyone?'

R.P. Singh gallantly offered to fetch her drink. 'For the intellectual enlightenment of one ignorant policeman, I say let's proceed with the debate.'

'Mehrunisa,' Raj Bhushan said, 'would you like to provide a spirited defence, like your uncle would have?'

Mehrunisa was neither an experienced Mughal scholar, nor did she have the proficiency of her godfather. But she *had* assisted him while he wrote *The Taj*. Recollecting what he'd written, she said, 'The Mughals had no written architectural theory. But the fact that no texts exist does not mean that architectural theory was absent from Mughal thinking. The monuments and formal gardens built by Shah Jahan and other Mughal emperors that survive to this day are living expressions of their architectural theory. In their case, we can derive the theories from their forms.'

Pamposh was not one to let go easily.

'Have you heard of P.N. Oak? He has founded an Institute for Rewriting Indian History, and has published an enormous body of writing to show how exaggerated the claims of Mughal Emperor-builders are.'

'Well,' Raj Bhushan cleared his throat as he warmed his hands by the fire, 'he also claims that all historic structures in India, and even abroad, that are currently ascribed to Muslim sultans—including tombs, gardens, canals, forts, townships, castles, bridges—are actually pre-Muslim constructions.' He gave an elaborate smile. 'Surely, you will agree one would need to take a barrel of salt to digest such information.'

Pamposh rolled her eyes, 'There has to be a reason behind such rumours, you know.'

'The rumours,' Mehrunisa shrugged her shoulders, 'are as old as the Taj. There are Western theories that the Taj Mahal was built by a European architect. Then there are guides' tales about the Second or Black Taj; the story that Shah Jahan killed the architect and the workers upon the building's completion so they would not build another like it...'

She glanced at her audience. 'One visit to the Taj can yield an assortment of exotic tales that have been spun around it by guides looking for gullible tourists. Quite a few of which can be found in a classic compilation of folk motifs across cultures. King kills architect after completion of great building—versions of this motif are reported from various parts of Europe. In a Muslim context, the legend appears earlier with regard to the Sassanian castle of Khwarnaq, which was considered one of the thirty wonders of the world in the early Arabic Middle Ages.'

Pamposh stifled a yawn, which Mehrunisa noticed, her eyes glittering. R.P. Singh did not miss that. Clearly, to Mehrunisa, the Taj Mahal was not just a beautiful monument. Her parents were dead; her godfather, the man who had devoted his life to the Taj Mahal, was critically ill; upon her return to India she had immersed herself in researching the Taj.... As he mulled over it, the answer became clear to him. What was to Pamposh and others a Mughal monument to spar over was, to Mehrunisa, a reflection of her own mixed heritage, and the repository of her godfather's lifelong devotion. It was something precious, something worth defending—and saving.

Pamposh slid off the high bar stool, tottering slightly. 'Methinks I am a wee drunk,' she chortled. 'More, anyone?'

R.P. Singh rose for a refill. 'I find this fascinating,' he smiled at Pamposh, 'a history lesson on the Taj Mahal!' He uncapped the Johnnie Walker, showing no sign that he was carefully studying their responses.

SSP Raghav had asked him why he was making the trip from Agra to Jaipur to see Mehrunisa—it could have easily waited till she returned. Feeling a little self-conscious, for reasons he was unwilling to examine, he'd told the inspector that he wanted a chance to talk to Raj Bhushan outside his office. Happily, the conversation was actually giving him something to think about.

'The subject matter, you mean?' Raj Bhushan laughed. 'The greatest erection of the great builder—surely one needs no other indication of his lascivious nature!'

Mehrunisa looked at him in amazement. It was obvious to Singh she had never heard the director speak in this manner before. Had the drink gone to his head as well? What he had said was a common joke, a crude description of the Taj Mahal. However, coming from the invariably suave and dapper Raj Bhushan, it seemed entirely inappropriate. He made a mental note to cross-check it with Mehrunisa.

At that moment, Pamposh cleared her throat, a bit too enthusiastically, as R.P. Singh looked on, his brows raised, his mouth bearing the faintest hint of derision. Raj Bhushan flushed, a look of consternation passed across his face. He sat upright as if mentally pulling himself up, adjusted his spectacles, and raising his right hand in a gesture of apology said, 'Sorry, ladies, for the inelegance.'

Mehrunisa remained silent, and sipped her drink. The fireplace crackled and she could not help thinking how convivial the setting would appear to a casual observer.

Pamposh flashed her generous smile at R.P. Singh, her eyes twinkling. 'Perhaps you should read the memoirs of Manucci and Bernier. Both maintain that Shah Jahan had adulterous liaisons with married women—usually wives of his noblemen.' Her cheeks were flushed, her hair tousled, her wide eyes glinting, and as she bit her lower lip, Pamposh looked sexy and sozzled.

Catching Mehrunisa's eye, Pamposh turned to her. 'Perhaps it is your Persian heritage that is unhappy with this line of thinking but,' she scowled, 'no one can deny that the emperor was a libertine.'

'Well,' R.P. Singh settled into his chair, 'at least there is consensus that the emperor was a man of love!'

'Surrounded by too many women to grieve over one dead wife. That should be proof enough that the great romance between Shah Jahan and his beloved Mumtaz was just an eye-wash by his court chroniclers. One that was swallowed wholesale by the British! And,' she threw a challenging toss at the ASI director-general, 'subsequent historians!'

'Whatever the truth of the particular stories,' Raj Bhushan, his hands in a steeple in front of him, spoke as if he were concluding the debate, 'one thing seems to be clear: after Mumtaz, Shah Jahan became promiscuous. But that never hindered a man from carrying on with the rest of his life. Maybe the story of the romance is a myth, but that does not disprove that he built the Taj Mahal.'

Mehrunisa looked at Raj Bhushan with some surprise: he'd spoken in the manner of a responsible director-general of the ASI, quite removed from his defiant posturing in the car ride earlier in the day.

After that the discussion petered out. Pamposh excused herself to oversee dinner arrangements after extending an invitation to R.P. Singh, and Mehrunisa switched on the music system and the twang of sitar filled the room.

R.P. Singh gazed into the whiskey and swore softly to himself. Damn these intellectuals! They had awakened him to the gamut of possibilities in the Taj Mahal equals Shiva temple claim, Raj Bhushan suavely straddling both sides of the argument. If not for Mehrunisa's erudite rebuttals, he'd have believed that yes, indeed, the monument could be Hindu.

But there lay the crux of the problem: Mehrunisa was erudite and rational; the public was gullible and emotional.

Agra

At the Taj Ganj police station SSP Raghav worked his luxuriant moustache as he brooded over the curious discovery of the python. His legs on the table, he was sunk into his chair.

'Anything the matter, Sir?' a constable enquired solicitously, depositing a cup of tea on the table.

Lost in thought, Raghav ignored him.

His distress was compounded by the forensics lab in Delhi, bogged down in bureaucracy. It had indicated that a DNA test on the corpse parts discovered in the python's belly would take at least a week—the forensics officer in the DNA profiling lab was on annual leave.

At that, Raghav had hinted darkly that he was working on the orders of the home minister himself. When the doctor on duty had remained unimpressed, Raghav made a great show of dialling the minister and thrust the phone beneath the doctor's nose. 'Speak!' he'd said.

At which the doctor, a few shades paler, promised to tackle the case right away. But the DNA result on the recovered torso would still take two days.

Meanwhile, the photographer he had caught in the Taj mosque had thrown up nothing of substance either, and time was ticking. It was R.P. Singh's surmise that the conspirator was working towards a huge hungama that would disrupt Republic Day, less than a week away.... If the man was a jihadi, it would serve his purpose to disrupt the one day when Indian pride and patriotism was on display. If it was Kriplani, he'd wrest attention to his fundamentalist agenda on a public holiday when folks were glued to television.

The BHP had made Taj Mahal its target before when, on the commemoration of the Urs of Shah Jahan, the monument was opened to visitors free of charge for three days. BHP youth activists who had gathered in Agra to celebrate fifty years of the party's founding went berserk at the monument, teasing women, urinating publicly, plucking flowers, and rinsing their mouths in the fountains, as officials watched helplessly.

In a classic case of locking the stable after the horse had bolted, a large police contingent had been posted at Taj Mahal after the rampage was over. Afterwards, a spokesperson explained that the city police were preoccupied with security arrangements for senior leader Shri Kriplani's impending visit for the BHP convention.

Senseless violence at a world-famous monument explained away so casually, and the ineffectuality of the police—all of it made Raghav's blood boil.

'Sir,' the constable intruded upon his thoughts as he laid the day's newspaper on his table, 'tea's getting cold.'

Raghav picked up the paper and started to sip his tea. After a couple of minutes he snorted and flung the paper aside.

'Sir?' the constable looked up.

'Central government has employed some new security personnel: langurs.'

'Langurs?'

'To scare away the monkeys around South Block! Defence, external affairs, finance—all these ministries have now been assigned the protection of langurs.'

'Why?' The befuddled constable scratched his chin.

'Apparently the list of monkey achievements includes stealing top secret documents, snapping power cables to computers containing sensitive data, screeching at foreign dignitaries, and biting an Army officer.'

'Re-ally,' the assistant said, hidden mirth making him brave as he adopted a convivial tone with his boss. 'The other day, a monkey brought down a sandstone flower vase from the turret at the Taj Mahal's entrance gate.'

As the SSP narrowed his eyes, he continued. 'You know the gate, Sir, from which tourists enter the Taj complex— the monkey took a flying leap from a nearby tree, landed on the turret, and down went the vase, smashing straight onto the entrance passage. Thankfully, no tourist was hurt.'

SSP Raghav snorted again. He reached for the paper, and read, '*The fearsome-looking langur monkeys now patrol South Block, to scare away smaller rhesus monkeys, at least 10,000 of which have taken up residence in South Block. The Army chief and his officers, as well as senior public servants at adjoining ministries, now take refuge in caged rooms!*

'A government and an Army both terrified by monkeys—no wonder terrorists are doing what they want,' Raghav's mouth was set as he shook his head. 'If things continue this way, we will be forced to become refugees in our own country.... Langurs, my ass!'

The assistant sighed his assent and turned to slurp his tea.

Jaipur

After dinner, Pamposh insisted R.P. Singh stay the night at the haveli. Singh said he would check into a hotel, but Pamposh, high on conversation and Scotch, trilled that that would be akin to spurning the hostess and the famed Jaipur hospitality—after all, the city was first painted pink in honour of Queen Elizabeth II, pink being the traditional colour of hospitality.

Singh was about to turn in when he remembered he'd meant to ask Mehrunisa the reason for her sudden trip to Jaipur. Since her room was across from his, he knocked on her door and, when asked to come in, looked around in astonishment at the size and opulence of her room. One wall was lined with mirrored French windows and a large chandelier held pride of place.

'Pamposh says this room,' Mehrunisa's arm took in the massive chandelier, plush carpet and magnificent mural on the wall facing the bed, 'has always been assigned to esteemed guests! I think she's pulling my leg,' she grimaced.

R.P. Singh, hands on his waist, grinned and declared, 'Totally over the top. And those lights!'

'Overcompensation,' Mehrunisa said, 'the bathroom is pitch dark.' She had a towel slung over one shoulder and Singh realised she had probably meant to shower.

'I can switch rooms with you,' he shrugged nonchalantly.

'I wouldn't want to inconvenience you,' Mehrunisa said eyeing him uncertainly.

'Not at all. Rest assured, I do not share your hygiene compulsions.' On that they traded rooms. As they moved their bags, R.P. Singh enquired about the reason behind her sudden trip. Mehrunisa updated him on the Jaipur map that Raj Bhushan was looking to source from the Jaipur royals.

'Interesting,' R.P. Singh said. 'One more question,' he smiled apologetically. 'Why were you so surprised at the director's joke?'

Mehrunisa looked puzzled.

'The one about the "erection",' Singh prompted.

'Oh! You don't miss much, do you? It, it was just, somehow, so *out* of character. Know what I mean?' she shrugged, a faraway look on her face. 'In fact, it reminded me of Arun, who was given to that kind of humour. With Arun, though, it was part of the complete package: the unkempt appearance, the slovenly scholarly air, the racy humour.'

Singh nodded. 'Well,' he said, 'I won't keep you any longer.'

Back inside his new room, R.P. Singh was soon less than thrilled: when he went to bed, the room did not plunge into darkness as tiny nightlights continued to twinkle on the chandelier's top tier. Now whenever he turned, he caught sight of his shiny pate or his stubbled chin in the row of mirrored French windows. Hideous, he muttered grumpily.

He also had too much on his mind, he reckoned. He pulled the blanket over his head and contemplated each person in the haveli.

Raj Bhushan was a self-proclaimed counterfactual historian; Pamposh was a Kashmiri Pandit refugee who ran an orphanage for Muslim children; Mehrunisa was a Renaissance scholar who was interested in Mughal art; the dead Arun Toor was a Jat who, unlike his destructive predecessors, had been responsible for the Taj. Why this duality? What did it tell him?

Time for a smoke, he thought and swung his legs off the bed. At a French window, he unfastened two latches and pushed. It did not budge. Trying again, he wedged his shoulder against it and shoved harder. No luck. He peered at the window. Layers of paint over the years had fastened the windowpane to the frame—it would break before it would open.

Frustrated in his attempt to smoke or sleep, Singh decided to put an ingenious end to the darned twinkle-twinkle in his room. Grabbing the white sheet beneath his blanket, he balled it and tossed it at the chandelier. The sheet unfurled as it fell, sheathing most of the lights. The room plunged into partial darkness. As he eyed the comforting darkness, his gaze fell on the wall lined with French windows.

His blood froze!

Behind one window was a lumpy form. A monkey cap shrouded the face. A dagger was visible in the right hand!

The mirrors in the French windows were one-way! As long as there was light in the guest room, the person on the other side was invisible. But the moment the room was dark, the mirror became like ordinary glass, allowing him to see the man clearly.

As comprehension dawned on Singh, there was a rush of blood in his veins. With a snarl he lunged towards the window. The next instant the man was gone!

Jaipur

R.P. Singh's loud attempts to open the windows roused the household. Within minutes, Pamposh, Raj Bhushan, Mehrunisa and the retainer were in the guest room.

Singh brushed aside their questions as he hurried into the hallway and out the main door to explore the area outside the guest room. A narrow annexe was tucked at its rear. It had been added later, Pamposh said, because the windows were never opened. Inside were stacked some old chairs, earthen flowerpots and gardening shears. Apparently a storage place for odds and ends, it was never locked. When he located the exact window through which he'd seen the man and probed the thin frame, he discovered a tiny knob in the top right-hand corner. He pressed it, and it opened to floor length.

R.P. Singh stepped inside the guest room and moved the casement back and forth. It swung easily.

'Well-oiled! Evidently, someone uses it regularly to access the guest room.'

He led the confounded folk, who'd trailed into the room after him, into the living room where he apprised them of his encounter with a dagger-wielding man after he had switched rooms with Mehrunisa.

Pamposh hands flew to her face. 'Why,' she whispered, 'would anyone want to kill a police officer in my haveli?' Her eyes rolled like a kathakali dancer's.

'The killer was targeting Mehrunisa,' R.P. Singh said quietly, as he explained how the rooms were switched. 'No one knew we switched rooms.'

Pamposh looked like she would faint. R.P. Singh caught her arm and led her to the study as she rattled on about the room. It was seldom used, she said, for she had infrequent overnight guests. And on the occasions that she did, she preferred to use the smaller room that R.P. Singh was using. She started to apologise to Mehrunisa, before fretting about the dangerous intruder, then turning to the safety of her orphans, her voice rising hysterically.

R.P. Singh sat her down and served her a shot of brandy. In a calmer voice, Pamposh said, 'This is what comes of inheriting mansions—skeletons in the cupboard.'

It became a midnight soiree as the group once again congregated in the study and the fire was rekindled. Questions flew from Pamposh. Had Singh recognised the man? Did he know him? Did Mehrunisa have any reason to believe she would have enemies, dagger-wielding ones at that?

All this while Mehrunisa sat quiet, a cardigan pulled tight around her. R.P. Singh's recountal made her weak-kneed, her spine like jelly, for she knew at once that the man with the dagger and a monkey cap shrouding his face was the same person who had attacked her in the Red Fort.

The man who had killed Nisar before he could tell her who had ordered the change in calligraphy on Mumtaz's cenotaph. Changes which Raj Bhushan, the director-general of ASI, had casually dismissed.

She shivered involuntarily. How had he tracked her to Pamposh's haveli? And how the hell did he know the access to the guest room?

It was the second attempt on her life—monkey-cap had no way of knowing it would be R.P. Singh and not her in the room. She had to unmask him before he succeeded in getting to her. An image of a bloodied dagger hitting the gravel in the Red Fort came vividly to her mind. She squeezed her eyes tight; before her nerves got the better of her she announced, 'I know the man.'

Pamposh gasped audibly.

Mehrunisa, meanwhile, was watching Raj Bhushan. Tired of his playing down the calligraphic changes on Mumtaz's tomb, of his double-speak, she had thrown down a gauntlet. She sensed R.P. Singh watching her discreetly, and realised that he was aware of what she was doing. The ASI director-general looked concerned, his hands steepled as he watched her attentively.

'Yes,' Mehrunisa said and proceeded to update the gathering.

When she finished, Raj Bhushan said, 'I wish you had told me about this earlier, Mehrunisa. I dismissed it as a conspiracy theory, but perhaps there is more to the changes in the calligraphy than I had thought. My sincerest apologies—'

Pamposh, who had sat stupefied thus far, interrupted him. 'Mehroo, you poor thing! With Kaul uncle ill and someone trying to kill you, you need someone to take care of you.'

Singh noticed Mehrunisa stiffen. 'This monkey-cap is clever and dangerous—not only did he trace Mehrunisa, he knew where she was sleeping and found an inventive access route to the room. How did he manage that?'

Raj Bhushan shrugged, 'Perhaps he was crouching in the garden bushes outside and spying on us. And the guest room does have access from the annexe, the door of which is kept unlocked.'

'Where he fortuitously discovered the one-way mirror that has access to the guest room?' Mehrunisa shook her head. 'Too much of a coincidence.'

Hoarsely, Pamposh asked, 'What are you implying, Mehroo?'

'Our monkey-cap *knew* about the one-way mirror and access, he didn't just discover it.'

'But that wouldn't be possible unless—' Pamposh gasped mid-sentence as comprehension dawned on her.

'Unless he has an accomplice,' Mehrunisa said. '*In* this house.'

'Who?' Pamposh glanced around the room, looking at each one in turn. 'My maid and retainer have been with my family for decades. There's the centre supervisor, the teachers, the peon, the gardener, the cook and a couple of more staff.... How do we even begin to find out who he's working with.'

Mehrunisa spread her hands out. 'I don't know. The thing to remember is that he's working with someone who is intimate with the Taj Mahal. Enough to understand how subtle changes in the calligraphy on Mumtaz's tomb can have a significant impact.'

In a half-mocking tone Pamposh enquired, 'And this same accomplice is also intimate with my haveli?'

'Perhaps,' Mehrunisa said simply.

For a short while there was a stunned silence. Until Pamposh started to laugh, mouth open, peals rippling through the room.

Pamposh finally composed herself and said, 'Sorry, I couldn't help myself. An accomplice who is intimate with the Taj Mahal and this haveli,' she held up her left hand in a 'V' sign. 'Surely, that throws up only two likely candidates: Mehrunisa and me.'

Pamposh walked up to Mehrunisa, who was sitting on a high bar stool. 'In which case, dear Mehroo,' she slung her arms around Mehrunisa's neck, holding her in a languid grip, 'either you were trying to fake a murder attempt on yourself, or I am trying to kill you.'

R.P. Singh watched the two friends. It was absurd, he knew. After all, the two had practically been sisters, thrown together for extended periods of time. Yet, the scene that had just unfolded reminded him of a cat playing with a mouse.

Before she struck it down.

Agra

One day a week SSP Raghav was vegetarian. Unlike other meat-eating Indians who observed such a practice for religious reasons—Monday for Shiva; Tuesday for Hanuman; Thursday for Vishnu; Saturday for Shani—Raghav did it for health reasons. Not that it helped much, he reflected ruefully, considering that the day before he fasted—what else would a vegetarian meal be to a hearty meat-eater?—he feasted invariably on shammi kebabs, followed by tandoori fish and biryani. Three hundred years on, the Mughal influence lingered in Agra's monuments and food.

Having promised himself he would not think of the Taj conspiracy for the one hour in which he would enjoy a relaxed meal, he rode leisurely through the narrow main street of Kinari Bazaar.

It was a winter's evening and the bazaar was congested with shoppers keen to accomplish their business before it got too chilly. Outside Haneef's, a mid-sized eatery that he patronised—the main draw being the shammi kebabs, silky and soft—he parked his motorcycle. That the eatery had grown beyond its humble origins was evident in the kebab stall that fronted it, where the elderly proprietor still sat frying mincemeat patties in a huge wok.

'Salaam, Haneef chacha!' Raghav called out a greeting to the proprietor.

Haneef was dressed in a cream-coloured pathani salwar kurta. Raghav marvelled how he managed to keep it spotless despite a full day's work with oil and meat and chutneys.

Haneef acknowledged the police chief with a genial smile, a tip of his head, and a firing up of his stove. 'No different this time, SSP Sahib?'

'The usual.'

A boy had run up to the nearest table and was wiping it clean. Throwing his raggedy kitchen towel on his shoulder, he indicated the table was ready. The oil in the wok was steaming now, its sharp mustard smell filling his nostrils as he watched Haneef lower the flame. Deftly, he took a patty in his fleshy red palms, rolled it once to smooth any misshapen bits, before sliding it into the wok. A sizzle erupted, and flavourful garlic-ginger-chilli assailed him.

Raghav had sighted heaven. Next, a teacup surfaced by his side. With a smile, he began sipping it.

Those who knew him well were aware of his preference for sugarless tea and Raghav noticed that Haneef chacha's tea boy had remembered. Of course, Raghav reflected, considering he was Haneef's most powerful patron.

Raghav surveyed the seating area that stretched beyond the kebab stall. Several tables were occupied and two waiters roamed the aisles, serving water, flicking flies, taking orders. Meanwhile, Haneef chacha's son Feroze, who was also the manager of the eatery, was by his father's side whispering into his ear. Haneef shook his head dismissively. The young man, around twenty, bit his lips. Catching Raghav's eye, he bowed his head.

'Business good?' Raghav enquired, unconsciously switching to his policeman's tone, one quite different from what he employed while conversing with the elderly proprietor.

'Yes sir—with your blessing.' Feroze cast a nervous glance at his father before giving him a tremulous smile.

'You look troubled.'

Haneef waved a hand, 'SSP Sahib, please,' he indicated the table, before turning to scowl at his son. He ladled the crusty-brown gleaming kebabs out of the wok and deposited them in a plate. His son garnished the kebabs with coriander leaves and added some mint chutney before bringing it over.

Raghav rubbed his palms before drawing the plate closer. 'Sit,' he indicated to the young man, and bit off a chunk of the kebab, savouring the smooth mutton. Smacking his lips, he brought his right hand to his forehead and flicked it briefly to indicate his appreciation. Satisfied, Haneef nodded and turned his attention to the wok again.

'Tell me,' Raghav commanded, 'you troubling your father?'

Feroze shook his head vigorously. 'No, Sir. But yes, *we* are troubled.'

Raghav chewed thoughtfully, watching the young man.

'Have you heard the rumours, Sir?'

'What rumours?'

'There is a rumour going around in Agra city. It used to be there, always,' he shrugged, 'one always heard it as part of the stories around the Taj...'

He eyed Raghav, whose face remained expressionless.

'Sir, there have always been stories around the Taj Mahal, you know. How Shah Jahan was planning to build a black Taj Mahal across from the white, how he chopped the hands of twenty thousand labourers who worked on building the Taj so it could not be replicated. How the Taj is actually a Hindu temple which was snatched by the Mughal emperor. In fact, they claim,' his tongue flicked out to lick a lip, 'that the calligraphy on Mumtaz's tomb says so.'

Raghav kept his face immobile.

'They say the inscription states that it is a false tomb—anyone who can read Persian can make it out. That is why it went unnoticed thus far—who in India today knows Persian anyway?'

'Who is your source?'

'One of my cousins, Sir, is a guide at the Taj. He told us.'

'Told you what?'

'That the Hindu guides have suddenly started elaborating on the story of the Taj being a Hindu temple. It was always part of their stories, but apparently,' Feroze went whispery, 'someone has paid them to inform all their tourists about the Hindu origin of the Taj.'

Raghav leaned forward, popped a whole kebab in his mouth, and muttered, 'Go on.'

He shifted in his chair. 'Not just that, Sir. In this market even, a lot of people have started to sing the hymn of the Taj Mahal's Hindu origins. I keep my ears open and more and more, I hear it. Now,' he hissed, 'there is talk of reclaiming what belongs to Hindus, one way or other. I have seen a couple of young men—they look like college students—roaming about in this market.

They look harmless but they have been going into shops methodically—mind you, no Muslim-owned shops—spending time with the shopkeeper and exiting without buying anything.' He regarded SSP Raghav.

'So that makes them suspect?' Raghav feigned a scowl as he wondered whether these were the same lads he had almost apprehended with the pamphlets. 'Perhaps, they are doing market research. You know these big marketing companies send people around asking questions on Lux soap and cooking oil and such stuff!'

'But they would target specific shops, right? Grocery stores or hardware stores? While these men go into every shop except the Muslim-owned ones.'

Raghav dipped an index finger into the mint chutney and licked it before turning his attention to the manager. The sweat beads on his forehead were not from the spicy kebabs alone.

'Perhaps they are college kids, doing a project.'

Haneef Chacha's son was unconvinced. 'No Sir. They are spending too much time inside those shops. Since when did a baniya start spending his time in idle chit-chat?'

Kinari Bazaar, it was then. He would send a constable in plainclothes to investigate it right away, Raghav decided. If his constable managed to unearth something suspicious, it would be time for a covert operation of his own: a swift distribution of Mehrunisa's pamphlets refuting the claim that the Taj Mahal was a Shiva temple.

'Will you recognise those college students? Describe them to me,' Raghav said. He had to catch these boys. They were a link in the chain that led back to the Taj conspirator.

Delhi

Mehrunisa did not need her regular black tea to rouse her that morning as she sat in the patio of Professor Kaul's house. The front-page headline of the *Hindustan Times* jolted her awake.

Sunni Waqf Board claims the Taj Mahal
An Indian Muslim organisation has declared that it owns the world's most famous monument to love, the Taj Mahal

She gasped audibly. That made the constable, sitting upright in his wood chair, look at her enquiringly. After the appearance of Monkey-cap in Jaipur, R.P. Singh had insisted on, and provided, police protection for her. The constable was supposedly her new shadow, though he was content to guard the house while Mehrunisa was inside.

'Everything's fine,' she waved, and turned to the newspaper.

The Uttar Pradesh Sunni Central Waqf Board declared on Tuesday that the Taj Mahal was a Waqf property and directed that the 17th century monument be registered in its name. A Waqf is a religious endowment in Islam, typically devoting a building or plot of land for Muslim religious purposes.

The chairman of the UP Sunni Central Waqf Board, Ameer Usman, made the declaration at a packed UP Sunni Waqf Board meeting in Lucknow. The Board says it owns over 100,000 properties in the state of Uttar Pradesh, where the spectacular marble mausoleum is located. It says since the Taj Mahal houses several Muslim graves, it falls under its jurisdiction.

Since 1920, the Taj Mahal has been governed, managed and maintained by the Archaeological Survey of India (ASI). Describing the Waqf Board decision as 'not in the interest of the Taj Mahal', a representative of ASI, who attended the hearing, said the organisation would challenge it in the courts.

The chairman of the Waqf Board said that in the meantime the ASI would continue to manage the monument, and the future management and sharing of revenue from the gate receipts will be decided in consultation with the state and federal governments. However, he added, the Taj Mahal needed better upkeep, and the Waqf Board would strive to improve its maintenance.

If the Sunni Waqf Board becomes the owner of the monument, it stands to get 7% of the income from this building by law. By one estimate, the ASI earns some 190 million rupees ($4.36m) from the three million-odd tourists who visit the monument every year. They Board would also collect revenues from the 80 villages *located around Agra for maintenance of the building and for arranging prayers.*

Some historians say that the Taj Mahal was indeed a Waqf property of which the Mughal emperor Shah Jahan was the custodian. However, the historian Sharmila Thapar is quoted as saying, 'The Mughal Empire and the emperor no longer exist. Who succeeds him as the custodian of the Waqf? There has been no claim for ages. Just because somebody makes a claim now does not necessarily mean that the monument goes to them.'

To take her mind off the Taj Mahal, Mehrunisa decided to cook the professor's favourite dish. Shah Jahan, the great aesthete of the Mughal empire, was regarded the creator of that dish. As the thought popped in her head, Mehrunisa grimaced: even in the kitchen there was no refuge from the all-pervasive Mughals!

Her hair tied in a knot, sweater sleeves rolled up, she rinsed the basmati rice in cold water a couple of times, before dunking it into a sieve. Turning to the counter she watched Mangat Ram who had laid out on a board the ingredients she would require to season the Shahjahani Pulao: black cumin, green cardamoms, sticks of cinnamon, whole cloves and bay leaves.

Outside, the sun broke through the clouds and its bright light lit the kitchen and washed her with happiness. Smiling, Mehrunisa walked to the window and looked out. Professor Kaul was sitting exactly where she had left him in his cane armchair, a shawl draped over his shoulders, his hands in his lap, his mind—God alone knew where.

As Mangat Ram shuffled away with a cup of tea for the professor, Mehrunisa sighed and turned to the rice grains. They had fluffed a little and she raked the mound of rice with her fingers, draining the remaining water. Kaul uncle loved Shahjahani Pulao for its intense aroma and the flavoursome fruit topping.

Mehrunisa started to sauté the spices in ghee, her mind on her uncle. His abrupt descent into that strange abyss frightened her; that such a great mind could be reduced to so little in a matter of days. Her greater fear, one she refused to acknowledge to herself, was the possibility that perhaps, in the manner of her father, her uncle would also disappear from her. Her father was legally dead, yet his body had never been found. He had left on a business trip to Syria when she was fourteen and never returned. Having quit the Indian Foreign Service, he had started a business of antiques out of Rome—both Maadar and Papa liked Italy enough to want to continue living there. The police had pursued the case for a year. The Indian Consulate had applied pressure on the Italian police, but to no avail. Harinder Singh Khosa had simply vanished. With a shake of her head, Mehrunisa determined not to follow the thought through.

The onions had browned to a crispness; she proceeded to add the basmati rice. A soft hiss rose from the pan, she stirred the contents thoroughly and lowered the flame. Covering the pan with a lid, she leaned against the counter and watched Mangat Ram shuffle in again. It was either the cold, or empathy with his weakening master, that had enervated the housekeeper as well. Mehrunisa smiled at the wizened old man, feeling immense love for him and gratitude for the comfort of his companionship.

'At least he still likes his tea,' Mangat Ram quipped, a smile bursting forth from the creased face. 'He will enjoy the pulao,' he added, turning to deposit the cup in the sink and running the water. 'The last time he asked me to make it was when you were about to visit. He said we should make it in your honour though he complained that I do not make it as well as you do. That day Bhushan sahib dropped in unexpectedly.'

Mehrunisa nodded. She hadn't met Raj Bhushan since their visit to Jaipur. Apparently the royal family had flatly refused his offer to buy the map.

'So I laid the table for two,' Mangat Ram continued, drying his hands with a towel, 'and Sahib, he was in a jovial mood. When I served the pulao to Bhushan sahib, he joked, "You should serve him khichri".'

Mangat Ram smiled at the memory. 'Why offer such a simple dish to a guest when there is rich pulao at home, I asked. Know what he answered?'

Mehrunisa urged him on with a smile.

'Aurangzeb was fond of khichri, Sahib said. His taste in food was unlike that of his father Shah Jahan, who favoured rich food.'

Mehrunisa's mouth fell open. '*Aurangzeb?*' Her voice was a croak. 'Who was he calling Aurangzeb?'

Mangat Ram seemed not to have noticed the incredulous look on her face. Reaching for a head of garlic, he sat on the tall wood stool and started to peel a clove. 'Bhushan sahib, who else?'

'But why would he call Raj Bhushan Aurangzeb?'

'It is a direct translation of his name. Aurang-Zeb. From Urdu, or is it Persian?' He wrinkled his nose at Mehrunisa. 'It means ornament of throne. Raj, ornament; Bhushan, throne.' Mangat Ram lifted his brows. 'Living with Sahib for forty years has made me into a small-time teacher as well!'

Delhi

Mehrunisa paused at the gate. She had headed out of the house after Mangat Ram's revelation, hoping some outside air would vacuum the fuzz from her mind.

Raj Bhushan was Aurangzeb!

It had been staring at her all the time, yet she had not noticed. How could she have missed the connection when even her uncle, in his state of amnesia, had been agitated enough to warn her. *Hang on*! She was moving too fast. Mehrunisa tugged her pashmina shawl closer around her and attempted to marshal her thoughts.

First: Aurangzeb was Raj Bhushan, there could be no doubt. Arun, who evidently knew the nickname, had mentioned that he was expecting Aurangzeb. The ASI director-general's presence in the Taj Mahal was natural—nobody would think twice about the director visiting the preeminent monument on his list. Thereafter, Kaul uncle had cautioned her about the dead Mughal emperor. And now Mangat Ram had divulged that the professor routinely teased Raj Bhushan with that moniker.

Second: Raj Bhushan did not reveal to the police that he had met Arun on the evening of his murder. Why? What was he attempting to hide? He might have been the last one to see Arun alive. He might have seen somebody who could be implicated. He might have witnessed the murder ... *He might be the murderer!*

On the last thought Mehrunisa gasped. Even the police was working on the premise that Aurangzeb was either the murderer, or directly linked to the murder. But this was too improbable. ASI director-general Raj Bhushan did not seem the murdering kind. Besides, why would he want to kill the Taj supervisor? They *were* dissimilar—were their relations strained? Had they had a falling out? But surely, as the ultimate authority, he could always have fired Arun if they had work problems—so why murder him? No. Then why not inform the police that he had met Arun on the night of his murder? Was he trying to avoid a scandal—the police would have questioned him and the media would have got nosy? Perhaps he had nothing concrete to disclose and decided therefore to stay silent?

Watch out for Aurangzeb! That was what her uncle had said. *What* should she be watching out for? What did the professor know? And how did he know it?

She would talk to Professor Kaul. While she may not know Raj Bhushan well, her godfather still did. If Mehrunisa voiced her misgivings, maybe Kaul uncle would be roused out of his state to say something.

She went inside to call R.P. Singh right away.

Delhi

Shri Kriplani was furious. So enraged was he that he was in danger of choking on his own animus: the glass of yellow piss he had drunk in the morning after his daily constitutional had tasted pungent enough to make him gag.

The first urine of the morning was a snapshot of his previous day: clear, with a pleasant aroma meant he had eaten healthy and thought pleasantly. However, the previous day's news report had put his mind in turmoil, his acidity had acted up, and he had slept fitfully as he strategized through the night; the result, therefore, was cloudy, foul-smelling urine. At such times he felt he should take an occasional break from urine therapy....

But the essence of urine therapy was predicated on harmony between input and output. It was a daily reminder to stay calm and think with a cool head. Today, he needed that.

The Waqf Board's statement asserting a rightful claim to the Taj Mahal had made headlines in all the top dailies.

The Board chairman had been interviewed on TV channels where, contrary to expectations, he turned out not to be a bearded, skull-capped mullah but a rather telegenic young fellow. Now, a TV crew was waiting to interview Shri Kriplani.

Any other time he would have had a field day.

The sons of Babur were a most militant minority. When not cosying up to their Muslim neighbour and assisting in terror attacks on Indian soil, they were bent upon usurping India's heritage!

If the plan of carbon dating the monument had worked, he'd have declared the Taj Mahal was indeed an ancient Hindu temple and delivered a body blow to these rabid foreigners. Instead, with that CBI officer on his heels, he had had to relinquish that effort. Things were looking bad....

He inhaled deeply. For a seasoned politician, every setback was an opportunity. It was time to play the elder statesman for TV cameras and assorted reporters gathered outside.

Shri Kriplani was a consummate performer as he parlayed his personal wrath into Hindu umbrage at the Muslim hijacking of Indian treasures. Legs crossed, his dhoti tucked in neatly, he faced the TV camera resolutely and began his withering speech.

'The Waqf Board has claimed the Taj Mahal. Tomorrow they will claim Qutab Minar, the Red Fort, Humayun's Tomb ... where will they stop? The Parliament House? Why not? They will claim the building was designed by a British architect but the labourers who worked on it were Muslims, mostly; so, rightfully the Parliament House should also be theirs. Once the ball is set rolling, where does it stop?

'Fact is, the Mughals were invaders. Where did the money for building these lavish monuments come from? From the Hindu masses. How did the Mughal Empire become the richest in the world? By robbing the Hindu subjects. Did they bring these riches and wealth with them from their mother countries of Turkey and Mongolia? Penniless, on horseback, they rode into our motherland and ransacked it. They looted us for centuries and today they want to legalise what they have looted. Shabash! What is the meaning of Hindustan, I ask? Simple. Hindu-stan: the land of Hindus. *The Land of Hindus*! This is my answer to the Waqf Board and any and all Muslim boards and to the Muslims of India. Understand the meaning of Hindustan, and live here.

'Ours is a great nation. Through the ages it has embraced outsiders and absorbed them into its fabric. A mother never lets go of her children, even when some of them persist in being difficult.

'In a few days the prime minister will give his annual speech from the Red Fort—it is a time for unity, not for petty squabbles. Jai Bharat! Jai Sri Ram!'

A satisfied, though dry-throated, Shri Kriplani sat back in his chair as the cameras switched off. He had played to the gallery yet ended his speech such that it would elevate him in the eyes of his countrymen, and deflate the communal rhetoric of his opponents.

Agra

R.P. Singh stood on the balcony of the Taj Ganj police station, munching roasted chana and contemplating the mist that still hovered around. It reflected the state of his mind accurately. Mehrunisa had called to say that she'd found out Raj Bhushan was Aurangzeb. She had explained her reasoning, but it was based on hearsay, not proof. Nevertheless, it added the latest twist in a case that already looked like a dish of seviyan.

As he ruminated on the multiple skeins of the case, people started to gather in the courtyard in front of him. They seemed to be leaking out of the mist and taking form in front of him, dressed variously in shawls, blankets, woolly caps, some coats. Had he missed a memo?

A young man separated from the mass and approached him. R.P. Singh beckoned him inside.

The man seated opposite him did not inspire confidence; less so, his fantastic story.

His mouth concealed behind a hand, Singh scrutinised the young man: long sideburns, longer hair, bell-bottomed jeans fashionably slit at the knees, a denim jacket over a polka-dotted shirt open at the neck—despite the cold day. He was the epitome of a local ruffian from Taj Ganj, the sort who trailed backpacking tourists, and in halting mishmash English promised to show them the best souvenir shops, best restaurants, best whores, best anything. So the logical question was: what was he doing in a police station of his own volition? He would hear the story again, this time for inconsistencies.

Singh wore his best saturnine expression and queried, 'Aamir? Tell me again why you are here.'

The young man seemed taken aback at the question. He had spent ten minutes detailing the previous night's event that had rattled the Muslim residents of Taj Ganj. Narrating his story with sound effects, he had made it as graphic as possible. Besides, he was best suited to tell it to the police and convey the fear of the residents: he was, after all, the one with the largest gora clientele. If he could communicate with the firangs, surely he could make one of his own countrymen comprehend him!

Perplexed, he mumbled, 'Sir, where do I start?'

'The beginning is usually a good place,' Singh's voice was toneless, yet laden with menace.

Aamir's Adam's apple throbbed nervously. He began. 'Sir, yesterday night we were asleep when—'

'Time?'

'1.15—I glanced at the clock. It has these glowing hands, you see.'

When R.P. Singh nodded, Aamir continued, 'So, the locality was asleep. All quiet, as it normally is that late, when a loud voice broke through the night! It was a terrible sound like, like ... a goat being slaughtered at Moharram. Plaintive, pleading. Then shrieks sounded, loud cries, followed by thrashing sounds, and a sound of crackling fire and the air being slashed.... Oh!'

Aamir shivered, his face crushed. Shaking his head vigorously, he whispered, 'It was horrible! Horrible!'

Singh watched the performance—it looked authentic. 'What happened next?'

Aamir shrugged. 'I was terrified but I was also curious. So I went to the window to see if I could make out the source. My room is on the first floor, see. The voices were getting louder. I looked out. And what did I see?' Aamir had clamped a palm on his mouth.

Considering it was a repeat performance, the boy was managing to render it with commendable passion and consistence.

'Outside in the street was a van. A Maruti gypsy van. Atop it was mounted a loudspeaker that was blaring those sounds!'

'And why would that be?'

'How would I know, Sir? That is why I am here—to beg you to do enquiry into this strange happening. Why would pre-recorded cries and shouts be blared into our neighbourhood in the middle of the night? The van took three rounds of our locality, going up and down the street, making sure everybody was awake and hearing the cries!'

'What did the sounds remind you of?'

Aamir went still. 'It seemed like a TV news report on a riot...'

Like any policeman, R.P. Singh knew how to mask his emotions. But at that moment, a terrible fear had gripped him. Cars speeding through neighbourhoods, playing pre-recorded sounds of riots and screams, had an ugly precedent. On the eve of the Babri Masjid demolition, most Muslims had fled the neighbourhood, scared out of their wits by such cars. In his mind's eye Singh saw TV images of urban youths in jeans and yellow headbands, and wild-haired, half-naked sadhus atop the central dome of the mosque. Matter-of-factly, he asked, 'You think they were trying to scare you?'

'Not me alone, Sir—the entire mohalla. We are a Muslim locality, mostly.'

'And why would they do that?'

Aamir's response was to shrug again.

At that instant he reminded Singh of a forlorn child. He saw a different youth: the long hair was lank with grease, the sideburns distracted from a pimply-red skin, his broken English was an attempt to hoist himself on the social ladder, and his nervously flicking tongue a pointer to his inner turmoil. A young Muslim boy raised in the squalor of the Taj's shadow, eking out a living in Taj Ganj like so many others.

'Perhaps,' Aamir's Adam's apple was bobbing furiously, 'they want to drive us out of our homes.'

'Is there anyone else who can corroborate your story? Any other witnesses?'

Aamir nodded.

'Well, call them in.'

'Sir, better if you could just step out to the porch again with me.'

R.P. Singh pushed his chair back and strode to the door. When he stepped onto the porch, the mist had cleared to show a group of forty to fifty people standing in the open courtyard, huddling in their shawls and jackets against the cold. In the midst of all the men with their hennaed beards and skull caps and the women with dupattas were a couple of white tourists. Pointing at them, R.P. Singh turned to Aamir.

'They heard it too, Sir, and said they would give evidence.'

'Hmm...' Singh wagged his head. With a raised palm he acknowledged the greetings from the gathering. His tongue probing the corners of his mouth, he turned to scrutinise the cement floor.

Aamir's narration had touched a raw nerve. In his mind he saw a shrieking mob dressed in camouflage-green uniforms, carrying assault rifles as they set fire to mud-and-thatch dwellings and shot at villagers who escaped.

Mao and Marx were two chutiyas whose guerrilla followers had plagued his life for a decade. However, their victims were tribals and police—so who was this new joker in the pack?

R.P. Singh dispatched SSP Raghav with the youth to investigate Taj Ganj while he left for Delhi. This development was red-hot. Time to drop in on the home minister, with whom he was acquainted from his Chattisgarh days. He needed his muscle to clamp down on Kriplani, in case he was the Joker; fire forensics to deliver the DNA results; and approve additional security for the Taj Mahal.

Delhi

It was dusk. The ASI director-general's office was quiet except for a faint clattering of a typewriter somewhere in the cavernous colonial building where Mehrunisa was awaiting Raj Bhushan. When she had called his mobile earlier he was on a field trip from which, he said, he would return late evening. She had been waiting for half an hour and would have preferred a stroll in the lawn, but a drizzle had started. She shivered. The room's high ceiling and large windows were meant to keep the place cool in the searing heat of an Indian summer, rendering it wholly unsuitable even in a mild winter. The occasional shiver she felt had nothing to do with her agenda for the meeting, of course.

The peon walked in, a steaming teacup on a tray with Marie biscuits. 'Bhushan sahib,' he said conversationally, 'was travelling a lot overseas. But when back in the office, he'd stay put. Lately, that has changed. He is visiting various circles.'

'Is that so?'

'And to way-out places! Surprise checks!' he grinned. 'Keeps them on their toes, he says.'

Hmm, Mehrunisa acknowledged.

'Now, he is so charged up—hardly ever in the office.'

Something in the man's words made Mehrunisa pay attention.

Car tyres squealed in the driveway and the peon turned to the window. 'He's here,' he muttered and made to exit hastily.

A short while later Raj Bhushan was sitting opposite Mehrunisa. His hair, probably moist from the drizzle, was slicked back, and despite the day spent working, he looked fresh and ... Mehrunisa's mind searched for the right adjective. Raj Bhushan was youthful-looking and had evidently freshened up in the washroom before joining her, but tonight he looked positively virile. *Virile*, yes!

Now he beamed at her, his smile making his mouth upturn wondrously like a monkey's. An instant later, as he heard her out, it faded.

Sitting upright in the straight-backed chair, Mehrunisa had coolly enquired, 'Why did you lie about your presence at the Taj the night of Arun's murder?' She had decided on a direct approach, betting that an accusation might ferret out the truth.

If a smile could turn menacing, Raj Bhushan's just had. It still curved in that deep U, but the mirth had gone out of it. His eyes held her in a fixed stare.

A snort broke the silence. 'In-your-face? Is that your preferred approach, Mehrunisa?'

'It has its advantages, don't you agree?'

'Meaning what? That I will be startled into coming clean? Why would I, for what proof could you have?' He leaned forward, his stare still pinning her to the spot.

'Considering I left none behind.'

The rain had gained intensity; raindrops fell like lead balls on the windowsill, ricocheting in her ears. She wanted to move, make a gesture, a sound, anything that would release her from the trap of Raj Bhushan's steady unblinking stare from behind his glasses. That stare was so intense ... and its intensity reminded her of someone else ... *Arun!* Yes, Arun had that same habit. Mehrunisa had seen him exercise it on his staff when he felt they were stalling on a request he had made: he would cock his head and subject his opponent to a mutinous protracted scrutiny. In a couple of intense debates, she had suffered that same treatment. Funny that Arun and his boss should have a similar mannerism. Before Mehrunisa could hold the thought any longer, Raj Bhushan interjected. His voice was soft, even.

Too even, Mehrunisa registered, for a man who had just been accused of a grave wrongdoing.

'I am a careful man, Mehrunisa. I pride myself on being rational. Too often human beings are driven purely by their emotions—as you seem to be now. You have come into my office, accusing me—although indirectly—of murder. You have not offered any proof in support of your hypothesis, and you sit there, presumably unarmed, in the presence of a supposed murderer. Is that sensible on your part, Mehrunisa?'

He was angry, no, furious, and in that moment Mehrunisa did not know whether Raj Bhushan was genuinely outraged, or if he was a sassy cat toying with an absurd mouse.

'Yes, I was present at the Taj the night Arun was murdered. But I did not see anything noteworthy,' he shrugged, 'anything that could have provided the police with leads. It was a routine meeting, we discussed a few details, and I left. Since I had nothing to reveal, I thought it prudent to avoid telling the police about the meeting. My first priority was to avoid any scandal around the Taj. You know the number of twenty-four-hour news channels in this country? A story like this would have given them fodder for weeks. It was bad timing; you know we're seeking additional funds for the conservation of the Taj Mahal.'

Mehrunisa continued to regard him stonily.

The director-general gave a long sigh and held up his hands. 'Look, you've heard the phrase: no free lunch. Well, Taj Mahal subverts that particular economic principle brilliantly. For a four-hundred-year-old monument, its structure is remarkably sound—it has survived earthquakes, lightning and floods. Yet, it suffers severely. Ten years ago, iron foundries, glass and leather industries, marble mining and the Mathura Refinery were the culprits, but now the Taj faces new threats. Vehicular population, chronic power shortage, and three national highways that crisscross the city, are adding to the pollution.

'The sandstone gets less attention, yet it is in a more precarious condition because of its porosity. Not to mention the wearing out of the pavement on the garden walkways and terrace floors from two million annual visitors! And that number is only going to increase. Forty-five million people voted the Taj as a new Wonder of the World—surely some of them will be trudging up here soon!'

Raj Bhushan paused. He stood up, hands on hips and looked squarely at Mehrunisa.

'The marble is rapidly being stained yellow, the Yamuna stinks to high hell, we are perennially short of funds for maintenance and conservation ... yet, who cares?'

His defence of the Taj Mahal, while spirited, had little to do with the murder of Arun Toor. Mehrunisa veered the discussion back. 'Why not let the police decide whether your disclosure could offer any leads?'

Raj Bhushan opened his hands and held them out in front of him, 'I ran the scene over and over in my mind, Mehrunisa. We met in Arun's study. We were alone. Nobody interrupted us. I left within an hour.'

'Why didn't the staff see you? The security guards?'

'It was a cold night, and wet. Much like tonight. Most of them were probably indoors, I guess, staying warm. And I usually use Sirhi Darwaza.'

The Taj Mahal complex could be entered through one of three gates leading into the Jilaukhana, the forecourt. The east and west gates were those commonly used by tourists. The south gate of Sirhi Darwaza—from Taj Ganj—was more difficult to reach.

'Why would you use the south gate? You've to go through a crowded bazaar to access it.'

'Routine—helps avoid the tourists.'

'At night?'

Raj Bhushan blinked. 'Habit, I said.'

'Was any staff aware of your visit?'

'I have a key to let myself in. Besides, my visit was not pre-planned. I happened to be in the vicinity, inspecting the new excavation at Fatehpur Sikri. I dropped in to discuss a few things with Arun.'

'Was he expecting you?'

Raj Bhushan smirked, 'You make a good interrogator, Mehrunisa—never losing track.' He paused before answering. 'I called him. From my mobile phone. I guess you will want to get the records checked?'

Mehrunisa stayed silent.

Gamely, Raj Bhushan continued, 'But you haven't told me how you figured out I was at the Taj Mahal that evening.'

Mehrunisa proceeded to divulge Arun's remark to her regarding a visit from Aurangzeb, and her discovery of that particular moniker in relation to Raj Bhushan. However, she refrained from disclosing Professor Kaul's warning.

Raj Bhushan looked amused, like he was laughing at some private joke. 'That's good deduction Mehrunisa, except it's not proof.'

'What is so amusing?'

'You. You would make a fine Miss Marple but for your age. So, what is the verdict? Guilty or not?'

Mehrunisa knew her one strength was a quality regularly attributed to her, albeit deprecatorily: glacial. Now, summoning her best imperturbable façade, she said with a hint of a smile, 'Inconclusive, shall we say, on grounds of insufficient evidence.'

'How courteous, my dear,' Raj Bhushan said with a tilt of his head. 'And now, you'll have to excuse me, I do have other matters to take care of, besides clearing my name.'

With a genial smile, he started to walk her towards the door. At the arched doorway, he said, 'My regards to Professor Kaul. Does he remember me?'

Mehrunisa looked him straight in the eye.

'He remembers Aurangzeb.'

Bateshwar

The head priest of the main temple at Bateshwar squinted his eyes at the pamphlet. It was late evening, the prayers were done and he was getting ready to close. The youth who had handed it to him was dressed in baggy pants, coarse sweater and an orange headscarf. In the glow of the brass lamps, the priest studied his face and knew he was not a local.

The youth started to speak in a curious monotone. His eyes, though, burned with fire as he narrated how his father was set aflame by the Muslims, how a guru showed him the way to Lord Shiva, how he was saved. The day of the great unveiling was on the horizon when the Truth would be revealed to all.

Read on, the youth jabbed at the paper.

The priest, befuddled, turned to the paper in his hand.

The Taj Mahal is a Shiva temple.

Why, he had heard that story before! He read the text slowly in the manner of one who doesn't spend much time reading. He had studied till Class 2 and then begun assisting his father. His family had been priests at the temple for generations. It was the largest of the riverfront temples, by virtue of which it had been ordained as the main temple. Which was the way it had been for a long time.

Now, though, visitors came for the Chambal safari, took boat rides to view the 101 temples and stopped for darshan. He had slowly seen the temple he presided over grow in importance. The gathering of Shiv bhakts over Shivratri had swelled. The temple coffers were brimming like never before. If, indeed, the Taj Mahal was to be declared a Shiva temple, the path ahead was paved with increasing prosperity. If the Taj Mahal joined Bateshwar as a Shiva pilgrimage centre, and even a fraction of its traffic came to Bateshwar's main temple....

He stopped reading midway. There was enough proof here for any doubter. Besides, whoever had crafted this document, was indeed very knowledgeable. A man stepped into the temple. He was dressed in a kurta-pyjama, sleeves rolled up to reveal bulging biceps, his hands clasping the orange muffler around his neck. His eyes bored into the priest as he sauntered forward out of the shadows. The priest gulped on recognising the Agra strongman who was also the go-to man for the local BHP leader.

He clapped a hand on the young man's shoulder and the youth deposited a briefcase in front of the priest. Eyes glued on him, the strongman urged him with his chin to open it.

'For you,' the youth said, 'to do as you're told.'

The priest realised his palms were suddenly moist. Wiping them on the shawl draped over his bare chest, he smiled nervously in the direction of the two men. He lifted the lid of the case—it was full of rupee notes arranged in neat rows. His eyes widened with wonder as if he had seen the Lord himself.

'Tell your people about the proof,' the youth resumed in his flat tone. 'Spread the knowledge that Lord Shiva's pilgrim centre includes what is known as the Taj Mahal.'

The priest was gazing at the youth blankly, the sight of so much money had driven all thoughts from his mind.

Suddenly the strongman bent down and slammed the lid of the case shut. The sound reverberated in the empty hall.

The priest recoiled as if he had been lashed at.

'The Lord will need his bhakts,' the strongman said in a voice that sounded like low thunder rolling across the hall. 'Can he count on you?'

The reputation of the strongman preceded him—he was famous for an extensive police record that included lynching, rape, rioting and murder, and the curious fact that despite that record he had never served a jail sentence.

The priest bit his lip as he nodded. A chill had caught hold of his body. He was shivering all over.

'Otherwise...' the man leaned in to the priest, bowed his head, and studied the priest's belly flab that was jiggling nervously. The dim light cast his face in shadow as it made pinpricks in his eyes.

'Otherwise,' he bared his teeth, 'you know me.'

Delhi

R.P. Singh gatecrashed the home minister's luncheon with the minister of tribal affairs. While the latter glowered at him, the home minister excused himself to talk privately with the officer he had handpicked to solve the Taj conspiracy.

He had grudging respect for Singh's work—it got results although his methods were debatable. However, the Oxbridge lawyer had learnt in his long years as a senior politician that some hands needed to get dirty to ensure the nation's gears kept churning. In his crisp white shirt and white mundu, he strode to his office. Instructing his assistant that they were not to be disturbed, he walked up to his desk.

'I presume this couldn't wait,' he said, in a voice that was curt and not to be trifled with. He had never laid store by small talk and, for a politician, he had the unusual reputation of a man who brooked no nonsense from anyone, be it journalist or industrialist.

He listened intently as R.P. Singh outlined the developments in the case. His face maintained its famous passivity as Singh's narration ended. A case that had started with the murder of the Taj supervisor, followed by an incendiary pamphlet alleging the Hindu origin of the Taj Mahal, looked set to turn even more serious if indeed vans with shrieking cries were roaming Taj Ganj. Singh was convinced of Kriplani's hand in the affair, but would the BHP leader, with his prior record, take such a gamble? Indicating that Singh take a seat, he swivelled in his chair to study a lush potted palm in one corner, bathed in wintry sunlight.

Finally, he asked, 'What sort of attack do you anticipate?'

'I wouldn't put anything past them, Sir. You're aware how two months back the BHP youth cadre vandalised the Taj Mahal by forcibly entering the monument on a Friday. They wanted to bathe in the small tank that is used for ablutions outside the mosque. When an ASI official ordered the tank emptied, they scribbled "Jai Sri Ram" on the walls of the Taj.' Singh wished the minister would look him in the eye. 'My advice, Sir, would be to prepare for the worst and hope for the best.'

'When do you think will be the date of attack?'

R.P. Singh spoke to the minister's profile. 'I expect it to occur in the run-up to Republic Day.'

'Why Republic Day?'

'By attacking the Taj Mahal, this conspirator is playing a high-stakes game, Sir. And he is ratcheting up the momentum. A significant day in the calendar will give him maximum impact.'

'That gives us four days.'

'Yes, Sir.'

'The additional security at the Taj Mahal that you've requested will be made available to you before the end of the day. The DNA test result, my PA will ensure you get it immediately. As for your suspicions regarding Shri Kriplani,' he said, a weary note in his voice, 'I'll deal with him.'

Unconvinced, R.P. Singh wagged his head. 'Sir,' he pleaded, 'I reiterate, the danger from the BHP leader is real. After all, he *is* one of the instigators behind the Babri Masjid mess. He did galvanise kar sevaks to converge upon the masjid. Where they went berserk and tore it down. And while they were at it, he issued feeble requests on TV for them to stop. He did it once, he can surely do it again!'

The home minister spun back to face him. Resting his arms on the desk, he reverted to his erstwhile advocate's demeanour. In that avatar, the articulate and very sharp man had argued for several multinational clients with resounding success.

'Kriplani and I, we go back a long way ... Babri was an uncut stone he picked up and polished. The Taj Mahal is a gem. A world gem. If it goes down, so does Kriplani—he is not that foolish. You have to look elsewhere.' A furrow broke through the phlegmatic mask.

'Have you ever failed before, Singh?' the minister asked quietly.

'Sir,' Singh looked puzzled, 'yes.'

'And that is what makes you who you are, one of our finest officers.'

The minister stood up. 'But this time,' he probed the dry edge of a palm frond, 'you don't have that option. This moment is when you face your biggest challenge.'

He walked to a cabinet, withdrew a pair of scissors and examined the brown tip of the frond.

'A mob looking for some violent sport at the Taj Mahal is a security nightmare. When religion comes into it, even a lathi charge will get beamed to every home in the country, and the ruling party will be declared traitors to Hindus. The conspirator knows that. You have to manage the mob and you have to manage the monument, and your best bet is to keep the two separate, that is, prevent a horde from descending on the monument.'

From behind his thick glasses he contemplated the policeman who sat like a leopard ready to spring.

'There was a reason I picked you. You are dogged, you don't give up, you follow every lead. And I am telling you the Kriplani lead is a dud.' With that he snipped the palm frond.

'Find the behrupiya, Singh, or we will end up paying a price we just can't afford.'

Delhi

The sky was darkening when R.P. Singh stepped out. After he spoke with the home minister, he had spent time with the PA who was arranging additional troops at the Taj Mahal. Then he called SSP Raghav and briefed him on the new security arrangements.

Outside the North Block Central Secretariat he checked his watch and saw with surprise that it was 4.30 p.m., and time for the bureaucracy to head home. Except, he glanced back in the direction of the office he had just left, the home ministry that was headed by a workaholic.

R.P. Singh proceeded to the Central Government Forensics Science Laboratory. Stalled at a traffic signal, he drummed the steering wheel with his right hand and squeezed a tennis ball with his left. What had started as a way to build strength in his wrists and hands had become a tool that he turned to when he needed to think or de-stress.

A natural right-hander, he could shoot equally well with his left hand. His training had started early, with his father, a general of the Army, who believed a shooting range was where a boy should spend a healthy amount of time. His mantra: defence is the best offence. The general would know, he was a war hero. But a hero can be his own worst enemy.

R.P. Singh felt the familiar bitterness wash his insides. But over the years he had developed the discipline to deal with it. He mentally closed the floodgates, stroked his bald head and turned clinically to the problem at hand.

Now, he worked the kernel of a thought that was niggling him: behrupiya.

The minister had used a word that very appropriately mirrored his own feelings about the case. A behrupiya was an expert at disguise and impersonation. And this case was laden with characters noteworthy for their duality: a Western-educated scholar researching Mughal art; a contrarian director in charge of India's monuments; a wealthy Hindu refugee running an orphanage for Muslim orphans; a Jat in charge of a monument his forefathers had ransacked.... Arun Toor's murder had started this off, and yet, investigations by SSP Raghav indicated it was not a case of personal enmity. In which case, the murder was tied to his professional capacity, a supposition supported by the increasingly sinister occurrences around the Taj Mahal.

Suddenly a pile of magazines was thrust in front of his face through the narrow gap where the window was down.

From behind his aviators he saw a malnourished boy, his thinness apparent despite his oversized sweater. He rolled down the window, pushed the magazines away, grasped the boy's hand in which he deposited a fifty-rupee note with a command, 'Go, have some anda-bhurji and milk!'

The signal changed, he pushed hard on the accelerator leaving a perplexed boy and exhaust in his wake.

His mind returned to his earlier train of thought. In the gathering of contrarians, Kriplani seemed straitlaced, a fundamentalist, plain and simple. A man infamous for his communal rhetoric and one of the founding fathers of a right-wing Hindu party.

Was the home minister correct in striking Kriplani off the suspects list? And was the behrupiya amongst the cast of known characters, or was there someone else, who had not yet revealed his face and was waiting to make a dramatic entrance....

Delhi

Mehrunisa fed Professor Kaul porridge, dabbing his listless mouth every now and then. It killed her, witnessing the ruination of a brilliant mind—on most days the professor was incapable of the simplest task. She looked past the dining table to the patio where the constable was sitting.

Apparently on guard duty, he had developed a daily routine of idling on the patio, walking down the lane to chat with the neighbours' domestic help or pressing Mangat Ram for a continuous supply of tea. And Mehrunisa had caught him eyeing her when he thought she wasn't watching.

She would talk to R.P. Singh and get rid of the nuisance. In any case, she was more capable than him when it came to defending herself. She had picked up the fitness regimen that she had neglected since her return to India: the aerobics video had been retrieved and the dumbbells dusted.

The constable heaved himself out of the chair and tugged his belt over his belly. With a shake of her head,

Mehrunisa returned to the cereal bowl. As she fed the professor she noticed several grey hairs had sprung on his ears—he probably trimmed them for she hadn't noticed them before. Mehrunisa made a mental note to add that to his grooming requirements, tasks she shared with Mangat Ram.

Most days Mehrunisa could cry at her tragic-comic situation. Instead, she looked for ways to distract herself.

Refusing to sigh, she scanned the newspaper headlines. A report caught her eye: 'New nuisance at the Taj Mahal'.

Her heart skipped a beat. She read it hurriedly.

Apparently monkeys were proving a big menace at the monument: shrieking at tourists, dislodging clay flowerpots, snatching food items from unsuspecting visitors.... In her visits to the Taj complex she had always encountered them, and as precaution, she never carried any food item.

Perhaps, she mused, there was a way to train these monkeys to guard the Taj against miscreants—a vanar sena, like the monkey army of Lord Hanuman in the *Ramayana*, for the Taj Mahal!

Agra

By the evening of January 25, two supplementary police units had arrived to beef up security in the outer Yellow zone of the Taj Mahal. A hundred additional armed policemen of the Provincial Armed Constabulary were deployed at various strategic points in the outer periphery of the complex. Sandbag bunkers, manned by police personnel with automatic weapons, were set up beside the outer entry gates.

On orders of the home minister, the air space over the Taj Mahal was to be sanitised until the dawn of January 27. Security had been tightened at different airports, railway stations as well as bus stations all over Uttar Pradesh.

At the Taj Mahal, the carrying of bags inside the monument was already forbidden, and in the run-up to Republic Day, additional restrictions were imposed on carrying water bottles or any other liquids into the complex. As SSP Raghav oversaw the new security arrangements, R.P. Singh strolled on the plinth, hands clasped behind his back, the mist swirling at his ankles.

He chased the skeins of the case in his mind, wondering what he was missing. Despite the enhanced security, despite the round-the-clock vigil, despite the new measures, he knew he was missing something....

He looked up and watched the mist roll in from the Yamuna as it blurred the contours of the marble monument, rendering it hazy. A similar fog had blanketed his reasoning, he reprimanded himself.

Where the hell was the bloody behrupiya hidden?

Delhi

Shri Kriplani had finished drinking a glass of clear urine. It would be a good day—he felt it in his bowels. Just then a call from the home minister came through.

A CBI officer was baying to put the BHP leader in jail and I am barely managing to restrain him, the home minister said.

Rana Pratap Singh! Kriplani recalled the arrogant CBI officer, the memory of whom threatened to despoil his disposition.

The home minister was continuing in his calm voice as if he were discussing a sitar recital. *The policeman had a reputation for being apolitical and honest.*

Kriplani flushed, despite the cool weather and the healing power of the urine therapy. He knew what the home minister was doing—claiming to be his friend while holding a knife at his neck. It was what politicians did.

He had an answer for that stratagem: brazen it out.

He countered the allegation hotly: 'This CBI officer, what proof does he have?'

None, the minister assented, but that wouldn't stop him from hauling a suspect in for questioning and imagine if media were there to live broadcast it.

'Tell me Home Ministerji, why would you waste my time—and yours—with such speculation?'

Looks like I have offended you, Kriplaniji. I was merely— warning—you, as a friend.

Shri Kriplani did not miss the significant pause and emphasis that bookended 'warning'.

Meanwhile, the minister continued blandly, *I have some information to share regarding telecom licenses, that is—if— Kriplaniji, you are willing to cooperate....*

The biggest supporter of the BHP was a large Indian corporate that was looking to enter the expanding telecom industry. A hint was enough for a seasoned player: Kriplani snorted and grunted simultaneously.

He had always believed in keeping his fingers in several pies....

Agra

January 26 dawned in Agra, wet and cold, a thin drizzle adding to the problems of the security personnel but doing nothing to deter the large number of visitors who had descended upon the monument on a public holiday. The additional security precautions drew complaints as people discarded their bags and bottles at the gate and were frisked twice by policemen with dogs. The lengthening queue of visitors snaked out of the forecourt, the squelchy ground steadily littered with candy wrappers, paper, crushed kulhars, and fallen food as cigarette smoke mixed with vapours and hung in the air.

SSP Raghav, from his post beside the great gate, and R.P. Singh, from atop the marble plinth, watched the proceedings intently. Plainclothes policemen who mingled with the crowd were keeping a lookout for any miscreants and were in constant communication with the officers.

As the day progressed, the overcast sky cleared and Singh could have sworn he heard a collective gasp from the vast throng. He quickly spun on his heel to identify the source that had elicited that shock—the late noon sun had emerged from behind clouds to drape Taj Mahal in pale light. Abruptly the monument had changed colour, its white marble blushing in the lambent winter sun. Relieved, Singh allowed himself a slight smile.

And much like any regular day at the monument, as closing time approached, visitors departed, the stragglers were ushered out by security guards, entry gates were barred, and the Taj returned to its serene splendour. The only incidents that day had been a scuffle between two youths and a monkey scare as the animal snatched a camera straight out of the hands of a Japanese tourist.

R.P. Singh rotated his tense shoulders and had a word with Raghav who spoke with the officers—there was to be no let-up in their vigil until dawn. Then he called the home minister and briefed him: there was no untoward incident to report.

The absence of a security incident at Taj Mahal should have been good news to the CBI officer but he was too experienced to believe in fairy-tale endings. The mysterious case of the Taj conspiracy still remained unsolved, and with the nameless behrupiya still to be identified, the conspiracy was very much a work-in-progress.

Delhi

Mehrunisa descended the steps. They were narrow, uneven, hewn out of rock, with tufts of grass poking out of crevices. The stairwell wound steeply, seemingly forever. When she craned her neck downwards, she saw nothing; around her, high walls barred any view. She had been on the flight of steps forever, yet had reached nowhere. As she rounded the corner, she came face-to-face with a severed head leaking blood that dripped on her shirtfront. Black hair swept back from a high forehead, sideburns streaked with grey. Coal-black eyes. A strong aquiline nose. Salt and pepper stubble.

It was Papa.

She tried to scream, swivelled to return, but the steps had vanished, and she plunged into a dark cavern.

Mehrunisa jolted awake. The scream was stuck in her throat, her chest was heaving and perspiration dotted her forehead. Her quilt was on the floor. She glanced around her room. The nightlight cast a pale amber patch on the carpet revealing a reassuring floor.

A cold winter night and she was perspiring as if it were a blazing summer day in Delhi, when the mercury soared and even birds fainted from sunstroke. Pulling herself upright, she gently turned her neck to ease the pain.

She had a name for these serial torments: the beheadings. Evocative, but not entirely original, for the old masters, painters whose work she had studied and admired, had deployed Biblical themes for inspiration, and tales of decapitations were abundant in the Bible, whether of John the Baptist, Saint Catherine or Goliath.

In Mehrunisa's case, 'the beheadings' was an epithet for the trauma from the unexpected loss of her father. Since her mother had revealed on her deathbed that her father was a spy, the nightmare had frequented Mehrunisa, and with the approaching anniversary of her father's disappearance, presumed death, the beheadings gathered frequency. It was her subconscious acting out her guilt—Mehrunisa had enough acquaintance with Freud to know that she blamed herself for not preventing her father from disappearing. If she had loved him enough, he would have returned.

The fresh nightmare had left her with a parched throat. Shivering, she swung her legs out of bed. The sudden motion made her wobbly. Steadying herself with an outstretched hand, she breathed deeply. Finding the jug on her dresser empty, she headed for the kitchen.

A shaft of light from the professor's room fell on the hallway floor. As she passed it, she cast a cursory glance inside the room. The curtains on the window were half-drawn, just as she had left them. Light came from a tall floor lamp positioned in a corner so the shade, which dangled at the end like some bulbous fruit, pointed at the professor's footboard. This way, it lit the room without throwing the light into his eyes. As Mehrunisa moved her gaze to the spot where her uncle reclined, she froze.

A click sounded; faint, but audible.

Mehrunisa looked quickly around the room. Nothing. She unfroze enough to lunge inside, throwing herself on the professor's bed. With desperate hands, she went for his head. For once she regretted not having long fingernails as she frantically strove to rip the plastic apart. It was distended with carbon dioxide. She grabbed the glass on the bedside drawer, flung the water, smashed the glass against the corner and plunged the jagged edge into the plastic bag. It ruptured, discharging air with a whistle, and collapsed about the professor's neck where it was fastened in a tight knot. Mehrunisa clawed at the plastic, shredding it into strips.

Professor Kaul's eyes were open but glassy. His face had the pallor of a dead man. He was unconscious. Clutching both his shoulders, Mehrunisa shook him hard. 'Uncle! Kaul uncle!' she screamed hysterically.

Getting no response, she flung his quilt away, then the pillows. She climbed the bed and holding the professor's legs, she dragged him flat and tilted his head back, his chin pointing up. Placing one hand under his head she lifted it gently. With the other she pushed his forehead down. Noiselessly, Mehrunisa listened. The tongue should have moved to open the airway. She brought her left cheek and ear close to his mouth and nose. No. She could feel no air!

The professor's chest was still. Mehrunisa opened his mouth and probed for any foreign matter inside. None. Maintaining the head's backward tilt, she pinched the professor's nose, inhaled deeply and sealing her mouth around his, blew four quick but full breaths as fast as she could.

She watched his chest for movement.

None.

Mehrunisa repositioned his head and tried again. This time she changed her rate to one breath every five seconds. After a minute or so, an exhausted Mehrunisa sat back. The professor lay supine in front of her. Tears filled her eyes. As she cradled his head, a faint sound reached her.

Mehrunisa bent to catch it. Yes, air was passing through the professor's nose. Drawing back she saw his chest move gradually. The dam within her burst.

Mehrunisa clung to her uncle, tears streaming down her cheeks into his woollen sweater, her torso shaking with emotion. The next instant rough callused hands were caressing her head, stroking her straight black hair away from her face. Mehrunisa looked up to see a forlorn Mangat Ram stooping beside her.

In a hoarse voice she said, 'Call the doctor. Tell him it's an emergency!'

Delhi

Mehrunisa was chilled to the bone. No heater, no quilt, no layers would help. Just that morning Mangat Ram had brought rather disquieting news. As he fetched milk from the Mother Dairy booth at the lane's end, he bumped into the night watchman who enquired about the midnight arrival of an ambulance at the professor's door.

When Mangat Ram assured him the professor was fine, just a minor attack, and made to leave, the watchman held him back. Placing a hand on his shoulder, he revealed that the previous night, as he was doing his rounds, he had seen a man coming out of the professor's house. As the man unhurriedly clicked the latch back on the gate, the night watchman hailed him. But the stranger refused to look, only pulling his cap more securely around his face, before he sped off on a motorcycle. He was wearing a coarse brown overcoat and a monkey cap.

If her nightmare had not roused her, her godfather would be dead. Monkey-cap expected the enfeebled professor to die soundlessly and had been brazen enough to walk into the house. The guard that R.P. Singh had deployed was bundled under his quilt on the cot in the patio, struck unconscious by chloroform.

Mehrunisa had learnt the basics of mouth-to-mouth resuscitation at a Girl Scout camp one summer. Only once before had she needed to perform it: when an elderly tourist had collapsed in the Florentine heat. The doctor had said a delay of minutes would have proved fatal for Professor Kaul.

An enraged Mehrunisa stood in the patio, fists clenched by her side. Once she had possessed a terrible temper. Papa said she inherited it from Maadar's cousin Uncle Massoud, the eccentric artist who splashed paint on his work or hurled paint cans at hapless servants when unhappy.

'You have to be strategic with your anger, Mehr,' he would counsel, 'channelise it into something useful.'

Mehrunisa struggled with that advice until the day her father disappeared. When all her angry fulminating did not bring Papa back, she had pushed the aggression deep inside and sealed it with a glacial mask. Now it was set to explode.

She had spent the day watching over her uncle in his hospital room. Mangat Ram had taken the night shift and she, back at home, was too beat to sleep.

Abruptly, Mehrunisa started to pace the patio, arms tight like a robot's. She wanted to climb a mountain, start the arduous journey from the foot to the rounded peaks, clamber over grassy hills, scale treeless ridges, trudge, trudge, trudge upwards until her breath was ragged....

In a corner, Mangat Ram's rickety bicycle reclined against the wall. She lunged towards it.

Pre-dawn mist floated in the quiet garden. Mehrunisa cut through it as the pedals spun furiously, tyres crunched the dewy grass, and the old cycle creaked alarmingly.

In her mind's eye she saw Maadar, forlorn at Tehran airport, Papa, kissing her on the forehead before departing for Syria, Kaul uncle, deathly still on his bed....

Round and round she went, new tyre treads smudging the earlier ones until the lawn was marked by a swathe of flattened grass and she was drenched in mist, sweat and tears.

Agra

Inspector Bharadwaj of the CISF strode down the central walkway of the Taj Mahal. He had just returned from dinner in the Taj Khema area and was reporting for night duty.

In the Taj Khema area was also located the office of the police constable who manned the CCTV cameras. There were eight such cameras that monitored the traffic approaching the monument and it was Karam Singh's duty to look out for suspicious vehicles and alert security. After his meal Bharadwaj had bought some paan and stopped by to chat.

As he took the offered paan, Karam Singh lamented that only one camera was functioning. The other seven had been rendered useless because squirrels had chewed the wiring. He had put in a written complaint but the matter was yet to be rectified.

Bharadwaj commiserated with the constable, clucked his tongue about delays, spat red juice in one corner and said he would make sure to convey his grievance.

Now, he surveyed the Taj complex with a smug smile. Within the monument, in the Red zone, all was well. Unlike the security outside in the Yellow zone, because, unknown to Karam Singh, his complaint had never reached the requisite authority. Between the CISF, the state police and the Provincial Armed Constabulary, there was enough red tape to ensnare such alerts. Not to count the Vibhishana in their midst.

Bharadwaj squirted a jet of orange juice into the shrubbery. Like the legendary traitor who brought down Lanka by revealing its secret, Bharadwaj would watch the marble monument get destroyed as he operated from within it.

Delhi

R.P. Singh and Mehrunisa crouched next to the hedge bordering Raj Bhushan's garden. The CBI officer was livid at the monkey-capped assassin's third murder attempt, this time on the enfeebled professor. Meanwhile, Mehrunisa, suspicious of the ASI director since the attack had come close on the heels of her accusation, wanted to scour his house for evidence of guilt. R.P. Singh didn't see the historian in a cabal of criminals with Monkey-cap, but all were suspects until he found his behrupiya.

Raj Bhushan was a bachelor with no full-time staff, and he was travelling overnight; his house was bound to be vacant, Mehrunisa had reasoned. It was a government bungalow, one in a row of similar white-washed erstwhile colonial barracks converted to provide housing in a capital city teeming with officials. Mehrunisa was familiar with such houses—at one time Professor Kaul had stayed in one—and knew that their decrepit state could be counted on to ensure that a window or a door or a door-plank somewhere would be loose enough to give.

Dressed in a midnight-blue tracksuit, hair secured in a ponytail, she approached a row of windows at the rear while R.P. Singh kept a lookout. Glass panes, no grilles—which was a relief—and a mosquito netting. She ran her right hand against the wooden window frame, her fingers seeking a vulnerable spot. On the third casement she felt a lower corner that jutted out.

Torch in mouth, she clasped it with both hands and tugged. The wood was swollen, which accounted for the protuberant part, and the casement had probably been jammed in. She tugged, pried, heaved, her fingers bruising, until she felt it give. A quick glance back at R.P. Singh who motioned all-clear.

The casement yielded stiffly. A mosquito mesh covered the window frame. She tugged at the bottom and the net peeled off.

Once she had clambered inside, R.P. Singh followed. They found themselves in a living room. As they waited for their eyes to get used to the darkness they observed the sparse furnishings: some wicker chairs, an ikat-patterned durrie against one wall, a bronze Nataraja.

The room's glory was the centrepiece: a glass-topped table. It stood out amidst the modest furnishings by its sheer size. It was also a curious shape ... Mehrunisa shone her light on it as she advanced softly. Yes. The glass was placed on an elaborately carved wooden door, the kind popular with havelis. The base consisted of a large black iron trunk. As she circled the table, Mehrunisa breathed in sharply.

'What is it?' R.P. Singh hissed from where he was examining a TV cabinet.

She beckoned him over. 'Unless there are two identical pieces, I saw this table last in Arun Toor's residence!'

'Are you sure?'

She nodded.

She had shared a couple of meals with Arun, one in his home as they worked over lunch. The beauty of the wooden door and its incongruous use as a centre table had surprised Mehrunisa. She had attributed it to Arun's eclectic style. Yes, there could be no mistaking the piece.

'Why would the ASI director-general remove Arun's table and place it in his home?' R.P. Singh asked. 'Kleptomaniac?' he grinned and bent towards Mehrunisa who was on her knees examining the table.

A *rat-tat-tat* crashed the stillness.

R.P. Singh dived, taking Mehrunisa with him. He lifted his head a few inches and scanned the room for a clue to the sound. Had the owner returned? Was there somebody in the house? Momentarily, he was distracted by Mehrunisa's heart throbbing beneath his forearm and the scent of mint in her hair.

A shadow fell across the rear windows.

Someone was prowling, tapping a thick staff against the windows, rattling them as he went. He had made sure to shut the window behind him. As the shadow disappeared from view, the rattling turned to a rhythmic tapping on the ground. It was the night watchman on his round, indulging in a routine inspection meant to deter intruders such as them.

He released air from his chest and relaxed.

As his hold loosened, Mehrunisa wriggled out rubbing her upper arm.

'Sorry,' Singh said, realising he had clutched her arm.

Mehrunisa waved it off with her hand, which struck the trunk and touched a cold lock.

She turned the torchlight on the trunk: it was a large modern brass lock.

They looked at each other, brows raised.

'Odd, hanh?' Singh grunted.

'For a man with Raj Bhushan's taste, it is out of character with the ornate table,' Mehrunisa added.

R.P. Singh fingered the heavy lock. 'It's clearly not an ornamental piece, it was meant to secure the contents. Question is—'

'What is in the trunk?' Mehrunisa finished

'Got a hairpin?'

Mehrunisa removed a barrette from her hair. R.P. Singh snapped off the clip where the ridged side turned into a U. Sticking the broken end into the lock, he twisted it one way, tugged at the lock, twisted it another way, tugged again. Outside, the wind must have picked up, for the house had begun to sigh like an old woman.

Several gyrations later, the wedge separated from the notch and the lock lay limp. He removed it and assessed the heavy glass top and the door that would need to be eased off before they could open the trunk. On their haunches, they began to push the thick glass.

It took a few minutes of shoving and sliding before they eased the glass and the door to the ground. As Mehrunisa sat back, breathing heavily, R.P. Singh lifted the lid of the trunk. A warm musty odour assailed them before R.P. Singh swore, turned his face away and banged the lid down again.

'What?' Mehrunisa demanded, scrambling forward.

Singh laid a hand on her shoulder, his eyes concerned.

'I have to see it, dammit!'

He gave a slight nod.

The contents hit her like a fist smashed into her belly. On a gasp Mehrunisa let the lid clatter back as she clutched her stomach and staggered. Nothing in the world could have prepared her for what she had just seen.

Inside the wooden trunk in the director-general's living room, like some pièce de résistance, was the perfectly preserved body of a woman!

R.P. Singh grabbed Mehrunisa by the shoulders and helped her into an armchair. Then he opened the trunk again. Beside the body was a notebook. He picked it up and flicked it open.

The stiff leaves were pasted with typewritten pages.

Delhi

Confessions of a nefarious mind. That's what the notebook sitting on the dresser in Mehrunisa's room could be titled. Partially filled, it had kept her up all night.

Standing at the window of her room, Mehrunisa watched Mangat Ram water a flower bed. The day had kept the previous night's promise, dawning bright and clear. The lush red lilies and plump white chrysanthemums against a backdrop of verdant green were beautiful, and Mehrunisa was happy to simply look at them. She needed the respite. It was February; an entire month of the new year had flown by, and she had barely registered it. Lately her life was like the weather: bleak and foggy. Was the bright day signalling a change in weather as well as her life?

Mehrunisa glanced at the diary, loath to touch it again. Inside its covers was evil, typed and pasted on the pages—the Devil had made sure not to reveal his handwriting.

The diarist was so fixated on his mother, he had killed a father competing for her affection, and upon his mother's death preserved for himself her dead body. One facet of the writer's identity was his Jat pride. Raj Bhushan was not a Jat. If Raj Bhushan had appropriated the coffee table, as she was convinced, then it rightfully belonged to Arun Toor. And Arun Toor was a Jat. He had once joked to Mehrunisa about the ransacking of the Taj Mahal in 1761 by the Jats of Bharatpur. Under their leader Suraj Mal, they had carried away the silver doors of the mausoleum that they contemplated converting into a Hindu temple. The irony, Arun had stated wryly, was that a modern-day Jat, himself, was the caretaker of the same Taj.

The occurrences thus far revealed a conspiracy to invalidate the Taj Mahal's Muslim origin, and now, Mehrunisa had unearthed what could be a critical link in the chain of events. She stacked the facts in their right order:

Arun Toor was the Taj supervisor.

Arun Toor was a Jat.

A Jat leader had once broached the idea of converting the Taj to a Hindu temple.

The Taj conspiracy was centred on disputing the monument's Muslim origin.

Arun Toor was murdered in the Taj.

No, no, no. It did not add up. If a conspiracy was afoot to discredit the Taj, and Arun was involved with it, why was *he* killed? And by whom?

But Mehrunisa was implicating Arun in the conspiracy because he was a Jat—what if that was just a coincidence? In which case the focus shifted to Raj Bhushan, in whose house the diary had been found. But Raj Bhushan was not a Jat, so the dairy couldn't be his. What about the body? Had he stolen the coffee table from Arun's house— after his demise—to conceal the body? Which begged the question: where had he hidden the body all along? R.P. Singh had said he'd ask for a DNA test on the woman's body but with scarce resources at Forensics, a DNA test on the corpse recovered from the python was first priority.

Mehrunisa looked at the clear blue sky and hoped for illumination. The one thing she knew for sure was the diarist was a psychopath. The question to be answered was: *who* was the psychopath—Raj Bhushan or Arun Toor.

Mangat Ram barged in. 'Sahib, he—he spoke—he asked for you—he—'

Mehrunisa started towards the professor's room and the housekeeper fell in step. He recounted that he had been dusting Professor Kaul's room when he felt his eyes on him. When he picked up the photo frame on the sideboard, the professor motioned for it. He stared at the picture and then started talking to it! When Mangat Ram tried to talk to the professor, he asked for her.

'"Mehr, Mehr", he said, repeatedly.' The disconsolate housekeeper watched from the doorway as Mehrunisa entered.

Professor Kaul was still holding the photo and in the midst of some narrative. Mehrunisa pulled a chair close to his bed and rested her head in his lap. In turn, he placed his palm over her hair. She could feel his hand, skeletal, brittle, as it lay on her head, making no attempt to pat her as he continued talking. He seemed to be repeating the same story. She sat up, removed the picture gently, and took both his hands in hers and listened intently.

Inder and his wife Indu were god-fearing. Once Indu's brother Sunder visited them. All three went to Goddess Durga's temple. First Sunder entered the temple. On seeing the idol of Durga, he was so overcome by devotion that he decided to sacrifice himself. Subsequently, he cut his head off in front of the idol. Then Inder entered the temple and saw his brother-in-law's dead body. Gripped by a sense of self-sacrifice, he too cut his head off. Finally, Indu entered the temple and saw the two dead bodies. Overcome by grief, she wept loudly and prayed to the goddess Durga to give her the same husband and brother in her next life. As Indu prepared to give up her life, Durga appeared. She said she was pleased with their devotion and would bring the two men back to life. Then she asked Indu to join the two heads to the respective bodies. When Durga put life into the bodies, Indu realised she had mixed up the heads. Now, Inder's body had her brother's head and her brother Sunder had Inder's head!

So, who would be Indu's real husband now?

Professor Kaul turned to look at her. For an instant Mehrunisa thought she saw a sign of recognition in those tired eyes. Whatever it was, it vanished in an instant. However, the professor's voice acquired urgency as he frantically repeated his query.

So, who would be Indu's real husband now?

Mehrunisa shook her head. She wanted so much to jolt her uncle awake, so he would stop treating her like a twelve-year-old and talk to her. But the professor persisted. In a strange high-pitched voice, he kept repeating the question.

To quieten him she said, 'The head is the body's most important part since that's where all thoughts and memories reside. The man with the husband's head had all the memories of Indu as a wife. So he was her real husband.'

As she finished, Professor Kaul went quiet. She continued to speak with him, attempting to locate the trigger that had set him on the narrative, but he had once again retreated into the shadows of his mind.

As she took the photograph back to the sideboard, she studied it, wondering what about it had set off the story. A group of men stood in front of the Taj Mahal: Professor Kaul, Arun Toor, Raj Bhushan, and a couple of assistants. The professor stood in the middle, flanked by Toor and Bhushan with the assistants standing deferentially apart. Arun Toor, clean shaven for a change, was dressed in his habitually creased kurta, baggy trousers, slip-on sandals; Raj Bhushan, on the other side, was dapper in his neat boxed beard, tailored trousers, brogues, and Nehru-collared shirt.

As she replaced the photograph, she wondered why her uncle had chosen to tell that particular story. What was it R.P. Singh had said about the previous story her godfather had told her? That the crux of it was the escape ... Mehrunisa stopped in her tracks. Both stories were about the *impression* of death, when not dead.

Agra

It was midnight at Taj Ganj police station. SSP Raghav and R.P. Singh sat discussing the DNA result that had come in two hours back. A half-empty bottle of Old Monk, a partially-depleted plate of oily samosas, and a radio humming in the background gave the impression that the cops were letting their hair down.

The next instant R.P. Singh hurled a tennis ball at the opposite wall as he snarled, 'He's making a chutiya of us!'

Singh collected the ball on rebound, got up from the chair and said, 'Let's go over it again.'

SSP Raghav worked the ends of his luxuriant moustache and started. 'We matched Arun Toor's DNA, sourced from personal articles at home, to the DNA of the torso recovered from the python's belly. And it didn't match. However, it did match the DNA sample taken from the pink kurta. Which means, someone was poisoned, as the post-mortem has shown, dressed in Arun Toor's kurta, and then fed to a snake!'

R.P. Singh paced the floor, juggling the ball in his hands. 'This person approximated the Taj supervisor in height and build. But the relevant specs are those of an average Indian male,' he shrugged. 'It would be easy for Toor to lose himself in a crowd.'

Singh's study of the notebook recovered from the trunk in Raj Bhushan's house had revealed a psychopath with twin obsessions: his mother and his Jat heritage. He walked to a board that had seen some furious scribbling and turned to a new sheet. On it he wrote two words—Mother, Jat—and eyed Raghav.

'Arun Toor was a Jat, Raj Bhushan is not.'

'But Mehrunisa is certain she saw the very same trunk in Toor's house. So, what is Toor-the-Jat's trunk doing in the house of his boss?'

R.P. Singh had tried to contact Raj Bhushan, but the office had informed him that the director-general was on tour in southern India for a few days and he wasn't picking up his cell phone.

Singh paused to refill the glasses with rum. 'Consider the possibility,' he said, his eyes glittering, 'this case started with a murder, yet the murdered man might be alive.'

'And laughing at us all this while! Watching us run in circles as he hides—' Raghav swore, dragging Toor's grandmother into the melee of curses.

'Hiding where, hiding where?' R.P. Singh had resumed his perambulation. He had been asking that question every single day since Republic Day, a fortnight back. Meanwhile, the additional security at Taj Mahal had been lifted since he could find no further justification for extra security.

Singh grabbed a samosa and chomped on it as he walked about, the peas popping to the floor. The radio was playing a peppy Bollywood number, its notes pulsing through the stale air.

'Boss,' Raghav called, his voice slurring from the rum, 'you realise we have a growing list of behrupiyas?' He held up his fingers as he counted. 'One: Kriplani. Two: Raj Bhushan. Three: Arun Toor.'

Singh nodded his head in assent. The home minister might have let Kriplani off, but he would follow every lead until he nailed the behrupiya. Then he chortled loudly. 'The third behrupiya is technically dead!' It turned into a snigger as he realised how ridiculous it sounded.

Raghav had started to sputter too, as he shook his head. When he couldn't stop his head from shaking he realised dimly that he was drunk.

'Boss!' he hollered. 'I think we are drunk. We should have a samosa each.' He wobbled around the table and grabbed two samosas. 'Some food helps reduce the a-aceta-acetal-de-hyde—got it!—in the stomach.'

'You are the one who's drunk!' Singh protested as he demonstrated a straight walk.

It was as straight as the jagged skyline of Taj Ganj.

He noticed the bloodshot eyes of his colleague, paused, and stood akimbo. In Chhattisgarh there was a swathe of forest that the locals called 'unknown jungle'. It was so impenetrable that even the government had not mapped it yet. During an operation a constable was kidnapped by the Maoists and secreted into the jungle. When he was released the Maoists sent a message on his person: every inch of his body was slashed with knives. The deep scars were meant to constantly remind the police not to venture into the unknown.

Since the murder in the mausoleum, the SSP had pursued the case with the zeal of one who had everything to lose. What scars was he carrying?

'Tell me, SSP, why are you losing sleep over the Taj conspiracy?'

Raghav looked up, suddenly alert, as if someone had shone a torch on his face. His mouth twisted bitterly. 'Remember Babri Masjid? I was on police duty when it was ravaged in front of my eyes—my orders were not to intervene. Never,' he shook his head vehemently, 'never before had I felt that helpless in life. Bas, after that I pledged to follow the path of right, regardless.'

On that he downed his glass of rum. In his mind's eye Raghav saw a frenzied mob tearing at the pristine marble of the Taj Mahal; gouging out the lapis lazuli, agate and jasper; stabbing the Quranic inscriptions; hammering the cenotaphs. Marble dust clouded the air, sandstone splinters flew into the sky, shards of red, green, blue scattered like confetti.... Was that the fate of the monument of love in an age of hate?

Angrily, he said, 'All it takes is a few mad men, the destruction of Babri Masjid has shown that.'

Singh nodded his head, his mouth pursed. He wasn't the only one who felt this case of the Taj conspiracy alluded to the infamous Barbri demolition. The grim thought promptly sucked fumes of tipple out of his head.

Wiping his mouth Raghav asked Singh, 'What made you such a dusht?'

'A proper devil, hunh...' R.P. Singh drawled and patted his bald pate. 'See this? I shaved my head on my father's death. After which I decided not to grow hair.'

Raghav was leaning on the table, face in his hand as he listened with interest.

'My father, General Jai Singh Sisodia, was a decorated war hero. The '71 war. Then he was sidelined in the Army because he resisted the corruption he saw around him. He died a disillusioned man. And I vowed to myself that I would race right to the top of my career, whatever it takes. You see,' Singh rested his palms on the table, 'the general could fight the enemy across the border but how do you fight the enemy within—the corrupt politician and the self-serving bureaucrat? The home minister and director special ops want the conspirator. But they don't want to go down the warrens that lead to such moles. So they call in pest control.'

He snorted. 'Me.'

'The general's mistake was that he saw only one kind of pest. But a pest control man must fight rodents and roaches and raccoons.' He paused. 'He must be able to get into the heads of all his pests.'

He pulled back, walked around the room with long deliberate strides before he pulled a chair and straddled it.

'Three things are clear: faking the murder of the Taj supervisor was pre-planned. A substitute—someone with close physical resemblance—was identified in advance. And the corpse was stolen from the morgue to prevent a post-mortem that would lead to identification. The death of the python,' he said, his eyes flashing, 'was very lucky for us.'

Raghav nodded. 'In the elaborate dance of deception, the puppeteer tripped up. In an otherwise perfect execution, he made one bad move.'

'This pest,' R.P. Singh banged the table with his fist, 'I've tunnelled inside his head. And no Aurangzeb-behrupiya-chutiya is going to escape me!'

'We'll get him, boss.'

The two men clinked their glasses, rum sloshed, and as the radio blasted a raucous drumbeat, they joined in, belting out the lyrics with off-tune fervour.

Agra

Pre-dawn fog shrouded the Taj Mahal complex. Everything lay quiet, cold and still. Only a continuous lapping of water sounded. A boat came into view, packed with a mass of huddled people. Another boat glided behind, and another ... the column of boats was long as it paddled up the Yamuna river towards the Taj Mahal.

The first boat stopped short of Dassehra Ghat, near the ruins of an old haveli, erstwhile tannery, now abandoned. The dilapidated haveli of Agah Khan fell within the Red zone under the purview of the CISF, and Inspector Bharadwaj had co-opted this, the residence of Shah Jahan's officer in charge of riverine security, to launch an assault on the monument. Men disembarked and ascended the slope, a man in the shadows briskly herding them into the ruins. Other boat people followed. Some looked ghostly, blending into the prevailing mist with their ash-smeared bodies.

Inside the ruins were arrayed the creature comforts of bedding, water and provisions. The youth of Taj Ganj, all with saffron headbands and fiery eyes, doled out food and blankets to the Shiva devotees who had paddled through the night from Bateshwar to witness the predicted Shiva miracle. Their instructions were not to let these men venture out of the ruins until the time was right. Meanwhile, the bhang and exhaustion would knock them out for several hours.

From his corner in the shadows Inspector Bharadwaj watched the proceedings, a thin smile on his sallow face—all was going to plan.

Delhi

The contents of the mysterious diary had spun her mind like a roulette wheel all day long and she'd slept fitfully as a result. Next morning, brain dead, she opened a book for some relief. *The Vatican Masterpieces* transported her to more idyllic days.

Upon completing her Renaissance studies, Mehrunisa had figured the best way to continue her education was to see the great Florentine and Roman museums on a daily basis. Since museum fees were expensive, and one needed a job to sustain a bare minimum lifestyle, Mehrunisa had done the next logical thing: signed up as a guide with an agency that provided Vatican tours. Thereafter, she spent two years shepherding eager tourists through the capacious museums brimming with treasures.

Her favourite galleries were the Sistine chapel and Raphael's Stanze. While the Sistine threatened to give her goitre—much as it did Michelangelo with the constant upward posture of his head and neck while painting the ceiling—the latter was easier on the body. It had been time well spent.

Now, whenever she felt the need to break away from the immediate world, she would open one of her art history books and lose herself in the lavish illustrations of either the Sistine or the Stanze. It was working, for the fresco of *The School of Athens* had drawn her in.

Of all the frescoes that decorate the walls of Raphael's Stanze in the Vatican museums, this, *The School of Athens*, was probably the most famous and most reproduced, as Mehrunisa had informed many Vatican tourists during her stint as a guide. Now, Mehrunisa studied the beautiful fresco in which young Raphael had painted a veritable who's who of Greek greats, accompanied by some Renaissance luminaries: the philosophers Socrates and Diogenes, the mathematicians Pythagoras and Euclid, and in a prominent place, the reflective figure of Michelangelo.

The two most influential philosophers of ancient Greece stood in the centre: Plato and Aristotle. With his right finger, Plato pointed to the sky. On the right stood Aristotle, Plato's pupil, his open right hand indicating the Earth. Thus had Raphael depicted the two thinkers and their different approaches to life: Plato's idealism alongside Aristotle's realism.

Mehrunisa studied the bearded Plato—his face, so historians said—resembling that of another Renaissance great, Leonardo da Vinci. Raphael had met him in Florence in 1504 and the encounter had left such an impression on the twenty-one-year-old that subsequently he abandoned the manner of his master, and moved closer to that of Leonardo. The portrait was the artist's homage to his ideal. And indeed, Plato looked like Leonardo of the self-portrait painted by the artist himself—the flowing beard, the balding scalp, the intent gaze.

In the fresco's right-hand corner, as was customary, Raphael had painted himself. Wearing a black cap, he looked at Mehrunisa with a soulful gaze. Almost all the other figures in the fresco—certainly all the artists—sported a beard; Raphael was the only clean-shaven one. And it seemed to Mehrunisa that if the beard of Leonardo, in the representation of Plato, were transposed to Raphael's face, the two would look quite similar. It had struck her before that while Raphael had painted Plato in the image of Leonardo, he had also painted him in his own self-image. Implying thereby that perhaps, young though he was, he was already claiming to be in the league of Leonardo.

Once again, Mehrunisa scrutinised the two faces, transplanting the beard from one to another. And, from somewhere, Pamposh's teasing statement when R.P. Singh had landed at her doorstep popped in her head: *the fun is in figuring what the fuzz conceals*.

One hand massaging the back of her neck, Mehrunisa glanced at her uncle. He had been asleep for the hour or so since she had been absorbed in her study. She sighed and looked away, her gaze trailing to the sideboard and the plastic tray on which were arrayed the multiple medicine bottles that were her uncle's daily diet. Her eyes skimmed the familiar contents: the professor's stack of books—neat, since he had not picked up any since his illness—the spare spectacle case, the round moneyplant vase, the group photo in front of the Taj...

The next instant Mehrunisa shot like a rocket from her chair and ran to grab the photograph. Her eyes bored into the picture, her mind transplanting the boxed beard from

Raj Bhushan's face to Arun Toor's clean-shaven face. It struck her then, with force!

The two men, the ASI director-general and the Taj supervisor, were of similar height and build. She was such a fool! The evidence had always been on the sideboard! The bell should have rung with her godfather's mythological stories of *apparent* deaths. His warning to watch out for Aurangzeb! The attack on the professor right after she accused Raj Bhushan in his office and mentioned that he had mentioned Aurangzeb. Mangat Ram's puzzlement over Raj Bhushan's sudden desire for walnuts. The frequent use of fresh mints to mask his smoker's breath. The strangely yellowing fingers of a non-smoking director. The occasional lapses into vulgar jokes by an otherwise suave director. Her own feeling that Raj Bhushan, whom she had never met before, seemed somehow familiar....

Oh! What a blind bat she had been! The swirling picture resolved into a face—one that she was familiar with. And one of his remarks recurred to her, delivered in that cocky, half-mocking voice.

The genius in the underprivileged world does not innovate; he transgresses.

Immediately she called R.P. Singh.

'An impersonation!' Singh exclaimed. 'Fits right fucking in.'

'Yes! And I think *he* left those clues in the tomb chamber along with Raj Bhushan's body.'

'Toor? But why would he do that?'

'I think he wanted us to assume there was a terrorist hand behind the murder—after all, the Taj Mahal has received several threats over the years—and hoped the clues would further deceive us. And they did, for a while. We thought the third eye on the forehead meant a calamity, that "chirag tale andhera" indicated a bomb, and the slit wrist that the Taj Mahal would be desecrated. That's probably why he told me on the phone that an Aurangzeb was coming to visit him. He guessed we would think Aurangzeb was a jihadi. Also,' her mouth twisted, 'it was a private joke, an allusion to Raj Bhushan whom he was planning to kill and replace. He thought while we wasted time following up the terrorist angle, he would have time to pursue his plan to reclaim the Taj Mahal as a Shiva temple.'

R.P. Singh shook his head, taking in what she was saying. 'He must have panicked when you stumbled on the altered calligraphy—it threw his plan off track.'

'Right! He played it down because it might have led us to discovering his actual plan.' Mehrunisa gave a bitter laugh and continued, 'The thing is, in his trademark warped way, those clues *also* revealed his actual plan. He was toying with us, testing whether we were clever enough to get his actual intent, and laughing while we scurried around trying to unravel the damned clues!'

'What do you mean?'

'Well, take the third eye—it was an allusion to the Shiva temple. Slit wrist? The penalty for theft under Sharia law is severing of the hand. Since the Mughals appropriated Tejo Mahalaya as Taj Mahal, in the spirit of Sharia—an eye for an eye, a hand for a hand—it would be rightfully stolen back and reclaimed as a Shiva temple.'

'And chirag tale andhera,' Singh said, 'is to do with a basement—as we'd deduced.'

'Yes,' Mehrunisa nodded, 'and the changed calligraphy. The alteration indicated two things: one, Mumtaz's tomb was counterfeit; two, something was concealed. I think it alludes to the sealed rooms in the riverside terrace.

There've always been rumours that proof of the Taj being a Hindu temple lies there. I think he's probably been smuggling in things that will make it look like an ancient temple.'

'That's why he killed Raj Bhushan, so he could have the run of the place.'

'Yes. As supervisor, he oversaw the change in calligraphy, which was accomplished in a couple of hours. But to change the basement rooms he needed time, and the certainty that he wouldn't be caught. Raj Bhushan was in the habit of dropping in unannounced, which was why he had to go.'

'Tell me, why didn't he mention the calligraphic change in the pamphlet?'

Mehrunisa snorted. 'That was very clever of him. All his points were allegations. Allegations that are scandalous and lend themselves to reinvention and rumour. Which is why the guides lapped them up—the allegations added to their existing store of myths and stories around the monument. But he had actually implemented the calligraphic change. If the police were to read about the change in the pamphlet, that would force his hand. The police would insist an ASI person verify the calligraphic change. It was in his best interest to let the change in calligraphy build through rumours.'

'Until?'

'Until what?' Mehrunisa asked, perplexed.

'Until now. Don't you see ... now is the time he'll reveal the changes; now is when he's planning the takeover.'

'How?'

'Beats me. But when I lay my hands on this supervisor Toor in director-general disguise, he'll spit it out. One last question: why was he trying to source the Jaipur map?'

'To destroy it. Evidence that the Taj Mahal was part of Shah Jahan's grand riverfront scheme would conveniently vanish.'

'He made a huge gamble that he would pull the deception off.'

'He headed the drama club,' Mehrunisa shrugged. 'He probably studied Raj Bhushan's mannerisms during their interactions, and then adopted those along with his dapper clothes and fashionable glasses. Despite their similar build and height, the two were as different as Burberry and khadi, and when the time came, Toor made the switch. I'm sure the lacerated right hand was just a convenient cover-up. Also, Bhushan was a bachelor—which helped. And after assuming his identity, Arun as ASI director-general spent time out of the city rather than in the head office. A perfect way to avoid interaction with Raj Bhushan's staff who might have figured something was amiss. Also, he was probably looking at a narrow window of three to four weeks—as you said, he's probably planning the takeover sometime now.'

Mehrunisa shook her head slowly, as if still in disbelief. 'Toor was the shape-shifting behrupiya all along!'

Singh muttered, 'Aurangzeb was the bloody red herring. Behrupiya-Bentinck-chutiya is the big fish to be caught. Bloody brilliant ... and brilliant deduction, Mehrunisa,' R.P. Singh said cheerily, adding he would immediately order DNA analysis on the personal items he had plucked from the mysterious Bhushan's house on the night of the intrusion.

Delhi

At noon, Mehrunisa sought refuge in the kitchen. The realisation that Arun Toor, presumed dead but actually alive in disguise, was a cunning deviant; that Raj Bhushan, Kaul uncle's good friend, was dead; and that the Taj Mahal was in imminent danger, caused a miasma to hang around her. Mehrunisa had turned to the one thing she relied upon to help focus her mind and lift her spirits: cooking.

When she deliberated on ingredients, chopped, pounded, stirred, a part of her, floating on a cloud of colour and smell, took leave. The act of cooking in some miraculous way engaged the senses and freed the brain. Now, pounding the tomato-basil-garlic into sauce, Mehrunisa was hoping for the same miracle.

Mangat Ram shuffled in and deposited a red hibiscus flower in the alcove above the kitchen counter. His palms folded, he bowed to the blue-grey statuette of Shiva seated on a tiger skin, a serpent coiled around his neck and a fountain emerging from his topknot. She had seen that idol for more than two decades since she had been acquainted with the housekeeper.

As he turned to her, she smiled.

'I'll go to the market for some ingredients for the puja,' he said. 'Do you need anything?'

Mangat Ram had a simple prayer routine. 'What ritual is this?' she said, curious.

'Shivratri is tomorrow. I'll get some bael leaves and incense sticks.' He turned to the wall-mounted water purifier and flicked the switch on. A low humming started as the machine readied.

'The puja is simple. You bathe the Shivlingam with milk, string up some bael leaves in the alcove and light incense. And keep a fast.'

At that Mehrunisa raised her brows: at the best of times Mangat Ram was no hearty eater.

With a wry smile, he said, 'It is good, occasionally, to free the stomach from its dependence on food.'

'And the story?' Mehrunisa grinned. Over her years with the professor and his housekeeper, she had figured that in India nothing was done that didn't have a story behind it.

'There are many stories, you take your pick. I like the one that says that after creation was complete, Parvati asked Shiva which ritual pleased him the most. Shiva said the thirteenth night of the new moon was his favourite. Parvati repeated it to her friends, the word spread, and the day came to be known as Shivratri. So tomorrow you can watch me do the small puja.'

'Tomorrow,' Mehrunisa acknowledged with a nod.

He peered at the Hindu lunar calendar hung beside the water purifier and confirmed, 'Yes, Friday is Shivratri.'

There was certainly a wide range of Shivbhakts about—overzealous ones like Arun Toor, habitual ones like Mangat Ram —

Friday is Shivratri!

Friday was the day the Taj Mahal was closed to visitors. The day when the mosque within was open and Muslims gathered for prayers. Friday was also Shivratri.

What better time to reverse the 'historic wrong' than Shivratri Friday when the Shiva temple, supposedly defiled by a Muslim mosque, could be returned to its patron Lord? A mosque with its Muslim patrons surrounded by a sea of Shiva devotees....

Could this Friday be the night when Arun Toor would mount the assault to reclaim the Taj Mahal?

Mehrunisa flew to call R.P. Singh.

Singh said he was in Delhi to arrest Raj Bhushan—DNA tests had confirmed her hypothesis: Arun Toor was alive and masquerading as Raj Bhushan. He was the behrupiya! Singh had an arrest warrant for him but the man had vanished.

Quietly, Mehrunisa divulged her theory that the monument would be usurped the coming day.

That took the wind out of Singh who broke into a string of expletives—his focus on January 26 as the date of the attack had him completely overlook the significance of Shivratri for the Shiv-bhakt Toor.

As he discussed the possibility with her, she heard him barking orders to SSP Raghav on another phone before he hightailed it to Agra.

Agra

Late afternoon admission to the Taj Mahal was abruptly halted. There was no prior notice, no explanation forthcoming from the stony security, and irate visitors who had been waiting in a snaking queue, were hurriedly hustled outside. Speculation filled the air and filtered to Taj Ganj and beyond.

Was it a VIP visit?

No-no, a bomb scare!

No! A miracle was expected—Shiva's trident would shake...

The police intercepted a call in which a person enquired if the suicide bomber was inside the Taj or not. A battalion of policemen began combing the Taj complex with metal detectors, sniffer dogs, batons and bare hands as they hunted for bombs and mischief-makers. On the commissioner's orders, two new units were hot-footed to beef up security in the Yellow zone. The security perimeter was extended with barbed wire and sandbags. All vehicles proceeding to the Taj were stopped and diverted. All police stations in Agra were mobilised for combing operations in different parts of the city. Vigil at bus stands and train stations was mounted. Bomb disposal squads had dispersed through the city's high-density areas and were attempting to do their work unobtrusively.

But, expectedly, one particular rumour had gathered urgency and Agra residents—in offices, bazaars, restaurants—were whispering about trouble anticipated at the Taj since a Shiva miracle had been predicted.

Within the Red zone, CISF had an additional posse of men to secure the monument. Snipers in the eight watchtowers, recently erected around the periphery of the complex, were on alert.

An irate monkey, upset by SSP Raghav's frisking, lunged at him. Vanar sena, he shook his head. Mehrunisa had called earlier with an idea—it struck him as totally bizarre but under the circumstances any help was welcome. He'd agreed to Mehrunisa's request and dispatched a man to Sikandrabad that boasted a large number of a particular genus of monkeys.

Now he mulled over the situation, having encountered nothing out of the ordinary—which was ominous.

R.P. Singh, heading back to Agra, was in constant communication with Raghav and, apprised of the situation, he was similarly nervous at the apparent calm.

Prepare to seal the city for tomorrow, he ordered.

Pakistan-occupied Kashmir

There was only one thing Jalaluddin prized above Kashmir—Islam.

Which was why he had struggled with himself the past few days after the news reached him. From his snowy hideout, he insisted on reading a few national dailies and his courier had to trudge on foot through the final miles—in winter that required considerable mountaineering skills for delivery, inevitably with a time lag.

Jalaluddin flung the paper aside. He had spent an inordinate amount of time on a news article. The new information necessitated the abrupt cessation of his bold plan. But, as he reasoned with himself now, the claim by the Waqf Board on the Taj Mahal made the change of plans imperative. After all, the concept of Waqf had been developed by the Holy Prophet.

His brows stayed dipped in concentration as he thought through his new course of action. Glancing at his young mujahid assistant he said, 'Inform our nephews that khala is on the deathbed no more.'

The mujahid gaped at this completely unexpected order from the commander. Jalaluddin shot him a withering glance. He knew what his trusted lieutenant was afraid to voice: General Ayub would be furious at the operation being called off. Khala, aunt, is on the deathbed—that was the coded message to stay on track. Recovery in the aunt's health was a coded message to abort the operation the general had sanctioned and backed with a large cache of arms and ammunition. The notion that the plan, once committed, could be rescinded, was out of question. Nobody crossed paths with the general. In the snowy Himalayan region, the enormity of his boss's action made the mujahid perspire.

Now Jalaluddin repeated slowly, 'Khala is on the deathbed no more. Understood? Neither the IJ, nor Kashmir, is beholden to General Ayub. He has sold his soul; we haven't. If the Sunni Board has declared a claim on the monument, we will respect that claim.' He paused, the prayer-bead eyes rolling in furious thought.

'As should every Muslim! Perhaps, we can get the general interested in some other Indian monument? And this time,' the brows dipped over the bridge of his nose, 'one that distinctly belongs to the infidels?'

Agra

Past midnight, R.P. Singh stood in the Jilaukhana as SSP Raghav updated him. The dense fog had blurred the contours of everything. The diffused streetlights hovered over floating trees, the ground below vanished beyond a few metres and, at a distance, it was difficult to make out friend from foe. The biting cold had driven them indoors, leaving behind an eerie silence.

Everything looked in order, Raghav assured him, but that only worried Singh more.

'Do another recce of the four gates,' he instructed him while he proceeded inside.

CISF patrolled the lawns, the watchtowers were manned with fresh snipers, shivering bodies marched the periphery of the Taj complex, their breath mingling with the enveloping fog. Except for the click of heavy boots, the monument lay in repose, wrapped in vapours that stirred in the breeze.

Nodding to the guard on duty, Singh let himself into the mausoleum and stood still, his ears straining for a sound. Mehrunisa had explained how the dome was constructed to amplify sound especially after it had lain quiet for several hours. Nothing. He went into the basement and checked the rooms in the riverfront façade, the very rooms where Jara had spent time doing housekeeping chores. Clearly, the monkey-cap had done a good job for Singh discovered nothing. He was speaking with the constable on duty when his phone rang.

Raghav's hoarse voice crackled into the quiet room. 'Boss!' he said in agitation, 'the cop manning the CCTV cameras is dead.'

R.P. Singh remembered that feeling of a warm muzzle on his forehead.

One night he had awoken in a government guesthouse in Bastar looking up into the twin barrels of a gun in the hands of a dreaded Maoist. In that split second before his mind took control, Singh prayed for the gun to be fired. Anything was better than being tortured by Maoists. What he was feeling now was distinctly worse.

'And only one camera was operational,' Raghav's voice crackled again with urgency. 'Shit! There is no time to repair the cameras...'

Singh jolted out of his stasis.

'Forget the cameras,' he barked. 'Whatever had to be brought in is already here. Start a thorough search of the complex. And post men on the riverside—any entry or exit from the Yamuna and you throttle the chutiya!'

Agra

The red sandstone terrace, atop which sits the marble platform of the mausoleum, has at its four corners four octagonal towers of three storeys. The towers are not open to visitors, yet they have a functional inner life. Two north towers facing the river have stairs that lead down to exits in the river façade of the sandstone terrace. Of the two south towers facing the gardens, the one south of the mosque houses an elaborate well construction, a baoli; the one south of the Mihman Khana contains chambers leading to toilets at a lower level.

It was two in the morning: while R.P. Singh roamed the Taj complex like a gladiator and Raghav reconnoitred the premises again, two people were not losing any sleep. Jara, in a thick brown overcoat and his monkey cap, was curled up on a sleeping bag in the circular room that ran deep into the ground in the tower to the south of the mosque. This tower had the same shape as the other towers, but it housed a baoli, a step well below the octagonal chamber of the upper floor, where an open well shaft cut through all floors, descending to three additional levels below ground.

Between the mosque and the tower to its south is a small windowless room from within which a stairway leads down to the floors below ground and to a landing above water level—it was in this circular underground room that, unbeknownst to the police, Jara and his accomplice rested. The door that led to the stairway was permanently boarded, senior staff had informed police when they began their reconnaisance. SSP Raghav, during his initial recce of the complex in the run-up to Republic Day, had insisted it be unlocked. He had trod down a musty stairway to a cobwebbed windowless cave and coughed his way back. The door was re-bolted, thereafter. It never occurred to Raghav that this room, apparently in disuse and permanently secured, could provide refuge to the man he was seeking.

But Jara knew the innards of the Taj Mahal better than a mother could read her child's face. For several months he had prowled the subterranean walkways of the complex. While police searched the basement rooms, he had hidden in another section of the underground labyrinth.

Now, he slept as there was still time. The other person in the room, though, sat in padmasana, meditating, his chest rising and falling calmly.

Above them, police corps scurried about, oblivious to what lay deep beneath their feet.

Delhi

Mehrunisa had started from Delhi early, hoping to benefit from scarce traffic as she drove the two hundred kilometres to Agra. Beside her sat Pamposh.

Late the evening before, Pamposh had descended unannounced upon Professor Kaul's house, greeting her uncle with, 'Herath Mubarak!'

'What's that?' Mehrunisa asked.

'It's Shivratri tomorrow,' Pamposh grinned, 'the most auspicious Kashmiri festival.' After fussing about her uncle, she commented on Mehrunisa's wan face, and insisted on accompanying her to Agra.

Now, early morning light glinted off the tiny mirrors in her red phiran—another one from her collection of embroidered Kashmiri robes—and lit her face with crystal parallelograms. Her dejihor caught the light as she swung her head to smile at her friend.

Mehrunisa returned a weak smile and turned to focus on the road.

As the highway approached Agra, vehicular traffic started to increase. R.P. Singh had ordered Agra to be sealed, so, as per SSP Raghav's instructions, she was to contact an officer at the police naka who would let them through. Mehrunisa slowed down as cars began to pile up ahead and behind her. A thicket of humanity had also sprung up on the highway. Suddenly Pamposh screamed. A monkey had landed on the glass window beside her. His turbanned keeper peered at the women from behind the animal. Mehrunisa checked to make sure the doors were locked before glaring at the man.

Taj! Taj!

She squinted at the traffic as the cries rang out. A young man with long hair, a bright yellow headband holding it in place, face scruffy with stubble, was herding a group along. Lowering her window, Mehrunisa poked her head out and shouted, 'What's happened?'

Before he could answer, a woman's head popped out from behind him. Her face was filled with awe as she raised her palms heavenwards and spoke in a sing-song voice. 'Praise to the Lord Shiva! His trident is summoning us.'

Before Mehrunisa could process the woman's gushing chatter, another face popped up, a man. 'The Lord is showing us a miracle. If you want to witness it, hurry to the Taj! Hurry!'

'Wait! What miracle are you talking about? What trident is this?'

'The trident on top of the Taj Mahal,' the youth in the yellow headband said eagerly. 'The pinnacle, haven't you noticed it? It is Shiva's trident and now it is shaking. Know what that means?'

As he paused, the crowd around him chorused, '*Har Har Mahadev! Har Har Mahadev!*'

'Come, sister,' the first woman said earnestly, 'come to the Taj Mahal, witness the miracle with your own eyes and offer your prayers to Shiva. Better still, take us with you!'

Abruptly, she grabbed the door handle and started to yank it. Meanwhile, the youth struck the pose of Nataraja, the dancing Shiva with one leg hoisted, arms flung out, jigging his head wildly. Others lurched around crying, *Jai Shiv Shankar! Har Har Mahadev! Jai Bholenath!*

As the various names of Lord Shiva were called in delirious profusion by the crazed devotees, the two occupants in the car sat in stunned silence.

Tutte le strade portano a Roma. All roads lead to Rome. In this case, Agra, Mehrunisa thought as she scanned the burgeoning sea of traffic for a break. The Sonata car was in the midst of a billowing mass of man and machinery as all humanity, propelled by various modes of motion, jostled to move towards the Taj!

Mehrunisa tried to imagine that kind of crowd milling around the Taj Mahal, and failed. It would amount to packing the Taj's daily tourist traffic of several days into the Jilaukhana's forecourt at one moment in time. The sheer pressure of such numbers could cause irretrievable damage to the monument that already suffered from 4,000 to 5,000 pairs of feet tramping over it daily.

Nobody could say where they had come from, or how they had heard the news, but it was as if a gigantic beehive had been ransacked and now the bees, buzzing, restive, feverish were swarming all over. Taj and Shiva were the two words on each tongue as people—barefoot, astride two-wheelers, packed atop jeeps and trucks, hanging out of cars—speculated fervidly.

Hands thumped the car as folks walked past or bent to peer inside. It was a powerful car, it would hold, but Mehrunisa was acutely aware of the curious glances at the capacious car with its two female occupants.

Agra

At daybreak, the fog lifted and crowds started to approach the Taj complex. A perplexed police officer stopped them at the barricade and informed them that the Taj Mahal was closed to visitors on Friday. Sullenly, they hung around.

Following that a horde of Naga sadhus—naked, sporting saffron headbands or red and gold scarves, their bodies smeared with ash, trishuls aloft in their hands—appeared at the East gate. Since they had a reputation for being fractious, the policeman on duty decided to inform them politely that the Taj was closed and ignore them thereafter.

However, neither silent treatment nor vigorous communication worked, for the complex kept filling with people. In a couple of hours, the entire forecourt was swarming, saffron headbands bobbing in their midst. SSP Raghav was urgently roused from the cubicle within Darwaza-i-Rauza where he had finally fallen asleep at a desk.

Hitching his crumpled trousers up, he marched bleary-eyed into the crowd and ordered them to scoot. Like some mammoth misshapen creature that had been prodded, the crowd rippled but stayed put. Raghav was sleep-deprived, his neck stiff from the position in which he had dozed, and his head was throbbing from the fruitless exertions of the night. They'd be thrown into jail, he shouted a hoarse warning at the upturned faces. It was futile. The lawless crowd of hangers-on was a mob deserving a heavy hand. He beckoned the constables to charge into them with their batons.

Suddenly, a woman thrust a mike at him. Dazed, Raghav spun around. Behind her a cameraman captured the melee as police thrashed a motley crowd of sadhus, youth and visitors sporting saffron bandanas.

'Hey!' Raghav yelled to the cameraman, 'Stop the filming! Now!'

But the fleeing crowd was between him and the camera crew who were capturing the commotion in the Jilaukhana of the Taj Mahal. The sickening realisation dawned on Raghav that the action was being relayed live to an early morning audience.

'Jai Bholenath!' a chant went up.

The crowd was responding to the camera, gesticulating and shouting slogans.

We are here to witness the miracle of Shiva!

Lord Shiva's shaking trident!

'Saala, gaandu,' Raghav thundered as he lunged at the cameraman over the heads of cowering men. 'I'll show you the miracle!'

He grabbed him by the neck as two cops nabbed his equipment.

However, unknown to Raghav, the cameramen and his team had accomplished their mission. An anonymous tip about the opportunity to record a sensational event at the

Taj Mahal at the dawn of Shivratri had made them hurry there. In turn they had secured a recording coup. Competing channels would scramble for footage soon but they had had a headstart. By the time Raghav got his hands on the camera, five minutes of live footage had been beamed by the sensationalist TV channel. It showed Shiv bhakts braving police violence in front of the Taj Mahal as they awaited a presaged miracle that morning. And it flashed repeatedly photographs that showed close-ups of the flowing calligraphy on Mumtaz's cenotaph. These were accompanied by a high-pitched voice-over declaiming that the calligraphy indeed stated that the tomb was masnooee, a fraud. In order to verify that particular allegation, the TV channel was locating an expert in Persian calligraphy. Meanwhile, the news reporter exhorted the audience not to go away, to stay tuned, as they continued breaking the sensational news.

Agra

As the number of people gathering in the forecourt continued to swell, R.P. Singh sent constables around the complex to investigate the area. Soon enough one returned with the information that, in the dilapidated Haveli Agha Khan on the east side of the Taj Mahal, adjacent to Dassehra Ghat, he had discovered bedding, clothing and food items. It verified Singh's grim assumption that the mob, despite the appearance of being spontaneous, had been pre-planned.

A troubled R.P. Singh sped into Agra city on motorcycle to assess how effectively his order to seal the city had been executed. Right in Taj Ganj he saw a swarm outside a shop watching breaking-news at the Taj Mahal on the owner's TV set. The reporter on TV passionately narrated how eager devotees had gathered to witness a Shiva miracle that was to take place at the monument at noon, then cut to a scene of cops lunging at them with batons, the outburst of Shiva slogans from the devout, and the 'high-handedness' of the police as SSP Raghav's threatening face zoomed into the frame, and to the mixed sound of swearing-crunching-ripping, the picture went dead. The gathering gasped, tittered, gesticulated, and planned to head to the monument and check for themselves the situation at the Taj.

R.P. Singh broke into a sweat, his tensed muscles trembling as if he were facing the slashing knives of a gang of Maoists.

Meanwhile, at the left bank of the Yamuna across from the Taj Mahal, Mehrunisa had arrived as per Raghav's instructions at Mahtab Bagh. There a cop watched over a gnome-like man settled beneath a neem tree with his simian mates. The dozen langurs with black faces and white bodies eyed her curiously and Mehrunisa had a sinking feeling that her plan to protect the Taj was underwhelming, to say the least.

Pamposh, with raised brows, retreated to the car. She had debated with Mehrunisa the considerable risk of approaching the Taj Mahal at such a volatile time, but her normally sensible friend was suddenly impervious to reason.

Mehrunisa, unable to sit, paced the grassy bank, eyes glued to the Taj Mahal across. Force of habit made her touch the kara she wore. Now, as stray shouts drifted across from the Taj Mahal, and policemen scurried like ants across the marble plinth, her eyes surveyed the marble monument as if fierce passion alone would stave off danger....

Agra

How does a sealed city spring leaks? Ancient Agra was a sieve—too many exits and entryways, including a riverine passage. And how was he to contain the excitement of locals without a curfew?

As he rode across the city, an alarmed R.P. Singh saw people huddled in corners, grouped at the milk booth, pausing in their morning walk, shouting across balconies, all excitedly trumpeting the purported miracle. Their faces shining with enthusiasm, these people were oblivious of, or deliberately ignoring, the Muslims gathered in sullen silence as they watched the jubilant proclamations.

It reminded him of the time when Ganpati idols were said to have started to drink milk, driving the entire nation into a collective frenzy as people abandoned offices, police their stations, doctors their clinics, as every Indian scrambled to reach an idol with a canister of milk in tow. The milkman was the only one who worked that day as milk was offered with such frenzy to Ganapati idols in the country that ultimately drains from temples ran milky-white. Except the 'milk miracle' was ultimately harmless, providing succour to a nation which liked its gods on-call. But the 'trident miracle'....

The staccato ringtone of his mobile cut his train of thought. It was the home minister. He'd caught the TV footage, he said. Agra in frenzy over Shiva miracle at the Taj Mahal! What the hell was happening?! Why wasn't he informed?

'We're taken by surprise, Sir,' R.P. Singh ground his teeth and admitted. 'But we are on it, Sir—'

The home minister shouted an expletive before starting to mutter under his breath. The man who was reputed to be a cold cucumber amidst the sizzle of Indian politics was beyond furious. 'What I see on TV is a Kumbh mela! You cannot fire into the crowd, you cannot arrest the thousands gathered, there are TV crews all over—just what is your plan?' he asked.

The colourful pulsating sea of people swam before Singh's eyes. Statistically, the minister was way off the mark, but he could be forgiven the exaggeration given the circumstances.

Icily, the home minister informed him that the matter had reached the prime minister. He was on the line.

R.P. Singh veered to the curb, braked, put one foot on the ground and breathed hard. Beads of perspiration that had sprouted earlier were finding their way down his creased forehead into the inner corners of his eyes. Eyes narrowed, he focused his entire being on the moment.

'Son—' he heard the prime minister, his soft voice weighed down, 'you don't need me to tell you we're facing a very grave situation...' a long pause, '...you are on the ground and you see it for yourself. I am told that you are one of our finest policemen. And the son of a brave general whose heroism in '71 saved our nation.

'This time the enemy has declared war from within. And he has chosen his target very cleverly—he strikes it, he strikes at our very foundation. Just as the colour white contains all colours within it, this monument of white embodies our innate, ancient pluralism. Save the Taj Mahal, Singh, that monument stands for India.'

Agra

Anyone would be forgiven for thinking there was a carnival on at the Taj Mahal.

SSP Raghav shook his head in disbelief at the massive crowds jammed into the Jilaukhana by noon. People were craning their necks to see if they could look beyond the imposing red entrance gate. Many had children hoisted on their shoulders. The din around them was a mix of chants, jubilant shouts, speculation, gossip. Vendors weaved through the crowd, selling tea in glasses, roasted peanuts in paper cones, even roasted corn cobs along with seasoning sachets of half-cut lime and chilli powder. In the treetops, lured by the profusion of food, more monkeys were becoming visible. Abruptly, a boy with glasses of a milky concoction in a wire rack surfaced, and he stopped to offer one to a woman.

'Milk?' she asked.

The boy, no more than eight years old, flashed a sudden grin. 'Bhang!' he supplied. 'Shivji's favourite drink. Go on,' he urged, 'no charge. Most people have had a glass or more.'

SSP Raghav lunged at the boy's elbow, rattling the glasses in the process. 'Why free?'

'S-saab,' the boy trembled, 'my seth, he said to distribute it free. He is a big Shiva devotee.'

'Where is this seth?'

'Not here,' the boy shook his head.

'How many boys are here like you, distributing bhang?'

He scratched his forehead. 'Fifteen, maybe twenty.'

'*Fif*-teen twenty!' SSP Raghav was apoplectic, his moustache aquiver. 'Out! Out of my sight! If I see you around I'll thrash you. And your buddies as well.'

The boy slipped away. As he was about to disappear, he said with a sly look, 'He is paying us well.'

Raghav beckoned a constable and ordered him to tail the boy and find his accomplices.

Anxiously, he surveyed the crowds. The mood was festive, the people were in eager anticipation, and the crisp winter air had warmed with the explosion of human beings crammed into a small space. Aromas wafted through the air: of cigarette smoke, masala chai, and the Agra delicacy candied pumpkin. People crunched on nutty gachak and salty dalmoth and quipped and waited while monkeys hopped about grabbing spillage. This bacchanal—his mind fleetingly acknowledged the pertinent word—could erupt into a riot any time. All it needed was one trigger.

✸ ✸ ✸

R.P. Singh watched the action from inside the great gate of the Jilaukhana complex. The milling crowd had, by some remarkable feat of physics, occupied more space than was available around the red sandstone and white marble gate.

In six hours the crowd had swelled to well over forty thousand. At some point they had sullenly watched defiant Muslims enter for their namaaz. That incident had passed without a scuffle as an entire battalion of policemen guided the worshippers into a phalanx and deposited them into the monument.

The multiple police and CISF contingents were armed and in place, the snipers were alert in watchtowers, a helicopter whirred overhead, yet Singh knew that the home minister had been correct in his estimation. Arun Toor was planning a very public heist and the only way out was to locate him, capture him and spirit him away before he revealed himself.

But where the hell was Toor?

He had severely underestimated the swell of religious fervour and the consequent public hysteria—something Toor had counted on as a fulcrum on which to successfully turn his plan.

The crowd was growing belligerent as shouts claiming that the trident was shaking rippled through the gathering. People craned their necks and heaved and shifted anew. Those who had clambered atop some nearby trees reported jubilantly at frequent intervals—at which the crowd broke into chants of 'Jai Jai Mahadev'.

Eager cameramen had descended on the scene to report the unfolding drama live. Star TV, Zee, Aaj Tak—the logos on their equipment proclaiming their identity—were besieged by devotees eager to share their particular experience. One news reporter, with frizzy hair and an aggressive twitch in the eye, was threading her way through the clamouring men, asking them why they were there, what they had seen, and the ramifications of a Hindu trishul atop the central dome of a mausoleum.

Gathering several cops, R.P. Singh headed to the mausoleum again.

* * *

The bhang boys had not been caught. And SSP Raghav, at the great gate, had witnessed its slow but sure effect on the gradually inebriated behaviour of many devotees. He wondered what the Muslim worshippers, who had gone inside earlier, were doing.

Throw open the gates! Throw open the gates! The demand rose again, followed by the chant *Throw open! Throw open!*

Out with the sons of Babur! Muslims in a Hindu temple, Hai Hai!

The crowd would look to break into the complex soon—he had seen several young men with saffron-headbands weaving their way through the throng. As he followed their movements he realised they were initiating the chants and declamations, which the crowd regurgitated. Clearly, those were the assigned troublemakers. And soon they would light a friggin match. He had conveyed it to R.P. Singh, with whom he was in constant communication.

Abruptly, a voice crackled through the air, carried over a powerful loudspeaker. A hush descended on the crowd as all eyes searched for its source.

Brothers and sisters! Welcome to Tejo Linga, the thirteenth Linga of our Lord Shiva! Forget the nonsense you have been told so far. This beautiful marble monument, famous around the world as India's pride and glory, was not built by any Mughal emperor. No! That is blasphemy! This is the ancient temple of Bholenath, our innocent Lord Shiva. For too long it has been sullied. But the time has come to correct the grievous damage. It is time to reclaim what rightfully belongs to us! And in this the Lord himself has come to guide us. Behold, as in fury, he has set his trident shaking. You all know what that means. Our Lord is in Rudra form, he wants his bhakts to witness his trident trembling. So, come forth! You will find the entrance door miraculously open— come in and witness with your own eyes Mahadev's trident shaking in fury!

Jai Mahadev! Har Har Mahadev! Jai Bholenath!

The next instant a stampede began. The mob, believing the door would open, headed toward it, forcing their way through. The multiple files of policemen attempted to hold their ground but were brushed aside like soldiers in front of marauding elephants of war. Bamboo staves flew through the air. Plexiglas shields were crushed underfoot. Cameramen crashed to the ground with their equipment.

Raghav flattened himself against the red sandstone wall. The next instant everything blurred as frantic, frenetic human motion obscured his line of vision. The watchtower snipers, the additional police, the chopper, all were useless against the rolling glob of unarmed fanatics.

The offensive on the Taj Mahal commenced from the south side and a simultaneous exodus began from the river-facing north side. The Muslims who had forged their way through a burgeoning sea of Hindu devotees in order to offer namaaz heard the loud chants, sensed the swelling numbers in the Jilaukhana complex, and understood that exit from the south side would be akin to inviting slaughter. An emissary was therefore despatched to

Dassehra Ghat to hire a boat. However, Friday being a lean day, no boat was moored on that bank of the Yamuna. So the emissary swam across the river, returning with a couple of dinghys in which the Muslims departed just as the stampede started. The ones who couldn't clamber aboard leapt into the water and started to swim, a few managing to stay afloat by hanging on to the helping hands thrust from the boat.

However, unknown to them, some 'Muslims' had elected to stay behind. Earlier, during prayers in the mosque, Jara, dressed for a change in Muslim garb, his face shrouded in a checked keffiyeh, had climbed out of his subterranean burrow, mingled with the crowd with his accomplices who were also masquerading as Muslim worshippers, and slipped to the boarded-up rooms in the riverfront terrace.

Inspector Bharadwaj of the CISF ensured that they weren't noticed by the security. He had taken care to put a particularly vigilant CISF officer out of action. Inspector Javed, overcome by chloroform, was slumped inside a locked police van parked in one corner of the complex.

Once inside, they retrieved the Shiva artefacts Jara had spent days storing in a location within the riverfront terrace rooms—in the ceiling of the last room a secret trapdoor opened into an overhead chamber. It was so well concealed as to escape the attention of anyone who did not have prior knowledge of its position. Not a word was spoken as, briskly, each man set to his task arranging the antiques intended for discovery by the Shiv bhakts who were storming in.

Like a tsunami the crowd rolled in, thundering through the gardens and the paved walkways. Squeezing through the narrow entrance, it burst with renewed vigour and diffused rapidly down the complex.

As the first wave approached the mausoleum, the loudspeaker came alive again, urging them to halt before the marble mausoleum. The devotees were to assemble in the gardens to witness another miracle. Once they had beheld the full glory of Mahadeva, the Shiv bhakts could enter and rightfully reclaim the temple. Meanwhile, the voice exhorted, look up, and witness the miraculous shaking trident!

Even as the loudspeaker was issuing its dictum, a cordon of Naga sadhus and young men with saffron headbands formed around the mausoleum. As they stood aggressively guarding the access routes, one of the CISF policemen brandished his rifle at them. The next instant a Naga sadhu leapt up, grappled with him and they rolled to the ground. Another Naga sadhu grabbed the rifle and examined it with glee. Meanwhile, a cop made to assist his colleague when the rifle rang out loudly.

The people in the crowd nearest to the mausoleum cowered and dived to the ground even as the Naga sadhus celebrated. The cordon shouted slogans, waved trishuls and exhorted the assembly to hunker down as the sadhu jigged and brandished the trophy rifle. Inspector Bharadwaj of the CISF shouted to his men to back off, their actions were exciting the crowd and people could get seriously injured.

SSP Raghav, unaware of the action ahead and surrounded by the eagerly muscling bodies in the crowd, allowed himself to be carried forward into the Taj complex. He narrowed his eyes and examined the trident. The pinnacle, viewed from that distance, was no more than a speck atop the dome. One could always claim it was shaking—there was no way to verify it. Nevertheless, people craned their necks, and rewarded their effort by agreeing wholeheartedly that the trident was indeed trembling.

Delhi

For once, reality had exceeded his wildest expectation. Shri Kriplani was glued to the television set, the glass of urine forgotten on the sideboard. The Lord fulfilled himself in many ways and here He was manifest in his devout bhakts. The omens were right—he was on track to seize the reins of the nation.

TV channels across the country were attempting to outdo one another in the coverage of the sensationalist development at the Taj Mahal. As they broadcast the continuing action at the monument live, they held panel discussions with eminent intellectuals, bureaucrats, statesmen, and artists in their studios, and laid siege to the headquarters of political parties in order to procure the views of leading politicians.

As the morning wore on, an army of media personnel took position outside. Not wanting to project any sign of excessive keenness, Shri Kriplani pretended to go about his daily business as usual. He was stepping out for a routine meeting when he was waylaid by the vociferous media. Yes, he would answer their questions, briefly.

Shri Kriplani of the BHP spoke directly into the cameras, his eyes bright, his smile sanguine, his black bandhgala jacket crisp against the starched white of his kurta.

No, Shri Kriplani shook his head mournfully, he did not approve of what was happening at the Taj Mahal—but then, it was the will of the people. The ordinary god-fearing citizens of India believed that the trident of Shiva rested atop the monument and was shaking. Surely, such faith could not be trivialised.

But, Sir, it might lead to bloodshed, a reporter quizzed.

Shri Kriplani held up both palms, his smile unfaltering. That is the task of police and security. We leave it to them. Jai Bholenath! Jai Shiv Shankar! He held up his hands in an elaborate namaskar and retreated into his waiting car.

Agra

Back at the Taj Mahal, R.P. Singh with several cops had gained entry into the mausoleum before the crowds began their surge into the charbagh. Near the base of the eastern riverfront minaret, at the head of the stairs that led down to the riverfront terrace, his ears pricked up. He came to a halt, motioning the men to be quiet. A snatch of muffled sounds had floated up to him.

The iron railing that closed the upper opening of the stairway was in place, but unlocked!

He held his gun in front of him and crept down the stairs, sliding against the marble wall as he went. It got darker as he descended and he took it slow, letting his eyes adjust. Behind him the men followed with similar stealth.

The gallery consisted of a series of rooms arranged in line along the riverfront. Mehrunisa had guided him through the plan first, after which he had checked the gallery himself a couple of times. The musty air was heavy with chill. A policeman coughed and quickly clamped a hand on his mouth.

The first room was ahead. Singh motioned for a torch to be switched on. He paused, beckoned two men to cover him, and then spun into the room. It was bare.

A smell of incense floated up the narrow corridor. Their noses twitched. The faint tinkle of a bell sounded, finishing even before it had begun. And a dull glow appeared up ahead.

Blood pounded in his ears as Singh sped softly down the corridor. He burst into the third room, surprising its engrossed occupants. In the dim light of a square room inside the Tahkhana of the Taj Mahal, a Shiva temple was in the process of being built.

A black stone lingam, garlanded with marigold, stood in the middle of a rangoli pattern. Two brass lamps were aglow in front of it. A bare-chested priest squatted beside it chanting softly, a tiny bell in his right hand. Two men were frozen in the act of positioning a marble Nandi bull against the east wall of the room. Clearly, the miscreants were not only intent on establishing that the Taj Mahal was a Shiva temple once, they were determined to set up a functioning temple right away! What better way to reclaim a temple than by initiating ritual puja.

For a couple of breaths, the entire room was in limbo as the two parties goggled at each other. R.P. Singh was the first off the mark as he pointed his gun at them and yelled, 'Don't move!'

Instead, two scruffy youths pounced upon him. The cops swung to apprehend the men, the priest started wailing and a thug kicked a constable in the shin and landed him on the floor. A fierce fight ensued.

The men were either fearless or high or both, and while lacking any martial moves they spun furiously, flailed their arms and attacked the cops with fisticuffs, kicks and blows. Brass puja vessels clanged in the room as they were struck amidst thumps and smacks. Finally, the ruffians were restrained and marched off. Singh, bleeding from a cut on his chin, instructed his men to hustle the captives to the riverside where they wouldn't be visible to the assembly in front of the monument.

Meanwhile, he ordered another unit to quickly remove all signs of a temple and restore the room to its original state. Singh had no knowledge of antiques, but he could have sworn the provenance of the lingam and Nandi was ancient. Arun Toor had ensured that the faking of the Shiva temple was, to all appearances, genuine.

Taking a few men with him he continued his search for the loudspeaker and the man inciting the mobs.

✻ ✻ ✻

It was nearly 4 p.m., and the feeble January daylight was dying. Dusk had descended abruptly, as it did in the north during winter. The cordon of Naga sadhus and manic young ruffians had held firm.

In the intervening hours, the heaving crowd had forced its way into every inch of available space in the complex. The enterprising folk who first entered the gardens had a ringside view of the mausoleum while the multitude had decided to bide its time. A few had curled up for a quick snooze, others were partaking of snacks and flinging bits to curious monkeys who descended frequently for a hasty grab.

Meanwhile, the ornamental pool—set into a white marble platform where the central walkway intersected the east-west walkway—had become one long pond for washing hands. The elegant cypresses lining the path became makeshift, open-air toilets for full bladders.

Somewhere in the charbagh, closer to the Mihman Khana, Mehrunisa slumped against the enormous trunk of a red silk cotton tree, attempting to straighten out her thoughts.

When the Muslim worshippers decamped from Dassehra Ghat, Mehrunisa, Pamposh, the gnome with his dozen langurs, all under the supervision of the cop assigned by SSP Raghav, had used the same boat to return. They had alighted on the eastern side and, crouching, made their way up to the monument where the cop and his team were allowed entry by the tense police.

Mehrunisa spotted several plainclothes policemen mingling in the crowd, quietly cornering the visible ringleaders and silently plucking them out of the crowd. The saffron youths, visibly intoxicated, were being similarly siphoned away. But it seemed too little, too late. Beside her, Pamposh watched the melee and studied her wristwatch anxiously.

Abruptly the loudspeaker crackled again.

Brothers and sisters, the time has come to witness the miracle you have been waiting for. Our Lord Shiva will reveal himself through his most potent form: the Shivlingam. Arise and behold the spectacle for yourself. So, when our future history is written, you can proudly tell your grandchildren that you were a part of it. Arise! Bring your hands together in prayer. And from your throats, pour forth praise to Lord Shiva! Har Har Mahadev! Jai Bholenath!

The next instant, the marble plinth on which the marble mausoleum stood was bathed in niveous light. From the ill-lit lawns it appeared to glow like a pearl, and the throng, as if with one pair of eyes, was fixated on it. A cylindrical structure swam up from the plinth. Its black stone radiated against the milky-white marble. A gasp rose from the audience. The shivlingam looked majestic as it rose upward, so smooth and noiseless in its ascent that it seemed like an apparition. A clamour broke through the audience as a delirium of sounds filled the air.

The crowd had started to swoon, literally and otherwise, as the effect of the intoxicating bhang and the miracle of a Shivlingam emerging from nowhere sunk in.

The loudspeaker came on again, announcing that since the devotees had witnessed the sign of Shiva, they were to ascend the plinth, perform their own abhiskekha, and bathe the lingam.

At the announcement, people scrambled to fetch water from the central channel for the ritual washing. Trampling over each other, they jostled towards the eerily glowing black stone.

The riverfront terrace yielded nothing more. R.P. Singh made his way back up the north tower and hurried across to the mausoleum with his men. He could hear the melee and knew that any minute the mob would be tearing inside the tomb chamber. He sent a few cops to man the chamber from outside.

Where was the damn loudspeaker? The transmitter, receiver, wires, audio source, something to give it away...

Around the octagonal chamber he went, flashing his light into corners that were bare as always. He searched in the niches, examined the filigreed screen, poked around the cenotaphs, scrutinised the patterned floor, but found nothing suspicious. He looked up at the cavernous roof faintly lit by the perennial flame of Curzon's lamp. Its shimmering bronze, inlaid with gold and silver, caught his attention. Flask-shaped, it was a natural storage area and likely to be overlooked. Additionally, it was positioned right above the cenotaphs.

With a silent apology for defiling its sanctity, Singh clambered atop Mumtaz's cenotaph, torch in mouth. Standing on tiptoe, he tilted the lamp to check if the transmitter had been placed there.

A shadow filled the doorway. Singh looked up. In the light of the torch he saw a masked man with a gleaming knife in his hand. Singh squinted, trying to read the face as he shone the light on him. The masked man swung his head to avoid the glare, and his kaffiyeh slipped to reveal a featureless face.

The psycho monkey-cap chutiya!

Singh ducked, removed the torch from his mouth and switched it off. The man lunged towards him just then, jabbing the air in front of his nose in the darkness. Singh caught his knife-wielding wrist and thrust his boot into the man's groin. With an *Aagh!* Jara dropped the knife and doubled over.

As Singh caught his breath a shot rang out. Monkey-cap had a pistol aimed at him. Singh scrambled, lost his balance and toppled. As the man made to pull the trigger again, a dark form flew at him, thrusting an elbow into the assailant's neck.

Jara gave a muffled yelp.

The man who had jumped into the fray swore and toppled sideways clutching his chest. Blood oozed thickly onto the marble floor. SSP Raghav had been shot.

Pakistan-occupied Kashmir

In his snowy hideout Jalaluddin listened intently to the radio his mujahid assistant had excitedly handed to him.

An anxious voice announced that a mob of Shiv bhakts had laid hostage to the Taj Mahal with the claim that the trident atop the mausoleum dome was shaking. They claimed that the trembling of Shiva's trishul was a sign that the monument was a Shiva temple waiting to be reclaimed. The grave male voice said the police estimated the number of people crowded into the Taj Mahal complex to be in the thousands. However, they affirmed the situation was under control.

Jalaluddin looked up with a smile of pure delight spreading on his rough face: bared teeth, crinkled eyes, whiskers twitching in humour. He laughed a deep-chested theatrical laugh as he handed the radio back to the young mujahid. 'Time for some fresh tea and toffee to celebrate! They don't need us,' Jalaluddin sneered, as the men gathered in the cave smirked joyously. 'The kafirs are their own worst enemies, they'll destroy themselves!'

Agra

Led by young men with shiny faces and manic eyes, eager people swarmed up the plinth of the mausoleum as they headed to the riverfront rooms where the promised proof of Shiva lay. However, the mob found nothing in the barren rooms and retreated sullenly.

They prowled through the tomb chamber, descended to the lower chamber— where the only items of note were the twin tombs—and the riverfront rooms, then ran across the sandstone platform in search of some visible signs of Shiva.

Single-minded in their pursuit, they did not notice a bleeding Raghav coiled up on the marble floor.

Meanwhile, R.P. Singh gave chase to Jara. As he reached the door the shuffling man disappeared into the crowd. However, to Singh's stupefaction, the crowd was in retreat.

It was a scene straight out of *Ramayana*, thought Singh. Like the vanar sena had descended upon the battlefield to rout the demon king Ravan's army, hordes of monkeys had now descended onto the gardens of the Taj complex.

Tumbling down trees, bounding over bushes, chattering wildly, they dispersed through the crowd. Swinging from one human shoulder to another, springing off backs, dangling from sari pallus, they scampered over the sea of humanity. In turn, their wild antics, loud chattering and furious flailing triggered the crowd into a panic.

Policemen, unsure thus far, swung into action as they captured the ringleaders who were attempting to stay the crowd.

Singh burst into loud laughter. The tension of the last several hours erupted into a roar, a *Hooha!*, as he pumped the air and filled his lungs with whoops of pure relief.

Next, he headed for the glistening Shivalingam, suddenly bereft of its worshippers. A few determined stragglers hung about. Singh walloped them and shoved them forward to examine the stone closely. A cheap, lightweight black stone imitation sat atop a jack that rested on the staircase leading below. Mehrunisa had explained how that staircase led to the rooms in the riverfront terrace. Toor had attempted to project that an ancient Shivalingam was rising from the basement of the Taj, but the duplicate was likely sourced from Kinari bazaar.

'Chor chutiyas!' he cuffed the men who were prancing around to escape his beating. 'Even the monkeys know better than you!'

As the men were handcuffed, Singh headed back to the tomb chamber with two cops. SSP Raghav's face was wan, his right hand clasped across his chest, his shirtfront was scarlet. He squinted in recognition and attempted to speak.

R.P. Singh gripped his hand fiercely. 'You saved my life, SSP.'

Raghav mouthed something but no sound came.

'We are in control now. But we have to rush you to a hospital—you've lost a lot of blood.' With one last firm grip, he let go of Raghav's hand and helped the men lift him up.

Delhi

Shri Kriplani had followed the events unfolding at the Taj Mahal with the jingoistic keenness of his countrymen when watching an Indo-Pak cricket match. Except for the one media interview, he stayed closeted in his office as the television set spit images of a saffron sea of bhakts surging against the curdled-milk of the marble. It was incredible, but things were working so well that this time he might have the result of Babri Masjid without the infamous association!

However, as the drama at the Taj Mahal fizzled out in front of his bewildered eyes, his political antenna set about recalibrating his response. After which he called for an emergency press conference that was telecast live.

In his persuasive professorial voice he urged people not to pay attention to a charlatan making false claims in the name of Lord Shiva about trembling tridents. The most feared and revered God of the Hindu Trinity did not require puny zealots to usurp recognisable Mughal monuments in his name. Shiva's glory was *aparampar*, limitless. He called upon devout bhakts to observe Shivratri in its true spirit of worship and meditation and purge their mind of falsity. Jai Shiv Shankar!

Agra

Mehrunisa looked around, amazed at the wave of humanity cascading down the Taj complex towards the forecourt. On the heels of the fleeing humans came the panicky monkeys, in turn fleeing from the fierce langurs. Her plan had worked.

Astonishing but true: the mob was in retreat.

As pandemonium rippled through the crowd, she racked her brains. Where could a man with his loudspeaker hide in the Taj complex and evade detection so successfully?

It had to be in the labyrinthine basement somewhere....

Now that the charbagh was free of the mobs, Mehrunisa walked across from the Mihman Khana to the west, lost in thought. A nervous Pamposh tagged along reluctantly, saying, 'Mehroo, we *have* to leave!'

With a finger to her lips Mehrunisa motioned for silence. Pamposh shook a rueful head.

Mehrunisa had reached the mosque and it struck her then that the octagonal tower to the south of the mosque housed a unique construction: a baoli, a well tower with three floors below ground level, unlike the other towers which had only one subterranean level! Functionally, the step well provided water independently of the waterworks outside the complex. Symbolically, it was connected to the mystical saint who found the Water of Life and gained immortality. For Hindus, Shiva was the Lord from whose locks Ganga spouted, and the act of pouring water over a shivalingam was replicating Ganga's descent from heaven. A water body was symbolically the perfect spot for a madman seeking eternal glory.

Mehrunisa's heart sank.

Licking her lips, she scanned the grounds for SSP Raghav or R.P. Singh but could not see them anywhere. She gulped. *Basement issues, Mehrunisa,* a tiny voice inside her cautioned. She swung her eyes from the mausoleum to the gate where stragglers were exiting. If Arun Toor was indeed hiding within the baoli, there *was* no time to lose. He might even have used the opportunity to join the fleeing crowd to make his getaway.

Which meant one thing: she would have to overcome her fear and descend to the basement.

Mehrunisa headed to the door in the southern wing of the mosque that would lead her to the passage that led to the baoli. Immediately, Pamposh's arm snaked out and gripped her wrist. Her eyes flashed as she said, 'Don't be a fool, Mehrunisa! Stay out of it.'

Mehrunisa gave her a puzzled look, thrust her hand away, and ran to the door of the windowless room.

She descended a dark stairway into a cool dank chamber. There was little light and she used her fingers to feel her way as she went deeper into the circular well shaft. The noise of the charbagh was left behind and all she heard was her own heart beating. Visions of the time when she was trapped in the Taj Mahal's labyrinth flashed before her eyes and she shut them out. Rounding a corner, she slipped and clutched at the cold mossy wall, her hands dragging until she recovered her foothold.

Breathe, breathe, she counselled herself as she reached the lowest landing.

A snarl greeted her and in the dim light she saw a man. The jaw twisted with wrath, his lips had disappeared, his eyes were pinpricks and his hair was ablaze. He looked like neither the Arun Toor nor the Raj Bhushan that she knew. It was as if he had shed his external trappings to reveal an accursed core.

'Why?' Mehrunisa asked, her voice distraught. 'Why destroy the Taj Mahal?' Her voice sounded tinny as she suddenly realised how foolhardy she'd been. She had rushed in, impetuous, without a plan, and now she was facing a madman with not even a stone for self-defence.

With an animal sound he lunged forward and slapped her. She cried out and staggered. He whipped out a pistol, smacked it against her temple, 'Move!' He walked Mehrunisa forward where an electric light blazed. Swiftly, he tied her hands above her head and handcuffed her to an overhead pipe.

As Mehrunisa struggled, a shrill voice sang out, 'Fool!' Heels clicked into the chamber.

Mehrunisa's stomach caved in as Pamposh appeared and slung an arm around Toor.

'Fool,' she rasped again, 'we've always hated the mongrel that you are, much like your precious Taj Mahal.' Her eyes were wide with wrath, her tiny frame swelled with loathing.

'But why attack the Taj? Why make it the symbol of your anger?'

Pamposh sniggered. 'How like you to ask an obvious question! In that sense, you are quite like the professor: you'll know everything there is to know about a centuries-old event, yet you fail to notice what is in front of your eyes. Haven't you seen enough proof that the Taj Mahal was never built by the womaniser Shah Jahan?! We have to restore it to the pristine form it was in before it was usurped by the thieving Mughal.' Pamposh paused, her chest heaving as she attempted to steady herself.

Toor watched with narrowed eyes. 'Don't waste your breath on her,' he hissed.

But Pamposh stepped forward and jabbed Mehrunisa in the chest with her index finger. 'Do you know what it is like to be driven out of your home? To have intruders occupy your bedroom, strange hands pluck the fruit from your apple tree, never again see the chinar you grew up with blaze with its fiery flowers? Do you, Mehrunisa? You who are *so* removed from reality, all you want to do is your project on Indo-Persian linkages! *Do you?*'

Pamposh's face was the simulacrum of pain—the sort of pain frozen by artists in their great works. It was surreal—her friend, a co-conspirator, in league with a madman?

In that susurrus tone she continued, 'Sun Tzu, have you read him? Keep your friends close, he says, your enemies, closer.' She leaned into Mehrunisa, her eyes agleam. 'And we have always been close, haven't we, Mehroo? Oh, how I have hated you, ever since we were children, and the best part is that you never knew! Imagine my plight—under the care of an uncle who was drunk on Mughal grandeur, playing with a Persian mongrel-cum-gypsy who had no roots. Where have you lived? Isfahan, Dubai, Rome, Delhi—do you even know where you belong? Is there one place you can truly call your own?' Pamposh snorted.

So this was the angst that Arun Toor had leveraged as he deployed Professor Kaul's niece against him.

'Quit wasting your time,' Toor sniggered. 'She is from the same region and religion as the bloody Mughals!'

Mehrunisa pulled against the manacles. 'Don't gloss your communal rhetoric with bullshit.'

'Oh! And she's an intellectual, I forgot to add,' Toor simpered. 'An art historian, hunh?'

'Any day better than a fraudster like you, right?'

Arun Toor lurched towards Mehrunisa and bared his teeth within inches of her face. 'Who's interested in history? What is critical is what people believe, what they want to believe. And we are this close,' he snapped his fingers, '*this* close to reclaiming the Taj Mahal as a Shiva temple!'

He swivelled, grabbed Pamposh and started to pull back. 'As a child little Mehroo got locked in the basement, remember? Now, we'll leave her here to die.'

He smirked at her, grabbed the torchlight, turned it off and the chamber plunged into darkness. 'Our work is yet to be finished,' he whispered.

Mehrunisa heard footsteps moving away. She squinted her eyes and tugged at the overhead pipe.

From a distance Toor's low voice socked her in the gut.

'After her, we'll finish the Mughal-lover Kaul. With the great expert on the Taj gone, let's see who can stand in our way!'

The memory of the professor, a distended plastic bag around his head, roused Mehrunisa and she started to holler. Twisting and turning she wrenched at the pipe. As she yelled and screamed, her voice started to echo. Mehrunisa paused suddenly. There was another sound beside the echo. Toor had forgotten to switch off the loudspeaker and her yells were resounding around the charbagh.

Mehrunisa filled her lungs and burst into a volley. 'R.P. Singh ... SSP Raghav ... Toor is in the baoli! The baoli in the south tower of the mosque. Quick! He's escaping ... The south tower of the mosque...'

In the gardens of the Taj Mahal complex the loudspeaker crackled to life again. But this time, instead of the exhortation to Shiva devotees, the voice pouring forth was an anguished woman's. Mehrunisa's appeal floated above the police and the CISF as they herded the troublemakers and cleared the charbagh. Her pleas reached R.P. Singh as he stepped out of the mausoleum with a prone Raghav. Singh froze.

The man who pursued the Naxals in Bastar was a hunter. In every successful hunt he underwent a state of extreme alertness—when his mind processed everything with slow deliberation even as his body sprang into action. He experienced that heightened consciousness now as with calm motions he handed charge of the wounded SSP to a deputy, silently beckoned his men to follow and shot towards the narrow door.

In the well shaft Mehrunisa heard Toor swear loudly as he realised his mistake. But she heard their footsteps hurrying—they must have decided to make a run for it. A desperate Mehrunisa struggled with the pipe. It held firm. She attempted to wriggle out of the rope shackle but it was futile.

The pipe had to be old, she thought, pulling downwards with all her strength. Then she crept her fingers along the pipe, grasped it and swung her feet up, folding her knees so her weight was suspended from the pipe. A creak. She swung harder. Using her right toe as lever, she lurched forward, pendulating awkwardly as her knee scraped on the return. As her hands slipped, she screamed in agony and outrage and anger.

Again she held onto the pipe, folded her knees and launched the oscillation. The rough rope cut into her wrists. She felt as if her shoulders would pop out. There was blood in her mouth from biting her lip. Crrr-eak. She swung again. The crunching sound grew and the pipe snapped, breaking free and hitting her head. She landed in a heap on the cool concrete. With her wrists still in the makeshift cuffs, she stood up, spun on her heels, and fell. Her knees were jelly, her shoulders seemed like footballs swelling from her neck.

Slowly she crawled on the floor till she reached the stairs where she started to drag herself up. As she squinted ahead to locate the fleeing couple, gunshots rang out.

Above her a scuffle erupted. Feet pounded on the steps. Something clattered down and landed above her. Pamposh's red high heel. A powerful torchlight shone. She heard Pamposh scream. Toor swore, then choked loudly. A shaky Mehrunisa craned her neck up from the step where she had collapsed.

The next instant footsteps bounded down. Powerful hands gripped her upper arms, and R.P. Singh eased Mehrunisa up.

Agra

A run Toor stirred uneasily on the mattress on which he
lay in a cramped cell inside the central police station.
The thin bedding and a narrow wood bench were the
only furniture, a barred window set high in the rear wall
the sole ventilation. In the distance he could hear the
murmur of traffic.

Since his arrest, Arun Toor had stayed silent. The
manner in which the ingenious plan had gone awry,
especially when he was so close to victory, was driving him
insane. He had failed his God. The marble monument
would persist in its false glory as a Mughal monument of
love—temple bells would not ring in praise of Shiva. The
Lord would not forgive him.

Growing up in the holy city of Varanasi, he had gone
every morning to the Dasaswamedh Ghat—where Lord
Brahma himself had paved the way for Shiva's return to
the city after a spell of banishment—for a ritual bath and
prayers to the rising sun. In the library of the Benaras
Hindu University, he had trawled through books on the

glory of the Jats. When he worshipped at the Kashi Vishwanath temple, he made sure to avoid even glancing at the Gyanvapi mosque, which clung to the temple like a leech. He had pledged to eradicate the curse of the Mughal conquerors and return his city's great religion to its ancient glory—but all of it had come to naught.

Arun stared at the dark ceiling, oblivious to what had appeared at the window. About three feet long and slim, it started to slither noiselessly down the wall towards the recumbent man. Its light brownish colour made it almost invisible in the dark, the brown-black splotches merging with the ill-lit shadows cast from a single low-watt bulb outside the cell. Nocturnal by habit, it was skittish at night. In addition, it had been prodded into irritability. Now, as it glided along the cement floor, it emitted a low rasping sound. Denied its daily diet of rats, field mice, birds, it was irascible as it approached the prey.

Sunk in his anguish, Arun became aware only when, raised above his chest, a head swayed. At the base of it was a pair of dark spots. His eyes followed the thin neck to its coiled body and he heard the hiss.

Shiva, the Lord of regeneration, had sent his emissary to put him out of his misery. It was time to submit to the master and fulfil his dharma, his sacred duty. The chapter, he reflected, had begun with snake venom and now it would end with the same. A full circle. But it was only one chapter—the story was longer, much longer. Shiva was also Ardhnarishwar, half woman. He might go, but his other half, the Shakti to his Shiva, would remain. And there was always Narada, the wise one. Arun closed his eyes and waited, trying to calm his breath.

With lightning speed the snake flashed to Arun's head and stung. The venom began to course through his body.

The poison, a potent coagulant, would soon destroy tissue and blood cells. Its reputation was fearsome: the Russell's viper accounted for most snakebite deaths in India.

There was a faint whistling, *oo-hoo-oo-hoo*, like a call, and the viper obediently started to slither back to where it had come from.

❋ ❋ ❋

The train to Dehradun clanked its way out of Agra station. In a second-class compartment, a man dressed in an olive green sweater and matching trousers sat on a single-seater, the seat opposite him occupied by a couple of bamboo hampers. At a casual glance, it would appear as if an Army orderly was carrying his memsahib's hamper while she travelled in the comfort of first class. That, however, would be wrong.

Jara, his face shrouded in a monkey cap and a muffler wound around his neck, was heading to his hamlet in the foothills of Dehradun where they still practiced a dying trade: that of snake charmers. He had joined police service to escape being condemned to the life of a snake charmer. However, since his career with the police had been cut short and left him bereft of even a face to call his own, he had turned to the art form. Pandit Sir's daughter had given him refuge—after all, he had been Omkar Pandit's loyal driver until the day a car bomb had struck—and on learning about his special skill, had found ways to employ it.

He had used it well: extracting venom from a King cobra, feeding the corpse to the python, training a Russell's viper to kill—these were skills that needed years of perfection. He had delivered.

Now, though, it was time to disappear—the message had been unambiguous.

He eyed the bamboo hampers: the bottom one was shaped like a large trunk, the top one like a semi-circular lidded basket. They looked harmless, more like some rich lady's extravagant accoutrements. Nestled within them, respectively in a large burlap and a cloth bag were a giant python and a Russell's viper. He hoped no nosy passenger would ask him to remove the hampers in order to take the seat. He had made the python sluggish, but the viper was especially tricky. It was known to bite through cloth and the slats of its bamboo hamper were a bit wide....

Jara bent his neck and burrowed his face within the muffler, attempting to appear unapproachable.

Agra

In the wake of the mayhem at the Taj Mahal, the Archaeological Survey of India announced special access to the basement rooms for two hours daily for a limited period of time. This was to enable people to see for themselves that there was no evidence of Shiva artefacts in the barren rooms, and to prove that the proposition claiming the Taj Mahal was a Shiva temple once was a complete hoax. Of course, they had quietly taken measures to correct the changes in calligraphy on Mumtaz's cenotaph, and restore it to its original state.

Meanwhile, the CBI swooped down upon the proprietor of the private TV channel that had broadcast pictures of Mumtaz Mahal's cenotaph, extracted the footage and instructed him to state, for all future reference, that a storage vault fire destroyed an entire archive of film including that particular footage. The proprietor, under investigation for tax fraud, was most compliant.

Deploying Mehrunisa's rebuttal-pamphlet, the ASI also issued a full-page clarification in leading dailies citing comprehensible evidence of the Taj Mahal being a Mughal monument. This advertisement also carried endorsements from renowned world historians—which included noted Indian scholars, the Austrian academic acknowledged to be an expert on Mughal architecture, a Harvard Indologist—who certified the marble monument's antiquity and provenance.

Additionally, the home minister announced an inquiry into the issue to be jointly headed by Shri Kriplani of BHP, the chief representative of the Sunni Waqf Board, and the newly-appointed director-general of the ASI.

❋ ❋ ❋

Meanwhile, SSP Raghav was recuperating from the gunshot wound in Agra Civil Hospital. Luckily, the bullet had hit the outside of the right shoulder where the thick muscle pad had borne the brunt and saved him, despite the blood loss. He would be in hospital for a fortnight, after which he could resume duty, though he would require a sling for a while. His wife declared she would not leave his side until he was perfectly all right; the children meanwhile were at a relative's.

The state police chief paid him a visit and conveyed that he had recommended Raghav to the prime minister for a gallantry award.

Late one evening, when visiting hours were over and the nurse had finished her night round, R.P. Singh snuck into Raghav's private room. 'Too much healthy food will kill your taste buds for sure, if not you!' he said, and set a bottle of rum and a bag of samosas on the steel side table.

Raghav guffawed.

R.P. Singh cast a look around and asked conspiratorially, 'The nurses, are they any good?'

'Not worth checking in for,' Raghav grinned.

R.P. Singh nodded, stood akimbo and looked at Raghav intently. He was pallid and the injury must hurt like hell. 'I ...' he started, patting his bald pate, 'What you did in the tomb chamber that night in the Taj, you didn't have to, you know.... You took a bullet for me.'

Raghav shrugged his uninjured shoulder. 'I'd rather share a rum with you alive than drink it at your funeral,' he said.

The two men grinned and nodded to each other. R.P. Singh walked to the side table, opened the Old Monk and, looking at Raghav said, 'I owe you one, my friend.'

'Ah! To have a dusht devil in my debt!'

R.P. Singh muttered an expletive as he turned to Raghav with upturned palms. 'Where the fuck do you keep the glasses?'

Delhi

R.P. Singh was invited to 7 Race Course Road for a half-hour session with the prime minister at his pleasure. What they discussed at Panchavati was not minuted. But when Singh stepped out and donned his aviators, he looked very satisfied. He had let the PM express his gratitude. His work, and the manner in which he conducted it—with absolute disdain for superiors—mandated powerful patronage. The PM's indebtedness would be of assistance.

R.P. Singh then swung by Professor Kaul's residence to visit Mehrunisa. It was a bright winter day and they sat on the patio.

'Feeling better?' he asked.

During her exertions in the baoli of the Taj Mahal, Mehrunisa had pulled a muscle in her shoulder.

'The swelling's reduced. And the anti-inflammatory tablets help. Otherwise, rest is best.' Mehrunisa grimaced.

'It was one hell of a job you did.'

'And yet, *you* got to be in the papers!'

'Oh! Hell.' R.P. Singh looked uncomfortable, his neck turning red.

Mehrunisa laughed. 'I was joking! You did your job. I'm glad I could help.'

'Exactly! I did my job. You ... did more.' He paused and looked in the direction of the house. 'The professor will be happy, Mehrunisa.'

She tipped her head in assent.

'As am I. If not for you, Toor would have escaped.' He bent forward and confided that Arun Toor had died in his prison cell with no visible wound marks. Post-mortem had showed it resulted from snakebite. However, the information was strictly confidential since they were still looking to nab the mysterious monkey-cap who was likely a snake charmer as well.

Mehrunisa nodded. 'What about Pamposh?'

The truth about her childhood friend had confounded her. But perhaps Pamposh was not such a contradiction. The lotus flower, her namesake, rose above the surface of water to bloom, bewitching all with its regal beauty. Yet, at night it closed and sank beneath the surface. In those eight to ten hours that it was submerged in the muddy waters, who could tell what it absorbed from those stygian forces? Every morning when the lotus showed its glowing face to the sun, how hard had it worked to mask the dark forces buried within?

'She'll be in jail on non-bailable offence until trial begins. She is being questioned on the co-conspirators. The police is also looking for Toor's ally in CISF, an Inspector Bharadwaj, who has disappeared. He was responsible for guarding the Taj from the riverside—the fact that boats from Bateshwar could sail up the Yamuna was clearly with his collusion.'

Mangat Ram brought in tea which R.P. Singh offered to serve. As he added milk, Mehrunisa said, 'So what do you plan to do now?'

'Enjoy my newfound "saviour-of-nation" status before I'm shunted to the boondocks again!'

There was more laughter and easy banter before it was time for him to depart. Mehrunisa walked him to the door, where he hesitated before turning to face her. Mehrunisa was tall, yet Singh was a head taller as he gazed at her, leaning against the doorframe.

'Some adventure, hunh?'

A faraway look came into her eyes as she thought of all that had happened within a month. 'Some adventure,' she concurred.

'When this dies down and you feel better, I'd very much like to take you out, Mehrunisa.' He looked intently at her.

A horn sounded shrilly, repeatedly. R.P. Singh refused to glance back.

Mehrunisa arched a shoulder towards the lane. 'Someone's in a hurry.'

He had parked his vehicle at an angle in the lane, which was upsetting some folks.

'Rrr-ight,' he drawled but did not move as he studied her. Her grey-green eyes were green now. He had observed them darken before, at times of intense emotion. The tip of her tongue flicked out as she tucked a strand of hair behind an ear. He wanted to run his hands through her hair and smell the mint in them.

Mehrunisa cleared her throat. 'Am I under surveillance here?' she said as a smile played at one corner of her mouth.

'You'd make an excellent prospect for a close watch.'

The horn pealed again.

'In case you've forgotten the question, Mehrunisa, I'd very much like to take you out.'

She smiled. 'First name terms would help.'

'Pratap.'

Mehrunisa tilted her chin at him. 'I'd like that too, Pratap.'

Delhi

Mehrunisa woke early. A cool winter morning was warming rapidly in a bright sun. She guided Professor Kaul to the garden where Mangat Ram would lay tea on a wicker table beneath the tree. Sparrows chirruped in the coral bougainvillea, the sky was an effortless blue. Mehrunisa decided to walk in the garden.

Mongrel gypsy—that was how Pamposh had described her. Indecorous, but accurate. She *was* Iranian-Indian and had grown up all over the world ... but the events of the past month had clarified some things for her.

She came to India to research her project, but she had been searching for something else—something that would crystallise what it meant to be Mehrunisa Khosa. Now, due to the elaborate Taj conspiracy, she knew. Pamposh had claimed that since she grew up everywhere, she belonged nowhere. But she had discovered the flip side of that very same coin: she grew up between worlds and so, perhaps, she belonged everywhere. The idea of home didn't have to be held hostage to physical coordinates—it could be an act of choice. Her roots were not fixed in a piece of land, they were within her. That freed her to love the Taj in Agra and the Duomo in Florence, the quarries of Isfahan where Maadar grew up and the mines of Makrana which gave marble to the Taj Mahal, to marvel at the beauty of Michelangelo's Pieta and lose herself in the music of Amir Khusro....

Mangat Ram walked in with tea and the day's newspaper. Mehrunisa joined her godfather and was serving him tea when her eyes fell on the front page. It carried a picture of the Taj Mahal, the monument burnished in mellow light as the sun rose behind it.

A lump was in her throat. She pushed it down, breathed deeply, and with a smile, held up the paper to her godfather. The professor blinked. His eyes flickered. As he scanned the newspaper she saw recognition on his face.

Delhi

At a tea party at the residence of the prime minister to celebrate Republic Day, R.P. Singh bumped into Shri Kriplani who congratulated him on saving the Taj Mahal.

'People should never take the Lord's name in vain,' he said with a regretful shake of his head.

Singh raised his brows in response.

'Now,' Kriplani said with enthusiasm, as if he were lecturing on his favourite subject, 'the Taj supervisor misused Shiva's name. And what did the Lord do? Sent a snake to punish him!' He paused and wagged his head.

From a gathering of politicians seated at a table in the centre of the room, a voice hailed the BHP leader. He glanced at them before turning back to Singh. Raising his hands skywards he said, 'It is all Lord's maya,' and sauntered off.

R.P. Singh, however, was rooted to the ground. That Arun Toor had died in his prison cell from snakebite was confidential—something only a handful of people knew. *How had Kriplani got to know?*

The next instant someone slapped him on the back. It was an old colleague who was now on the PM's security detail.

'What man?' he jogged his brows. 'Shri Kriplani was falling all over you! If that man congratulates me, I watch my back. Narada!'

R.P. Singh frowned.

The cop leaned in and whispered, 'Narayan Ram Das Kriplani. Na-Ra-Da. Always looking to topple the government. Know of the latest wedge he drove between the coalition...'

R.P. Singh led his friend to the porch. As he smoked, his colleague prattled on about the machinations of the Opposition leader which had earned him the nickname 'Narada', which was incidentally his Hindi acronym. But Singh was processing a parallel thought.

Kriplani was inextricably linked with the Taj conspiracy. He was Arun Toor's college teacher, colleague to Professor Dixit, assorted thugs caught at Taj were acquainted with the BHP's Agra unit ... several times in the investigation the trail had led back to Kriplani but the politician always had an alibi. Except, this time, perhaps.

Through a cloud of cigarette smoke Singh scrutinised Kriplani: was he the real behrupiya behind the Taj conspiracy?

Acknowledgements

Certain monuments come to define their nations: the Eiffel Tower, France; the Statue of Liberty, the US; the Taj Mahal, India. And yet, few Indians really *know* the Taj, beyond its fabled beauty and the legendary love that inspired it. They're even less aware of the alarming vulnerability of the monument in the face of increasing pollution, a depleting Yamuna, and rising terror. I have attempted, through this book, to create a greater appreciation for the monument that is more symbolic of our heritage than we realise.

To borrow from a character in the book who, at a critical juncture when the Taj Mahal is facing an extraordinary threat, exhorts a police officer thus: '*Just as the colour white contains all colours within it, this monument of white embodies our innate, ancient pluralism. Save the Taj Mahal, Singh, that monument stands for India.*'

This book is based on years of research and I owe much gratitude to the scholarly works of several Taj historians such as Amina Okada, Mohan C. Joshi, Gilles

Tilottson, amongst others. I would, however, be remiss if I didn't make a special mention of Ebba Koch and her marvelous book, *The Complete Taj Mahal*. I am so impressed with Ms Koch's dedication to the Taj that I have based the scholarship of a character in the book— Professor Kaul—on her.

To the best of my knowledge, all descriptions of architecture, artwork, calligraphy, documents, and urban legends around the Taj, are accurate. There is one secret trapdoor that I've had the impunity to add in a room inside the Taj Mahal—that is a thriller writer's privilege which, I hope, Shah Jahan shall deign to overlook.

I consulted people in the Indian police for valuable insight on security matters, and I thank Anjaneyulu for allowing me to pick his brain. I am grateful to V.K. Karthika for an initial reading of the manuscript and her valuable feedback. My agent, Jayapriya at Jacaranda, is a friend who has never stopped championing my work. My editor, Deepthi Talwar, for her evident enthusiasm for the book, and a sharp eye that misses nothing—the manuscript is stronger because of you.

I'd like to acknowledge the artisans who work at the Taj Mahal on ridiculously low wages as they chisel and saw and inlay the parchin kari to keep the world's most beautiful monument pristine. And the security personnel who guard it, both within and without.

I am blessed to have an ustad like Gulzar saab—I could not have hoped for a more inspiring mentor as I continue my writing journey.

And now I must turn to the people who have provided laughter, support, love, red wine, re-readings, and cards filled with little hearts as I strove over the years to complete my book: my daughter Malvika and my husband Prasanna. Writers are notoriously difficult people to live with and this writer can, at the best of times, be tetchy. Thank you, my family, for your loyalty, love and stoicism—Mumtaz must have been a kindred spirit for having inspired Shah Jahan thus!

Manreet Sodhi Someshwar trained as an engineer, graduated from the Indian Institute of Management, Calcutta, and worked in marketing, advertising and consulting. An award-winning writer (Commonwealth Broadcasting Association), and copywriter (Creative Abbey), she is a popular blogger as well.

Her debut novel, *Earning the Laundry Stripes*, released in 2006 to critical acclaim, with *India Today* calling it 'an enjoyable tale of a sassy girl's headlong race up the corporate ladder...' Her second novel, *The Long Walk Home*, published in 2009, has garnered critical acclaim and hit several bestseller lists in India. Legendary poet-lyricist Gulzar has called it 'a narrative of pain that knows no borders'.

She has featured at several literary festivals including the Singapore Writers Festival, the Shanghai International Literary Festival and the Man Hong Kong International Literary Festival.

Her articles have appeared in the *New York Times*, *International Herald Tribune*, *South China Morning Post* (Hong Kong) and several Indian publications.